PRAISE FOR MEGAN CHANCE

"A powerful and thought-provoking story that is impossible to put down."
—Kristin Hannah, *New York Times* bestselling author of *The Four Winds* and *The Women*

"Chance's knack of introducing quiet menace into her novels pulls the story along at breakneck speed. I couldn't let go! Highly recommended."
—*Historical Novels Review*

"This thought-provoking historical mystery is destined to become a book club favorite. Its timely emphasis on women's autonomy (or lack thereof!), not to mention its twists and turns, will keep you reading all the way to its unpredictable, but fully earned, ending."
—Christina Baker Kline, #1 *New York Times* bestselling author

"A page-turner of a historical mystery that rips along to an unexpected and immensely satisfying ending. This is Megan Chance at her best!"
—Meg Waite Clayton, international bestselling author of *The Postmistress of Paris*

"I have loved Megan Chance for a long time, and this is another dazzling gem from her oeuvre."
—Barbara O'Neal, bestselling author of *When We Believed in Mermaids* and *This Place of Wonder*

"I've loved every book by Megan Chance I've read (and I've read them all), and this is by far one of the best. This is a stunning novel that shines brightly as it shines a strong light on the deep and abiding emotions of the characters."

—M. J. Rose, *New York Times* bestselling author of
The Jeweler of Stolen Dreams

"Absolutely engrossing. I literally only put the novel down once—to catch an airplane—then obsessively kept reading through to the final page."

—Joy Jordan-Lake, bestselling author of *A Bend of Light* and
Under a Gilded Moon

GLAMOROUS
NOTIONS

GLAMOROUS NOTIONS

A Novel

MEGAN CHANCE

LAKE UNION PUBLISHING

Published by Lake Union Publishing, Seattle

www.apub.com

Amazon, the Amazon logo, and Lake Union Publishing are trademarks of Amazon.com, Inc., or its affiliates.

ISBN-13: 9781662515774 (paperback)
ISBN-13: 9781662515781 (digital)

Cover design by Faceout Studio, Spencer Fuller
Cover image: © Walter Carone / Paris Match Archive / Getty Images

Printed in the United States of America

Los Angeles, California—1951

The street and traffic lights streaked past the car windows, reminding her of the neon of Rome as she told them the story of what had happened to her there, how well it had started and how terribly it had ended, with the escort to the Rome airport and the warning not to return. After the last fifteen hours she'd spent on the plane, with all of its luxuries and strangeness, she felt lost in a dream, moved from one self to another and back again, forced to return to a life she'd never intended to come back to, and yet . . . here she was.

She finished to silence.

Charlie stared out the passenger window as he said, "What do you think you were involved in?"

"I'm not sure."

Soberly, from the driver's seat, Harvey said, "I don't think you should tell this story again. Not to anyone. You can trust us to say nothing, but this world now is strange. Now that the Soviets have the bomb, McCarthy and his cronies see spies everywhere. I think it's safer to just keep this to yourself."

Charlie agreed. "You don't know who's watching. Or listening. Just forget it ever happened. Forget you ever went to Rome."

Their words frightened her, though she knew they were true. "I don't think I can forget."

"Then take it as a warning. You're lucky you're alive and not in some Italian jail. You don't want to end up in an American one," Charlie said.

Harvey's hands tightened on the steering wheel. "Treat it as if it happened to someone else in a faraway land. You're going to have to become someone new here. Someone they can't find. We can help you with that." He looked at Charlie. "Can't we?"

Charlie nodded. "You'll need a new name. A birth certificate. With that you can get anything else. Fortunately, we know an artist or two . . ."

"I told you they'd come in handy," Harvey said.

Charlie rolled his eyes. "I'm going to pretend you never said that. And you, my dear, are saying goodbye to the past. Hopefully forever. Don't ever mention Rome again."

"I won't," she said. "I promise."

PART ONE

The Remaking of Elsie Gruner

CHAPTER 1

Los Angeles, California—1948

On the postcard she sent to her parents in Ohio, Elsie wrote, *In Los Angeles, CA, living my dream!* But . . . not really, not yet. The duplex in Edendale was halfway up a hill, reachable only by a precariously steep street that ended at a narrow set of equally steep stairs. The Ford protested and backfired on every trip up the road, and they parked it at the bottom of the stairs, next to the house of a Mexican family who rented their dirt yard out to a flock of chickens. Mr. Evans, their neighbor in the duplex, had parties at his house every Friday that ended with loud music and people drinking in the yard. The house on the hill above them belonged to a Slavic couple, who were very quiet but whose dog was not, and at the very top of the hill was an architect's house whose huge glass windows sent a blinding glare over everything on any sunny day, which was nearly always.

Elsie's new husband, Walter, had picked the place because it was cheap but also because he'd heard it was close to some film studios. That had once been true, but most of the studios had moved out of Edendale by then. Walter thought it would be easy to visit them personally for auditions, but it turned out that wasn't how it worked; he had to meet with casting agencies and agents and go to "open calls," and so he and Elsie still spent every night at the pool halls, rotating between the venues to keep their faces "fresh," as Walter put it.

Not fresh enough, Elsie feared. They'd been in LA only a month when she noted the whispers and frowns that greeted them more and more frequently. She mentioned it to Walter.

"It won't be long before we won't need the pool halls anymore," he told her from the sagging sofa they'd rescued from the front yard of someone two streets over who'd left it with a sign saying **FREE**. "I've got another audition tomorrow. I have a feeling about this one."

He had a feeling about all of them, but she didn't say that. He came back from that audition as he came back from all the others, dejected, snappish, an excuse ready in hand. "They were looking for a blond. I told them I'd bleach my hair, but . . ." or "They wanted someone with more muscles. Maybe I should go to a gym. What do you think?"

She shrugged. Walter was tall and skinny; she wasn't sure he *could* turn into a muscleman.

"I wonder if that's the new fashion. Tough guys. Maybe I'll try a few weeks at the weights."

"We need money for that."

He made a face. "Let's go play some pool."

"Walter . . ."

He grinned and pulled her close. "You just twinkle those pretty brown eyes at them and smile."

But when they got to the hall, the owner met them at the door and said, "Not tonight, Walter. You and your hustle can go somewhere else. I don't want to see either of you here again."

Walter spread his hands in innocent dismay. "I can't help it if I'm lucky."

"A little too lucky a little too often," the owner said. "I've gotten complaints. More than a few. You take your business elsewhere."

"Fine." Walter's dark eyes flashed. "Fine. The Royal will be happy to take our money."

"Don't count on it. And don't count on the Sun Court either."

"What? You guys start a club or something?"

"Or something." The owner hooked his thumbs through his suspenders. "We run legit businesses here, not scams. Get a real job, Walt, before someone breaks your skull with a pool cue." He sent a hard look to Elsie. "You hitched your wagon to a loser, girlie. Don't let him steer you to jail."

Walter grabbed her arm and jerked her from the hall. "Goddamn ass," he snapped when they were outside. "Who does he think he is?"

But Elsie was too disconcerted and embarrassed by the man's last words to pay attention to Walter's.

When he said "Let's try the Royal," she shook her head.

"No. You heard him."

"He was lying."

"I don't think so."

"We won't know until we go there."

"Walter, I'm not doing that," she said firmly. "You can go if you want, but I won't. That was humiliating."

He looked surprised, but he relented. "Okay. Okay, baby. We won't go today if you don't want. But you can't let people push you around like that. People lie all the time, you know, to get what they want."

She nodded, but she was hardly listening, and she was relieved when he drove them back to the duplex, though he was moody and silent the rest of the evening.

~

She was twenty, and the way she'd managed to get out of her parents' pig farm in Zanesville was by hitching her wagon to Walter Maynard. She thought she'd be in that town forever, helping her mother run her dressmaking business and trying in vain to convince anyone to order one of her own modern designs and stinking of her father's pigs, until the night Walter showed up at the grange dance and complimented her dress—orange-red taffeta and her newest creation. That night he'd taken her to the pool hall, where she'd never before gone inside, and when every man in the place looked at her hungrily as if she were a steak dinner, she understood why her parents had never let her go.

When she stood at the end of the pool table to watch Walter, and the man he'd been playing botched his next three shots, Walter said, "You're a pearl, baby! My good luck charm! You keep doing that and we'll make a fortune!"

"Doing what?" she asked.

"That smiling thing. You're a natural. Say, do you have another dress like that one?"

"Sure."

"Can you wear it and meet me here tomorrow night?"

It was the first time anyone had asked her to wear one of her own designs.

Elsie stared at him in surprise when she realized what else he was asking. "Do you mean a date?"

"Yeah, a date." He grinned. "Absolutely."

It turned out she *was* a natural at helping him hustle pool.

"You look so sweet. Why, you're my own Donna Reed, aren't you?" Walter said.

She'd never been compared to a star before. She wore no makeup— only loose or married women did in Zanesville—and with her wavy brown hair and brown eyes, she'd never turned heads until she found her calling in the pool hall. Three weeks later, they'd eloped and were on their way to LA, where Walter meant to be a famous actor. Elsie had never been so happy to see anything as she was to see Zanesville recede in the rearview mirror. She told her parents via a postcard from Cincinnati, where she and Walter made two dollars at a pool hall the first night out, and afterward stumbled into a dark little shack of a place where music leaked from between the wooden siding into the night. The music sounded a little like the songs Elsie's uncle played when he felt down, but it had a different rhythm, a twistier melody.

"Jazz," Walter said, pulling her inside. The club was full, the light was low, some people moving sinuously on the dance floor but not many. Most sat listening and shaking their shoulders or gyrating their hips in their seats, and the ones dancing did so in almost obscene ways that Elsie had never seen before. Not only that, but there weren't only white people in the club, but Negroes too.

Everyone danced in the same indecent way. One man had his leg shoved between the woman's; they were so close there was no light between them. Walter's hand went to the small of Elsie's back as if he were trying to create that same kind of closeness. The music got into her head, winding, looping, hot and cool.

The music set her on fire, and when they got back to the hotel, she wanted him so much she could hardly control herself. Walter said, "You're like ten different people in one girl," and she drew away, stung, but he pulled her close again and said, "Don't get all prudish on me, baby. Let's try it this way."

The next day he bought her a bottle of perfume at the drugstore, L'Air du Temps. He gave it to her with a sheepish grin, and though she took it with a smile, she wondered why he'd bought it, if it was because the smell of pigs was still on her skin. God knew she still smelled it, every time she opened her suitcase, no matter how many times she bathed; there had been nowhere to wash her clothes. She wondered if she could ever get rid of the scent, and wished she could throw away every piece of her clothing and start again. She had a new name now: no longer Elsie Gruner, but Elsie Maynard. She was ready for the new life that came with it. She threw herself into her role at the pool halls in a rush for that new life. The more Walter won, the sooner they'd get to LA, the sooner she could rid herself of Zanesville and the world she was still afraid might jerk her back. It seemed strange that leaving the city hadn't changed her more completely, but it would, she was sure of it. Once they settled in LA and Walter was a famous actor, she would have all-new clothes, which would help. She spent the hours in the car drawing them, much to Walter's amusement.

"When we're rich, you can have that famous guy you're always talking about design your stuff. What's his name?"

"Flavio," she said.

"Yeah, that guy. You said he does all the movie stars, right? What about movie stars' wives?"

"He does their gowns too."

"Then he'll do yours," Walter said with confidence. "But for now, baby, you just concentrate on what you do best. I have a good feeling about the pool halls in Joplin."

But now, in LA, they couldn't go back to the pool halls. Walter wasn't getting any roles. *"You hitched your wagon to a loser."* She wouldn't believe that. It was only a matter of time before Walter got the part that would make him a star. Elsie had escaped Zanesville and come all this way, and she refused to believe it wouldn't turn out the way she'd envisioned. They needed money and Walter needed to continue to audition, which meant it was up to her to make things work for now. It was just . . . What could she do?

When she walked by the little café on Hope Street, only a few blocks from the house, and saw the **HELP WANTED** sign in the window, she felt as if the universe was smiling down on her, because the woman who ran the place—a heavyset brunette with an overbite, named Anita Nelson—hired Elsie immediately.

"Can you start now?" Anita asked, which was how Elsie found herself in an apron and a hairnet and running dirty dishes to the kitchen and glasses of water to customers that very morning. When she went home, she felt accomplished and satisfied. Walter would be pleased that she'd taken the job. She'd bought him time if nothing else.

But Walter had other news.

"I got it!" He pulled her into his arms and swung her around. "I got the part!"

"You did!" Elsie laughed in relief. "What is it? Tell me!"

"It's just a small part, but what do they say? There're no small parts, only small actors? It doesn't pay much, either, but it's a start. An 'emerging' playwright. He's going to be big someday, I know it. Of course, it's just a little theater off Pershing Square. I wish it was someplace else."

"Why?"

"Pershing Square?" Walter made a face. "How can I expect any movie producers to brave all the cruising fairies there to come see me?"

"Well, I—"

"I'll be rehearsing almost every evening," Walter went on. "I know you'll miss me, baby, but it'll only be a few months, and this way I can keep auditioning during the day."

"I expect I'll manage. I might get a—"

"Maybe you could clean or something." He swept a bunch of her fashion sketches from the sofa.

"Maybe I could get a job. Maybe that little café down on Hope Street needs someone."

Walter frowned. "Why do you need a job now? I just got a role. My career's on the way up."

"Yes, but—"

"No buts, baby. One day I'll be in *Photoplay*, and you'll be there on my arm, wearing a gown by Flavio."

She didn't tell him about the job that night. He had an audition the next morning, so she had no chance to tell him then, and she went to work. When she got home, exhausted, she realized that Walter had already arrived. She heard him before she saw him, slamming dishes around in the kitchen, a sound she had spent the entire morning listening to, but the noise Walter made didn't have the benign and organized music it had at the café. She closed the door softly behind her. Walter charged out of the kitchen.

He was furious. "Where have you been?" he demanded.

"I got a job at the café," she told him. "I'm a bus girl."

He stared at her as if he had suddenly forgotten English. "A what?"

"They hired me yesterday. I didn't have the chance to tell you. What's wrong?"

"What's wrong? What's wrong?" His voice rose with every subsequent word. "I thought I told you I didn't want you to do that!"

"What does it matter?"

"I'm going to be famous. I can't have a wife who works in a café. It will look bad."

"But you're not famous yet," she said reasonably.

Walter's frown deepened. "I guess not."

"In the meantime, I've got a job. It will help a little bit, don't you think? It'll make it easier for you to focus on your career."

"At the café down the street?"

She composed her voice, gave him a smile. "Just clearing tables a few days a week. If it's . . . okay with you. I thought it would be, because you're trying so hard and you can't do everything. You know how I help you at the pool hall? This is just the same. Just helping. It's only until you make it. Just to help out. You won't have to worry then."

Walter took a deep breath and nodded slowly, a bit uncertainly. "Sure. My lucky charm. Yeah . . . yeah, you know, you're right. It will help. But only until I get a part in the movies, baby. Then we'll be rich enough that you'll have a maid and a nanny and you can spend your whole day by our pool. I can make that happen for us. Do you believe me?"

He was so intense, and the dream was so hard in his eyes, and she understood it, that wish to be something, to be more than everything around you, that feeling that you were different, that you *had* to be, or what was the point? She wanted to dream his dream, too, despite that nagging little echo. *"You hitched your wagon to a loser, girlie."*

"Of course I do," she said.

CHAPTER 2

The next two weeks, Walter was gone all the time, auditioning, or at rehearsal, or sometimes he went out drinking with the theater company afterward.

"It's all part of the business," he told her. "You never know who's going to make it and give you a leg up. I have to make friends."

She spent her spare hours sketching, which was how she'd spent her time in Zanesville too. She'd stuffed the cardboard box beneath her bed full of her own designs. All pointless—her friends laughed at her sketches until she started to laugh too. *"No one will ever wear anything like that, Elsie,"* Mom said so often it was nearly rote. *"What we need are new patterns for housedresses."* Dad said, *"Don't be so frivolous. When the Soviets have the bomb, there won't be any need for party gowns."*

But if nothing else, LA gave her hundreds of ideas; she'd never felt so inspired. The limp laundry hanging in the Slavic couple's yard prompted a bright tunic dress, the colorful scarves and blankets sold in the Mexican stalls and stores in El Pueblo—the old town across from Union Station—spurred an entire series of skirts and boleros and a con-quistador trouser set that she particularly loved. The southwest corner of Sunset and Gower, where the actors gathered hoping to be noticed, provided a kaleidoscope of styles to borrow, mix, and match, and the burlesque joints on Sunset, mixing with the fancy stores and the clubs jumping with movie stars, lit fires in her head. Sometimes she went there in the evenings just to watch them arrive.

She couldn't get her ideas down fast enough. Her sketches were strewn all over the house, much to Walter's irritation—they had to move them to eat or sit down or even to make love. On Saturdays, when she didn't have a shift at the café, she went to the matinee house nearby and whiled away the hours lost in the drama and glamour of old movies like *Wuthering Heights* and *Ninotchka*, *Jezebel* and *Camille*, along with B movies specializing in melodrama and mystery, *The Cobra Strikes* and *Half Past Midnight*. They fed her passion for fashion just as they had in Zanesville.

The café became the best part of her day, not just because she had people there to talk to, but also because Edendale was populated with a fascinating mix of artists and leftists and old movie stars and bohemians, some shabby, some in cashmere, some flouting every fashion convention. She began to recognize the regulars: the old man she knew only as Mr. Allen, who leashed his Great Dane out front; a woman who used to be a B movie actress, according to Anita, but who Elsie didn't recognize, and who always ordered pancakes with peanut butter; and two men in their thirties: Harvey and Charlie, who always smiled and asked how she was doing when Elsie refilled their coffees or brought them water.

One atypical slow day Elsie took her break at the end of the counter, nursing a Coke and sketching.

Harvey called, "Elsie, what are you drawing?"

She was surprised to find that he and Charlie were watching her with interest.

"Would you like more coffee?" she asked politely. "I'll get Jan to—"

"No, no." Harvey waved her over. He was tall and stooped and looked like a strong wind might blow him over. His cornsilk-colored hair was so fine the pinkness of his scalp showed through it. "You look lost to the world. Charlie and I wonder what has you so rapt."

She was used to people's curiosity—and their uninterest when she explained her drawings. It was easier to shrug it off, which she did. "Oh, it's nothing."

Charlie, who was Harvey's opposite—beefy and black Irish—grinned. "It's not nothing if you're concentrating so hard."

"Charlie's an animator at Disney. He knows concentration," Harvey put in.

"Oh." LA was full of people who worked for studios, but somehow she had never imagined Charlie in the industry. "Well, that's—"

"Are you an artist?" Harvey asked.

"It's clothes," she said. "I like to draw clothes."

"Now there's art," Charlie said—admiringly? Was that admiration? Or was he sarcastic? She was used to dismissive sarcasm, but just when she had decided that's what it was, he said, "Bring it over. Let's take a look."

Harvey puffed on his cigarette and nodded. "Yes, let's see."

She'd never shied away from real interest, it was only that real interest had been rare. She brought over the sketchbook.

"Break's over, Else," Anita announced.

Harvey smiled at Elsie's obvious dismay. "Go ahead—do you mind if we look through it without you?"

She didn't mind, and just then a group came in and she couldn't linger, but she couldn't help her curiosity over Charlie and Harvey's reaction to the sketches. They were really looking at them, she realized, not just leafing through but spending time with each one, and she wasn't sure whether to be relieved or pleased. The waiting to find out grew unbearable.

She saw them pay their bill. She didn't think they'd leave without saying anything. But then they rose. She couldn't step away; a couple waited for her to clear a table. Charlie set her sketchbook next to the cash register. Dirty coffee cups filled her hands. Charlie gave her a smile as he headed to the door, and a surge of desperate disappointment raced through Elsie until she realized that Harvey stood right behind her.

"You've a gift," he said to her. "Can you come over when you get off work? We're only a few blocks away. Come and have a beer. We want to talk to you about your work."

She didn't know them except from the café. Walter would not like the idea at all. They could be kidnappers or . . . murderers. She'd heard about that Black Dahlia murder last year. It was still unsolved. People were still jumpy about it.

"We have no nefarious intentions." It was as if Harvey had read her mind. He grinned as he put a piece of paper into her apron pocket. "Come or not, as you like."

He followed Charlie out the door.

Elsie had no time to think about it further. She was swept into the chaos of the café lunch hour. But when her shift ended, and she retrieved her sketchbook and pulled the piece of paper from her pocket, she saw it was their address. *"We have no nefarious intentions . . ."* Sure, but wasn't that what a murderer would say even if he did? Elsie thought of how thoroughly they'd looked through her sketches. They wanted to talk to her about her work, and she wanted to hear what they had to say—she yearned to hear it. Charlie was an animator at Disney. An artist.

Elsie went to Anita, who was slicing a cherry pie. "Harvey and Charlie asked me to come over for a beer. Do you think that's all right?"

Anita looked surprised. "Did they? Well, I've never known them to do that before."

"Do you think I'd be in any danger?"

"Only of being talked to death. Or maybe recruited. They're active with the CRC, you know."

"What's that?"

"The Civil Rights Congress. They want equal rights for Negroes." Anita leaned close. "The rumor is that those two hold Communist Party meetings as well, but I wouldn't know about that."

"Oh." Elsie frowned. She didn't want to mess around with anything like that, but as long as she didn't attend those meetings, what did it matter?

She glanced at the address Harvey had given her and then at the clock on the diner wall. Walter wouldn't be home for hours. She had time, and her curiosity won out. She would go.

～

Their house was small, a yellow stuccoed Spanish-style bungalow with a red roof and an overgrown pink bougainvillea weighing down a tumbling side fence. Charlie answered her knock with a smile and "You came!" He ushered her in. Harvey was already approaching with a beer.

"As you can see, we're perfectly normal." He handed her the beer and gestured about the room. Bookshelves laden with books—*The Atomic Age Opens* prominently displayed—lined a wall next to a red chenille sofa. Armchairs in multicolored floral flanked the fireplace. They'd hung posters—one of a Picasso exhibition at the Art Institute of Chicago, and a movie poster for *The Grapes of Wrath*, as well as a framed autographed photo of Dorothy Dandridge. It was a comfortable room.

"Oh, we're much more interesting than normal," Charlie said. "Sit down, sit down! Tell us about yourself. Are you from LA?"

"God, is *anyone* from LA?" Harvey teased.

Elsie sat on the red chenille sofa. Harvey grabbed two more beers, and he and Charlie listened intently as she told them about coming from Ohio with Walter, and how her husband was going to be famous someday and she was just working until he made it.

"What about you?" Charlie asked.

"Me?"

"Don't you have ambitions for yourself?"

"I—um . . ."

"Your sketches are amazing." Charlie looked at Harvey, who nodded.

"Fantastic." Harvey held out his hand for her sketchbook. "Look at these, they're gorgeous!"

He had turned to what she thought of as her "bird designs," the cardinal-inspired trouser ensemble with its little tufted hat, the blue jay gown, the crow dress with its bustle-like back of pleated and layered tulle.

"I can't believe you got away with this in Ohio," Charlie said, pointing to a slinky sheath with scrolling up the sides and beneath the breasts, meant to enhance and allure.

"I didn't," she said. "I never made it. My mother said it was obscene."

"It would be a crime for you not to go to Chouinard."

"What's Chouinard?"

"An art school. It's where I studied animation. But they teach fashion illustration and costume design too. I can give you a letter of recommendation if you want, but you won't need it. Not once they see this."

"It's here? In LA?" she asked.

Charlie nodded. "Over in Westlake."

An art school. It was something Elsie had never imagined. She hadn't even known there was such a thing. A school that taught fashion? It sounded impossible. "You mean they teach this?"

"You could be a fashion designer, Elsie," Charlie said. "My God, you have the talent."

"And they let women in?"

"They do, though right now GIs have priority. But it would be a crime for you not to go."

She could not be still. It was alarming how much wanting could bloom so quickly. It threatened to eclipse her. Fashion design, school . . . in Zanesville she'd never dreamed so big. Taking over her mother's shop one day had been her only expectation. She'd never imagined it was even possible for her to be a . . . *fashion designer*—the words held worlds within them, and those worlds left her breathless.

"A few years at Chouinard . . . ," Charlie went on.

A few years . . .

Elsie's excitement died. She hadn't thought about Walter. Walter, who had to agree. Walter, who had to want this for her too. And the money . . .

"What is it? What's wrong?" Charlie asked.

"I have to talk to Walter. This wasn't our plan."

"Plans change," Harvey said. "Tell him you have a recommendation from a Disney man. That should convince him."

Yes, of course, Harvey was right. She and Walter had never talked about it. He liked the dresses she wore—it was what had drawn him to her in the beginning. Why wouldn't he like an idea that might make her famous too?

She left half-drunk, elated, though when she got home her doubts returned. After all, despite Walter liking her dresses, he'd seen her sketches and never mentioned the potential Harvey and Charlie said she had.

She waited up for him, her sketchbook on her lap, nervous but determined.

Walt came home late and sauced. "What are you doing on the couch?"

She rubbed her eyes. "I was waiting for you."

"The play's coming together. You should have seen us tonight, the whole thing really just gelled, you know? It's going to be great, and I was talking to the fellas tonight and I had this idea to send out flyers to the movie producers. You know, announcing my debut. Inviting them all to come." He was talking fast, excited. He pulled her from the sofa and up the stairs to the bedroom in a flurry of talk.

"Wait—Walt, today I met these two men . . . well, I knew them before, but—"

"What?" He frowned at her in confusion. "What two men? What are you talking about?"

"At the café. Harvey and Charlie. Charlie's an animator at Disney."

"I heard Disney is full of commies."

"Where did you hear that?"

Walter shrugged. "That's the rumor."

"I don't think that's true."

"Look, baby, you're home all day. You don't hear the things I do."

"I'm at the café. I hear about things. Like the CRC." She wasn't sure why she said it except that his condescension irritated her.

"The CRC? Where did you hear about that? Are these guys part of that?" Walter looked worried now. "You stay far away from them. You should report them."

"Report them to who?"

"The FBI, I don't know."

"How would I even talk to the FBI?"

"I don't know." He took off his shirt. "You don't want to be anywhere near those crazies, Elsie." He took off his pants and his underwear, then crawled naked between the sheets. "Like I said, communists. Stop talking about that kind of crap and come to bed."

"They saw my sketches and they think—"

"Who saw your sketches?"

"Charlie and Harvey."

"The commies?"

"Charlie thinks I have talent. He thinks I should go to art school."

"Art school?" Walter looked surprised. "Why?"

"He thinks I could be a fashion designer."

"Why would you want to be that? I thought you hated your mom's business."

"Well, no. I mean, I did, but—"

"Besides, the wife of a famous actor can't be making dresses. She *has* her dresses made, by that Flabioso—"

"Flavio."

"Yeah. It's not what we planned, baby. You'll be too busy shopping and having babies and looking gorgeous as the wife of Walt Maynard. Which reminds me . . ."

He went back to the play, and how he'd discovered a perfect mannerism for his character that really made everything *work*—it was the answer he'd been looking for; he couldn't believe he hadn't seen it before, everyone commented on it.

"Bernard told me I had it in me to be a movie star like Rudolph Valentino."

"Rudolph Valentino? But . . . he's so old fashioned."

"It was a compliment." Walter was obviously stung. "He meant that I should be a leading man like that. He said I should think about going to that place called the Actors' Laboratory over on Laurel."

"I've never heard of it," Elsie said.

"They're doing interesting stuff over there. Training actors in the new styles coming from New York City. Now that you have that job, I might look into it."

Elsie's heart sank.

"Maybe you could get a few more hours. What do you think?"

"Sure," Elsie said. "Sure."

He sighed with happiness. "It's all turning around, baby. We'll be in *Photoplay* before you know it."

CHAPTER 3

"We don't have the money for both Chouinard and the Actors' Lab anyway," Elsie told Harvey and Charlie when she explained that Chouinard would have to wait. "I'm going to have to work more to pay for even one of them. And you said they'd take GIs before they took a woman anyway, so I probably won't get in."

"You're more talented than any of those GIs," Charlie grumbled.

"Those GIs fought the Nazis," Harvey pointed out. "You can't begrudge them."

Charlie sank onto the sofa. "I know. I know."

It was obvious from the way they talked that neither of them had fought, which was strange, given that they were both the right age to be veterans. "Neither of you went to war?"

Again they exchanged a glance, one full of meaning that Elsie couldn't read.

"No, sadly," Harvey said. "We tried but we were . . . unwelcome."

He did not elaborate. Elsie remembered what Anita had said about the rumors of Communist Party activities and thought maybe that had something to do with it.

"We're all in the same boat now anyway," Charlie said glumly. "All hoping we aren't vaporized by the bomb."

"At least not until our girl here has a career," Harvey joked.

"When Walter makes it, then I'll have my turn," Elsie said.

She did not miss their obvious doubt.

"You really think he will?" Harvey asked. "Not that I question your faith, but Hollywood is full of actors who don't make it."

"I've seen him convince a hundred players that he's bad at pool, and he's good enough to be a professional."

Charlie frowned. "You know that's just a hustler, right, Elsie?" He passed around a bowl of potato chips.

Elsie took a handful. A rapid knock on the door startled her into spilling some on the floor.

Charlie lurched to his feet and went to the door. Whoever was there kept his voice low—he and Charlie exchanged a few terse words, and then Charlie came back.

Harvey gave him a questioning look.

"They were at it again," Charlie said quietly.

Harvey's mouth thinned.

Elsie stared at them, bewildered. "Who's at what again?"

Neither of them said anything for a moment, and Elsie felt them measuring how much to say.

"Is this about your meetings?" she asked.

Charlie looked surprised.

"Anita told me," she explained. "It's hardly a secret that the two of you are leftists, you know."

"There're all kinds of secrets in Edendale," Harvey said soberly. "You want to be careful what questions you ask. It's not that we don't trust you. It's that we don't want to drag you into trouble."

"The FBI has been amusing themselves by going around Edendale asking questions the last month or so, checking license plates, things like that," Charlie explained.

"Asking questions about what?"

"They want to know what people think their neighbors are up to."

"Are you in trouble?" Elsie asked. "Can I do anything to help?"

"We're not in any more trouble than anyone else in this neighborhood," Harvey told her. "They find all artists suspicious. They don't like anyone who thinks differently, and that's half of Edendale. They can't shut us all up. It's nothing to worry about."

So Elsie tried not to worry, but it didn't escape her notice that they'd told her they didn't want to drag her into trouble. It was as if they expected it.

Still, she didn't stay away. Harvey and Charlie were her closest friends, and she was alone more often than ever now, as Walter's rehearsals became more intense. The play opened in a week, and he was in a fever of excitement, jittery and unable to keep still. He hardly slept. He'd brought home the flyers he'd had printed up for the movie producers. She'd spent all the next day addressing envelopes and stamping them.

"When they see my performance, I'll be in like Flynn," he said.

Elsie wanted to go to the dress rehearsal, but Walter said no, he wanted her there on opening night instead.

"That's when I'll be in all my glory, baby. I want you to see me then."

The day before the play opened, Harvey and Charlie stopped in at the café. They were both smiling broadly, both obviously bursting with some kind of news.

"What is it?" she asked as she poured their coffee. "You two look like cats who caught the canary."

"You want to tell her?" Charlie asked Harvey.

Harvey shook his head, still grinning. "It's your doing."

"What?" Elsie asked.

Charlie reached into his jacket pocket and took out an envelope, which he handed to her.

Elsie set down the coffeepot and turned the envelope over to look at it—strangely, it was addressed to her, at Charlie and Harvey's address. The return address was Chouinard. It had been opened already.

"What is this?" she asked, but her heart began to pound, her heart already knew. Elsie took out the letter, her fingers trembling as she unfolded it and read the words. "Oh my God, what did you do?"

"You've been accepted," Charlie said. "I know you said you were waiting for Walter's class, and maybe you didn't want this, but we went ahead and applied for you. I sent it in myself. I told them you were the most talented fashion designer I've seen. Elsie, you're accepted to Chouinard! Even over the GIs!"

Harvey and Charlie looked jubilant. Elsie was jubilant. She had tried not to think of it, she had tried to put it aside, and yet the dream remained, and she could not deny she wanted it.

"Oh." She pressed her hand to her chest, unable to say what she felt, and then she realized Anita was watching from behind the counter and she was smiling and no one asked Elsie for more coffee or water, and everyone seemed to know that something special was happening, and Elsie wanted to cry with sheer happiness.

"I don't know how to do this," she managed. "Walter won't—"

"Well, after tonight, Walter's going to be a star, isn't he?" Harvey asked. "And we're going to help you, honey. You're going to be the best investment we've ever made."

~

She decided to wait until after the play on opening night to tell Walt about Chouinard, when they would be celebrating his success too. Everyone would be jubilant. The movie producers would be there, one would offer Walt a contract, and his star would rise with hers. They would be on their way.

She decided to wear the orange-red dress with pink organza overlay—it was her good luck charm, and his, too, since she'd been wearing it when he first realized how much she could help him. When she came downstairs in the dress, with her hair up, she expected him to appreciate the symbolism, but he was obviously too distracted. He barely noted her.

She kissed him. "Tonight's going to be perfect."

He straightened and nodded shortly. "We'd better go."

Walter had reserved her a seat in the front row. The theater was mostly full. She wondered which of the men she saw were movie producers. Maybe that one in the gray suit, or the one over there with the glasses who looked very well groomed. She opened her program and scanned it until she found Walter's name: *Man in Bar... Walt Maynard.* So he'd decided to go with Walt as a stage name. She had pushed for Walter. It sounded more dignified. Like Humphrey Bogart or Orson Welles. Two-syllable first names had more heft. But Walter said he liked the livelier, more assured sound of Walt. *"It makes me sound like an ace, don't you think?"*

The lights went down. Elsie closed her program and settled back to watch the play, excited for Walter to appear. The first act went on and on with no sign of him. The second act opened in a bar and there he was, looking handsome where he sat, wearing the linen suit she'd first seen him in at the grange in Zanesville. The director had asked the actors to costume themselves, and the suit was the best he had, and she'd agreed that it would be perfect. How different it had made him in Zanesville, how it had made him stand out.

But the suit looked old fashioned on the LA stage, compared with what the other actors wore. It even looked seedy, and in it, Walter, with his six lines, certainly made an impression—just not a good one, which would have been fine, had that been the character.

It wasn't.

His words so broadly articulated, that flamboyant gesture he'd thought so perfect looked like it had come straight out of a silent movie. Dark-haired, handsome Walter. *"Like Rudolph Valentino...,"* the other actor had said, and now she understood what he'd meant. Not just Walter's looks, but also his melodramatic delivery belonged to another time.

It was all wrong for this play. The crowd laughed, but his lines weren't funny.

Elsie sank into her chair, cringing for her husband. The gesture was ridiculous—why had no one told him? Why hadn't the director said something? And the suit . . . the character was a man-about-town. He needed a dark suit; she would have said charcoal. Double breasted. A richly colored tie to signal confidence and discernment. Superbly tailored.

She was relieved when the scene ended and Walter left the stage. Unfortunately, now Elsie knew a truth she did not want to face. If there were movie producers there, none would be offering Walter a contract based on that performance. She did not want to think about what the critics would say. There was no way Walter would be a star. Not after tonight. Not after any night. She knew that with searing, swift certainty.

The truth was that Walter wasn't good. The truth was that her confidence in him was not just shaken but broken. Again, she heard what the pool hall owner had said. *"You hitched your wagon to a loser, girlie."*

Had she?

The answer came to her with blinding clarity. *Yes, you have.*

But she couldn't admit it out loud.

Afterward, she went backstage and smiled and hugged him and kissed him and said, "That was wonderful! I enjoyed it so much!"

"Did you? You really did?"

"I'm sure the play's going to be a hit," she assured him, though she knew it wouldn't be.

On the way home, Walter said, "I think the crowd really responded to me, didn't you? Did you hear them?"

"Yes, I did."

"You see what I mean about the gesture? How it really brings the character into focus?"

How to say it without hurting his feelings? Elsie searched for the words. "Well . . . honestly I think . . . you know, it might be a little old fashioned."

"Old fashioned? How do you mean?"

"Your character is supposed to be sophisticated, right? He's supposed to know what he's talking about. So I don't think they'd trust someone who's so . . . flamboyant and old-style."

Walter went very quiet. The car felt uncomfortable. Elsie looked out at the passing buildings, the other cars.

She tried, "Your lines aren't supposed to be funny, are they?"

Walter threw her a quick look.

"I mean . . . you know, maybe the gesture doesn't work the way you mean it to. But I might be wrong. Those movie producers tonight—"

"There were no movie producers there tonight," he snapped. "None of them came."

"Oh."

"This is not going the way I thought it would!" He slammed his hand on the steering wheel. "There weren't even critics there tonight!"

"It's only the first night. I'm sure once they know about it . . ."

"Yeah." Walter spoke as if he were trying to convince himself. He stared ahead. "Yeah. But you know what else? I have to audition to get into that Actors' Lab thing! Me! Can you believe it?"

"Oh, well, about that—I've been thinking—"

"I agree. I've been thinking too. Who needs it, right? I don't need any of that fancy acting crap. I'm good without it, right, baby? I can be a star just the way I am. It's all about the right look, you know. The play's going to build, and soon I'll get another part—the right part—and now that you've got that job, I've got time, I've got all the time I need. I'll keep auditioning, and it'll happen. You watch."

Elsie said nothing.

"So maybe it doesn't go as quick as I expected. So what? Someone's looking for the new Rudolph Valentino. Someone wants Walt Maynard. I'll be in *Photoplay*. One day it'll be my name on the marquee—it's all going to happen."

How embarrassed she'd been for him in that theater.

"You hitched your wagon to a loser."

He nervously thumbed the steering wheel *rat-a-tat-tat*, that intent stare, those Valentino eyes, and suddenly she saw herself at the end of the pool table, making it all happen for him, and she knew another truth she hadn't wanted to admit—he needed her. She had made the hustle work. Without her, they wouldn't be here. Walter couldn't have made it to LA on his own. He was good at pool, but he wasn't *that* good. Her ability to distract the other players had allowed him to win as often as not. *She* was the key.

She had wanted out of Zanesville, and he had taken her out. She had lied to herself about what he was. But Charlie was right. Walter was just a hustler. He was a loser. And if she stayed with him, she'd be a loser too. She would keep working to support Walter, live in a duplex forever, and Walter would keep auditioning and maybe he'd get small parts but he would never be a star. He would only ever be dreaming, and she would never get to Chouinard. She would never be anything but a diner waitress and wife. The vision leaped into her head with an insistence she couldn't ignore. Exhausted from days at the diner, laundry hanging on the line and a baby in her arms and toddlers crying. Waiting for Walter to come home from another audition, another small part. Every night a few hours later. Every night more drunk.

The horror of it, and the clarity, startled her. This was not what she wanted. This was never what she'd wanted. There would never be enough money. Her life would be worse than it had ever been in Zanesville, more a trap, because once she had children, she'd never leave them.

"You believe in me, don't you, baby? You believe I can make it?"

They were at the top of the street. The stairs loomed before them. She could keep her wagon hitched. Or she could unhitch it.

"No," she said steadily. "You know what? I don't think you can."

It took her a moment to realize she'd said the words aloud, and they surprised her as much as they obviously did Walter, who stomped on the brakes in the middle of the street, jerking them both forward. "What?"

"I don't think you can," she repeated slowly, letting the truth sink in.

Elsie opened the car door and got out. She slammed it behind her and started up the steep steps.

"Elsie!" Walter yelled out the window. "Where are you going? Goddamn it, Elsie!"

She kept going. Past the quiet chicken coop, the hens inside for the night.

"Elsie!"

He couldn't leave the car there; he'd have to park it before he could come after her. She dodged down the street, passed their duplex, and turned onto an alley.

"Elsiiee!" Walter's voice came plaintively behind her. Then, explosively, "Don't you run to those Reds! I know who they are, you know! I'll call the FBI! Elsie! You unnatural bitch! Come back here!"

She ran. Down more stairs, down another steep, twisty street. She was so busy listening for Walter to come after her that she was at Harvey and Charlie's block before she knew it, and then she saw the lights blazing—too bright, shadows crossing, noise. She stopped. All the commotion came from her friends' bungalow, and people parading from the house into the darkness, herded by men in suits and police officers. It was obviously a raid on a meeting of some kind. Harvey and Charlie and their fellow travelers were being arrested.

She fought the urge to race forward to defend them. That would be stupid and she knew it. They would just haul her away too. She could not go there. But she did not want to go back to Walter. She had nowhere to go.

She heard a man shout. Someone pointed to where she stood at the end of the block.

Elsie turned and ran down the hill, past one set of darkened houses, farther, a roundabout way, avoiding the road, until she reached the café. It was the only place she knew to go, though she also knew Walter would check there before long. It was closed. But the lights were on in the bungalow behind, where Anita lived. Elsie pounded on the door until Anita opened it.

"What the . . . ? Elsie?"

"I'm sorry," she said. "I've left Walter, and I . . . could I just come in for a minute or two? Please."

Anita stepped back quickly, her gaze moving beyond Elsie, searching the night as she ushered Elsie in. "My dear, you can stay much longer than that. Get yourself in here."

~

Anita put her in a spare bedroom and told her to stay away from the café for a few days, which was good advice, because Walt came by the next afternoon.

"He said to tell you he's done with you," Anita said. "You want my advice, Elsie? Maybe that's true and maybe it isn't, but if I were you, I'd clear out for a while, hmmm?"

Elsie had the money she'd saved for Walter's Actors' Lab classes, but she was now going to have to find a place to live, and not only that, but working at the café wasn't an option. It wasn't that Elsie thought Walter was a danger, but . . . he could be persuasive, and she didn't want to be persuaded to be with him again. It was just better to put it all behind her. She wanted to move on. She wanted a future that didn't include Walter. She was in LA with the chance to start new, and she meant to do that. She'd look into getting a divorce soon, but for now a new job, a place to live, and then . . . What about Chouinard? She'd been accepted, but Harvey and Charlie were arrested. She had no idea where they were or what to do about that. She was on her own. She would have to get the money for tuition herself.

"Who knows when they'll be out or what they'll do then," Anita said over a cup of coffee one Sunday morning. "That they're Reds is bad enough, if the feds discover they're fairies too—what? Don't give me that look. Don't you know a fairy when you see one?"

Anita's words were a little shock, though now that she'd said it, Elsie wondered why she hadn't noted it before. She'd never seen Harvey and Charlie touch, really, had she? But now . . . well, of course. It was obvious that Harvey and Charlie were a couple. The way Harvey handed Charlie the sugar before he asked for it, the small comments, "*Better get Harvey his coffee quick. He's sullen this morning.*" Things like that. The way they looked at one another, the way they seemed to know what the other was thinking.

Elsie tried to figure out how she felt about it. It was one thing to know that homosexuals existed. But to see a couple, to imagine them as a couple . . .

Yet she truly liked them, and they were . . . they were just normal people, and it was those little things, wasn't it? No different from how she'd been with Walter, she supposed. She could not look at Harvey and Charlie and think *degenerate*, or *morally enfeebled*. Quite the opposite. They were two of the most principled men she'd ever known. They were friends. They had helped her. This new revelation didn't matter.

Anita laughed. "I surprised you, I see. You don't know what to say. Tongue tied! You know what you need, Elsie? Confidence. You let Walter walk right over you and he was nothing. But you . . . you've got something. I'm not sure what it is exactly, but you could do something with yourself. You should get a good job and go to Chouinard, the way Harvey and Charlie said. See what it makes of you."

The next evening, Elsie went down to Charlie and Harvey's. The house was dark and locked up. No one was there. She walked over to the duplex she'd shared with Walter. He wasn't there, fortunately, and she hastily gathered her things. All of her in one suitcase. She did not leave a note.

It was a relief.

The idea of starting new, alone, frightened her, but Anita's words about her needing confidence stayed with her, and Elsie knew her friend was right, and that maybe Walter had seen that, too, and it had let him think that Elsie would do whatever he wanted. She had, too, but she had learned some things since then.

Walter had taught her how to make people notice her when she wanted them to, and Anita had told her she had "something." Harvey and Charlie had said she had talent.

Now all Elsie needed to do was turn those things into a future.

CHAPTER 4

Los Angeles, California—1950

Polly's on Olive was an old nightclub and its glory days were behind it, but the tips Elsie earned as a cocktail waitress paid the rent at an all-women's boardinghouse and the tuition at Chouinard, and that was all Elsie cared about. She treated the shin-length slit skirt, heels, striped shirt, and jaunty scarf of her uniform as a costume, and when she wore it, she focused on her role as a vivacious cocktail waitress. When she finished her shift, she was once again Elsie Gruner, fashion design student, intoxicated by Chouinard. In every spare moment she drew and practiced; she filled sketchbooks with drawings and notebooks with notes, went to breakfast with other students and wished fervently that she could do just this, only this. That she couldn't, she knew full well. Work paid the bills. Work paid for tuition and books, drawing materials, everything. She was a dedicated student, as dedicated as she could be. She declined when the other staff at Polly's invited her for drinks. She tried to avoid the constant conversations about what the US should do now that the Soviets had the bomb too. She had no time for existential dread, and she didn't want to discuss the bestseller everyone but she had read, *How to Survive an Atomic Bomb*. She had homework. She had design on her mind. She owed it to Harvey and Charlie, who believed in her and who she tried, unsuccessfully, to find. She owed it to herself.

She was one of the top of her class. Not *the* top, that honor belonged to Jasper Rutledge. Everyone liked him. Well, everyone but Elsie, who found him to be what her father would have called a brownnoser and her mother an apple-polisher. That he was talented was unarguable. He was also a full-time student who didn't have to work.

"Bound for a top fashion house," Mr. Matthews, their professor in Fashion Illustration, said once, grinning as proudly as a father, and Jasper strutted around annoyingly for a while after that.

"It's too bad," Jasper told Elsie. "But it's not your fault, really."

"What's not my fault?"

"That you're a woman. Everyone knows women designers are second best," he said.

"Why should that be?"

"They've got husbands and children, that's why. They can't focus their whole attention on a career."

"Can anyone these days?" asked another student. "There may not even be a future. This may all be a waste of time."

Jasper rolled his eyes. "I'll worry about the bomb when I'm dead."

Elsie said, "There are plenty of women designers. Claire McArdle, Schiaparelli, Lanvin."

Jasper made a face. "Will they be around in a decade? Probably not. But you do have some talent, Gruner. For the few years before you start having kids, you'll do all right. I'll tell you what, look me up when you've graduated, and I'll find you a job in my atelier."

The others laughed. Elsie didn't tell him that kids were unlikely since she'd left her husband and had no idea where he was and no desire to find him. She clenched her charcoal so hard it crumbled.

Then she saw the announcement on the bulletin board in the hallway, the offer of a six-month internship at the American Art Academy in Rome. She nearly passed it by, but then the words *scholarships available* caught her eye. She couldn't afford it. She couldn't afford to give up her job for six months. It was crazy. She shouldn't even think about it.

But it wouldn't leave her mind. There was something about it—fate perhaps? Something else?—that nagged at her, that told her it was what she needed. The best fashion houses were in Europe. What edge could such an internship give her?

Elsie filled out the application. She filled out the request for the scholarship. She got a teacher's recommendation from Mr. Matthews, and another from Mr. Teske. She put together her portfolio with care and took the entire package to the administrator's office to send to the academy. The secretary had stepped out for a moment, so Elsie sat down to wait.

The open window beside the secretary's desk let in a spring breeze. The papers on the desk ruffled; one threatened to fly onto the floor, and without thinking Elsie grabbed it to anchor it. That was when she saw a manila envelope similar to the one she held, addressed also to the American Art Academy in Rome. Written below the address, just as it was written on hers, was *Internship Application.*

The return address was Jasper Rutledge's.

Elsie's heart sank. She hadn't known he planned to apply. He was graduating in June; there was no possible way he wouldn't win the internship. She might as well not even try. He was talented, he was a man, and he was ready to embark upon his career. He would probably brownnose his way into a European atelier, which he hardly needed. The teachers' recommendations could get him on at any house as an intern, or even as an assistant. He had money. He had everything she didn't have. It was unfair. He didn't need the internship, and she did. She had nothing except her own will and her talent.

This chance in Rome was everything to her. She did not know if she could win it, but she knew she would not if she was in competition with Jasper. It was that simple.

She thought about stealing his application, throwing it away. The urge was nearly overwhelming. The secretary was gone. It would be easy. But then . . . she would always wonder if she could have got the scholarship on her own. She would never trust her talent. Anita's voice whispered, "*Confidence*," and Elsie couldn't ignore it. How else did she get confidence except by believing in herself the way Harvey and Charlie had?

She left Jasper's application on the desk. When the secretary came back, Elsie handed the woman her application with a smile, said "Thank you" when the woman wished her good luck, and left.

~

A month later, the administrator called her into the office to tell her she'd got the internship at the American Art Academy in Rome, along with a scholarship.

Jasper Rutledge went around telling everyone he hadn't really wanted it anyway. He was going to Milan when he graduated. It was the center for Italian fashion anyway. After that, he was bound for Paris.

Elsie only smiled.

CHAPTER 5

Rome—summer 1950

She'd taken a ship and trains to get to Rome, and during the journey, Elsie's excitement had grown so much that she thought the reality of Rome and the art school could never measure up to it, but when she arrived at the elegant and winding drive bordered by tall trees and ending at a soft pink villa with a tiled roof and jutting square towers, she realized she was wrong. She hadn't had enough imagination to envision this. Elsie paused, exhausted and sweating, and dropped her suitcase. It landed on the flagstones with a thud. She flexed her hand, imprinted now with the stitching from its cheap and fraying leather handle, and stared at the American Art Academy in Rome, wondering again at the will she'd manifested to get herself here. Here, she was sure, her life would change again.

She picked up the suitcase and made her way to the large and imposing iron door that stood three times her height, with great pull rings. One side was wide open, and she walked into a foyer with a pink marble floor inset with great white granite medallions, white pillars holding up arched frescoed ceilings, and bustle.

She found the academy office down the expansive hallway, and it was like no office she'd ever seen. Massive red stone desks that looked as if they'd been lifted from some palace, chairs with upholstery that could have suited French kings. Sun slanting through huge windows overlooking a fountain of a veiled woman pouring water from a jug. The place didn't look quite real. It was about as far away from anything in LA or Zanesville, Ohio, as you could get, and since those were the only places she'd really been, she couldn't help staring in awe.

"Can I help you, miss?" the woman at the nearest desk asked with an inquiring smile.

Elsie approached. "I'm Elsie Gruner. New intern?"

"Ah." The woman nodded, took up a pair of heavy black-framed glasses, and turned to a vast wooden card catalog behind her. "Welcome to the American Art Academy, Elsie. I'm Mrs. Brown. Spell your last name?"

Elsie did. Mrs. Brown pulled open a drawer and skimmed through the cards. "Here you are. Fashion design—is that right?"

Elsie nodded.

"You're in the Villa Augusta, the female dormitory."

"Are there many other women interns?"

"Only three this summer," Mrs. Brown told her. "But we've only been taking female students since the war, so . . . there are two other resident artists. You won't be lonely."

Loneliness was the last thing Elsie had thought to worry about. She'd be too busy to be lonely. She'd quit Polly's on Olive. Chouinard she'd taken leave from, not knowing if she would return, and sent a postcard to her parents saying she was going to Italy for the foreseeable future. Whatever the academy brought her in the next six months, she meant to leverage however she could.

"Rob," Mrs. Brown called out. A young man with a head of brown curls popped up from behind another wall of card catalogs. "This is Elsie Gruner. Would you please show her to the Augusta? She's a new intern." She turned back to Elsie and handed her a manila envelope labeled with Elsie's name. "Here's all the information you'll need."

Rob sprinted over with a smile and an extended hand. "Rob Phillips."

She shook his hand and he took her suitcase, nearly wrenching it from her in his enthusiasm.

"Have you seen the gardens yet?" he asked, leading her from the office and back into the massive hallway.

"I only just arrived."

"You'll love them. Off to the side there, follow that hall straight out." He shrugged the direction. "Sometimes they hold classes there. Are you studying archaeology? You'll dig the Palatine—I was there yesterday. Or you could help out with—"

"Fashion design," she said.

"Oh. Well, I don't know anything about that." A quick grin. "But I can tell you all about the Etruscan origins of early Roman sculpture."

Elsie grinned back. "I'll know who to ask if I have any questions about it."

He jabbered on, but she was too busy looking around to pay much attention as he led her through a back door and onto a loggia with an elaborate cast-iron gate, and then down worn, cracked steps that might have been centuries old, past trees bearing foliage shaped like huge pom-poms and shrubs she didn't know the names of, and the fragrance of flowers mixed with that of smoke and petrol wafting from the Via Flaminia beyond. Another winding path, also worn and very uneven, led to a low-slung, two-story, whitewashed, tile-roofed building midway down a slight hill.

"It's hardly a villa. It was a stable once," Rob said as they approached. "But don't worry, they've done away with the stalls."

He took her to the door, but then stood back. "I'm not allowed inside. Only women, you know. They're not very strict about us mixing, except for the residence halls."

"I see. Thanks for showing me the way." Elsie eyed the heavy shutters on the windows, dark green and closed against the hot afternoon.

"You're welcome. Hope I see you around!" He set down her suitcase and was off, whistling as he climbed the path back up the hill.

This would be home for the next six months. Elsie swallowed a mix of excitement and nerves. She was already in love with the place—how could anything bad happen where a pot of splashy red carnations beckoned so welcomingly at the door?

The lever pulled easily in her hand—unlocked—and the door opened to reveal a narrow foyer of cracked black-and-white tile, and a painted table that held a pair of soiled gardening gloves and a filthy clay ashtray. It was quiet.

Elsie ventured into the great room. A kitchen was off to one side, and stairs on the other. The room opened onto a loggia at the far side, overlooking the downslope of the hill and a grove of palms, a park below and the spread of Rome beyond that, and all she could think was, How could *Elsie Gruner* live in a place like this? She was nobody, a farm girl from Ohio, and this was *Rome*. She turned away, overwhelmed at how out of place she felt, but then she caught sight of the books, notebooks, sketchbooks, pencils, paints—the evidence of art everywhere—and felt immediately comforted. This she knew. If she concentrated on art, she would find her way.

"Hello?" Elsie ventured.

There was no answer.

She set down the suitcase carefully, gripped by the impulse to be as silent as the building, and glimpsed the kitchen, which was a mess: pots and pans helter-skelter, something spilled and burned on the stove, a half-drunk bottle of red wine beside the sink.

"Who are you?"

The voice startled Elsie and she cracked her shoulder on the doorframe as she jerked around to see a woman who looked to be her age padding barefoot toward her. The woman was stunning, with wide-spaced catlike eyes, a wide mouth, long, waving chestnut-colored hair. She wore loose trousers and a blouse without a bra, and Elsie immediately felt like a tired frump in her polka-dot dress, wrinkled from traveling. Not only that, but she was tongue tied.

"Well? Who are you?"

"Elsie Gruner. I'm an intern."

"In what?"

"Fashion design."

"With that name?" The woman laughed. "Oh God, no. You can't possibly be serious."

Elsie didn't like feeling at a disadvantage. She felt trapped against the kitchen doorway, and this woman was odd and disconcerting. "It's my name," she said stiffly, stepping into the space the other woman had claimed. "I suppose yours is much better."

"Julia Keane," said the woman.

Yes, of course it was better. Of course she had an appealing name. Of course it matched this woman, who seemed to have inhaled elegance. A name was just a name, wasn't it? Until Elsie realized as she stood in the hot summer air of a Roman villa that it was one more thing that marked her as a farmer's daughter from smack in the middle of Zanesville, Ohio, in way she'd never considered before.

Elsie managed, "Are you studying fashion design too?"

Julia smiled and shook her head. "Archaeology. Don't worry. We're not competing."

"I wasn't—"

"Oh yes, you were." Julia's smile broadened. She had a vague accent, very slight, one Elsie could not place. "But that's okay. I know just the room to put you in. Then we'll have some wine and I'll tell you all the things to avoid here this summer and all the best things to do. But I'm not going to call you Elsie. That's the name of that Borden cow, and you're no cow. Besides, you're going to be famous one day, and Elsie just won't do, will it?"

"No," Elsie agreed softly. "It won't."

Julia smiled. "You smell good too. What is that?"

This time, the smell wasn't pig shit. "L'Air du Temps."

"It's nice. I like it. Come with me."

CHAPTER 6

The students had mandatory dinner in the dining room three nights a week, and that first night was one of them. Julia showed Elsie the way.

"You have to participate in the conversation du jour," Julia explained. "But don't worry. It's not that hard."

Still, Elsie worried. It was only her first night, and what if the chosen subject was something like—what had that boy said when she arrived? Ancient Etruscan pottery or something? *Confidence,* she told herself.

The academy dining room was as stunning as the rest of the main building. Its frescoed ceilings were a colorful garden, the faded gold brocade wallpaper mostly covered with what Julia said was a constantly changing gallery of student work. The brass-nailhead-trimmed mahogany chairs and tables and rugs had obviously been chosen for their venerable age rather than comfort. The food was good and nothing like Italian food Elsie'd had before, no ketchupy spaghetti, no pillowy garlic bread soaked in butter. Instead crispy fried artichokes, pasta Amatriciana flecked with pork and chilies and tomatoes, chewy bread, revelatory wine, and perfectly ripe cherries and melon for dessert. Afterward, the leading professor, Pietro Basile, rose to introduce the topic he'd chosen for conversation: "In what ways has the ancient Jewish ghetto lived on in Rome?"

Julia snorted. "The better question is, In what ways has it not? Countries have a habit of capitalizing on the suffering of those they subject. Rome is no different. They've turned the ghetto into cultural tourism. Those artichokes we had for dinner? Those were a ghetto recipe. I doubt the privileged ever thought to eat thistles until the poor had no choice but to do so."

Laura Mesner, a summer intern from New York, and the other resident at the Augusta, who Elsie had just met, retorted, "God, I get tired of hearing you talk about the poor. Like you would know. You're at the American Art Academy in Rome."

Julia shot her a withering look. "At least I don't suffer from poverty of the soul."

Laura rolled her eyes.

"Anyone else?" Pietro Basile boomed. He was a tall, muscled sculptor, the hair on his arms still dusted with dried clay slurry. "We're talking of the ghetto, remember, not the poor."

At another table, another student began to talk about the spiritual legacy of the ghetto. Julia leaned close to Elsie and whispered, "Let's go down to the Babuino tonight."

"What's the Babuino?" Elsie asked.

Laura, on Julia's other side, said, "Oh, that sounds fun! Yes, let's."

And then the suggestion traveled all around the table, and instead of just the two of them planning for what Elsie began to understand was a night at the cafés and bars on a street called the Via del Babuino, there were six. After dinner, Elsie changed into her best dress, one she'd designed at Chouinard, a sleek sleeveless sheath with a bow at the empire waist and a bit of lace at the high neckline. She'd only been able to afford a polished cotton of sage green, but it gave the dress a sheen that in some lights turned it satiny, and she was pleased with it. With gloves and a short bolero jacket—which she'd also made—she thought the outfit had a certain sophistication.

Or at least, she did until she saw the dress Julia wore. It was black, pleated silk, with broad straps ending at a banded bodice, simple and beautiful, and the way the skirt moved made Julia look so free and unencumbered that Elsie felt immediately imprisoned by her fitted sheath. Julia wore no gloves, while Elsie's hands were sweating in hers, and the evening was too warm for the jacket. She slipped the button loose and pulled off her gloves, then shoved them impatiently into her purse.

Julia's gaze swept over her. "Pretty dress."

It seemed all right then. The dress. The jacket. "It's my own design," she said proudly.

Julia flicked her fingers at her own collar. "The lace too?"

"It's too much, isn't it?" Elsie said.

Julia smiled. "I didn't say that."

"I thought the lace was too much. It makes it fussy."

Julia leaned close. Her lips brushed Elsie's ear. "Never admit your doubts."

The flicker of a touch sent a shiver through Elsie—a surprise. She didn't know what to do with it. "Where are the others?"

"I told them to take the boys and go ahead and we'd meet them at Il Baretto."

Elsie frowned. "Did I take too long?"

"No. But you and I aren't going to Il Baretto. Unless . . ." A pause. A careful look. "Unless I've mistaken you. Maybe you'd rather spend the evening with them."

Elsie recognized a challenge in her words. "No," she said. It had taken her only a few hours to understand that Julia was clearly a leader here, and Elsie wanted to belong. "No. Where are we going?"

"It's a surprise. But a good one. I think you'll like it."

Elsie followed Julia out of the residence hall and down the hill, where they plunged immediately into a group of nuns.

"Be prepared," Julia warned her, weaving through them. "It's a Holy Year. The faithful are everywhere."

"What's a Holy Year?"

Julia laughed. "Not a Catholic, I see."

"No." Her parents, like their neighbors, were suspicious of Catholics. All that ritual and incense. "Are you?"

Julia dragged on her cigarette. "Religion is a drug. It keeps you from thinking too hard about anything important."

Elsie had never heard anyone speak like that. She'd gone to church every Sunday with her parents and never questioned it. Julia's words gave her an uncomfortable feeling, as if she were edging up against some invisible border, a world she couldn't understand. "So you don't know what a Holy Year is either?"

"Sure I do. The pope declared this year one of jubilee. We've all been granted universal pardon. So I guess if you're going to sin, now's the time to do it."

"I see." Somehow that didn't seem quite right. Elsie couldn't imagine the leader of any church saying it was okay to sin. But she didn't know, really, and Julia seemed so certain.

The neon signs were coming on with twilight, casting colors onto cobbled streets that shone from the wear of centuries. Crowds in the Piazza di Spagna loitered about the stairs of the Trinità dei Monti, and the boat-shaped fountain at the bottom. Then Julia veered into a narrow street crowded mostly with men: men smoking, men talking, men staring at her with their expressive Italian eyes and vaguely obscene smiles, their "*cara, cara, cara*," their whistles and chittering. Elsie wanted to hide. If a man had acted like this in Zanesville—or even LA—she would have called the police. But Julia waved them off dismissively. When they passed an odd fountain bearing theatrical faces and a bucket of paintbrushes at the top, Julia said, "It's the street of the artists. Via Margutta."

The buildings were tightly pressed together, the shabby plastered surfaces ochre and russet that took on deeper tones in the twilight, neon signs glowing, creating red-, green-, and yellow-hued umbras, lights coming from the clubs and studios and cafés, music eking from inside. Cigarette smoke hung in clouds about the vined walls, twined about the branches of a tree—a tree, rising from a tiny plot beside a front door, crowding the street more.

Raucous talk, laughter, from the crowded streets and from the vine-covered balconies overlooking them and from hidden courtyards;

Elsie felt watched on all sides, as if there were hidden dimensions, layers and layers of shadows, of caverns and chambers, of secrets. Fantastic and strange, magical and delightful and romantic. Graffiti marked some walls, drawings in chalk; here and there someone had hung a painting. Before a door were mounds of stones, some carved, some awaiting the chisel or the mallet.

"Over there is a brothel." Julia pointed to a second floor with closed, chained shutters behind a balcony. "There's another one a bit farther down. A few of them."

"Oh." Elsie couldn't hide her shock. She'd never seen an actual brothel. Only streetwalkers. "Really?"

"Here we are." Julia stopped before a group of men smoking in front of a large green door with a cast-iron fanlight. Music—jazz—emanated from inside, and shadows moved behind the single foggy window. "Hey, Tony!" Julia called, and one of the men detached himself from the group and came toward her, dropping his cigarette on the way and grinding it beneath his shoe.

"Cara mia." He enfolded Julia in his arms. His hands went to her hips, trailing down, gripping her buttocks and pulling her closer until she gave him a rough shove and said something in Italian.

He rolled his eyes and stepped back with a grin. He turned to Elsie and started talking.

"She doesn't speak Italian," Julia said. "Yet. This is . . . um . . . Isabella. No, that doesn't work, does it? How about . . . Maria?" A frown. "Too common, I think."

Tony laughed. "She has forgotten her name?" He was tall and trim, with muscled arms and broad shoulders and an undeniable appeal. His thick dark hair held a touch of curl. He reminded Elsie of Tony Curtis, but this man's eyes were very brown.

"We don't like her name. We're looking for a new one," Julia told him.

"I have always liked Julia," he said.

"There are already a thousand Julias in Rome," Julia said. "We don't need another."

He studied Elsie with mock seriousness. "She looks like a Bianca."

Elsie frowned. "Doesn't that mean 'white'?"

"You don't like Bianca?" he asked teasingly.

"It's just so . . . bland."

"She's not bland," Julia told him. "This one's special, Tony."

Elsie stared at her in surprise. Julia smiled back—it sent a disconcerting flutter through Elsie, as if Julia saw something she could not possibly know.

"I see." Tony turned to the green door. "Come have a drink, not-Bianca. This is my club. La Grotta."

He swept her to the door, Julia following close behind. Music poured out as if it meant to imprint itself upon the smoky twilight, that hard messy beat, that low moan of the saxophone turning the evening dark, sneaking into those deep and longing parts of Elsie, reminding her of the jazz that night on the road with Walter. She hadn't heard it live since. The audiences at the nightclubs in LA preferred mambas and sambas and cha-chas, so that's what the bands played. Everyone wanted to dance these days, but this wasn't cha-cha music. This was *I want to get under your skin* music. She felt Tony's hand at her lower back with a tingling awareness. The smoke in the place felt dense and solid. *La Grotta.* It didn't take much to translate that into something she could understand. A grotto, a cave. Yes, it felt like that here.

Dim and smoky. Scallop-shaped sconces were few and far between and lit the brick walls in limited wedges of light. Tables crowded the place, some with small oil lamps flickering, pressing futilely against the smoke and the darkness and the physicality of the music from the small stage—barely a stage—at the back of the building, which held a quartet. No one was dancing, but every table was full, and the chairs against the walls were full, too, and people stood in front of the windows, blocking any light from the street. Some people talked, but mostly everyone listened intently to the band. Shoulders jerked in time, heads bobbed, bodies gyrated in their seats.

The bar was crowded too. Elsie swayed as she watched the band, aware that Tony and Julia spoke intently in low Italian before Tony went back to the bar. His place, Elsie supposed he had business. But then she noted the way Julia watched him go, studied and careful, and she followed Julia's gaze. Tony disappeared into the crowd at the bar. Then she heard Julia's voice in her ear. "I'll be right back."

As if she'd been waiting for Tony to go. Elsie nodded. Julia did not follow Tony, as Elsie half expected her to do. Instead, she wove her way through the tables toward the stage, half-hidden by the smoke. Then she veered to the left and just . . . disappeared.

Elsie blinked. It took a moment before she discerned the black curtain to the left of the stage, which obscured some room or alcove or hallway from the rest of the place. That's where Julia had gone. Elsie watched that curtain so intently it dissolved again into the misty darkness and she couldn't decide if it was really there or she'd imagined it. Something glinted on the olive oil cans stacked near the stage stairs, a reflection from a cigarette, the glint off a ring as someone else approached the curtain. A man. Elsie narrowed her eyes, trying to focus in the faint light, trying to decide if she really saw him, or if he was just an imagined shadow within a shadow, a man dressed in black slipping behind a black curtain.

The band ended the song to applause and people banging their hands on the table, and Elsie tore her gaze from the curtain long enough to watch the sax player gulp from a drink at his side and pick up his instrument again. He began a long, soulful solo, mesmerizing. For a moment she forgot the curtain, and when she looked back again, Julia was coming toward her.

"Ready for some fun?" Julia asked.

"Isn't that what we're already having?"

Julia took Elsie's hand, her fingers tight, her touch stirring those vague longings that the music had already raised. "Come on."

Outside, the night had grown darker. Julia took only a few steps and turned down a *vicolo* that Elsie hadn't noticed before, disguised as it was by a narrow gate, crowded by a pot with an overgrown laurel. Julia nudged the gate with her shoulder; it creaked open and then they were in a short, covered passage smelling of must and cat urine, and there was the cat, too, giving them a baleful look as it meandered toward them. The passage opened into a courtyard, small and dirty, with terra-cotta urns of bent and scraggly palms and more cats, some lounging in the urns, others watching from the tops of brick walls half a story up, most of them with tails undulating mistrustfully. A lamp shining from someone's window above made silhouettes of a line of laundry; between the sleeves and the trousers peeked a narrow piece of sky that was intensely, deeply dark blue.

Julia released Elsie's hand and sat on the edge of an urn, the pleats of that black silk falling over her knees. She reached into her purse and took out what looked like a hand-rolled cigarette, and then motioned for Elsie to sit as well. She did, on the urn opposite, though her narrow skirt gave her little room to maneuver and she balanced awkwardly. The lace at the collar tickled her throat in the sweaty warmth. She wished she hadn't put it there, and decided she would remove it as soon as they got back.

Julia put the cigarette to her lips and pulled out a silver lighter. She held the lighter to the tip, the click, the fleeting stink of naphtha, and then the stink of something else: the smoke didn't smell like tobacco, but weedy and skunk-like. Elsie knew immediately what it was, not because she'd ever tried it, but because she'd smelled it sometimes outside the pool halls.

Julia took another drag and wordlessly held out the reefer to Elsie, and it was clear in the lamplight that she expected Elsie to take it. And Elsie, who knew when she was being dared, reached out and took it from Julia's fingers. Then she put the marijuana cigarette to her lips and inhaled.

The smoke choked her. She coughed hard, her eyes watering. She went hot with embarrassment, but Julia only watched her with that unreadable gaze and said, "You know you shine."

Elsie was so stunned that she forgot about the cigarette burning in her hand. Julia motioned for her to smoke it. Elsie put the thing to her lips again, and this time she didn't cough so much. She didn't feel anything either. She wasn't sure what she was supposed to feel.

"You're not like everyone else here," Julia went on.

"What makes you say that?"

"I don't know. You have a *look*. I can't define it. Where are you from?"

"Ohio."

"Oh, well. I don't know Ohio. Is it a different kind of place?"

Elsie laughed. "Different from here. Where are you from?"

Julia ignored her question. "So how did you get here?"

Elsie told her about Walter, the pool halls, leaving him, and Chouinard. Julia listened intently. When Elsie finished, Julia said, "Walter sounds like a jerk."

"He was a decent pool player. And he got me out of Zanesville."

"Sounds like you played the game better," Julia noted.

Elsie grinned. "Maybe. I'm a good learner."

"I hope he taught you not to listen to liars."

"Like people who tell me I 'shine'?"

Julia handed back the reefer. "Yes. Except for me. I'm telling you the truth. I'm not wrong about you, am I?" Julia spoke with a quiet intensity—how did one deny such a question?

Elsie could not. She swallowed and took another desperate drag, nearly choking as she tried to talk through her exhalation. "No, no you're not. I mean to be somebody someday."

Julia gave her a curious look, a small laugh that made Elsie wish she hadn't said it. But then Julia took the reefer and sucked it down to the end.

Elsie babbled, "What about you? You're studying archaeology, you said. What will you do with that? Are there many women archaeologists?"

Julia tossed the cigarette to the ground. She contemplated it for a moment. "Not many." Then she looked up at Elsie with that same look, the look that made Elsie want to curl inside herself, so penetrating it was. She thought Julia meant to tell her something else, something important, but instead Julia said, "Come on, let's go back to La Grotta."

She grabbed Elsie's hand to help her to her feet. It was only then that Elsie realized she was a bit woozy—or something; she couldn't quite say what, but the conversation fell away. She felt languid and loose and the night felt addictive; she wanted to drink it up, warm and fragrant with cat, murmuring with strains of music leaking from the nearby club and talk from Via Margutta, that blue of the sky in the narrow space between the buildings a blue she could not get over.

The creaking squeak of a window opening cut through the other noises, and with it a louder music from just overhead, someone's apartment, their record player, haunting horns and piano blasting through the night in a song Elsie had heard a hundred times before. "Stormy Weather"—how strange to hear it in Rome, on a crowded street, floating from above—and then a man keening "Leeeennnaaaa! Leeeennnnnaaaa!"

She looked up, but she couldn't see the window he called from.

"Leeennnnaaa!"

Elsie stood there, arrested by the music and the man's desperation, his crying into the deep blue night. "He sounds like he's dying for love."

"For something, anyway."

"No, really, Julia. He sounds like he's dying."

"Leeennnnaaa!" The cry came again, louder this time, more plaintive. They both looked up.

Julia straightened from picking up her purse from the ground and gave Elsie a look of such powerful revelation that Elsie's breath caught. "Hey, that's it," Julia said. "It's perfect."

"What's perfect?"

"The name! The way it came . . . it's like a sign. It fits you. Lena."

Elsie stared at her. *Lena.* The name draped like silk, settling into Elsie's every dip and curve.

Lena. Elsie murmured the name, liking the feel of it in her mouth, her tongue against her teeth. *Designed by Lena.*

"Yes," she said.

CHAPTER 7

Julia insisted on Elsie's name change, and before the week was out, everyone called her Lena. Elsie was surprised at how the name inhabited her so easily, as if it had been meant for her, and even she stopped thinking of herself as Elsie—she was Lena now, and it was astonishing how much more self-assured Lena was, how much more sophisticated. The name influenced everything she did, in ways she would not have imagined. Her designs had always been so radical in Zanesville; Lena made them more so. While Elsie might add a bit of organza to soften a low neckline, Lena let it stand. Lena took chances Elsie didn't take, she experimented with mixing fabrics that didn't seem to go together, she juxtaposed patterns, she didn't question her more flamboyant impulses. Would anyone in Zanesville know her now? Her parents would hardly recognize her.

She felt as if everything she'd done since leaving Ohio had led her slowly to Lena—getting into Walter's car, the pool halls, making friends with Harvey and Charlie, applying for the scholarship. The parts of her that had nearly succumbed to that autocratic, tradition-bound future—staying so long in Zanesville, letting Walter determine what she would do, being a nobody . . . those things were Elsie. She did not want to be Elsie anymore.

Rome made her feel the way she'd felt when she first stepped into a pool hall. Daring. Exciting. New.

Or maybe it wasn't Rome so much as it was Julia.

Julia loved Lena's designs the same way Harvey and Charlie had. She talked about Lena's talent to anyone who would listen. "She's going to be famous. You watch." Echoes of Walter's words, turned around, with Lena at their center instead. It was heady, it was alluring. Julia made Lena feel the *shine* inside in a way no one else ever had, and as the days went on, she found herself cherishing each moment with Julia, looking forward to the next—no, *longing* for the next.

Rome was the most wonderful city in the world. Julia made it so.

~

If Rome was the most beautiful city in the world, then La Grotta was its magical center. There were clubs all over Rome: those on the Via Veneto, where the fashionable played, and those on the Via del Babuino, including Il Baretto, an artists' bar. There was the Piccolo Slam, a nightclub with a jukebox that played American songs and where patrons could gamble or get drugs, and all the piano bars and dance clubs where the bands played the Latin songs everyone wanted to twist and shake and cha-cha to. But La Grotta was for jazz, and only for jazz. It was Julia's favorite spot, and it became Lena's too. It was where the musicians went after hours when they were sick of playing "Luna rossa" a dozen times a night.

That was the best time to go—late, after the other bars had closed, and Tony had kicked out everyone but his friends. They sat around and ate spaghetti with eggs and drank wine and listened while the horns and bass and pianists and drummers jammed, lively tunes that set them all on their feet, or—Lena's favorite—those mournful, deep-into-your-soul songs that made her feel she was turned inside out. La Grotta was where she first heard songs like "'Round Midnight," and "On Green Dolphin Street," and "Donna Lee."

Lena swayed in her chair, half-drunk, eyes closed, as "C'est si bon" wound to a close. The small, cheap table shook as someone ground out their cigarette in the ashtray. Someone else laughed, and a voice she recognized as Marco's called out, "Anyone want more bread?"

Marco was a sculptor with cropped brown hair and a studio down the block. Lena opened her eyes to see him standing near the stage holding half a ciabatta. There were no takers. Tony washed glasses behind the bar. Julia stood beside him, talking animatedly. Renato, a ruddy-headed painter with a matching beard, listened avidly, and Tony shook his head. *No no no.*

Beside Lena, Petra Schiano ran her finger idly around the rim of her wineglass. She was a photographer, who, according to Julia, was semifamous for her scenes of Roman dereliction juxtaposed with little signs of modern life—a solitary piazza with a cigarette butt, or a headless statue with a pigeon perched upon its shoulders—*"melancholy but pretty,"* Julia had said. Petra had soot-black hair she wore piled on her head, and eyes that looked equally black in the dim light of La Grotta. She and Lena had barely spoken more than ten words since they'd met, but now Petra turned to her and said, "Where do you come from again?" A heavy Italian accent, almost aggressive.

Lena had had enough to drink that she didn't take offense. She opened her mouth to say *Ohio*, her usual answer, but then she remembered Julia saying *"You shine,"* and surely people who *shone* weren't from Ohio. So she said "Los Angeles," and felt gratified when Petra looked moderately impressed.

"Los Angeles, huh?" Petra took a sip of her wine. "Julia likes you. A lot."

Lena smiled. "I like her too."

"She thinks you could be one of us."

That was puzzling. One of them how? Wasn't she already one of them? Wasn't she here in La Grotta with the favored crowd? Lena didn't know what to say. She settled for, "I love Rome."

Petra laughed shortly. "That's because you don't know it. Yet."

"I've only been here a few weeks."

"How long will you stay?"

"I don't know yet. As long as I can. As long as I can afford to."

"Hmmm." Petra looked thoughtfully toward the bar.

Lena followed her gaze. The heated conversation between Julia and Tony had ended. Julia was watching him put glasses away, but she looked toward Lena and Petra and her expression was . . . measuring, Lena thought, but she couldn't be sure, and didn't know why it should be measuring, or why she thought so.

The band started up again, a few notes, and Petra got to her feet, hurrying toward the small stage, her ample hips churning in her tight skirt. She seated herself on the edge of the stage, and when the song revealed itself as "Nature Boy," she began to sing. She had a deep, plush voice that massaged those words and quivered over Lena's skin. Petra sang the song as if it were nothing to sing it, as if she had been made to sing it, just this song, and from the way everyone went still to watch, it was clear that she'd sung it many times and that everyone was as mesmerized by it as Lena was. Petra's voice was like a spell. The song was like a spell, winding her in its spool, binding her, keeping her from escaping even as she did not want it to let her go.

And then, she felt the pull, the pull of a gaze, a pull like a demand she could not refuse, and Lena tore her gaze away from Petra and turned in the direction of that pull.

Julia. Julia staring at her with a soft smile.

Just a smile, but the smile and the song wove together and landed with a breathless force, and Lena knew she would always remember this moment, and felt it as a weird inevitability—a meant-to-be moment, that this friend, this city, all of it, were both the present and the future, and one she would never escape, and she was blindsided by the feeling, strangely struck.

Then it was gone, and she was left with nothing but that soft smile. Lena smiled back.

~

The city was in its afternoon shutdown and would not wake again until the evening, all the cafés closed, most of the shops except for those that catered to the bedraggled tourists determined to fill every moment of their vacations with proof that they'd been in the Eternal City. Shutters everywhere had been pulled.

Lena spent the morning at the Forum with the rest of the class. It was a brutally hot day, but the visit had inspired her, and when she got back to the Augusta, she hurried to her room to draw the idea she'd got from the Basilica Giulia, the heart of the Forum—a tight skirt cut at the side into a flowing panel of something filmy, maybe pleated, an asymmetrical bodice and short sleeves that had a bit of a gladiator look . . .

The moment she opened her sketchbook, Julia appeared in the doorway.

"Leeeeeena," she sang.

It had become a joke between them, that poor man's moan in the Roman night. But Lena saw the question in Julia's eyes. She groaned. "Whatever it is, it has to wait. I've got this great idea—"

"It will still be in your brilliant head later, my darling, and I need you to do me a favor. Please. You're the only one I trust." She sat on the bed, her shoulder brushing Lena's, a feminine intimacy Lena had never known. "Please. I'll buy your favorite *sfogliatella* when you get back."

"When I get back from where?"

"The Forum."

"But I just came from there, and it's hot."

"Make it *supplì*, wine, *and sfogliatella. And* I'll take you out."

Lena groaned again. "Why can't you do whatever it is?"

"I have a class and it has to be done now. Please, Lena." Julia leaned close and gave Lena a hopeful, pleading look. "I'll love you forever, and I'll owe you one."

Lena let out a sigh. "Okay. Okay. You *will* owe me one, and I want two *sfogliatella*. And a bottle of wine."

"Done." Julia sat back with satisfaction.

"What do I have to do?"

"I need you to go to that shop by the Arch of Titus to get a pack of cigarettes and take them to Petra, that one with the sign out front that says Paolo's Tabaccheria."

"There are cigarettes at every *tabaccheria* in Rome. Why do I have to go clear to the Forum? And why can't Petra do it?"

"Because I said I would. Tell the man you need the Muratti's in the green box."

"Do they come in a green box?"

Julia made a face. "It's a kind of code. He makes a special mix there."

"So they're not really in a green box?"

Julia shook her head impatiently. "They're just in a regular box, but if you don't say the green box, he won't know what you mean."

"Why not just tell him they're for Petra?"

"No, no. Don't mention Petra's name at all."

"Okaay." Lena frowned. "So ask for Muratti's in a green box."

"And take them to Petra at La Grotta."

"Though they aren't really for Petra. Or are they?"

"You're asking too many questions," Julia snapped. "None of that matters. Just do what I say." Then, calming. "I'm sorry. Please."

Lena considered her. "Is this something illegal, Julia?"

Julia sighed and then laughed lightly. "You're really far too clever. No wonder your Walter wanted you."

"Don't call him 'my' Walter. What do you mean?"

"You know how you hustled pool with Walter? How you helped him? This is kind of like that. Just . . . distraction. The cigarettes are not what they seem."

"I see."

"It's a game. You'll get your share of the money too. Didn't you tell Petra you could stay in Rome as long as you could afford it? This would help, wouldn't it?"

Lena laughed. "You're *smuggling*?"

"Nothing anyone can get in trouble for. Not really. You'll help, won't you? We could use you, and I know you like a challenge, don't you? We all do it."

Again, Lena had the feeling that Julia knew her better than she knew herself. "Like a game, huh?" She grinned. "Okay. I'll play."

~

Julia asked for more and more "favors." Some of them were strange, like picking up street maps of Rome from one of the many kiosks selling souvenirs to tourists, or decks of playing cards with the great sights of the Eternal City. But the pickups always required that Lena ask questions precisely, like, "Can you tell me the way to Babelio's Forum?" Such a place didn't exist, but the man handed her the map and said, "B3." Or, "Do these cards include the Santa Maria della Salute?" which of course was in Venice, not in Rome. The vendor shuffled to the back of his kiosk and retrieved a pack of cards with a gold border along the top, unlike the plainer ones in front. His gaze shifted furtively. "God be with you, signora."

So serious. Lena wanted to laugh. The game was fun. She felt like a spy in a movie, though when she dropped off these items to Petra or Tony or Julia, they treated them like they were nothing that important. Julia slung the playing cards onto the bedside table without another look.

"What is that really?" Lena asked her.

Julia widened her eyes in mock warning. "If I told you I'd have to kill you."

"Ha ha."

"Microfilm of very important documents."

Lena let out her breath in exasperation. "Really, Julia."

Julia laughed. "Hashish, Lena. A small bit for one of Tony's artist friends."

"Hashish?" Lena felt a frisson of excitement.

"Not enough to get anyone arrested." Julia shrugged. "Does that scare you? Do you want to stop?"

Lena threw herself into the striped armchair near Julia's bedroom door. There it was, that sense of herself that she loved, that sense that she'd never felt in Zanesville except for those moments in the pool hall with Walter, being daring, being what no one expected. The feeling had driven her to Los Angeles, and, just as she had liked Walter's admiration then, she liked the same admiration on Julia's face, that bit of surprise, that *look at you, you're not what I thought you were.* "I'm not going to get caught anyway," she said.

"No, you're not," Julia assured her. "You're not because you're perfect at this. You're a natural. I'm so glad I recruited you. You're not like anyone I've ever seen. Have you always been so game?"

"Julia, until I came to LA, the most exciting thing that ever happened to me was the county fair. I feel like I've spent years waiting for something *interesting* to happen."

Julia laughed lightly, and again Lena saw that curious expression, that searching look she couldn't quite read. "You are something, Lena."

"Oh, yes, I *shine*," Lena joked. "Where are we going tonight? I'm in the mood for Menghi's."

"You know what? I've got a better idea. I've been thinking: you'd be gorgeous as a blonde. Have you ever considered it?"

"A blonde?"

"Like Veronica Lake. You have such good bones. Blond hair would really accentuate them." Julia surveyed her as if she were seeing her for the first time.

Lena laughed.

"I'm not joking. I know a place that can do it too. Not far from here. They did Petra's hair."

"Petra's hair isn't really black?"

"Sort of a mousy brown."

Like her own. Lena put a tentative hand to her hair. The idea appealed, though surely Julia was exaggerating. Lena had taken on a new name, and blond signaled another adventure, like the couriering, something new. Something exciting. "I can't afford it."

"I can." Julia smiled. "Don't argue—it's my gift to you for being so indispensable. You're my right hand. I don't know what I'd do without you. You deserve it. Please . . . just try it. For me?"

It didn't take much convincing.

"Put on your best dress," Julia said. "The dark blue."

Lena had designed and made the dress while at the academy, inspired by that first night at La Grotta. Fabric in Rome did not cost what it had in Los Angeles, and she'd found a silk in the same shimmering night blue of the courtyard sky, and made a dress like the one Julia had worn that night, with a pleated skirt, but instead of a banded bodice, Lena had shaped and cut it into triangles with an open V tied at the cleavage. It was too fancy for a beauty parlor, but Julia said they'd go to the Via Veneto after, and it wasn't too fancy for that.

The salon, if that was what you could call it, was just down the Via Flaminia. It was hidden away, small, and smelled of some particularly noxious and acrid chemical that swept into Lena's sinuses and set them afire. There was some consternation when the woman who obviously ran the place saw Julia in the doorway.

"Beatrice," Julia said sternly to the woman without even a *buongiorno*, and the short, slight woman with elaborately bouffant black hair frowned and shook her head definitively at a question Julia had not asked.

Julia responded with a long burble of Italian that had the other three women in the place looking at her curiously.

Beatrice sighed. She gave Lena a once-over—very cursory and yet at the same time penetrating enough that Lena stiffened. Then she said, "*Sì, sì.*"

Julia smiled and squeezed Lena's arm. "She'll take you. I'm going to leave you here. I'll be back for you in a few hours."

"Julia—" Lena started to protest.

"It will be fine. Remember, Veronica Lake. When it's done we'll see what kind of a reaction you get on the Veneto."

Julia slipped out the door. Lena settled herself nervously on one of the worn seats and picked up a magazine covered with photos of Ingrid Bergman and Roberto Rossellini and their new baby. Americans considered it an adulterous scandal, but, as far as Lena could tell, the Italians viewed it as a beautiful love story.

She waited, feeling Beatrice's annoyance at having to fit Lena into an obviously busy schedule with the woman's every movement. Lena didn't know what Julia had said to convince the beautician, but soon enough Lena was in the chair, her hair covered with that chemical that now, in intimate proximity, burned through her sinuses into her brain. But when it was all done . . . when it was done, Lena could not believe the transformation.

Every trace of Elsie Gruner had truly been wiped away. She could no longer see a pig farmer's daughter in the woman who looked back at her in the mirror. Beatrice had set and brushed out her hair, and it lay in a straight, shining golden mass over her shoulders. No more mousy brown. She couldn't even pretend to be her old self with this hair. It was impossible to be anyone but Lena.

Lena didn't expect Julia to recognize her, but when Julia returned, her eyes went straight to Lena, as if she'd already envisioned the transformation and knew in her soul of souls what it would do. Julia's smile was as bright as Lena's hair.

"Oh my God. It suits you just as I knew it would. Look at you! Just look at you! You're beautiful, Lena."

She felt beautiful then, as she never had. The closest she'd ever come was when Walter had put her at the end of that pool table and told her to smile and she'd distracted the other players and felt powerful and in control. But this was so much more. She felt . . . invincible. And when they went to the Via Veneto, Lena didn't feel as she always had before on the fashionable street, as if she should hide, an imposter. She felt as if she belonged there, as if the stares that came her way, and Julia's, were owed to her, as if her life had not really begun before this moment, but now that it had . . . she was ready for it.

CHAPTER 8

It was an attitude, a style; Lena learned to adopt it. When you walked into a bar, you ignored people looking at you askance because you were a woman alone—you were not Italian, you were American, you were *apart*, you were *someone to be reckoned with*. You sent scathingly sympathetic looks to the men who stared at you—*ah, no, this is not for you, my lad*. You crossed your legs elegantly when you sat and did not tug down your skirt. You acted as if everyone in the place watched your every move. You ordered Negronis when they expected you to order an Americano, no, no soda for you, thank you, nothing to take the edge off pure liquor. You smoked as if the cigarette were an extension of your erotic dreams. You danced the mamba with an extra twist of your hips and moved to jazz as if the music had taken possession of your soul, and you stared into Julia's eyes with an expression that made the mouth of every man water because he imagined you might be lovers.

Lena did her best work in Rome. Her teachers loved her. She loved the world. She wanted to stay forever. Julia had taught her how to be the woman Lena wished to be. She would have done anything for her.

~

She had just come from another *tabaccheria* near the Monumento a Vittorio Emanuele, after picking up "Muratti's in a pink box"—also nonexistent—and was on her way to La Grotta to drop it off. By the time Lena got off the sweaty, crowded tram, she felt nauseated. She was near the Via Veneto. Since the Veneto catered to tourists, it stayed open in the heat of the afternoon, and crowds sat at the tables of the sidewalk cafés, and the wealthy went in and out of the doors of the Excelsior, and expensive cars dropped off elegantly dressed people with expensive luggage, and everyone strained for a glimpse of a movie star, though why any stars would be there at this time of day was anyone's guess.

Still, Lena slowed her step, as always, on the lookout for one, curious to see what they would be wearing. If she were a movie star, she would come here to soak up the adulation. She'd sit there, at that table near the door of Strega. She'd wear big sunglasses and a hat and pretend she didn't want to be recognized. Like that woman there, at the far table, talking with a man in a leather coat who looked a little like a blond Tyrone Power.

Then Lena realized that the woman was Julia.

She started toward her, then stopped. What was Julia doing here, and with this man? And this Julia . . . this woman, while undeniably Julia, was a Julia Lena did not know. There was a haughty chill in Julia's manner that Lena had never noted before. Everything about the scene felt furtive. The way the man kept his head bowed so you couldn't really see his face. The way Julia kept looking about.

Was it her, really? Lena couldn't help herself, she had to be sure. She stepped forward, into Julia's line of vision. She noted the moment Julia saw her, the way Julia froze, and then . . . then the frown, the quick wave, undeniable in its message.

Go away.

It was odd, and it stung. Not the Julia she knew, not the smile of welcome, but clear frustration and irritation. Lena pulled back into the shade of a cluster of umbrella-ed tables, and then stepped farther down the street until she was certain Julia could no longer see her. But she didn't leave. She stood and watched Julia and the man argue until the man nodded abruptly. He put an envelope on the table, which Julia immediately covered with her hand. She smiled, the man grimaced and left.

Julia glanced around, seemingly casually, but Lena knew her well enough to see her tension. Julia rose and left the table, and Lena remained in the shadows. She didn't like what she saw. There was something wrong, or even . . . ominous about this. Lena hesitated, wondering what to do.

Make the delivery was the obvious answer, and so she made her way to La Grotta, which of course was closed.

Lena pounded on the door until Tony answered. "What is it, Lena?"

"Where's Petra?"

He opened the door wider to let her in. There were a couple people in the small kitchen behind the bar, Marco drinking coffee and Paolo gnawing on a sandwich.

"She's in the back," Tony said. "You want espresso?"

Lena shook her head and went through the curtain and out a narrow door into what could hardly be called a courtyard, just a narrow fenced-in brick square in the alley with the trash bins and a grill Tony sometimes used. Petra sat in a chair she had angled back against the railing, her eyes closed. Petra's hair, as usual, was artfully piled on her head, looking ready to fall at any moment.

"Hey," Lena said. "I've got something for you."

Petra opened her eyes lazily. She held out her hand so languid and smooth it was as if she hadn't moved at all.

Lena reached into her purse and took out the cigarettes, then placed them into Petra's palm.

Petra made a face. "I told her American cigarettes. I'm not smoking these." But she slipped the carton into her pocket. "Do you have any Camels?"

"Marlboros. Who's Tony selling the hash in there to?"

Petra wiggled her fingers in request and Lena took out her pack and gave Petra one. Petra lit it, inhaled, and said, "Hash? Is that what Julia told you?"

"Isn't that what it is?"

Petra laughed lightly. "She doesn't trust you."

Another sting. This time a confusing one. "Why do you say that? She says I'm her right hand."

"Does she?" Petra shrugged. "Okay."

"I saw her today at Strega. With some blond guy."

"Mmm. Mr. Bon Bon. Very good to her, that one is."

"Who is he?"

"A mystery man." Petra widened her dark eyes dramatically. "Ask her yourself, Lena, but don't tell her I said anything. And give me another one of those, *sì*? For later."

~

Petra would give her no more answers. Lena went back to the Augusta and knocked on Julia's bedroom door. "It's me."

The door opened. Julia had changed into a lounging pajama set with flared legs and a top that tied around her neck and left her arms bare. "Did you get the cigarettes to Petra?"

"She complained that they weren't American." Lena sagged against the doorjamb. Then, because she couldn't help herself, she teased, "Then she threw them away."

Julia's expression went immediately concerned.

"She put the pack in her pocket," Lena corrected. "But you looked worried there for a minute. What else was in there besides cigarettes?"

"Hashish, as usual." Julia walked back into her bedroom, trailing the scent of talc and marijuana.

Lena followed her. "That's not what Petra said."

Julia raised her brows in question. "What did Petra say?"

"That you don't trust me."

"Petra likes to cause trouble. You know that's not true." Julia sat on her bed with a bounce and leaned back against the headboard.

70

Lena hesitated, then . . . "Are you going to tell me what you were doing with that guy at Strega today? You looked so . . . different. It was like you were a stranger."

Julia reached for the reefer in the ashtray on the bedside table and lit it, then she offered it to Lena. "Want some?"

Lena took it. "Who was he?"

"He's a customer," Julia said.

"What does that mean, exactly?"

Julia tilted her head, considering. "Are you jealous?"

Lena had been in the middle of a deep drag. She choked on a laugh. "Jealous? That's ridiculous." But she felt a niggling discomfort. She pushed it away and handed Julia the reefer.

"Is it?" Julia met her gaze straight on. "You know what Petra thinks, Lena? She thinks you're in love with me."

Now it was Lena's turn to say nothing. She had no idea what to say. The discomfort was back and something in Julia's expression unsettled her. The marijuana was having an effect, too; along with her discomfort came a fullness. She was tender; she was soft. Was she in love with Julia? How else to explain this intensity of feeling, this wish to be part of Julia, to be . . . inside her? But then . . . no. It was more elemental than that. It wasn't that she was in love with Julia so much as that she wanted to *be* Julia.

"It's okay if you are," Julia said.

Now Lena felt hot. It was impossible to describe how she felt. Not love, and yet, how fierce it was, how undeniable. "No. I told you. I—I'm married."

"What does that matter? What does that even mean?"

"To a man. I'm not . . . I'm mean I'm not . . ."

"Really?" Julia tilted her head, a little smile, a knowing that crept into Lena in a strangely confusing way.

"Yes, really."

Julia rose from the bed. She handed Lena the marijuana and went to the record player and flipped the switch, picked up the stylus and put the needle to the record on the turntable. "Nature Boy"—Petra's song, the song from that night at La Grotta—began its eerie tune. Lena wondered if the choice of song was to remind her of that night, Julia's enigmatic smile.

"It's like I said, Lena. Petra likes to cause trouble. That man is no one. A client. He has nothing to do with us."

"Julia, I'm not—"

Julia laughed. It was light and free. She gave Lena a look that filled her with relief. "Oh my God, Lena, you're so funny. The look on your face. I'm kidding. Really. Dance with me." Julia closed her eyes and swayed. "I'm a little drunk. Come and dance."

Lena felt strange. Relieved, yes, but also confused at Julia's strange mood. Still, she went to dance with her friend. Julia opened her eyes and opened her arms and Lena walked into them, that smell of talc and marijuana all around her, the silkiness of Julia's hair, the warm smoothness of her bare arms, just being surrounded, bathed, cloaked in Julia's essence. Julia pressed her lips to the corner of Lena's mouth and then slid away, elusive, there and not, so Lena wasn't sure if it had happened and was left only with the shock of it, and Julia swaying against her.

The music spun on. They swayed to the winding song, the seductive words, and when the song ended, Julia sighed as if it was the saddest thing in the world and pulled away. She grabbed the half-drunk glass of wine. "We are so good together, Lena. Don't you feel it?"

Lena wasn't sure what to say—how was it possible to feel both abandoned and wanting to be gone?

"Together we can do so much," Julia went on. "All you have to do is admit that you want more than what the world wants to give a woman."

"I don't know what you mean," Lena said warily.

"Yes you do," Julia went on softly. "You walked away from Walter. You just *walked* away. That was amazing. You got the scholarship here. You're a woman and you won the scholarship. You're willing to take risks, but you have to choose well. Here they only see one direction for a woman. If you're not careful they'll direct you right into designing for little boutiques and stupid tiny ateliers. For God's sake. You're better than Coco Chanel. You could be bigger."

Lena laughed quietly. Julia's words were so alluring.

"I see what's really inside you. But it's so easy to give in to what the world wants, isn't it? You can be so daring. But you can't be afraid. It's not a game to us. Once you start, you can't stop. Not ever."

"What do you mean?"

"What do fashion designers do? Usually? What's your plan?"

Lena shrugged. "Learn everything I can. Get a job at a fashion house—"

"Not start your own?"

"No one just starts their own atelier, Julia."

"No? So it's years of sweat for nothing?"

"Not for nothing. You move up. Then one day, hopefully, you become a designer for a house like Chanel, or Dior or Balenciaga."

Julia regarded her, tilting her head, considering. "What about the movies?"

"What about them?"

"Why not become a costume designer for a studio like Cinecittà? You could stay here in Rome. Think of it"—Julia looked into the distance, obviously imagining Lena's future—"your designs, on a big screen, influencing every girl in the world. Like what's his name—Flavio. You could be the Flavio of Italian movies. And then . . . who knows? Maybe you could eventually go back to LA. You could be bigger than Flavio. What do you think?"

To stay in Rome. To work for the movies. Lena thought of all the times she'd sat in a darkened theater, the movie star paper dolls she'd designed for as a child. *Cinecittà*. But mostly, she wanted to stay in Rome.

"I know people at Cinecittà," Julia went on, gently persuading. "I can help you. Or . . . I would. But to do that you have to trust me. We have to trust each other. Can you do that?"

Can you trust me?

Lena understood what Julia didn't say. No more questions, not about her life, Mr. Bon Bon, or anything else, and though there was a part of Lena that protested, Julia's imaginings fed Lena's own longings, her passions. Julia thought so big, she created vistas easy for Lena to see. The choice was no real choice: go to Cinecittà when her internship was over and stay in Rome with Julia, or go home to LA and continue to toil on at Chouinard? Hadn't Lena promised herself to make something of Rome? Here it was, the opportunity she'd wished for.

"You'd do that? You can get me to Cinecittà?"

"I can and I will. But that means you have to stop listening to people like Petra. It means you don't let *anyone* come between us."

"Why does Petra want to make trouble? I thought you were friends."

"See? That's what I mean. Petra doesn't matter. None of them matter, Lena. It's just you and me. Yes? Or no."

Julia had given Lena everything; she had made Lena. Not only that, but Julia was the closest friend Lena had ever had.

"Yes," Lena said.

CHAPTER 9

Lena spent the next weeks with the dream of Cinecittà sparkling before her. Beyond classes, and the courier jobs for Julia, she worked on sketches for her portfolio. Her professors helped when she told them that she was hoping for an interview at the Italian movie studio, though Signor Basile gave her a faintly disappointed look. "I had hoped to see you as a fashion designer one day with your own house," he told her. "You have enough talent. The movies don't deserve you."

Julia said, "You see? They're doing just what I said. Pushing you toward working for another designer."

"He did say my 'own house,'" Lena pointed out.

"Hmmm. It's so *small*, Lena. Think about how many people watch couture fashion shows compared to how many watch movies. Think of how much more influence you'll have. American movies show all over the world. England, Spain, even the Soviet Union."

Lena snorted. "Yes, I imagine I'll be very influential in the Soviet Union."

"You never know," Julia said with a shrug.

"Don't the Russians only dress in gray?"

"It's not just the clothes, Lena, it's *culture*." Julia spoke the word as if it held the secrets of the universe. "The best way to change the world is through the things people love, not through politics."

"I didn't know we were trying to change the world."

Julia laughed. "Of course we are."

Lena took it as a joke. People trying to change the world were like poor Harvey and Charlie—she still wondered what had happened to them. Men who belonged to organizations like the CRC, who risked being arrested and jailed, who went to protests and whose homes were raided and who were blacklisted and professionally exiled. But here in Italy she rarely heard concern about world affairs, nor about the bomb, and hardly any political talk. When she did, it was whispered and fleeting. Italy still stung from the days of Mussolini and the Nazi occupation, and with the Christian Democrats now in power, no one admitted to being an anarchist or a communist even if they were. No one talked about the war or what role they'd played in it. In Rome, no one wanted to resurrect the bodies; whatever ghosts haunted its citizens, they pretended not to see.

Summer turned to fall. Lena found she loved Rome even more when the heat faded, and with it the tourists, though the Holy Year still drew pilgrims by the thousands, and the streets were still so choked with monks and nuns that Lena was starting to be able to tell the Franciscans from the Dominicans.

There was something else that came with autumn. Strange shadows. At first Lena thought them cast by the ubiquitous pigeons and crows, and then . . . just flashes from the corners of her eye. Slips in her peripheral vision. She would be at a kiosk on one of Julia's errands and there it would be, a glimpse of movement, nothing she could pin down. The hair on the back of her neck would prickle, and she'd turn to find nothing there—or at least nothing curious, nothing surreptitious.

Lena brushed it off. And kept brushing it off. But then, one rainy day when the worn-smooth cobbles of the street were slick as oil in the wet, she felt it again as she came out of a pharmacy on the Via del Tritone with not a jar of the toothpaste she'd asked for, but a box of emetic (who knew what it really was), and she turned quickly, just in time to see a man in a black coat flit around a corner, or at least try to.

Too fast; his heel slid from beneath him; he went down with a crack, his bowler hat rolling into the street.

She hurried over to help him. She wasn't the only one. He was no one she would normally have remembered. He was very flustered from the fall, dark haired, like countless other men in the city. But when she offered her hand, he pulled abruptly away, and he wouldn't meet her eyes. He got to his feet and didn't thank anyone, but hurried off, leaving the good Samaritans who'd tried to help looking at each other in puzzled irritation, grumbling at his rudeness.

When Lena got back to the academy and gave Julia the package of emetic, she told the story.

Julia went very still. "Really? Had you seen him before?"

"No. Why would you say that?"

"No reason." Julia shrugged, but Lena felt her tension.

After that, Lena was more aware than ever of those strange, peripheral movements. She became convinced that she was being followed, though it was more a feeling than something she could say with any certainty.

"I think that man was following me," she told Julia. "Maybe he's not the only one. I never see anyone really, but I feel them. Why would someone be following me? Do you think . . . do you think the police are onto us?"

Julia half snorted. "You sound like a character in a movie. The police have a whole city of criminals to worry about. Why should they care about us?"

"I just . . . I'm not imagining it."

"I didn't say you were. Maybe it's just the way you look now." Julia flipped the ends of Lena's hair. "Italian men love blondes."

"Maybe." But she detected something in her friend's voice that didn't quite ring true, and it was the first time she'd heard such a tone, and Lena wasn't sure what to make of it. Something was wrong, she knew, but she wasn't sure what.

When they were at La Grotta next, she asked Petra about it, but Petra only gave her a lazy look and said, "Julia's got a lot on her mind, you know? You shouldn't bother her with your silly suspicions."

"I don't think they're silly," Lena snapped.

"Rome is haunted. Maybe you're only seeing ghosts." Petra smiled. "You are becoming more Roman every day, Lena."

That was Petra—an insult followed by an assurance of belonging, leaving Lena perpetually off balance. She went to get a glass of wine and tried to forget about it.

~

The next day, Julia came bursting into Lena's room. "We're going to Venice."

Lena stood at the window, brushing her hair, and she turned. "What do you mean? Who's going to Venice?"

"You and me."

"What about classes?"

"I've talked to all the professors already. They've promised to grant us the days away if we visit the Doge's Palace and the Basilicas of San Marco and the Salute and write our impressions."

"They've said that for me as well?"

"Of course for you as well!" Julia was ebullient. "Four days, Lena! Four days in Venice! Just the two of us."

"When?"

"In two weeks. The most beautiful city in the world. Gorgeous light, ancient architecture, gondoliers singing sad songs . . . we'll drink wine and get lost. It will be wonderful."

"But . . . what brought this on?"

"Don't you want to go? I thought you'd be pleased."

"Yes, of course, but it's so out of the blue."

Julia stretched her neck. "I need to get out of this city for a few days. It's feeling claustrophobic. And you're starting to see things—"

"I see. Petra's making trouble."

"Petra has nothing to do with it."

"Petra said I was having silly superstitions about being followed."

"Well, you are," Julia said firmly. "And we both need a vacation. So I'm giving us one. Tell me if you don't want to go."

Lena could think of nothing she wanted more, in fact, than to go with Julia to an ancient city where they knew no one, where they'd have no jobs to do and no classes and only talking and laughing and drinking wine. "I want to go."

～

Three days later . . . "We have a small problem," Julia confessed. "Mr. Bon Bon."

Julia had revealed—eventually—that Mr. Bon Bon was a client that she'd once made the mistake of sleeping with, and who she now felt obligated to entertain whenever he was in town, which was this week. "He buys a lot of commissions. I can't just ignore him even though I'm not sleeping with him anymore."

"What kind of commissions?"

"Oh, you know, paintings, sculptures, things like that." Julia spoke dismissively.

Lena let it go, but later she realized Julia had never picked up a single painting or sculpture, and she'd never actually seen or known Julia to do any kind of business with those kinds of commissions. But Lena told herself that maybe Julia had done that sort of thing before Lena knew her, and pushed it away.

"He wants to go with us to Venice," Julia said. "So we need to convince him not to."

Lena was appalled. "Just tell him no."

"I can't really do that. He's too important. Look, we're going to meet him at Club LeRoy. I need you to do something for me. Flirt with him, fight with him—I don't care which. I just need to be able to get angry with him about it. It's the only way I can think of to get him to leave me alone for a few days. He's been so *clingy*. Otherwise he'll insist on showing us around Venice. Please, Lena."

It was easy to agree. The last thing Lena wanted was for that dangerous-looking man to ruin their holiday.

The night they were to meet him, Lena dressed carefully in one of her own designs—a pink A-line off-the-shoulder cocktail dress with elbow-length sleeves and a peekaboo dotted tulle in the skirt. She'd begun wearing makeup in Rome, under Julia's tutelage, and was stunned at the difference it made in how she looked. Elegant, almost. Sophisticated.

"Yes, the ribbon is better." Julia leaned forward to adjust the bow in Lena's hair. "That's perfect."

Lena twisted her head, watching her blond ponytail flip in the mirror, the fuchsia ribbon bouncing with it, and even she could tell how it changed her look, how it made her carefree and even . . . frivolous.

"You see?" Julia handed her a pink lipstick. "Now try this. See how easy it is to change who you are just with a few little things?" She laughed as Lena applied the lipstick. "Look at you! No one would take you for anyone boring at all. Which is perfect for today."

She rubbed her lips together and then blotted them. "So all I have to do is flirt with him?"

"That's it. Just so he notices you—really notices you. Maybe you could tell him about your misspent youth."

Lena caught Julia's gaze in the mirror. "But I—"

"Not the truth." Julia rolled her eyes. "Make a story for yourself, Lena. You're . . . Katharine Hepburn or Betty Grable or Ingrid Bergman. Yes, Ingrid Bergman. A woman capable of beguiling a director like Roberto Rossellini."

Lena laughed dryly. "Oh, that won't be hard at all."

"It won't. Believe me, he thinks he's irresistible." Julia turned away from the mirror and riffled through her purse until she found her own lipstick, a bright cherry red.

Club LeRoy was on the Veneto. It had been the hottest place in the city since it opened in the spring, a nightclub where all the actors and musicians working in the nearby theaters went after their shows to eat spaghetti or steak and drink and listen to the orchestra or the new acts the owner brought in from all over Europe. The club held theme nights every Friday—that night honored the Americans at Cinecittà shooting *Quo Vadis*. The staff wore togas and gilded laurel crowns and the orchestra played Roman numbers in between the mambas and rumbas. The lounge was decorated with shields and lances and brightly glimmering swords.

Mr. Bon Bon's name was really Terence Hall, which was not so interesting, though up close he looked even more like a blond and blue-eyed Tyrone Power. He had that same adventurous, dashing air. He looked like he should be striding the deck of a pirate ship or swashbuckling his way through a musketeers movie. However, he dressed like a hipster or a bohemian, which ruined the vision a bit—a black turtleneck beneath a tweed jacket, slacks. He looked like some of the actors in the place. You could spot them a mile away, talking loud over the music, smoking and bandying their drinks about like extensions of themselves, sweating charisma.

Terence Hall already had a table, and Lena and Julia joined him. Julia leaned to kiss him. "This is my friend Lena. I've told you about her."

"Yes." Hall smiled politely. "So nice to meet you."

He had a British accent that added to his mysteriously intrepid air. He raised his hand to call over a toga-clothed waiter and ordered them Americanos without asking what they would prefer. So he was arrogant too. But handsome, handsome enough to flirt with, and so Lena pulled her chair a bit closer to his and said, "Julia tells me you've lived in Rome for a while."

He nodded. "A few years."

"I've only been here since June, but what I've seen I love. I think I'd like to live here."

He made a dismissive gesture. "It's not a city to admire. Too many poor. Too much corruption. Julia, have you not educated your little friend on the evils of Rome?"

"She's been too busy seeing the sights. She's at the academy."

"The school of the privileged." He snorted and took a sip of his drink. "Americans."

Lena peeked at Julia, who ignored her. "You don't like Americans?"

"America is what is wrong with the world. You are American, yes?" His gaze swept over her disdainfully.

She was saved from having to answer by the arrival of the drinks. Lena took a deep gulp of the Americano, which was not very cold, but then, nothing was in Rome. The orchestra launched into a mamba, and couples pushed their way through the tables to the dance floor, their hips already swaying in anticipation.

Thinking it might loosen him up, Lena said, "Do you like to dance?"

He shook his head and looked at Julia, who was idly stirring her drink. "No."

"Too bad." Lena tossed her ponytail. "I'm a good dancer."

"Most Americans are, I hear. They have nothing better to do with their lives."

"You're very dour, Mr. Hall. And I heard you were such fun. Julia, you've misled me."

Julia's smile was wry. "Did I?"

"You said your Mr. Bon Bon was delightful."

Terence Hall frowned. "Mr. Bon Bon?"

"Don't you like our nickname for you?" Lena took another sip of her drink and leaned closer. "Shall I tell you a secret, Mr. Bon Bon? You look like you could be a pirate, but you act like an accountant. Boring, I'm afraid."

Julia laughed. "She sees right through you, Terry."

He seemed taken aback. "Boring?"

"Am I wrong?" Lena put her elbow on the table, resting her cheek on it, leaning closer, pouting just a little. "Maybe you could tell me a joke?"

"I don't know any jokes."

"How about poetry? You're dressed like a poet."

"I'm afraid poetry is not my favorite thing."

"What do you do then, Mr. Hall? What do you like? You don't dance, you don't tell jokes, you don't know poetry . . . or maybe . . . maybe it's just that you don't like me."

"I don't know you well enough to dislike you."

"This is the first time I've worn this dress. Do you like it?" She twisted in her chair, posing for him.

"You Americans care too much about how you look."

"I made it myself. I designed it."

She'd caught his interest at last. He looked impressed. "You designed it?"

"Um-hmm. I'm a designer."

"It's very pretty." He spoke almost reluctantly.

She pretended she didn't notice. "What part do you like best? The peekaboo skirt?"

He waved off her question. Julia reached into her purse for her cigarette case. "Tell him about the décolletage, Lena."

Lena smiled. "It's very special. My own design. You see how it lays just so—" she traced the neckline, watching him follow her finger across her cleavage—"pretty but not the least bit scandalous, not until I lean over and then . . ." She leaned, moving closer to him at the same time, close enough that she could smell his cologne, which was piney and arctic, knowing the way the neckline would lower with her motion, revealing cleavage, the round tops of her breasts. His gaze went obediently to where she'd directed and she let him linger there, embracing the little surge of power she felt before she straightened with a smile. "You see? Do you like that, Mr. Hall?"

He regarded her with a dispassionate stare. "American women are decadent. I'm not surprised you designed a dress to show off your bosom."

Julia extended her hand across the table to offer her cigarettes. Her gaze had gone icy. "But you looked, didn't you, Terry? Doesn't that make you a tiny bit decadent too?" She snapped the case closed before he had time to take one and turned to Lena. "Drink up. I'm bored already. We're leaving."

Lena frowned. "But—"

"It's fine. Terry's in a mood. Let's go to Petra's. She'll be more fun tonight."

"Don't be a bitch, Julia," Terence said in a low voice.

Julia motioned with her eyes toward the door. They were really leaving then. Lena didn't know why Julia had changed her mind, but she was happy enough to leave Terence Hall. She took a long drink of her Americano and rose.

"It's been lovely to meet you, Mr. Hall," she said. "Maybe next time you'll want to dance."

"Julia—" Terence warned.

"Good night, Terry." Julia grabbed her purse. "Call me when you're not so *dour*."

Once they were out of the club, Lena said, "I'm sorry. I tried."

"It doesn't matter." Julia seemed distracted. "Let's get out of here quickly, before he decides to come after us."

The night was full of late revelers, the cafés crowded. Cars meandered down the narrow street while Vespas and motorcycles zoomed by. A siren blasted into the night, a police car trying to make its way through. Julia took Lena's hand and pulled her off the Veneto into a *vicolo*, onto a less fashionable street, obviously so lost in thought that Lena wondered where Julia's mind was. The meeting with Terence Hall had felt odd; he wasn't what Lena had expected, and nothing had gone the way either of them had planned.

At Petra's building, they went past the closed flower shop on the lower floor and into the dimly lit cracked checkerboard of the foyer, leading the way up the much-traveled stone stairs to the third floor. They heard the noise from inside before they reached the landing: jazz music blasting, talk and laughter. The smells of garlic and funky pecorino and smoke perpetually hung about Petra's hall as if they'd permeated the walls for a hundred years or more.

Lena didn't bother to knock. She opened the door; people spilled out. Over by the window, Tony uncorked a bottle of wine. Marco handed around a bowl of pasta. Petra and Renato and Paolo gathered around a table full of Petra's photos. Everyone called a greeting as they came inside, but Petra—Petra gave Julia the strangest look. Lena couldn't decide what it was. Questioning? Angry? Discouraging? Julia shrugged in response, and then she laughed and accepted a glass of wine, and Lena poured her own wine and took a bowl of pasta and joined the others and soon lost herself in conversation and the review of Petra's photographs, which were different from her others.

These didn't feature the juxtaposition of the ruined and modern Rome. The photos were extraordinary and disturbing, of the working-class districts like Pietralata, where people lived in dilapidated housing. They were pictures of broken sinks and rusty buckets of water and children in ragged clothing and filth, an apartment that housed three families in cramped quarters. Lena remembered what Terence Hill had said at Club LeRoy, that Julia had neglected Lena's Roman education. She had never seen these places, or seen this level of poverty. The duplex in LA had been bad, but they'd had running water and plumbing that mostly worked. They'd been poor, but nothing like this.

"You see?" Petra asked her after Lena had enough wine that the night had started to blur. "You see what we are fighting? You understand now what you're part of?"

"It's horrible! Why doesn't the government do something about it?"

Petra laughed dryly. "They do only the minimum—or better yet, nothing, if they can. The government is not the people, Lena. But one day we will change that."

Lena was too drunk to wonder what that meant. She didn't remember how they got back to the Augusta that night, but when she woke the next morning, her head pounding, her ponytail hanging awkwardly askew and her mouth still stained pink from the lipstick she had not removed before going to bed, she had a flashing, intense memory of standing at the Pincio Terrace and staring out at the lights of Rome in the very early morning and Julia whispering something in her ear—what was it? Something about her being a good partner? *"The best ever . . . I think I'll keep you."*

Lena shook the memory loose and wandered downstairs in her pajamas for a glass of water—no Roman tours of antiquities for her this morning. The table was still spread with remnants of breakfast, but there was no one else there; they'd already gone to their classes or tours. Lena poured herself some orange juice and caught a glimpse of *Il Messaggero* as she poured—and then did a double-take, startled by the photograph on the front page of the newspaper.

Terence Hall.

She put the juice down and picked up the paper. She had learned a little Italian—very little, not enough to understand the caption beyond the word *morto*. But *morto* was pretty clear. Dead. Terence Hall was dead.

She stared in shock at the paper. When she heard the footsteps behind her, she knew who it was. She knew the sound of that walk in her bones, that presence that never failed to lift her spirits. This morning, however, it filled her with a strange dread. Lena turned to see Julia looking as hungover as Lena felt. She held out the newspaper. "He's dead. Mr. Bon Bon is dead."

Julia reached for the paper and scanned it, as dispassionate as Terence Hall had been last night. "Hmmm."

"What does it say?"

"He was found in the street last night near Club LeRoy. They think it was a heart attack." Julia set the paper on the table and picked a straw-berry from the bowl. "Are all the others gone?"

"A heart attack? Then why is he on the front page?"

Julia shrugged and turned away, wandering to the kitchen. "I guess because he's a foreigner. Poor Terry."

CHAPTER 10

Terence Hall was in the newspaper the next day too.

"He was that important?" Lena asked Julia.

"I guess it's bad for the government when foreigners die on Rome's streets."

Julia left for her class, but when Laura Mesner came down, she raised her brows at the sight of Terence Hall's picture on the front page. "Wow. That's crazy."

"What's crazy?" Lena asked.

Laura picked up the paper. "Didn't you read this?"

"I can't read Italian."

"Oh. Well, this guy was a diplomat—the assistant to the diplomatic representative to the Holy See from Great Britain. He was poisoned."

"Poisoned? Julia said he had a heart attack."

Laura gave her a funny look. "Yeah. Caused by poison. They're looking for anyone who might have seen him in the hours before he died. Why? What's wrong?"

"Nothing," Lena said, and nothing was, was it? She had not poisoned Terence Hall. When she and Julia had left him, he'd been very much alive. So why did Lena feel so uneasy? Why hadn't Julia mentioned that poison was the cause?

Lena felt worse when Julia came home that afternoon and said, "I've moved up our holiday. We're going to Venice tomorrow instead of waiting for the weekend."

"I have a project due tomorrow."

"Professor Basile has already given you permission to be gone, hasn't he?" Julia asked.

"Yes, but—"

"There's a reason, Lena—I finally got a chance to speak to my friend at Cinecittà. He wants to interview you on Monday!"

Lena stared at her in stunned surprise.

"Isn't it wonderful?"

"Oh—oh my God. Oh. I've got so much to do. I can't possibly go now . . ."

Julia squeezed her arm. "You've got everything you need, Lena. The sketches are perfect. We're going to Venice on the afternoon train, and when we return, you'll be relaxed and ready. Repeat after me: relaxed and ready."

Lena took a deep breath. "I'll be relaxed and ready."

Julia laughed. "The afternoon train, yes?"

"Okay."

"It's going to be perfect. I just need you to do one thing first. There's a pickup at the Piazza Fiume."

"Julia," Lena moaned.

"You'll have plenty of time. You can do it in the morning and meet me at the train. From Fiume you can take a tram right to Termini Station."

Lena sighed. "What do I do?"

"There's a little news kiosk at the edge of the piazza. The boy you talk to will be wearing an apron advertising Campari. Ask him who's going to be at Mario's this weekend. He'll ask if you like New Orleans jazz. Tell him you love it. That's it. Then bring what he gives you to the station and we'll be off." Julia stretched her arms over her head. "Four days away from here, and then everything will change."

The excitement of Venice and the interview at Cinecittà swept Terence Hall and her uneasiness from Lena's mind. The next morning she packed her bag and went to the small and unimpressive Piazza

Fiume, where she found herself in the middle of a funeral procession—a phalanx of nuns trailing mourners following a funeral carriage decked with flowers and palm fronds. It took her aback, the creepy chanting and crying set against the everyday life of the piazza, cars spewing exhaust and signs advertising NAZIONALI CIGARETTES and CINEMA TEATRO and the disconnect of the ancient section of the Aurelian wall and the Porta Salaria standing incongruously amid modern buildings. The clear blue sky and the crow-like shadows of the nuns fluttering on the stones and the heavy specter of death, and abruptly she thought of Terence Hall and poison and the authorities asking who had seen him in the hours before he'd died. The hair on the back of her neck stood on end; it all felt strangely portentous.

She was anxious to go. She hurried to the news kiosk, wanting to get away from the mourners as soon as possible. She found the boy in the Campari apron behind a stand holding *Grand Hotel* magazines, with their brightly romantic illustrated covers.

Lena approached him as he sliced open a box of new issues of the magazine. "Who's playing at Mario's this weekend?" she asked.

He glanced over his shoulder, his shock of dark hair falling into his face. "The Roman New Orleans Jazz Band. You like New Orleans jazz?"

"I love it."

"I have a record you'll like." He rose and led her to a stack of boxes behind a stand of *Turf* newspapers. Stealthily he reached between the boxes and drew out a record—*The Duke*. Not New Orleans jazz at all, but an old Duke Ellington album. He grabbed an issue of *Grand Hotel* from a nearby pile and shoved the record into it, handed it to her with a wink, and said, "Have fun."

Lena put the magazine into her baggage. She had two hours yet before she had to be at the station, so she dodged into a trattoria off the square, away from the mourners. She ordered a Coke and drew her sketchbook from her bag, thinking of Cinecittà, but she'd barely started work on a ball gown before two suited men stepped up to her table.

"Elsie Gruner?" asked one of the men—the shorter one, with dark hair and sunglasses.

Something in his look set off an alarm—along with the fact that he knew her name, her real name. "Yes?"

The taller man, with light brown hair and hazel eyes, pulled out a chair and sat down.

Her disquiet grew. Carefully, she set down her pencil. "Who are you?"

Now the other man sat as well. He shoved up his sunglasses to reveal icy blue eyes. "Miss Gruner, I'm Mr. Dunsmore, and this is Mr. Harrison. We're with the CIA."

"The . . . what?"

"The Central Intelligence Agency. For the United States government. We'd like to ask you about Terence Hall."

Now she was afraid. "I don't know anything about him," she said, trying to keep her voice even.

"Are you saying you don't know him?"

Lena had no idea what to say.

"You should tell us what you know," said Mr. Harrison. "You'll gain nothing by lying, Miss Gruner."

"I met him once."

"At Club LeRoy?" Dunsmore asked.

"Yes, but how—"

"We've been watching him for some time," he said. "You were there with Miss Kovalova?"

"Miss—who?"

The two agents exchanged looks. Dunsmore sighed. "You know her as Julia Keane."

"She . . . she has a different name?"

"A few," said Harrison. "You were there with her and Mr. Hall that night. Did you note anything unusual?"

"Like what?"

"Why don't you tell us what happened that night?"

Lena started to rise. "I think I should go. I have a train to catch—"

Dunsmore grabbed her wrist, stopping her. "Sit down, Miss Gruner. Trust me, you want to answer our questions."

"But I don't know anything. I haven't done anything." She sat again.

"We're just looking for some information, that's all. Tell us about that night."

"We met Mr. Hall for a drink. I tried to be nice to him but he was a jerk. Julia said that she'd call him when he was in a better mood and we left."

"Where did you go?" Dunsmore asked.

"A few bars. I don't remember. I got very drunk."

"Hmmm." Dunsmore looked thoughtful.

Harrison said, "You said you tried to be nice to Hall. Why?"

"Julia asked me to."

"Why would she ask you to do that?"

"Because he wanted to go to Venice with us. She wanted me to . . . you know, flirt with him. Or do something so she could start a fight with him so he wouldn't go."

"I see." Dunsmore looked thoughtful. "Did you?"

"I tried. He didn't seem to like me."

"How close were Miss Keane and Mr. Hall?"

"I don't know."

"Close enough that your flirting with him meant that she could start a fight?"

That had not occurred to her. It should have.

"Did Miss Keane offer him anything while the three of you were at the club?" Harrison asked. "A mint? A drink? A piece of gum?"

Such an odd question. Lena frowned at him. "No. He had a drink when we sat down. Other than that . . . no. I mean, she offered us both a cigarette, but he didn't take it."

Harrison sat back in his chair and let out his breath. "Classic pill drop," he said to Dunsmore, who nodded grimly.

"Wait—" Lena said. "Are you saying . . . what are you saying?"

"Thank you, Miss Gruner," Dunsmore said, rising. "You've been very helpful." Then, with as little ceremony as when they'd arrived, the two men left.

It was over, but instead of feeling relieved, Lena was more confused than ever. She waited only a moment to make sure they were gone before she shoved the sketchbook back into her bag and raced from the trattoria. Men in black suits. The CIA. She hadn't imagined being followed. She had to tell Julia. She wasn't sure whether Julia was in trouble or not—she wasn't sure what that whole conversation was really about, but there had been that strange "*classic pill drop*," that . . .

Lena slowed. What the hell *had* the whole thing been about? "*Did Miss Keane offer him anything?*" Were they accusing Julia of poisoning Terence Hall? And what about the weirdness with the names? "*She has a few.*"

Lena couldn't bring herself to think of it now. Julia would explain things. She had to get to Julia.

She hurried to catch the crowded tram, trying to slow her racing mind. When she reached Stazione Termini, the station was so busy it took Lena several minutes to reach the ticket counters, where she was supposed to meet Julia, and several minutes more to confirm that Julia had not yet arrived. Lena checked her watch, and then looked anxiously at the departure time for the Venice train. Julia was late.

Half an hour later, and Julia still had not appeared. Impatiently, Lena scanned the crowd. Her distress from the meeting with the CIA agents only grew with the noise and confusion of the station; she felt pressed on all sides, somehow culpable and criminal—but for what? Where the hell was Julia?

Fifteen minutes more, and the Venice train pulled in and disgorged its passengers. Lena shifted her weight. Any second now, Julia would be racing toward her, an apology on her lips. Julia would explain everything. She'd put all Lena's fears to rest. Lena wanted desperately to believe it, but what the agents had said kept circling back. "*Miss Kovalova.*" Different names.

"Classic pill drop . . ."

The heat of the station and the crowd, the train's belching steam, Lena's own anxiety, made her feel ill. The minutes ticked by. Still, no Julia. They announced the loading of the Venice train, and Lena's apprehension shifted to worry. It wasn't like Julia to be tardy, especially since she'd been so insistent on leaving today.

Lena watched the passengers board. She watched the doors close and heard the announcement of the departure of the Venice train. With a grunt and a chugging groan, an exhalation of steam, the train ground its way out of the station, and again Lena felt the skin on the back of her neck prickle. She glanced around, never more aware of the possibility that she was being watched.

Now she knew too much to discount it. She felt the danger as a visceral crawling thing. She picked up her bag, looking over her shoulder, looking for a suit, sunglasses. But there were too many suits and sunglasses in the train station, and where the hell was Julia? The stink of fear crept into her pores as surely and permanently as the stink of pig.

She hurried out the station doors and into the Piazza dei Cinquecento. The cars, the horns, the noise of arriving and departing trains and trams—the sounds were all too loud, churning in her head. Desperately she searched for the tram she needed, already losing her bearings though she'd arrived only an hour before.

"Lena!"

The shout stopped her. *Julia?*

Lena spun around, searching the people rushing into the station, desperately searching. There was no Julia. She wanted to hear Julia's voice so badly she'd imagined it.

"Lena!"

There it was again. Where was it coming from? All around, inside her own head, nowhere.

And then a hand landed on her arm with such force it nearly knocked her down. Julia, her hair falling from its pins, panic in her eyes, sweating and breathing hard with exertion.

"There you are! Where have you been? I—"

"Listen to me, Lena. It's all gone wrong. I need you to hide, do you understand? Hide, and stay hidden. I'll find you."

"Hide?" Lena frowned.

Julia gave her arm a little shake. Her face was harder than Lena had ever seen it. She looked like the version of Julia that Lena had seen at Strega, the first time she'd seen her with Terence Hall. "*Listen.* I was supposed to let you take the fall. I couldn't do it. I need you to do what I say now."

"I don't understand," Lena said softly. "What do you mean? What fall?"

"You're in danger. Don't let them find you. Go." Julia slipped away.

It was then Lena saw the men—suited men coming from one direction, and a black-coated man from the other, the same man she'd seen fall outside the pharmacy weeks ago. They eased from hidden corners, converging, shouting in languages Lena did not understand—Italian? English? Something else? She didn't know. She ran. Across the square, dodging through parked cars and those coming to pick up or drop off passengers, ignoring the horns and the shouts and the people who stared after her. Her bag bounced hard against her back. She kept running, now toward the remains of the ancient Servian Wall at the edge of the station. If she could get there, if she could somehow get behind it, hide, find a way to get lost in the streets . . .

But she was too slow and the men were too fast. They were right on her, she heard their breathing, their hard heels on the stone. One of them—the man in the coat—grabbed hold of her bag, jerking her back.

Lena lost her balance, crashing to the ground at the same time she heard a gunshot followed by screams of passersby. She was dimly aware of people crying out, fleeing, racing for cover, but mostly she heard the man who'd grabbed her bag let out a gasping grunt. He let go. Lena scrambled to her knees, her bag sliding over her shoulder, banging into her chest as she desperately looked for where the shot had come from, where next to run, and then she saw Julia, only a few yards away, next to the jutting stone of the old Servian Wall, a gun—a gun!—in her hand, and she realized that was where the shot had come from, and the other men chasing Lena had stopped and stood still, watching Julia, waiting for what would happen next.

Chaos erupted around them, but Julia's voice carried easily as she said, "Leave her. It's me you want. Let her go."

One of the men shook his head. "Not so fast. She's part of this too."

"She doesn't know anything." Julia leveled the gun at him, and Lena's thoughts ran in bewildered and astonished circles. "Lena, I want you to get up, and I want you to run away from here."

"I—"

"Now," Julia said.

"Don't go anywhere, Miss Gruner." The man who'd spoken to Julia put up his hand. "You can't escape."

"I don't even know what this is!" Lena said in desperation. From the corner of her eye, she saw the man in the black coat, who had been lying motionless, flinch. Maybe. She didn't want to take her gaze from the others, and Julia had already shot him. He was going nowhere.

"Get up, Lena," Julia ordered.

Lena did, and at the same moment, the man in the coat rolled and grabbed her, pulling her to him. She felt the gun in her back, heard his heavy breathing. She didn't think, she only reacted, a kick in his shin, and he buckled and released her, but the gun in his hand jerked and his finger on the trigger jerked too. The shot rang in her ears, his gun, and Julia, whose eyes had been on Lena—Julia, to whom Lena owed everything—put her hand to her chest, a bloom of red, crumpled, and went down, motionless.

Lena cried out, and started toward her, but then . . . then the man who'd told her she couldn't escape spun toward her, and she heard the shouts and screams of witnesses and Julia's voice in her ear, "*Run!*" though she couldn't have heard it because Julia had been shot, Julia was dead, and Lena turned and ran. She ran as fast as she could and as far. She ran with Julia's *It's all gone wrong. Don't let them find you* in her head. She ran without looking back. She ran until she cramped and her lungs felt they would burst and she couldn't go one step farther, and then she stumbled to a stop at the first tram station she saw.

She ignored the looks she got when she boarded the tram—more accurately, she saw nothing but Julia folding in on herself, that flower of blood, Julia falling like a rag doll. Julia still. Lena transferred from one tram to another before she realized she had to go back to the academy to report what had happened. She needed the police, the carabinieri. And yet . . . what would she report? They needed to find Julia's body and the men who had killed her and who were these men? They weren't the CIA agents who had questioned Lena in the Piazza Fiume. Lena had no idea who they were or what they wanted. CIA? Or something else?

"She's part of this too."

Part of *what*?

"You can't escape," that man had said.

"I was supposed to let you take the fall." Julia's words. The fall for what? A *"classic pill drop"*?

"I couldn't do it." Julia was dead because of her. It was her fault.

It took Lena two hours to discover where in Rome she was, and to navigate her way back to the academy, and she wanted to cry with relief when she arrived to its soothing pink marble floor and pillars and vast ceiling, though she wondered if there was any place she would feel safe again.

Not the academy, it turned out. She'd no sooner come inside when she was greeted by the director, Emilio Collie, whom she'd only seen from across the room at a dinner or two but had never actually met. A serious expression marked his already gaunt face, making him look forbidding, and Lena felt another rush of fear—what had happened to make him look that way?

Julia was dead.

He said in a low voice, "Miss Gruner, the carabinieri would like to have a word with you."

It was about Julia. It had to be. They'd found her. Lena had been gone for hours. Of course. "Is it about Julia?"

To her surprise, Mr. Collie frowned. "Miss Keane? No. They've said nothing about her. If you will . . ." He gestured down the hallway, and only then did she notice that they had an audience, that everyone in the building had paused to watch, and that farther down the hall, in front of the library, stood two carabinieri, arms crossed, waiting.

Lena's mouth went dry. "But if it's not about Julia . . . what do they want?"

Mr. Collie said quietly, "I cannot stop them from questioning you, Miss Gruner. I received a call from the American embassy. They've asked you to cooperate."

"Am I in trouble?" she asked.

The director shrugged. "That I cannot say."

She had an overwhelming urge to run again. But she had nowhere to go, and she knew she wouldn't get ten yards before she was stopped.

Her pulse jumped as she followed the director down the hall to the library.

The two carabinieri stepped aside.

"There is nothing to fear," one of them said. "We are only asking questions."

About what? The last hours became a weight she could not breathe through. She had already been asked questions by the CIA, and she was already afraid, and all she knew was that she didn't want to be here in this moment, or to be alone with the carabinieri.

But she obviously had no choice. Dr. Collie didn't come into the library with her.

He closed the door behind them after the two police officers followed her inside.

"I want to report a murder," she said.

The policeman who was obviously to be her main interrogator raised his heavy brows. *"Si?"*

"In the Piazza Cinquecento. A few hours ago. I was with my friend Julia Keane. We were pursued by three men, and one of them shot her. He wore a long black coat and . . . and he had dark hair. You'll know him because . . . because . . . because . . ." They looked at her with polite uninterest. "Because she shot him first. I don't know where she hit him, but he was wounded, that I know."

"I see. Won't you sit down, Miss Gruner."

Lena took a seat in one of the armchairs.

The main policeman sauntered over and pulled up another chair to sit before her. "Are you comfortable, signora?"

"My friend . . . aren't you going to do anything about it?"

"If what you say is true, the police at the *stazione* will be involved already." He seemed completely unconcerned.

"It *is* true. She's dead."

"Then there is nothing to be done, *sì*?"

"But—" Lena felt as if she were falling into darkness. "But these men . . ."

"In a black coat. Yes, I see. It all sounds very interesting. I'm sure we will hear all about it. In the meantime, we will try to make this short."

"I don't understand. You mean this isn't about Julia?"

"Now, I did not say that." His smile was chilling. "Perhaps you could tell me why you're in Rome."

"I'm an academy student," she said. "I'm here to study fashion design."

"From where?"

"The United States. Los Angeles."

"Ah." The man sat back. Again that little smile. "California, *sì*? Hollywood?"

Lena could not smile back. "Yes."

"How many communists do you know there?"

The question came out of nowhere. "What?"

"How. Many. Communists. Do. You. Know. There?"

"I . . . none." It was a lie, of course, but they couldn't know that, and why were they asking that question anyway?

"You're a student?"

"I just told you I was."

"In Hollywood."

Lena nodded.

"But you do not know any leftists."

"I . . . I . . . no."

"Liar." The man's little smile disappeared. "How often do you go to the Via Margutta?"

"I don't."

He turned to look over his shoulder at his fellow officer, and they exchanged a laugh. He turned back to her. "I am asking you again, signora. How often do you go to the Via Margutta? To a bar there called La Grotta? Do you know it?"

The walls felt very close. "Could I have some water please?"

"After you answer the question."

"I've been there once or twice," she confessed.

"To communist meetings?"

"To listen to jazz."

"Did you ever meet a man by the name of Terence Hall?"

Lena froze. "Once. I met him once."

"What was the nature of this meeting?"

"I met him at the Club LeRoy. He was a friend of Julia's." Julia, who was dead. "That's all. I talked to him a bit. I asked him to dance. He said no. We left."

"Do you know who he was?"

"I heard about it later. I didn't know when I met him."

She waited for them to ask her about a pill drop, about poison. They didn't, but the questions went on and on and on. Most of them about her associations in Los Angeles, and why she was really in Rome, until Lena's mouth was dry and she thought she would cry with frustration and worry and fear.

"Do you have friends here in Rome?"

"Yes, of course. I just told you one of them was dead."

"Who are they? Their names please." The man gestured to his partner, who took out a pad and a pencil.

"I—uh—don't remember."

"You don't remember your friends' names?"

"Well . . . they're Italian, so . . ."

"Please list them."

Lena cleared her throat. "Julia, of course. She's a student here, and Tony, who owns La Grotta, but you must know that, and there are some people who are always there, but I don't know them well . . . I don't remember really? Marco, maybe?"

"You are a messenger for them?"

"A what?"

"You deliver messages? Codes, contraband, things of that nature."

She was tired. "Cigarettes. I've brought them cigarettes. That's hardly contraband." A bit of hashish, and there had been that emetic that she was sure was not emetic, and . . . Terence Hall had been poisoned—*no, no,* she refused to believe it. He'd been alive when they left him. "Yes. Yes. Cigarettes."

"Just cigarettes, signora? Are you certain?"

Even through her exhaustion and sorrow she felt the danger in the question, and she knew then that Julia had lied to her. *"She's part of it too."* Whatever Lena had been couriering was not harmless, not just drugs, but something bad enough that men had followed her for it. It had been bad enough to get Julia killed. Bad enough that Julia had felt the need to protect Lena. And those men were still out there. *"You can't escape."*

This was not the game she'd thought it. It was no harmless hustle as it had been with Walter. She was in trouble, and she was not only grieving, she was also terrified. "If it was anything else, I didn't know. I didn't *know.*"

More questions. She lost track of time; it felt like forever. Finally, her questioner looked at his watch and sighed. He signaled to his partner, who rose and opened the drawn curtain over the window. The pink of dawn light filled the room.

They'd kept her there through the night answering the same questions. Whether she'd given them the answers they wanted, she had no idea. But she was relieved and stunned when her questioner rose and said, "It is time for you to leave Rome, signora." His voice was firm, but his dark gaze was not unkind. "You should not come back. We will escort you to the airport."

Lena stared at him in shock and confusion. She wasn't going to jail. It took her another moment to realize the rest. No interview at Cinecittà. Her internship, gone. The future she'd planned for, gone.

None of it mattered just then. Julia was dead. And those men Julia had died to save her from were still out there.

"You have twenty minutes to pack your things."

"What about Julia? And those men?"

"Best to worry about yourself. You should pack quickly, signora. We have orders to take you ready or not."

His eyes might have been understanding, but Lena also saw the resolve in them, and she knew the two of them would have no trouble manhandling her to the airport. They would carry her kicking and screaming onto the plane if they had to, and no one in Rome would question the carabinieri. No one would dare to, even if they handcuffed her to her plane seat. She had no idea who had given the order for her to be removed from Rome, but she had no doubt that it would be carried out with or without her cooperation, especially since—what had Dr. Collie said?—they'd been told by the American embassy that she should cooperate.

Her questioner's mouth settled into a thin line. "It is better if you don't ask questions. For your own sake. Now hurry, signora. You have a plane to catch."

They released her to go to the Augusta and waited outside while she gathered her things. She threw it all, including the bag she'd packed for Venice, into her suitcase, too upset to organize anything. Before the day ended, Rome would be a heartbreaking and confusing memory; she was on her way back to LA.

CHAPTER 11

It was her first time on an airplane, but she was too numb to appreciate the luxury of it. She stared out the window at the endless sky and thought it all must be a dream. She wasn't really leaving Rome, leaving the future she and Julia had planned. Julia had not been shot. Julia was not dead. The CIA had not stopped Lena in the trattoria and she had not been chased by dangerous men who'd threatened her or questioned for fifteen hours by the carabinieri.

God, the way the people at the academy avoided looking at her as she left, the humiliation of being brought to the flight gate flanked by carabinieri, the way people stared and then looked away as if they were afraid just looking might stain them with whatever stained her. She could see them wondering what she'd done to be brought to the airport under guard. The questions flashing through their eyes: *Who did she murder? Was she dangerous? How dangerous? Where was she going and how could they avoid that flight?*

Julia was dead. Lena could not stop reliving it. The shot ringing out. Her friend slumping to the ground. *"Get up, Lena." "Run." "I was supposed to let you take the fall but I couldn't do it."*

Finally, exhaustion took hold. Lena closed her eyes, but she couldn't sleep. She saw the face of her questioner, she heard those endless questions: whyareyouinRome whoareyourfriends youwereamessenger . . . and the CIA man, those piercing eyes, pill drops, and Julia with two names—no, a *few* names. Miss Kovalova. What kind of a name was that?

A Russian name.

Lena tried to push the thought away but it would not go. A Russian name, and she remembered Petra saying, *"You understand now what you are part of?"* and the man at the station saying that Lena was part of it too and there was no escape and the carabinieri asking if Lena had communist friends and telling her not to come back to Rome.

Julia, at the Pincio Terrace, brushing her lips against Lena's ear. *"You're a good partner. I think I'll keep you."*

Was that what she'd said? Was Lena remembering correctly?

A Russian name. Communists. *"You were a messenger,"* and the many jobs she'd done for Julia, the code words, the way Julia had distracted Lena with friendship and praise . . . Had it been deliberate? Had it all been a lie? *"You're a good partner."* Just like Walter. Julia had taught her how to play a game. Julia had used her. Lena had been enchanted but the entire time Julia was only taking advantage of her, and she'd put Lena, unaware and stupid, in danger.

"I was supposed to let you take the fall . . ." Was that the truth? Lena wasn't sure. What had she really known about her friend? Nothing. Julia had evaded every question. All of it could have been a lie. What did it matter? It didn't keep Lena from grieving, or from being afraid. Whatever the truth was, Julia had saved her and now Julia was dead and the danger was still there. Those men were still out there. And the CIA—they were unlikely to stay in Italy and they knew her name. Those men who had killed Julia . . . who were they? Would they follow her to LA? What had they called her? *Miss Gruner.*

Lena's sight blurred. She had been a fool, and she wavered between grief stricken and terrified. By the time she landed in LA, she was wrung out by emotion. When she got off the plane, she half expected CIA agents, or police officers, or whoever those men were to be waiting for her. She was relieved to see no one, but she didn't quite believe it, and she suspected every too-interested look.

But it also wasn't until she had landed that she realized she had nowhere to go. She'd given up her apartment and her job. The next session at Chouinard didn't start until September, and how could she go there? They would know to look for her there. She couldn't go back to Polly's. After months in Rome, how could she return to who she'd been? She was no longer Elsie Gruner. She was Lena now, but . . . not legally. They'd be looking for her. She had to find a way to hide.

She caught a glimpse of herself in the reflection of glass fronting—blond, elegant. No, not Elsie Gruner. Julia had made her into someone else. She *was* someone new. Could she continue to be that person? Was it possible to disappear into the Lena she'd become?

She couldn't just stand there in the airport all day. For one thing, if anyone was looking for her, they'd easily find her here. But where to go? Who did she know in LA anymore? Walter was gone and she didn't want to get anywhere near his opportunistic ego. Anyway, she didn't trust him and he'd expect her to be Elsie and she would not—could not—go back.

Lena dragged her suitcase to the nearest pay phone. The battered directory nearly fell apart in her hands, but she flipped through the pages, hoping someone might occur to her. She flipped through the *A*s, the *B*s . . .

Someone came to stand behind her, waiting for the phone.

*C*s . . . *D*s . . .

Disney. Lena stopped short. The memory flew into her head. Charlie saying he was an animator at Disney, that he'd gone to Chouinard, that he could write her a recommendation. Harvey with excitement in his eyes, "*We're going to help you, honey. You're going to be the best investment we've ever made.*" She hadn't seen them since the night of the raid on their house, but . . . they'd been the closest friends she'd had in LA once. Nearly two years ago now. Who knew if they were still in LA?

It was the only option she had.

Quickly she turned back to the *C*s, looking for Chesterfield, not expecting to find anything. But it took only a second to spot his name. Harvey Chesterfield.

She picked up the receiver and fumbled for change, ignoring the impatient sigh of the man behind her. She put her finger in the dial and then paused, remembering the parties at Harvey and Charlie's house, the CRC—a communist organization. The questions from the carabinieri about her associations in LA came back to her. What if she was being watched?

The man waiting said, "Please, miss."

Harvey and Charlie were probably the last people she should call, given the trouble she'd been in. But who else did she know? It had been some time. Maybe they were no longer involved.

She just needed to get herself situated. She just needed a little bit of help for now.

She dialed the number.

The phone rang, and rang.

"Hello?" It was Charlie's voice, Lena would have recognized it anywhere.

"Charlie! Hello, I'm sorry to call so late. This is—"

"Elsie? Elsie, is that you? My God, I can't believe it! Where have you been? Where are you?" He sounded genuinely glad to hear from her.

Lena couldn't help laughing. "I'm here. I'm here in LA. I just got in from Rome—"

"From *Rome?*" She heard a muffled voice from the background. Charlie said, "Quiet! Yes, it's really her!" Then, back to Elsie, "I'm sorry, Harvey's asking questions."

"It's a long story—"

"Say no more. Tell me what you need."

"A place to spend the night, if that's all right?"

"Absolutely. Where are you?"

"At Los Angeles International Airport."

"The *airport?* You *flew* from Rome? That's a pricey trip."

"I didn't pay for it. Actually . . . I don't know who did."

More talk in the background, Charlie saying to Harvey, "Yes, we're going to get her, just a minute—We'll be there as soon as we can. We'll meet you at Arrivals."

The phone went dead. Lena put down the receiver and smiled at the man waiting, a complete stranger. "My friends are coming."

~

She had to wave them down. The old Chrysler nearly drove right by her.

"My God, we didn't recognize you!" Charlie said when she got into the car. "Look at you! Your hair—"

"Do you like it?"

"It's more than that," Harvey said. "There's something else . . . seriously, you have been *transformed*." He ushered her into the front seat between them and pulled the car back onto the road.

"You two look just the same," she said, which was true.

"Ha! That's kind," Charlie said. "But we have been speculating the entire way here about why you were in Rome—an expensive plane trip, with a mysterious patron?—and it's obvious you're very changed and if you don't tell us what happened, Harvey will no doubt explode."

"Not just me," Harvey protested.

"Well, I didn't have much of a choice on the trip," she explained. "I had a scholarship from Chouinard to the American Art Academy."

"So you did go to Chouinard!" Charlie nearly crowed. "We wondered."

"Walter didn't make you wait. Thank God." Harvey frowned. "Where is Walter?"

"I left him. That is, we left each other. But mostly I left him." Lena took a deep breath. "You were right. He was no good. I went to tell you, but that was the night you were raided. I saw it. I saw you get arrested. I wanted to help, but I didn't know what to do. I couldn't find you after that. I tried."

The two men exchanged a grim glance. "There was nothing you could do," Harvey said. "It's good that you didn't get involved. It's been a nightmare since that night, frankly."

"Some of which could be avoided." Charlie spoke almost beneath his breath.

The quick tension between them was palpable. "I'm sorry if I raised a sore subject," Lena said.

Charlie laughed shortly.

"I didn't know if you'd still be in LA," she went on carefully. "Or if you were in jail."

Harvey said, "It turns out it's not actually illegal to hold activist meetings in your house. Free speech, you know. But our landlord did not appreciate it, and we're not living in Edendale anymore."

"Venice Beach," Charlie said. "A lovely little bungalow fit only for seagulls. But it's what we can afford."

She looked at him questioningly.

"Charlie was fired from Disney," Harvey explained. "For holding subversive views, though they didn't say that."

"They'll never say that. Instead I got a negative job review. Out the door the next day. I believe someone told them I was a member of the Communist Party, or the CRC, or possibly that I lived with another man, or . . . who knows?"

"We think it was the FBI," Harvey confessed.

An uncomfortable chill slid down Lena's spine. The shadows of the academy library, the carabinieri crowding around her, her questioner's relentless gaze flashed before her again.

"It's a simple time. Only simple views allowed," Charlie said.

"I know." Lena sighed.

"Now, that is a telling sigh." Charlie twisted in the seat to look at her full on. "You aren't giving us the entire story, Elsie."

"I'm not Elsie anymore. I'm Lena. Or . . . I *need* to be Lena. And I need a new last name. And a whole new identity."

They went quiet.

"This sounds serious," Charlie said.

"I know I can trust you, but . . . I think . . . I don't want to bring you trouble, but I don't know where else to turn."

"Best to tell the story in the car then," Harvey said. "We're not entirely sure the house isn't bugged."

"By who?"

"Who else? Our illustrious FBI," Harvey said.

Lena closed her eyes briefly. *The FBI.* And yet, who else could she trust but Harvey and Charlie? "Am I . . . should I be . . . is it safe to be at your house?"

Charlie said, "You know, it might be very confusing for them, in a good way, to hear a woman's voice there, but tell us your story, Els—Lena, how interesting, that might take me a few days to get used to. When you're done, we'll tell you what we think."

So Lena told them. The street and traffic lights streaked past the windows, reminding her of the neon of Rome, as she told them about Julia and the pickups and deliveries, and then Terence Hall and the CIA and the chase in the Piazza dei Cinquecento, Julia's death and then the carabinieri grilling her about her associations in LA and on and on until she'd been escorted to the airport and out of the city with the warning to not return.

She finished to silence.

Then Charlie said quietly, "What do you think you were involved in?"

"I'm not sure. But I think Julia was a communist and . . . they said she had a few names, and Kovalova, well, it's Russian, isn't it?"

Neither of them answered. They didn't have to.

"You didn't know what you were picking up and delivering?"

"No, but they made it sound . . . suspicious."

"And that attaché was poisoned. By Julia?"

"I—I don't know."

"Els—Lena," Harvey said. "These men really said you were part of it and you couldn't escape?"

She nodded.

Soberly, Harvey said, "I don't think you should tell this story again. Not to anyone. You can trust us to say nothing, but this world now is strange. Now that the Soviets have the bomb, McCarthy and HUAC see a spy in every communist or fellow traveler. The House Un-American Activities Committee is no joke. I think it's safer for you to just keep this to yourself."

Charlie nodded. "You don't know who's watching. Or listening. Just forget it ever happened."

Their words frightened her, though she knew they were true. "I don't think I can forget."

"Then take it as a warning. You're lucky you're alive and not in some Italian jail. You don't want to end up in an American one."

Harvey's hands tightened on the steering wheel. "Treat it as if it happened to someone else in a faraway land. You're going to have to become someone they can't find. We can help you with that." He looked at Charlie. "Can't we?"

Charlie nodded. "You'll need a new last name. A birth certificate. With that you can get anything else. Fortunately, we know an artist or two . . ."

"I told you they'd come in handy," Harvey said.

Charlie rolled his eyes. "I'm going to pretend you never said that. And you, my dear, are saying goodbye to the past. Hopefully forever. Don't ever mention Rome again."

They had reached the Ocean Park amusement pier, battered and neglected, but still busy on a Friday night with the Aladdin Ballroom. The old luxury hotels of the promenade were pensioners' slums now, and beyond them the shadows of insect-like oil derricks split the horizon, eerie in the streetlights and through the fog coming off the ocean. Finally Harvey stopped before a small house with a sinking roof set back behind a hedge of wild rose. Lena frowned; it did look hospitable only for seagulls. The porch light revealed flaking paint and a sagging stoop, and behind the house an oil derrick towered menacingly.

"It takes up the whole backyard," Charlie confessed. "Harvey hangs washing on it."

Forty-eight hours ago, she'd been on her way to Venice; how ironic to end up in Venice Beach instead. The thought caught and twisted her sorrow. A faintly fetid sewer stink blew in with the breeze and mixed with that of the salt from the ocean and the dank fog and the roses. They took her inside—a small living room, a kitchen with ill-hung cupboards, and a bedroom and bathroom beyond. But they had the same furniture, and the posters and pictures on the walls, the books and the bookcases from their Edendale house, and in that way it felt like home. Still Lena was dismayed to see that the loss of Charlie's job meant that all they could afford was this mean little place.

"The couch is yours," Harvey told her, bringing out blankets and a pillow. "You're welcome to stay as long as you want."

"Only until I can get my feet underneath me," she promised. "I don't want to put you out."

"Don't worry about that. Charlie works at the liquor store on Pacific. I do Saturdays at the Jewish bakery because the owners can't. We won't be walking all over each other."

"A liquor store? Oh, Charlie. And Harvey—a bakery?"

He grinned at her. "I don't mind it, actually. I meet some interesting people."

Harvey threw her a pillow. "They have delicious babka. I'll bring one home when I'm off."

PART TWO

The Undoing of Lena Taylor

CHAPTER 12

Two weeks later, Lena had a new birth certificate and a new name: Lena Taylor. The last name had come to her in a flash, as if she'd been subconsciously ruminating on it all this time, and it was perfect, wasn't it, for the daughter of a dressmaker who wanted to be a fashion designer? Taylor/tailor . . . she liked the play of it, the way it so easily rolled off her tongue, and that perfect play gave her even more confidence. She told Charlie to make her older on her birth certificate. She was twenty-six now instead of twenty-two—it seemed a more respectable age for a fashion designer.

Now all she needed was a job. She spent hours perusing the classified ads, and when she wasn't doing that, she sketched and tried hard not to think of Rome, or Julia, but it was difficult. Everything reminded her of Julia—the blond hair that Julia had suggested, the makeup Lena now wore religiously. *"You have such good bones."* Everything Lena had become had been Julia's doing, but it was so much more than that. Julia's scent, her smile haunted Lena at the oddest times, so she would spin around, half expecting to see Julia behind her, and when she wasn't, Lena could barely contain her tears. She reminded herself that Julia had lied to her, but that only made it worse. Grief and fear were a terrible combination and an unbearable weight.

Lena strolled Ocean Front Walk and listened to the sounds coming from the seedy amusement park and watched the fog roll in and out and jumped at every shadow. She'd thrown the bag she'd meant to take to Venice in the closet, unpacked. She couldn't even look at it without feeling too many things she could not unravel. There was nothing in it she needed. She couldn't wear any of the clothes she'd packed without remembering the anticipation with which she'd packed them, and how everything had ended up.

Harvey had told her to pretend it never happened. She tried.

Then one Sunday, Harvey pulled on his jacket to go out.

"Tell me you aren't going," Charlie said, looking up from the newspaper. "What have I told you about this?"

"Going where?" Lena sat on the couch, working on one of her designs. It was Sunday, and the smell of the toasted babka and coffee they'd had for a late breakfast still lingered.

Harvey rolled his eyes. "It's interesting, and I'm bored."

Charlie told her, "Remember the artists I told you about? Harvey's taken to hanging out with them and the degenerate poets they waste time with."

"Degenerates?"

"They aren't degenerates," Harvey protested.

"They talk of revolution and making art when the bombs fall and kill us all, when what they really mean is that they're going to smoke reefer and write bad poetry. What is that but degenerate?"

"Revolution?" Lena was instantly wary. "You mean they're communists?"

Harvey put his finger to his lips, reminding Lena that the house might be bugged. "Oh no, I doubt it." But he didn't sound convinced, or more likely, it was a deliberate lie, given Charlie's grimace. "Most of them don't know what they are except young and rebelling against whatever they can. They're harmless fools. The talk is interesting, though. It reminds me of the old days."

"The old days being what got us arrested—at least part of the reason." Charlie lowered his voice to a bare whisper and rattled the newspaper to muffle his words further. "And some of them are dangerous enough that they've forged Lena a birth certificate."

"I think I agree with Charlie," Lena said. "You're on an FBI watch list, Harvey. It's probably not a good idea—"

"They're bohemians, not Reds, and they idolize Charlie Parker, for God's sake. I told you they're harmless. Come with me if you want, Lena. You can tell Charlie I'm right."

Charlie met Lena's gaze and shrugged. "Go ahead. You can tell Harvey I'm the one who's right. In fact, I'd appreciate it if you would."

Lena set down her sketchbook. "Where is this meeting?"

"At a guy named Larry Lipton's place. He's in his forties, and he's a writer. I think he likes the whole benevolent-benefactor role. Very professorial and kind of a hipster. You'll like him. Come on, let's go."

Lena went only because she was worried and wanted to help Charlie convince Harvey that attending was a bad idea. She shouldn't associate with anyone who sounded remotely like a communist, and neither should Harvey. If what Charlie said was true, these people were probably being watched. She was in hiding, and she'd had her fill of all that in Italy.

Larry Lipton's cottage was on Park, between the seedy promenade and Pacific, which marked the better neighborhood beyond. It was bigger than the houses around it, with an upper- and lower-story sitting porch, and a shallow yard that looked like it hadn't been mowed in a month or more.

"Every Sunday he has this gathering," Harvey explained to her. "All the artists in the neighborhood go. I think it's partly because he serves lemonade and beer and potato chips and for half of them it's the only thing they eat all week."

The living room was already packed when they went inside, every square inch of seating taken up, the couches and the chairs but also every inch of floor. Wineglasses and beer bottles, spilling ashtrays, several bowls of potato chips spread about. There were mostly men, but a few women, and Harvey urged some to move closer together to make room for the two of them to sit on the floor. She expected him to introduce her to their host, but Larry Lipton was moving busily about, and there didn't seem to be a need. Lipton was short, with a round face and large eyes behind his round-framed glasses, and Lena watched him curiously while everyone got settled. He was the oldest person there, and Harvey was right, he had a professorial air about him, or so she thought, until he went to the record player below a long shelf of records—the collection was massive—and pulled one from a pile he'd obviously selected for the meeting.

"Let's start the magic circle with Bird today."

Harvey hadn't been wrong about the idolization of Charlie Parker. Everyone murmured in agreement, the record started, and someone brought out a can of pot and began rolling cigarettes. The room was already heavy with tobacco smoke from cigarettes and from the cigar Larry Lipton puffed away on. In a way it reminded her of Rome, and La Grotta, though there wasn't a bar and the only drinks were beer and wine and lemonade, and no one was making pasta. But it had the same atmosphere of free thought and artists and no one caring about how they dressed or convention, and the jazz winding through everything, and Lena half expected to see Julia leaning in a corner, smoking and smiling, though there was no one here like her.

But the memory, which was both good and heartbreaking, also made Lena acutely uncomfortable. She had a fleeting memory of her parents warning her about such things, something she should have remembered in Rome, she thought ruefully. Though truthfully she'd been too awestruck there to see it. Now she knew better. Maybe Harvey could lie to himself about how dangerous meetings like this could be now—all this free thought could lead to authorities like the FBI classifying a person as a radical. She would remind Harvey of that the moment they were out of here.

"I spent the whole week in Glendale," said one of the men on the floor. "Taking classes. I'm not going back. It feels good to be here after that. The squares, the teachers, the academics, man, they stifle real thoughts."

"What's a square?" Lena asked.

The man, who was blond and rangy, said, "Someone who worships success and work and *things*, man. Like your dad or my dad. Like all parents. Like that guy on the radio selling cars and toothpaste. Who cares if the world is blown to smithereens tomorrow? At least we'll have white teeth and a Chevrolet."

The curly-haired man rolling the reefers shook his head. "Man, that is bleak."

"It's true, though. The 'people's capitalism.' What a joke. Like we're partners with our corporate overlords. Yeah, man, we all share in prosperity. Any of them been to Pension Row lately?" The blond man spoke of the old luxury hotels on the promenade, too derelict to renovate but too expensive to tear down, that were now slums that housed the poor elderly. "Ha. It don't matter though, we'll all be gone in a blast." He made an explosive sound, followed by a gesture, fists violently opened, fingers flung wide. "Sayonara, baby."

The curly-haired man winced and shook his head. He lit the reefer and inhaled, took another drag, and then passed it along.

Another one said, "At least we're living the life until then."

"What does that mean to you?" Larry Lipton asked. "'The life'?"

"Simplicity," one called out.

"Art and beauty," called another.

"Freedom!" shouted a third.

"What does *freedom* mean, though?" Larry puffed on his cigar. Charlie Parker's saxophone wailed.

"Resisting the machine!" said someone else.

"Saying no to the system!"

"Or maybe . . . infiltrating the system. Changing it from the inside out."

All the rest had sounded naive and a bit stupid, but not that. Lena looked to its source. The man who'd spoken sat across the room, on the floor, his knees drawn up, though he looked tall. Tall and dark and slim. He had a weary air about him, too, as if the world had tired him out, and in that way he appeared different from the others, who had that innocence that came from book philosophy and poverty taken on like a mantle, that art-for-art's-sake sort of suffering when the suffering was your choice.

He didn't have the shabby look of the others, either, but wore tan trousers and a Hawaiian shirt. Even so, he didn't stand out. Somehow, he belonged in this crowd; and yet . . . he also wasn't like anyone else here.

When she looked at him, he met her gaze straight on, and his was interested. Interested enough that she looked away again.

The conversation went on, and Lena tried to pay attention, but she couldn't keep from glancing at him throughout the evening. He was the first thing in weeks that distracted her from thoughts of Julia.

When the meeting finally drew to a close, she went looking for him, but she couldn't find him anywhere, and she and Harvey left. On the way home she asked Harvey about him, but Harvey didn't know his name. "I know he's a veteran because he said something about it once. Everyone booed. Not me, of course."

"Why did they boo?"

Harvey said, "Most of them escaped service because they were students or too young. But you know, they all think soldiers are blind followers of the government."

"Oh." Lena thought for a moment as they walked through the foggy streets back to the bungalow. "Does he come every Sunday?"

"He has been. Why are you so curious about him?"

"I don't know. He seems interesting."

"Ah, a budding romance?" Harvey teased.

She ignored the tease. "He sounds like a subversive, Harvey."

"But he's good looking."

"This is how you get in trouble with the FBI."

"They're harmless, most of them, don't you think? Poets, artists, blathering on about changing the world but smoking enough marijuana to make them too stupid to move. What will they ever do, Lena?"

She said nothing. Again, she thought of Rome and Julia and La Grotta and the questioning of the carabinieri. Harvey liked the scene and she understood why, though she agreed with Charlie. He should not go there, and she shouldn't, either, not after what happened in Rome. It was a bad place for either of them to be, and she shouldn't go back, and yet . . .

Maybe once more. Just to learn his name. Just to see him again and satisfy her curiosity. Just one more time.

∿

Two days later, Charlie nearly shoved the newspaper at Lena while she sat eating a cinnamon roll. "Lena, you've got to look at this. It's perfect for you!"

She grabbed the newspaper before it landed in icing and scanned it. The classified advertisements. *Salesgirl Wanted, Clerk Wanted, Secretary Wanted, Bookkeeper Wanted, Sketch Artist Wanted—*

She stopped. At first she thought she was seeing things. But then, no, there it was. A job opening for a *Sketch Artist at Lux Studios, $50 a week. Send résumé and sketches to Richard Flavio, POB 6148, Culver City. Flavio.*

She had no experience as a costume sketch artist, but she could do this, she knew. Julia had thought so too. It had been the original plan, hadn't it? Cinecittà and then LA . . . *the scheduled interview at Cinecittà, had that been a lie?* Lena shook away the thought and the sorrow it brought. The fact that this job was listed here, now . . . well, it was meant to be, wasn't it?

"Well?" Charlie asked.

"What?" Harvey came out of the bedroom. "What is it?"

"Sketch artist for Lux Studios," Charlie told him. "For *Flavio.*"

"I don't have enough on my résumé," Lena said.

"So?" Charlie tapped her sketchbook on the table, and she knew he was right. Her résumé couldn't get her the job, but her sketches could. She could. If she could show them in person, she knew she could convince Flavio that she was the perfect person for the job. "*You shine,*" Julia had said. Maybe it had been a lie. Maybe Julia had just said it to manipulate her, but maybe it was true. Maybe Lena could make Flavio see the same thing within her.

If she could just get to him.

"I have to go there," she said. "In person. If I can show him what I can do, I can convince him. I've got those sketches I drew for my interview at Cinecittà."

"Say no more," Harvey said. "Let's go."

She changed, and they piled into the car.

The main building of Lux Studios looked like a southern plantation, long, pillared, with arched windows along its front. It was peach colored, with an art deco **LUX PICTURES** in gold across the top of the roof, and a stylized woman holding a flame on either side of the words. A parking lot was off to one side, a building next to that, and other buildings stretched behind it. What Lena hadn't counted on—what she hadn't even thought about—was the guarded gate bisecting the road into the parking lot. She had no appointment. Why in God's name should they let her in?

But that was Elsie talking, she told herself.

Charlie and Harvey both gave her a "What now?" look.

"I'll get in. Somehow," she told them. "Let me off here."

She took a deep breath and imagined the building was a nightclub on the Via Veneto. She got out of the car, straightened, and walked up to the gate, and when the sunglassed and visored man leaned out to ask what she wanted, she said:

"Lena Taylor. I'm here to see Flavio."

She met the guard's gaze, though she had to imagine where that was through his sunglasses, and she lifted her chin, waiting with what she hoped was a suitably haughty impatience as he called the costume department to announce her.

But of course there was a pause. Of course no one there had ever heard of her.

The guard looked back at her. "Miss . . . Taylor?"

"Lena Taylor," she said. "Is there a problem?"

"I'm afraid you don't have an appointment."

"I certainly do," she said irritably.

The guard frowned. "Oh, I—"

"It was quite an effort for me to get here on time from the airport. The least he can do is see me."

The guard looked flummoxed. He got back on the phone. She heard him say, "But . . . well, yes. She came from the airport. Um . . . she's insisting . . . okay . . . um, Miss Taylor?"

"Yes?"

"What is this regarding?"

"What do you think it's regarding? Fashion, of course."

"Oh, of course." The guard said back into the phone—warily this time—"Fashion."

Someone spoke for a long time on the other end. Lena tapped her foot. She looked impatiently at her watch. She took out her cigarettes, lit one, and smoked it with the bristly exhales and attitude of a woman who was rarely kept waiting and when she was, did not suffer it well.

"Listen," she said, "if he hasn't the time to see a woman who's flown all this way to see him—"

"No, no," the guard said. "You're to go up, Miss Taylor. The costume department is that building over there, past the parking lot. They're waiting for you."

"Thank you." Lena started toward the building, smoking now to calm her nerves, which were screaming at her bravado.

At the costume department she ground out her cigarette and took a moment to gather herself. *Confidence.*

She went inside. The secretary turned in her chair. "Miss Taylor." The woman was clearly flummoxed. "I'm so sorry. We didn't mark down an appointment, and—"

"I understand," Lena said. "Things like that do happen."

"Flavio is a bit late."

"I can wait." She sat herself down in one of the chairs against the wall. "Do you think he'll be long?"

"He's fitting Lana Turner."

"I see."

"She can be . . ."

Lena waved her hand to signal her understanding and opened her sketchbook as if she were so busy she had to make use of every moment.

She had waited an hour when she heard "Where is this confounded woman?" from down a hallway, followed by a quiet female voice saying, "She's waiting," and a bitten-off curse.

Lena looked up, and there he was. Flavio. She'd seen him in the movie magazines, of course. Tall, patrician looking, with dark hair swept back from his forehead, and his signature cravat. He looked the very picture of a costume designer—had she been called upon to describe one, she would have described him just this way. He stopped in front of her, his hands in his trouser pockets, and looked down his fine Roman nose at her, and said, "I'm sorry, I'm afraid I've completely forgotten any meeting we had. When did we last speak? And you are?"

She stood and offered her hand. "I'm Lena Taylor."

He took her hand and bowed slightly over it, though he looked confused. "You're from where?"

It was time to be honest. Lena raised every bit of her self-confidence, smiled, and lifted her sketchbook. "I wanted to show you my sketches. I'm applying for the sketch artist job."

She'd never seen anyone look more taken aback. Perplexed, a flash of anger, and then, just when she thought he was going to turn to his secretary and ask her to escort Lena to the door, Flavio laughed—a percussive burst so startling she stepped back.

He looked at his secretary. "Did you know this?"

"No, sir."

"Do you believe this?" Another laugh. He looked at Lena. "Miss Taylor, do you have any idea what difficulty you have caused me today?"

"Well, I am sorry about that, but I hope you'll find the trouble worth it."

He lifted a fine brow. "Well then. As long as you've scrambled my afternoon . . ." He motioned with his fine long fingers for the sketchbook she held. "Let's see it."

She gave it to him, and he gestured for her to follow him through the door that led into his office, which was a mess—a desk and chair, a love seat and low round table with other chairs around it, all covered with sketches and fabric swatches. An easel held a pad of paper and beside it was a small, tall table with pots of paint and a can of brushes, a box of pastels, and a bin of colored pencils. Its stool had been loaded with research books. A dye shade grid perched haphazardly on top.

He told her to have a seat, and then he shoved aside the sketchbooks on his desk chair to sit himself. She didn't see any horizontal surface that wasn't littered, so Lena carefully moved an estate auction catalog from the nearest chair and put it on the table. Flavio didn't complain; he was too busy flipping the pages of her book. She sat nervously, not wanting to watch him, unable not to.

His face remained expressionless; she couldn't tell what he thought about anything. He didn't pause, but spent exactly the same amount of time on each page, which by her estimation was about two seconds. One after another after another. Her mouth was so dry she could not swallow, but she tried not to listen to the conversation in her head that poked at the edges of her brain: *You're not good enough. What made you think you could do this? You haven't enough experience . . .* Elsie thoughts, not Lena thoughts.

Then, abruptly, he stopped. He closed the book and looked at her. Just a long, steady look that told her absolutely nothing. "All I need is a sketch artist," he said finally. "You'd take the thumbnails I gave you and make them into full sketches, color them in, that sort of thing. Have you done that before?"

"At school."

"How old are you?"

She was glad she'd decided to add those extra years to her age. "Twenty-six."

"You'd be one of three others. You'll be in the workroom too. Helping the seamstresses and the cutters. Can you do that?"

"I make my own clothes," she told him. "My mom was a dressmaker. I helped her from the time I was old enough to hold pins without swallowing them."

Flavio nodded. "All right then. I admire boldness, but not stupidity. So don't be stupid, Lena Taylor, and you're hired. Can you start tomorrow?"

"Yes," she said eagerly. "Thank you, sir. You won't regret this."

"Call me Flavio," he said.

~

On Monday, Lena arrived at Lux Studios so early that Flavio's secretary blinked owlishly at her and said, "He won't be here for hours. And anyway, you won't be up *here*."

The girl took Lena downstairs to the workrooms, which thrummed with activity. She took in the tables with big rolls of fabrics, and men cutting it into pieces, pattern makers, and the sewing room, which hummed and pounded with the throttles of sewing machine pedals and the steady churn of needles and which had a rhythm all its own, so many machines it sounded like a kind of music.

Estelle was the matron in charge; she kept things on schedule, and in case you forgot, a huge chalkboard at the foot of the stairs showed what costumes were in production, and at what stage and who was assigned what. Flavio had three other sketch artists who took his croquis, or thumbnails, and enlarged them into full scale sketches and painted in the colors.

The sketching room was small, set with easels and shelves holding paints and pencils, pastels and everything needed for the work of fashion illustration, and immediately Lena felt at home.

All four of the easels looked to be in use, but one of them was surely hers, and so she took the one she liked best. She clamped paper in place, penciled out Flavio's design—a gown in lustrous shades of blue, draped over the bodice and wrapped around the hips until it flowed like water into a full and trailing skirt. It was so lovely that she felt the thrill of it into her fingertips; to think that this was her job, to think that she was translating Flavio's designs into something for others to look at . . . for a moment she paused, feeling the weight of it, the naivete of her boldness in approaching him. She had so much to learn, and yet, he'd wanted her here. He'd thought her worthy of this job.

Another impossible thing.

She had started to paint when she felt someone else come into the room. Lena didn't bother to look over her shoulder; she was too immersed in the job. But she felt someone come up behind her, she felt the scrutiny, and finally it was too distracting. She turned to see another young man—it was mostly young men in the workroom, with several women at the sewing machines. This one was tall and skinny, with round glasses and blondish hair.

"Hello," she said politely.

"You're the new one." It wasn't a question, and he did not look like he approved.

"Lena." She held out her hand to him. "Lena Taylor."

"You're at my easel."

She looked at the others, which all stood empty. "I didn't know which one was mine."

"They aren't assigned. But I always work at this one."

"Oh. Well. The paint's wet. It would be hard for me to move it now."

"I'm sure you'll manage."

Lena smiled politely. "There are three open ones."

129

He let out a breath and said, "Look, you're new, so maybe you don't know, but I'm Flavio's favorite, and you're the only woman sketch artist here. That means you're at the bottom of the ladder, and I hate to tell you this, but that's probably where you're going to stay."

He was smug, and so confident. Lena looked at him and thought, *It's my first day. I don't want to make an enemy.* But then, like a sneaking little whisper, she heard Julia's voice in her ear: *"It's so easy to give in to what the world wants, isn't it? You've been daring before. You can't stop. Not ever."*

Lena turned back to the sketch. "Thanks for the advice. The other easels are open."

He was quiet and still for a long moment. Then he said, "You said your name was Lena? I'm Mike. Do you like jazz?"

~

She sent a postcard to her parents telling them that she was back in LA and working for a fashion designer (she didn't mention the movies; her parents would only look down their noses at that, and she did not mention Walter, and hadn't for months), but the truth was that she hardly saw Flavio at all; she stayed in the workrooms with the others, working on sketches, and then she took the bus back to Venice Beach, where she slept on the couch at Harvey and Charlie's and saved money for her own apartment.

She loved her job. She loved everything about it. She loved the sketching and what she learned simply by looking at Flavio's designs, and the work slowly soothed her grief and confusion over Julia. Most of the women in the costume workroom had husbands or boyfriends, and the men had wives or secrets they hushed up about whenever she walked by. But she had friends, including Mike, who was arrogant, yes, but could be funny, and was a wonderful source of gossip: the stars, the movie sets, what was going on at soundstage five, and who hated who or who was having an affair with whom, and then one day Lena heard one of the men talking about the jazz clubs down on Central Avenue, and that time when they saw Humphrey Bogart and Ava Gardner there and how wild it was.

She remembered the jazz clubs in Rome, and the longing hit her hard. A drink, the music, the bodies moving in the smoke . . . it was what she wanted, a palpable reminder of a place and a time she knew she could never get back.

But when she asked these men which clubs on Central were the best, they shook their heads. "You'd get thrown out now," one of them, Bob, said. "It's not the same. They started cracking down on whites after the war. They don't want *mingling*. No one goes there anymore."

"Too many drugs," said Mike. "You wouldn't get two steps before the police would be escorting you back to your car."

"Or someone'd be trying to sell you heroin," Jerry piped up. "Go to the clubs on Western Avenue instead."

She didn't go. She was still feeling her way around, still in hiding, and now she had a job she loved too much to lose. She hadn't stopped looking over her shoulder, and memories of Rome were still too close to revisit. She hadn't managed to shrug off the fear, despite her new name. She kept her hair blond, long, and straight. She dressed differently, always in her own designs, even her casual clothing. Charlie and Harvey constantly commented on her transformation. No one in LA would mistake her for the Elsie Gruner she'd been. She was careful to stay away from anything that might bring her into the sights of the CIA—or whoever those men in Rome had been.

Except for one thing. One stupid thing.

Much to Charlie's dismay, she went again with Harvey to Larry Lipton's.

"Be watching for FBI agents checking license plates," Charlie warned them as he cut roses in the front yard.

"I don't think anyone there has a car. Maybe Larry," Harvey said.

Charlie pleaded, "Lena . . ."

"Leave her alone. There's a man there she likes." Harvey grinned.

Lena said, "No there's not."

"I'm playing matchmaker. I expect to be best man at your wedding."

Charlie gave her a chiding look. "Is he telling the truth? Is there a man there you're interested in? Please don't tell me he's a communist. Don't forget Rome."

"I'm not going to forget," Lena said darkly.

"And for God's sake, don't say anything about it. He might be an undercover agent himself."

"My God, you're suspicious. You didn't used to be so suspicious," Harvey said.

"That was before I spent a couple nights in jail. Be careful, both of you."

Charlie's warnings put a damper on the whole thing; again Lena told herself not to take the risk. Again, she found herself stepping up the porch stairs, going into Larry Lipton's crowded living room. The man was there again. He acknowledged her with a nod when she came in with Harvey, and she gave him a smile. Someone passed around the marijuana, and she watched the man smoke along with the others.

Larry put on a jazz quartet she didn't recognize, and then finally Bessie Smith, and that was when everyone settled and they talked about different planes of existence, and what plane creativity was on—as if it were a definitive one—and how the bomb impacted that creativity and existential crisis changed the trajectory of the subconscious.

There was only one reason she was here, and she told herself it wasn't good enough. She'd stopped paying attention to the conversation. It meandered in and out; she could barely keep track of it, meaningless words, arguments—no, here Larry was careful to call it "heated discussion."

She couldn't sit still any longer. She should tell Harvey she was leaving and drag him along. When someone said, "I thought the working class was the hope of the world once, too, yes? But they said that while they were listening to Stalin, and so . . . ," she couldn't bring herself to listen. She was done with all of it; Italy had cured her of any interest. Lena wove her way through the bodies on the floor, most listening intently, several intent only on mind alteration, and went to the kitchen, where a woman Harvey had pointed out as Larry's wife was opening another box of potato chips and lifting out one of the twin bags inside. She poured the chips into a bowl as she asked Lena, "You all right?"

Lena nodded. "I'm Lena. I just came in for more wine?"

"Right there." Larry's wife pointed to a jug of Almaden and went back into the living room with the chips.

She didn't really want more wine. What she wanted was the meeting to be over so she could address the reason she'd come, and she was afraid that, like last time, he would disappear before she had a chance to talk to him, and the whole Sunday would be a waste. She reached for the bottle and was splashing more into her glass when she heard someone come into the kitchen. The dark-haired man. The sight of him made her hitch; she spilled wine over the edge of her glass and cursed beneath her breath and grabbed a nearby towel to wipe it up.

He stopped. Today he wore a simple short-sleeved blue shirt. Not expensive, but again, not shabby. A man who cared how he looked.

Nervously she said, "Did you want something? The beer's in the cooler. Here's wine." She held out the bottle, then realized he had a bottle of beer in his hand.

"No," he said. "Is that your boyfriend?"

"Excuse me?"

"The man you're with?"

"Oh. Oh no, he's just a friend. I mean, I live with him and his . . . friend, but . . . we're just friends."

He frowned a little. "I see."

"Just down the street, actually. It's only temporary. I'm going to move as soon as I save enough money."

"Where do you work?"

"Lux Pictures. In the costume department. I'm a sketch artist. For Flavio. You know him?"

He nodded and took a sip of beer. "Can I get your autograph? It might be worth something when you're famous."

"Ha. I'll never be as famous as Flavio. He's far too good."

"The future is uncertain." His face clouded when he said it, but only for a moment. "You never know."

"I never finished my schooling, you see, so it was a miracle that he chose me, especially because I had no experience," she confessed, then wondered why she'd said it, and to this stranger, but she couldn't stop babbling on.

"He must have seen a great deal of talent."

"I think so," she said seriously.

He laughed. "You need more confidence."

"I'm working on that." She knew that he'd been joking, but she was not. "What do you do?"

"I'm a screenwriter. Or . . . I hope to be. I haven't actually sold anything of substance yet."

"What's your name?"

"Paul Carbone."

"What are you doing at Larry Lipton's?"

He set his empty beer bottle on the counter. "Where are you from? There's something in your voice I can't place."

"I asked first."

"Questions are problematic these days, aren't they?"

"You're spending your Sundays talking about socialism and anarchy and all the wrongs of a capitalist society."

He was silent.

"That seems odd for a veteran."

He raised a thick dark brow. "You've been asking questions about me."

"I thought you looked interesting."

"I like to think of myself as open minded. But I don't imagine the head of Lux would take well to finding out someone in his costume department spends her days with bohemians talking about 'socialism and anarchy and all the wrongs of a capitalist society.'"

"Funny," she said. "I'll keep your secret if you keep mine."

"It's a deal. So where are you from?"

"Ohio," she said.

"Ah, Ohio. That's the accent I heard." He nodded, satisfied. "So you're unattached?"

"I am." She didn't try to hide the smile that came with the words, or the simple joy she felt at saying them.

"Then I guess I'll see you next Sunday, Lena?"

She hadn't told him her name. "I see you've been asking questions about me too."

His smile involved his whole face. "I thought you looked interesting."

He walked past her to the back door, and she watched him go down the steps to a car parked there, an iridescent red Oldsmobile Dynamic—a flashy car that, like everything else about him, both matched and contradicted. When he drove away, she felt a loss, an impatience. He'd done that the last time, too, the quick retreat. She heard the murmurs from the other room: the meeting was breaking up.

But this time she'd learned his name, and he'd said he would see her next Sunday, and now she wanted the week to speed by.

It wasn't until that night, tucked in on the red chenille couch, that she wondered why she'd told him she was unattached, when she most certainly was not. There was Walter. She was still married. Or at least, Elsie Gruner was. What that meant for Lena Taylor, Lena didn't know. But married was married, wasn't it?

CHAPTER 13

"Lena!" Estelle stood at the doorway of the art room, looking exhausted and frustrated. "We need your help. The production censor needs a change immediately."

Lena turned from the easel, where she was enlarging a croquis for *Summerland Express*. "What kind of a change?"

"The costume for the Queen of Sheba is showing too much cleavage, for one—"

"Just use souffle." She was puzzled why Estelle needed her to come up with that solution; it was standard to use the sheer fabric for things like that.

"Yes, of course, it's not only that. I need all hands on deck. They want the costume changed to pastel. Pink."

"But it's stunning in red and black."

"Soviet Union colors," Estelle explained. "The censor believes we're signaling some subliminal communist message. It can't be bleached. It has to be remade."

"Was pink a color in Sheba?" Mike asked from his easel. "Wait—where was Sheba, anyway?"

"It's a nightmare. Please come. I have a continent of beading work."

Lena hurried after Estelle, noting that neither Mike nor Royal, who were also working on croquis, was called to help redo the costume. *All hands on deck* apparently meant only women.

She joined a group of other dressmakers gathered in the sewing room. Estelle handed her a bandeau of pink velvet and a bowl of crystals. Painstakingly, Lena began the laborious process of sewing them on. After an hour, her neck and shoulders began to hurt. After two, her fingers joined the pain parade. Three, and her eyes burned. She pulled the light closer—she might actually be going blind. She was so focused on wondering if that was true—could one go blind staring at transparent crystals?—that she failed to hear the fluttering until it went silent.

She looked up to see that Flavio had come into the workroom. Lena had been at Lux nearly six months—six months not just doing the work she loved, but also this kind of brutal, backbreaking detail work—and she hadn't seen him since he'd hired her. Immediately, she spilled the bowl of crystals. She put aside the bandeau top to pick them up—they had scattered everywhere, sparkling across the floor in little prisms of light. The workroom sweltered, sweat beaded on her forehead. She heard footsteps, and then Flavio stood in front of her—she recognized those wingtip shoes.

Lena looked up.

"There you are." He frowned. "Good God, are you ill? You don't look like yourself."

"I—I'm fine."

"Are you sure?"

"It's hot down here."

"We need more fans. I'll have some sent over. Well, come along then. I haven't all day."

She was unsure at first that he was speaking to her. Then it became obvious he was. She said, "I've got to pick these up—"

"Estelle, can you assign someone else to the beading? I need this one."

"Of course, Flavio." Estelle hurried over. "Of course."

Flavio offered Lena his hand. She took it, half-dazed. When he pulled her to her feet, she felt she was in a dream. She followed him upstairs, aware of the frowns and surprised looks of her fellows. He led her to his office. She hadn't been inside since the day he'd hired her, but it was just as scattered and messy. She saw three of the sketches she'd enlarged for him laid out on the low table, on display, and Lena's surprise shifted into dread—why did he have those laid out? What had she done wrong? Or right? Why had he brought her here? She wasn't sure whether to be excited or anxious. Was she going to be fired, or . . . or something else?

Flavio motioned to the illustrations. "You did these?"

Lena nodded warily. "Yes, sir. I did. Is there something wrong with them? Whatever it is, I can fix—"

"There's nothing wrong," he said. "I've been watching your work since I hired you. Lena, isn't it? Lena Taylor?"

"Yes."

"My assistant is leaving. I need a new one. I'd like you to be that person. What do you think?"

She stared at him, disbelieving. "Your assistant? I would love to be your assistant."

"Good. I'm leaving for Rome next week. I'll need—" He broke off with a frown. "What is it?"

"I can't go to Rome."

"Have I asked you to go to Rome? Wait—you *can't* go to Rome? That's an odd thing to say. What do you mean, you can't?"

"I'm . . . not allowed."

"Your husband won't let you?"

"No, not that."

"Then . . . ?"

Charlie and Harvey had told her never to tell this story, but neither of them could have anticipated this. "I was . . . escorted out. They told me not to come back."

"Well." Flavio leaned back on his desk and crossed his arms. "That's interesting. I've never heard of anyone but Mussolini getting escorted out of Rome. Are you some kind of—I don't know what, actually. You look quite harmless."

What was she to do? It would be dangerous to tell him, and more than that, she didn't want to lose her chance. "I was at the American Art Academy, but . . . I had some questionable dealings, and—"

Flavio held up his hand, stopping her. "No—stop. Don't tell me. It's better that I don't know. Well, tell me one thing: You were really kicked out of Rome?"

"They were quite adamant about it."

Flavio nodded slowly. "Are you a danger?"

Yes, no—she didn't know. She had not lost the habit of looking over her shoulder, and Julia's warnings haunted her dreams. "I'm a sketch artist," she said steadily.

He smiled. "Ah, good answer. Very good. Excellent. The next time someone asks you to go to Italy, tell them you're allergic to the country and you'll meet them in Paris. Do you understand me?"

"Yes," she said. "I'm sorry I can't go to Italy with you."

"I said *I* was going to Rome. Not that you were. I need you here to take over the sketching next week. It will be insanity, but I trust you can do it. The croquis are mostly done, and I've ideas written out for the script. You'll have to take over from there. If you need help, my current assistant will be here another week—you've met Jonny, I think? He's headed back to New York, but he'll teach you what you need to know."

Lena nodded.

"You'll be overwhelmed, and I need you to focus completely on the tasks at hand. Do you think you can do that?"

This was her chance. She would not mess it up. Lena nodded. "I can do whatever you need, Mr. Flavio."

"Just Flavio," he said.

CHAPTER 14

That next week, Lena plunged into learning the role that Jonny was giving up. The steady older man had been Flavio's assistant for only a year, and he was returning to New York City and stage design. Jonny viewed Lena's inexperience as a liability. Lena overheard him saying to the secretary, "I hope he knows what he's doing."

Lena planned to make sure that Flavio did.

They had a going-away party for Jonny on Friday. On Saturday, Lena went to the studio to set up her own tiny space—an anteroom next to Flavio's office. Flavio was due to return Monday morning, and Lena was so nervous she couldn't stay still. Sunday, she went to the meeting at Larry Lipton's, and when she saw Paul Carbone, the first thing she said—even before hello—was "Flavio made me his assistant. Me! It's unbelievable."

"You don't really think that," he said with a smile.

She laughed. "I'm nervous. He's been in Rome and he gets back Monday."

"He's a smart man. He wouldn't have lasted so long in this business if he wasn't. He knew what he was doing when he picked you. You'll do great."

His words were like a warm blanket; she wasn't sure why he could soothe her when no one else had been able to, or why his confidence in her should matter when he hardly knew her. But his were the words she thought of when Flavio came back, and his confidence was what bolstered hers.

As the weeks went on, and she grew more and more busy with work, she didn't give up Sundays at Larry's, though she knew going was stupid. The truth was she didn't care about the artists, or their talk, and she thought too much about Rome and Julia and the dangers she wasn't sure she'd left behind. She knew Harvey was right; these artists weren't like the ones in Rome. They talked, but she didn't see any evidence of *doing*.

Still, talk was more dangerous than ever these days, and every Sunday she told herself not to go. But she always did and her stomach was tight when they arrived; the memories of La Grotta and Julia were too strong and she never stepped onto that porch without wanting to turn around and leave again.

But then she would see Paul and tell herself *One more Sunday. Just one more.* He was the only reason she came. She had friends at work, though fewer since her promotion to Flavio's assistant, and she had Harvey and Charlie, but Paul was different. He never failed to ask about her work at the studio; he appeared fascinated about the inner workings of the costume department. He loved the stories about Elizabeth Taylor and her menagerie of pets, and how Lena had seen young Natalie Wood at a party flirting with older men as if she were a thirty-year-old woman, and how Flavio sometimes asked Lena to do a sketch on her own and then asked her to consider it and rework it for different body types. Paul seemed genuinely interested in how much she was learning and her struggles with the jealousy of the other sketch artists who'd been there longer and had hoped to win the position. Mike, for example, could barely look at her now.

In some ways, Paul reminded her of Julia, in the way he listened to her and encouraged her. Lena liked, too, that Paul shared his own struggles. She knew he was having trouble with a screenplay, that he had written a few B movies that had been produced but hadn't made much money.

"*Invasion from Venus*," he told her with a laugh. "You know it?"

"No," she confessed. "I'm sorry."

"Don't be. I wrote it on commission. It wasn't very good. Lizard creatures and a maiden needing rescuing."

"Ah. I can see how that's changing the system from the inside," she teased.

He sighed and shrugged, a little smile. "I'm working on it slowly. It's not easy, you know, with the blacklist, and the Motion Picture Alliance almost as bad as HUAC in their hunt for subversives. You have to be more subversive than the subversives."

The Motion Picture Alliance for the Preservation of American Ideals had Cecil B. DeMille and Hedda Hopper as members, and to Lena's eye they almost reveled in the fear and ruin they caused. Lena smiled. "Did I ever tell you about having to change the Queen of Sheba's costume from red and black to pink because they thought we were signaling that she was a Red?"

Paul snorted. "Was that the censor or the MPA?"

"The production censor, but I wouldn't be surprised if the MPA had a hand in it."

"I'm surprised they didn't change it to red, white, and blue."

"Too obvious."

"I don't think anything's too obvious for them," he said glumly. "But I'm determined to write what I want to someday. Or die a very poor man."

She never saw him beyond those gatherings. She didn't even have his phone number, and he'd never asked for hers. He never attempted anything. He didn't have to. His smiles were as confusing as a touch; sometimes they left her speechless. His presence prickled her skin. She couldn't deny the connection between them.

"You should be going out," Harvey told her one night as she helped him clean out the closet. "You should be dancing the night away. Why are you here doing this boring stuff?"

She pulled out a tennis racket. "Which of you plays tennis?"

"I did once. Not for years," Charlie said. "Harvey's right. You're so young. You should be dating."

"Call Paul. I'm sure he'd love to take you out," Harvey said.

"I'm too busy and I don't have his phone number."

"Why not?" asked Charlie.

"The two of you spend more time talking at those meetings than Larry," Harvey said. "It's obvious he's interested in you."

"Harvey, I'm *married*."

"Are you really? I mean, is Lena Taylor?" Charlie picked up the tennis racket they'd thrown on the couch and took a couple of practice swings.

"I don't know. That seems a technicality, doesn't it?" Lena asked.

"Better not to rattle cages," Harvey noted. "What do you have to do to get a divorce? Aren't there papers he has to sign? Don't you at least have to serve him? And what happens if you don't and you marry someone else and he finds out?"

Lena winced. "Exactly. I don't want to do anything that would bring attention. Not from anyone. Especially him. He wanted to be an actor. What do you think he'd do if he knew I was working at Lux? All he ever talked about was being in *Photoplay* with me on his arm."

Harvey pulled out a bag. "What the hell is this? Charlie, do you know what this is?"

"Oh, that's mine." Lena grabbed the bag away from him. "That's the bag I packed for Venice when Julia and I were going to go. Before she . . . before."

She opened it and rummaged through, taking out clothes she hadn't seen in more than a year. A polka-dot sundress, dungarees, sandals, the *Grand Hotel* magazine . . .

"An Italian magazine? Do you read Italian?" Harvey picked up the magazine she'd thrown aside, and when he did, a record slipped out. "What's this?"

The Duke. Lena stared at it, the memories clashing, a lapse in time, and she was back in Rome, the kiosk, the boy putting the record inside the magazine. One of the many pickups she'd done for Julia. Lena had no idea who the record had been intended for, or what importance it had, but the sight of it spurred a sick, regretful, sorrowful feeling deep inside her. She didn't want to think of it now, not now, not ever again.

"What is it?" Charlie asked. "Why are you looking like that?"

Waiting at the train station. The train doors shutting, the groaning huff of the train pulling out. Everything after. *"It's all gone wrong . . . Hide . . . I'll find you."*

"It is time for you to leave Rome, signora."

"Lena?"

"You must never tell that story again."

It was over. It was done. She didn't know what this record held, and she didn't care. It had nothing to do with her life now, there was no reason to share what it had been.

Lena forced the memories from her head. "Nothing. It's nothing."

"Duke Ellington." Harvey got to his feet, the record in hand. He went to the phonograph behind the sofa.

Lena went still, not knowing what to expect, but no, it was just a record, nothing more. She watched as Harvey put it on the turntable and flicked the switch to turn the player on. He put the needle on the record. Static, buzzing, the bump of the needle on a well-used record, and Lena froze again, half expecting a spate of Russian, or some other language, some kind of code.

But it was just music. Just big-band Duke Ellington. Scratchy—really scratchy. Hard-to-listen-to scratchy.

Charlie winced. "You brought this all the way back?"

"Sentimental, I guess. You two can have it if you want."

"Hmmm." Harvey let it play, but the scratchiness didn't improve, and finally he took it off. "It's in pretty bad shape."

Lena went back to her bag and took out everything else, piling it on the floor. "I'm going to give all this away. I'll never wear this stuff again."

Charlie said, "Be careful, Lena. You don't want to give away good memories too."

"There aren't any," she told him.

~

Lena twisted to see better in the full-length dressing room mirror. Her gown—a Flavio design of chartreuse silk—was the most beautiful thing she'd ever worn. She was serving as a mannequin of sorts for Eleanor Parker, because the actress would be at the Marie Limerick gala tonight, and Flavio wanted Miss Parker to see a sample of the gown he planned for her to wear in her next movie for Lux Pictures, because she objected strenuously to the green, and Lena had her same coloring.

"She'll see how it looks on you," Flavio said, "and she'll understand."

This was Lena's first gala, and she was going with Flavio and his wife, Sheila. She felt both excited and nervous. She wasn't who she said she was, and her instincts screamed to stay hidden, to shy away from any limelight, and it wasn't just because of those men in Italy, but because of Walter too. This was the dream Walter had for the both of them when they'd left Zanesville for LA, but it wasn't Walter she wanted beside her now, helping her dress, telling her she was beautiful.

Maybe Charlie was right. Maybe it was time to find Walter, to get a divorce. But Walter was her only remaining link to Elsie Gruner in Hollywood, and she didn't trust him. Also, there was no need. She and Paul were only friends. He'd never made a single move toward anything more—besides asking her if she were attached. He'd never tried to touch her. Or to kiss her. All they did was talk.

It was better that way, she told herself. She was devoted to her job. She'd never told Paul about Walter—how would she bring him up now? *Oh, by the way, I'm married . . .*

Flavio's chauffeured car waited for her out front. It was gleaming and gorgeous, and Lena shimmied with pleasure when she got into the back seat with Sheila while Flavio sat in the front.

"You look perfect," Flavio told her.

"Oh, you do," Sheila agreed. Sheila was beautiful, almost regal in her bearing, his perfect foil; and she never for a moment made Lena feel lacking. They arrived at Marie Limerick's home in the newly popular, ever-growing neighborhood of Beverly Hills to such a glare of lights and music and pure glamour that Lena was blinded. But she avoided the photographers, and when Flavio insisted she be in a photo with him and Sheila, Lena dropped her head to let her hair hide her face.

The evening was like nothing she'd ever known, and she spent it speechless, stunned by the candlelit pool and the band and Eddie Fisher singing and the fact that she actually ran into—*ran into*, nearly spilling her glass of champagne—Cary Grant. That was Ava Gardner chatting at the bar, more beautiful and strangely more buxom in person, and when Flavio called her over to show Eleanor the dress she wore, Eleanor Parker took up the skirt and fingered the fabric and spun Lena around as if she were a model. She said, "The color becomes you. You're Flavio's new assistant? What's your name?"

But Lena detected tension in the air. Flavio frowned and leaned down to whisper, "Get lost, my dear," and she felt that she'd done something wrong, though she'd done exactly what Flavio had told her to do.

Once again, she did what he said. She stayed as far away from Eleanor Parker the rest of the night as she could.

After that, nothing was quite the same. Lena felt an imposter, surrounded by too many men in dark suits. More than one of them watched her with a ravenous, curious stare, so that she was thrown back into the Piazza dei Cinquecento, and over there . . . was that a flash of chestnut hair?

But God no, it was a ghost. Nothing real. It was all gone. It had all gone wrong.

Lena was exhausted by the end of the evening. The champagne had gone straight to her head, and it was the first time she'd ever tasted caviar, or lobster. Flavio told the driver to take his wife and Lena home; he still had some celebrating to do, he said.

The chauffeur let her off in front of the bungalow, and she shivered when she got out and couldn't help the involuntary glance behind her to see—what? A pursuing car? Another ghost? The car's strong headlights sent rainbows into the fog. Lena went inside, longing to talk to someone, but Harvey and Charlie were asleep already—it was after 2:00 a.m. Lena sank into the couch and wondered where Paul Carbone was, and if he was still awake, and what he would think of Hollywood parties and the lovely chartreuse gown.

~

The next day was busier than usual; they had four fittings that afternoon, and it was Lena's job to coordinate with the wardrobe assistant. One of the fittings was with Sylvia Vayne, who was known to be picky. Flavio was good with actresses like that; he would just give them this steady dark stare where it seemed he was contemplating the problem they'd complained about, while at the same time making it seem insignificant, and suddenly the actress would change her mind and declare that she was just being silly.

But that day he'd come in late, in one of his darker moods. Lena assumed he was hungover from the night before; she had a headache herself. A cup of coffee would help. She brought him one and he gave her a grateful smile, but he looked drawn and tired, and as the day wore on, he seemed even more so. At Sylvia's fitting, nothing he did appeased the actress. The gown for the lunch scene was too tight; did he really think that blue was the right blue? Wasn't it too green for her coloring? The cut of that jacket was too frivolous for the character. She had, of course, already seen the sketches for all the costumes, which had been approved.

Everyone was in a mood.

"I don't know," Sylvia said. "I think we should start over."

The vein in Flavio's forehead stood out. He looked undone. Lena couldn't remember seeing him that way before.

A bit desperately, she said, "Lucy is meant to show her happy side in that scene, isn't she, Miss Vayne? I should think the jacket would help you get into character. It's such a happy piece of clothing, don't you think?"

The actress's expression lightened. "Hmmm."

"We could maybe put a flower there in the lapel? Something . . . pink, maybe? To highlight your beautiful coloring?"

"Oh. Well yes, I think that might help . . ."

Flavio said, "Lena, I left my glasses on my desk, would you mind fetching them?"

She'd overstepped. She should have stayed quiet and left it to him. For all she knew, a pink flower in the lapel clashed with the set design. She remembered the night before at the gala, when he'd told her to get lost, and she'd squirmed in his displeasure. Two days in a row. Not good. She felt she was on a tightrope, but she wasn't sure how to make things better, or even if she could. He might fire her. He was in that kind of temper.

Lena hurried back to his office. She found his glasses sitting on the desk. She picked them up. Lying beneath them, half-crumpled as if he'd meant to throw it away and forgotten, was a receipt. The name on it was very clear.

Moxy's.

Moxy's was a bar near the beach that was notorious for its gambling and badger girls—young women who had come to Hollywood hoping for stardom and who found instead a life of pimping for the mob, sleeping with the famous for blackmail purposes, and urging customers to bet more and more. That Flavio had a receipt could mean only one thing, and she remembered last night, him saying that he wasn't done celebrating, Sheila's indulgent little smile.

Lena was surprised at how unsurprised she was. Since she'd been in LA, nothing startled her anymore. She knew that this wasn't something Flavio could possibly want known. The gossip columnists would have a field day. Hollywood's most famous costume designer . . . it would destroy Flavio's career.

Lena picked up the receipt and slipped it into her pocket.

She brought him his glasses. Sylvia had changed her tune. The jacket was perfect, and she'd misjudged the blue and she'd been slumping when she tried on the dress. It fit beautifully; she wasn't sure what she'd been thinking.

When she left, Flavio lit a cigarette and offered Lena one. She inhaled and said, "I'm sorry. I shouldn't have said anything to her. I won't do it again."

He said nothing for a minute. Instead, he blew a smoke ring. "I've made some tactical errors lately. More than a few. I don't know what it is. I've grown old, perhaps. There are times lately when I've found placating spoiled women and arrogant men to be boring. Because of that, I've lost discernment."

She was unsure what he meant. She remained quiet.

"Sylvia Vayne changed her mind because of what you said. When you reminded her what a costume is for. I've been out of sorts all day. You brought me back to myself. You saved the fitting session."

Lena felt herself grow hot beneath the praise. "I learned from the best."

He waved off her words. "I've made too many mistakes. Last night, for example. I should have known not to put you in that dress. Eleanor Parker will never wear it now."

"But she said it was beautiful."

"On *you*. She was jealous. She sees you as competition now. There's a reason I only wear black and white, with the exception of my cravats. I do not compete with the stars. I have failed to tell you this. You're young and pretty, my dear. Movie stars are the most insecure people on earth—this is always true. You should disappear when you're fitting them or showing them sketches. Whenever you're around them, in fact. One day, you'll be the head costumer here. You must never let them think you are in any way competing with them."

The other words faded away. *One day, you'll be the head costumer* shouted in her head. "What did you say?"

"Never compete."

"No—I mean . . . the head costumer part."

"I've decided you're my protégé. You'll take my place when I retire."

"Me? But . . . why me? And what do you mean? You're not planning to retire, are you? Not anytime soon?"

"No, not soon," he said. "But my time is coming. I'll admit it: my days are becoming boring and my nights are catching up with me."

She thought of the receipt in her pocket.

"Don't do what I've done, Lena. Don't develop a taste for risk and excitement. Not in this industry."

"I won't disappoint you."

"You haven't yet," Flavio said.

She reached into her pocket and handed him the receipt without a word.

He gave her a look. In it she saw questioning; what did she mean by it? What would she do?

"I didn't know if you meant to throw it away. They search the trash, you know. I—I didn't want you to get in trouble."

He squashed the receipt in his fist. "Thank you."

She gave him a short nod. She had done right. "Well, I'll get these costumes back to the seamstresses. Should I have them let the luncheon dress out?"

He sighed and nodded. "I've made the markings. You know, Lena, that I made the right choice when I picked you. Never forget that. I'm never wrong when it comes to talent."

"Well, it was me or Mike," she joked. "And he can't draw hands."

"No," he said. "He hasn't a spark of genius."

That would sustain her for a long time.

CHAPTER 15

MYSTERIOUS RISING STAR AT LUX—"Lena Taylor is the
biggest talent I've seen in years," says Flavio, but Tinseltown wonders how such a young woman climbed to
protégé status so quickly. There are ladders and there
are *ladders*. Is it talent? Or something else?

Harvey finished reading the item in Hedda Hopper's gossip column
out loud and tossed the paper down with a sigh. "This decides it, I'm
afraid."

"I'm afraid it does," Charlie agreed.

Lena scrambled to grab the paper and shook it out to stare at the
words. "I can't believe it. How can she say such things?"

"You'll notice that she didn't say anything. She only implied."

"But it's not true, whatever she's trying to say."

"Which is nothing," Harvey noted. "She's only bringing you to
people's attention."

Charlie poured a cup of coffee and handed it to her, then motioned
for her and Harvey to follow him onto the front porch. Lena knew by
now what that meant, a conversation away from any possible listening
device.

When they were all outside, Charlie said, "You're on the list now."

"What list?" she asked.

"The list of notable people," Charlie said. "Hedda will probably have a private investigator tailing you within days. If she doesn't already."

"Which means it's time for you to go," Harvey said sadly. "Long past time, honestly, honey. We've loved having you, and we don't want you to leave, but you can't keep sleeping on the couch of a couple of fairies."

"Don't say that. I hate it when you say that," she said.

"But it's true," Charlie told her. "We haven't wanted you to go, so we've said nothing, but Lena . . . What do you think will happen if they find out where you live? Or frankly, if they find out you're going to Larry Lipton's every Sunday?"

It was all true, she knew.

"They'll destroy you. You can kiss your future as head costumer goodbye before it starts."

Harvey gave her a sorrowful look. "You should find an apartment in Hollywood and never visit again."

"I can't do that!"

"Lena, we're on the FBI watch list," Charlie said. "We've been arrested as communist organizers and we're still radicals, if not in the same ways. You can't be seen with us, and you can't be seen going to Lipton's. For the same reasons you can't reveal your connection to Rome. Just because you haven't been found yet doesn't mean you won't be, and it doesn't help *at all* to have Hopper blabbing on about you. Please don't tell me you're going to take a stand on this. Everything we've done for you will be for naught."

"I can't just forget you're my friends," she said.

"For a while, you can," Harvey told her. "In this climate, you can. We know the truth. That's enough."

Lena's vision blurred. "This is horrible. I don't want this."

"You're going to be famous. You're going to make a million dollars. When we're old and crippled, you can pay our pension—will that make you happy?" Harvey asked.

"You're my best friends. I'm not putting you in a slum. I'll buy you a house."

"That would be fine," Charlie said, smiling. "We'll hold you to it. But no more Sundays at Lipton's. Starting now."

"Oh, but . . ." Lena blinked away tears. "I have to go once more."

"No—"

"Paul. I have to tell Paul."

"Let me tell Paul," Harvey said.

"One more Sunday," Lena insisted. "I have to tell him myself."

～

As she and Harvey walked that Sunday to Larry's, Harvey kept looking over his shoulder. "Don't turn around, but have you seen that car before that's behind us?"

They stopped, and Lena bent as if she meant to take a pebble from her shoe. The car went past, a dark Ford that frankly looked no different from a hundred other cars.

Harvey let out his breath in relief. "I'm wrong. Not following us. Sorry, I'm afraid I'm always on alert now."

Somberly she said, "Do you think it's true what Charlie said? Do you think those men are looking for me?"

"The CIA questioned you, right?"

She nodded.

"Then yes, they're looking for you. Someone is. Whatever it was you got mixed up in there . . . it's not over." He sighed. "It's never over. Don't come back here."

"How do you live like this?" she asked quietly.

Harvey shrugged. "You'd better get used to it, my dear."

"I don't want to."

He squeezed her hand. "Let's take the back way to Larry's."

Harvey turned up the street, away from their usual route. Then he cut through an alley, between buildings, through a gate into a backyard, and out the gate on the other side. It wasn't just a back way, it was a roundabout. He took her through the Jewish bakery where he worked and out another alley, and all in all they must have traveled a good mile out of their way before they arrived at the back door of Larry's house, where Paul's Oldsmobile Dynamic was parked.

Harvey said, "Look, don't go inside. I'll send Paul out. Tell him you won't be coming back. Even if that means you won't see him again."

"It would be better if I don't see him again anyway," she said.

He gave her a look. "That's not what I mean."

"I can't get involved with him. Or anyone."

Harvey sighed. "We disagree about that. This is just about the meetings."

"I know." She knew things couldn't stay the same. A part of her hadn't really believed this would be her last Sunday. But after the article in the paper, and the things Harvey and Charlie said, she knew it had to be. Her time at Venice Beach was over. She could not risk it.

Harvey went inside. When he opened the door, the talk floated out; Lena stood tensely waiting, not very long, it turned out. Paul appeared so quickly she knew he'd been waiting for her to arrive. He stepped out, already frowning—she wondered what Harvey had said to him—and then came quickly down the stairs to where she stood by his car.

"What are you doing out here?" he asked.

"Waiting for you." She ran her fingers across the hood. "This is quite a car for a poor screenwriter."

"It's my one indulgence."

Funny, how her body seemed to lean toward him—or no, it approached, it advanced, it tried to bridge the space between them while at the same time it didn't move at all. She didn't know how to say what she needed to say, mostly because she feared that maybe she had imagined something between them, that maybe he would shrug off her goodbye and say, *Nice to know you.* But then again, wouldn't that be best? She could not pursue a relationship with him. It couldn't go further than this. She was married. She was still a part of whatever had happened in Rome. She was not who she said she was.

She said, "I've got to tell you about Ciro's. Flavio and Sheila took me there Wednesday night, and it was wonderful. Have you ever been?"

He shook his head. He came to stand beside her and leaned against the car. They weren't touching, but he stood close enough that she felt him. "Too rich for my blood."

"You simply have to go. It was so elegant. And the music! You know, I've never asked you: What kind of music do you like?"

He regarded her curiously. "All kinds, but if I had to pick, I guess I'd say I like jazz the best. When I was in Rome, there were all these little clubs I used to go to. They were amazing."

Lena's heart thudded hard in her chest. She struggled to keep her voice even. "You were in Rome?"

"I was there at the liberation. With the army."

"Oh."

"It was a mess, but you know, I loved it. I'd love to go back someday. Have you ever been?"

She had already lied to him once, about being unattached. She didn't want to lie again. But this was more important, and she heard Harvey and Charlie's warning. She shook her head.

"I think you'd like the clubs. Small and steamy. Great music. Full of bohemians. The real thing, not the pretenders."

"The pretenders?" she managed.

"Not like these guys," he said, gesturing back to the house. "They talk a good game, but it's all talk."

"Then why do you come to these meetings?"

"At the beginning I thought they'd turn out to be real. Now . . . isn't it obvious?"

Again, the rapid thud of her heart, but Lena was afraid of herself, she couldn't answer his question, or acknowledge it. "How long were you there? In Rome?"

"Not long enough. I was sorry to leave it. But I'll go back. It would be more fun to go with someone, though."

"Oh?"

"To stroll through the Colosseum in the moonlight. Sit on the Pincio Terrace and look out at the city. Dance the night away in a little club near the Veneto."

Lena swallowed hard. "You sound like a writer."

"Rome is made for romance."

"It would be just like a movie."

"It could be." He was suddenly intent. Those eyes . . .

Lena could not keep his gaze.

"Why are you out here, Lena?" he asked.

"I wanted to tell you I'm not coming back."

"Because of Hedda Hopper's column?"

She looked up in surprise. "You read that?"

He laughed lightly. "I think everyone reads it, don't they?"

"Harvey thinks I'm now on the list of important people, and they'll start watching me, and I . . . you know, I can't risk it, not for—"

"Pretenders," he finished.

"Yeah." She nodded. "But I wanted to tell you, because I didn't want to just stop showing up and I'm going to miss our conversations, and I wanted to say it was nice knowing you—"

Before she knew it, he was right there. His hand came to her jaw, anchoring her, and then he kissed her. Gently at first, testing, then more deeply when she didn't pull away, when she kissed him back because it was what she'd wanted from him from the moment she'd seen him in Larry Lipton's living room, clashing with her memories of Rome, and she did not know how to be otherwise.

CHAPTER 16

I've got a promotion, she wrote her parents, another postcard, where she could be brief. *All is well.* Better than ever, in fact, though as usual she left out every other detail of her life. It would only trouble them.

Paul helped her find an apartment on Highland, an Italianate-style building of beige stucco with arching windows. Her apartment was on the second floor, and she had a narrow balcony overlooking a tree that shoved its branches through her cast-iron railing and half blocked her view of the street below, which was nice, because most of the view was a row of storefronts and other apartments and the Lucky 8 tavern. A living room, kitchen, bedroom, and bathroom—all small, but with tiled floors. It reminded her a little of Rome, and she wasn't sure whether she loved that or was discomfited by it, so she tried not to think of it, though sometimes, on certain evenings, when the warm LA air eased through the windows, she couldn't help remembering those sultry nights in Italy, and the life all around, the sounds of Vespas and talk and music from the cafés instead of the silence of LA's empty side streets, and she felt abandoned and alone.

The apartment was also the first place that had belonged only to her. She wanted it to reflect who she was now, Lena Taylor, assistant costume designer to Flavio, but she couldn't decide what that meant, and so she'd decided to decorate it classically and ended up with boring. Everything beige and off shades of brown and white.

Beige, it turned out, was her color, too, in that she wore it every day, following Flavio's dictate that she should never compete with the stars. Beige was the perfect camouflage for an assistant trying to persuade an actress to look like a drab maid when she was supposed to be playing a drab maid but wanted to look glamorous doing so. Lena still designed her own clothes—if they had to be beige, at least they would be perfectly cut and made from the best fabrics she could afford.

The only time Lena did not wear beige was when she went out with Paul. She took him to Ciro's and Mocambo. She introduced him to the producers she knew. She told people who asked that they were just friends. But it was true what Harvey and Charlie had told her. She was being watched, and there was speculation, even about the assistant to a costume head. *"What up-and-coming costume designer is dating a new screenwriter? Lux costume designer Lena Taylor and screenwriter Paul Carbone—could this be love?"* They avoided photographs—she told Paul she was camera shy, and used the excuse of not wanting to compete with the stars. She stayed in the background always. Wearing sunglasses and hats and sitting in the shadows. She never appeared in pictures in the paper except as a blur or hidden behind someone else or with her face camouflaged by her hair.

She tried not to be as in love with Paul as she knew she was. She tried not to want him, but the truth was she did, sometimes so badly she couldn't think. This could go no further. There was no point in it. She told herself that over and over. She was not going to sleep with him. She would kiss him. She would maybe go a little further, but beyond that . . . How could she go beyond that? Marriage could not be in their future. She didn't dare find Walter for fear of whatever trouble he would bring, and her life was one constant, hovering sense of doom. She couldn't involve Paul in what she didn't understand herself.

She resigned herself to it. She knew she could be strong. She told Paul the truth when she could. When he asked when she'd come to LA, she simply said she'd come three years ago to study fashion and didn't mention who'd brought her here. "There was nowhere to learn fashion design in Zanesville. Not on a pig farm."

"A pig farm?"

"Didn't I tell you? My dad was a pig farmer."

"I think you skipped over that."

"Well, it was embarrassing. The smell gets into your skin and your clothes. It never comes out, no matter how many times you wash."

He leaned closer, sniffing. "You don't smell like pig. You smell like—"

"L'Air du Temps." It had not occurred to her until then that she still wore the perfume that Walter had chosen for her. "But I'm thinking of changing it."

"Why?"

"I'm tired of it. Unless you like it."

"Whatever you want," he said. "You'd be yourself whatever you smelled like."

She laughed. "How do you always know just the right thing to say?"

"I'm a writer. I think about these things."

"You have them all planned out?"

"Sure." He blew cigarette smoke out in a steady stream. "There's narration going on in my head constantly."

"I see. What is it saying now?"

"It's saying: He puts out his cigarette and kisses her passionately."

"Ah." Lena smiled. "Not so fast. I want to know what brought you to LA."

"Oh. Well. That's easy. I was born here."

"Paul! You never told me that. You mean your parents are still here?"

"No. My father died the year before I joined the army. My mother long before that. He was a painter, she was his model."

"That sounds romantic."

"It was, for them. They didn't care about anyone else. I was mostly a nuisance." His voice was wry. "There was never any money. My father . . . he lied to everyone. If you listened to him, we had a hundred relatives, all of them sick and dying. That's the reason he gave every debt collector when we couldn't pay our bills. But we didn't have any family at all, or if we did, they were back in the old country. Who knows? He never told the truth about anything."

The anger in his voice made her pause.

"I don't want to be like him. He had a kid the way he did everything, without giving a thought to how he'd manage it. My mom was no better, but at least she loved me—or I think she did."

His words made her uncomfortable. His father had been a liar. She didn't think he'd like knowing how much she hadn't told him about her own past. He looked far away; he smoked as if he were taking everything out on the cigarette, frustration and bitter memories. Finally he turned to her, attempting a smile. "I don't want a life of lies, Lena. Not for me, not for my children."

How serious he looked, how . . . that look . . . Lena swallowed. "No, I don't suppose you do."

"You're the first woman I've told that story to."

She didn't know what to say to that. She didn't know what to do with the sinking, blooming combination of emotions she suddenly felt—regret and joy and fear and a flickering excitement and anticipation. He still didn't know so much about her. There was Walter. There was Rome, and everything that had happened with Julia, and all the other things she could not say. She wished she could do what Harvey and Charlie had advised and pretend it had happened to someone else. She wished she could put her old self into a little box and store it away and never think of any of it again. She tried. But then she'd see the flash of a shadow behind her and turn in fear, or a chestnut-haired woman in a crowd and break out in a sweat of panic, or she'd come home to the sense that someone had been in her apartment before her, and she'd look at Paul and think *He doesn't know* and feel as if she were somehow betraying him, and yet she knew she must keep these secrets. She could not take the risk of looking for Walter and bringing him back into her life, not now. He knew who she'd been. He would tell everyone that

Elsie Gruner was back in LA, and the sacrifices she'd made and was even now making—keeping her distance from her closest friends—would be for naught. She had to stay hidden. Hollywood was ruthless in its search for communists or fellow travelers. She would be destroyed, and Paul with her. Walter was a secret she had to take to her grave.

～

It had been a hard week; the production censor had turned a nightclub scene with Bob and Mikey, Lux Pictures' most popular comedy duo, into an extravaganza. The duo was popular overseas, and producers wanted to emphasize American abundance, and so a scene with a handful of musicians and a few dancers had morphed into a chase scene through an elaborate cabaret number with dancers in costumes with giant hats and huge fans and choreography. "Comedy gold!" the censor proclaimed it.

It had taken several days of staying late to redo the costumes, and Flavio and Lena were exhausted.

They had just finished the last fitting and Flavio lit one of his European cigarettes and said, "It's a Saturday night. What are you doing here so late? Go out."

She laughed. "We still have the cocktail waitresses to do."

"I'll throw them into something from Western Costume." They often rented from the costume house for minor characters. "They'll never notice. The girls are in the shot for half a second. Go. You're young. Have fun. Call your man."

So she did. It was a hot night, and she and Paul went to the Waikiki Inn and she was tired to the bone and maybe that's why the place affected her the way it did. Maybe that's why the memories came on so strong, and even though the place smelled of LA and sweat and Aqua Velva and Chanel No. 5 and spilled beer and pineapple juice and smoke, she smelled Italy. She felt Rome. She couldn't hold the memories back, and something about the jazz the quartet played reminded her of the shining cobbled streets and the deep blue sky of night and the roar of motorcycles and Vespas. There was something about the way Paul held her, about the way they danced, close and slow, that threw her back to that night when Petra had sung "Nature Boy" and the whole world had seemed so good.

Then Paul murmured in her ear, "This place always reminds me of Rome. Isn't that weird?" and at once Lena wanted it to go away, all of it, to bury it so deep that it could never escape. But before she could do anything about the feeling, the music stopped, and Paul pulled away, and she felt someone behind her, a nudge, a poke, against her back that threw her into shocked stillness—she was no longer in the Waikiki, but in the Cinquecento, with a gun in her back. Panic leaped through her, but then she saw Paul's expression, bored tolerance, and she turned to see it wasn't a man in a black coat at all, but Mike from Lux, and her relief was just as hot as her panic had been, until she saw the maliciousness in Mike's eyes. They shouldn't have come here. The Waikiki was a favorite of the costume department.

"Mike," Paul acknowledged—of course they'd met.

Mike inclined his head in greeting, then said, "Hey, Lena, I have a friend who swears he knows you."

"Is that so?" she asked.

"He's over at the table. Come and say hello."

There wasn't any stranger in LA who said he knew her whom she wanted to see. Lena's skin already prickled with warning, and she didn't like the look on Mike's face. His jealousy since she'd been elevated to Flavio's assistant had made her forget that he'd ever been a friend. "They're getting ready to start another song."

"Come on. Just say hi. He's a famous designer."

No, she did not like Mike's expression. She reached for Paul's hand. "The only famous designer I know is Flavio."

"Then you'll meet another one." Mike put his hand on her shoulder and lightly pushed her toward their table, and Paul, who of course saw no reason not to, started in that direction, and so Lena found herself going woodenly toward the table.

They were only a few feet away before the faces became clear in the glow of the tiny lights in the center of the table. There sat Joe and Billy, and Royal from Lux, and sitting between them, almost unrecognizable because of his different hairstyle and the very French scarf around his neck, was Jasper Rutledge from Chouinard.

It took all Lena's self-control to keep her expression blank. He had gone to Milan to apprentice at an atelier there, she remembered, and then he planned to go to Paris, and it looked like he'd done just that. She knew she looked nothing like the brown-haired innocent he'd known at Chouinard. Charlie and Harvey had not recognized her, but maybe it wasn't enough to fool Jasper.

She felt a sweep of rage. She would make it be enough. She had disliked Jasper Rutledge at Chouinard, and nothing about the smug way he looked at her now changed her mind. Not only that, but she had no intention of allowing this arrogant man to upend what she'd spent the last years building. She wondered if she could pull off what was sure to be one of the biggest acting challenges of her life.

"Lena Taylor, may I introduce Gaspard Renault," Mike said with a little smile. "From the Parisian house Iconique. Perhaps you've heard of him."

"I'm afraid I haven't," she said. "I'm happy to meet you, Mr. Renault. This is Paul Carbone."

Jasper-Gaspard gave her a snooty purse of his mouth. "Have we met before, Miss Taylor? I was just telling Mike that you reminded me of someone."

"I doubt it very much. I've never been to Paris."

"Oh, I'm not from Paris."

"Really? You have such a *French* name, I'm sure I would remember it if we'd met."

She thought she saw him flinch and wondered if he would own up to changing it. He did not. "Yes, I know it's unusual. But I'm from LA. I graduated from Chouinard. I wonder if that's where I know you from?"

"I'm not from here." She felt Paul's hand flex in hers, a little impatience. Her own hand was moist with sweat that she hoped he didn't notice.

"You're sure you didn't go to Chouinard?"

"I think I'd remember that too."

"You've moved up *quite* rapidly at Lux. Where did you get your training?"

"At Lux," she said. "With Flavio."

Jasper-Gaspard frowned and glanced at Mike. "But . . . Mike says you had an impressive portfolio."

"Did he?" She smiled at Mike, who looked flustered to have been caught out complimenting her. "He was kind to say that. I've always liked to draw clothes, that's all. Flavio saw that I could be trained."

"I see." So much confusion in Jasper's eyes. "You seem so familiar."

"I must have a doppelgänger somewhere." She wanted to run before it dawned on him where he'd seen her before, before he managed to blink away the blond hair and the fine tailoring and the poise and see through it all to the girl she'd been before. "It was nice to meet you, Mr. Renault, but we really must be going." She squeezed Paul's hand and rushed him from the Waikiki.

They were at the door before he said, "Were we done dancing?"

Her panic had left exhaustion in its wake and in that exhaustion was fury. She was furious with Mike for his stupid jealousy that had obviously made him think Jasper had some secret about her. It didn't help that Jasper did, or that the reminder of Chouinard and the close call had left her undone. It was always going to be like this, she realized. So much hiding, so many secrets. Clubs like the Waikiki reminding her of Rome, threats from her past. "I didn't realize how tired I was."

That Paul sensed something was clear. He frowned, obviously confused. "Okay." He took her back out to the car.

They were quiet as they drove to her apartment, and she felt his disappointment as he parked and walked her to her door.

"I guess I'll see you later," he said, bending to kiss her good night. She put her arms around his neck and pulled him so hard into her that he stumbled. She opened her mouth to his. It was not a good night kiss. It was a *don't leave me* kiss. It was a *fill that place that Rome left in me* kiss. She didn't know what he knew or what he felt, only that he pulled away and looked at her in question.

"I want you to come in," she said steadily, forgetting all her resolutions. She was Lena Taylor, and Lena Taylor did what she wanted. But more than that, Lena Taylor needed to exorcise her demons tonight, and she knew Paul could help her do it.

He didn't misunderstand. Paul swallowed. "Look, I want to . . . I really want to, but I can't offer you . . . I'm not in a position to . . ."

"Let's not talk about the future." The relief of saying that, of knowing it was what he wanted too, was overwhelming. "We both have things to do first. Just . . . don't make me pregnant."

His laugh was a whisper of sound. "No, I won't."

"I'm not a virgin," she said quietly.

"I don't care about your past."

She didn't quite believe that, but it was a reassurance she wanted for now, it absolved her from telling him what she didn't want to tell him. So she led him inside, and his kiss reached down inside her and yanked hard, she was aware of wanting him more than she ever had, and that was saying something, because she had wanted him so fiercely before. She led him to the bedroom, and he pulled her close, as if reassuring himself that she was real, and the kiss that had been so passionate before turned her into someone she wasn't sure she knew. She peeled away his shirt to bury her fingers in the hair on his chest as he slipped his hands up her bare arms, sliding down the sleeves of her dress to reveal her bra, and then that too was gone, and his mouth was on her breasts, his hands were all over her, and hers were on him, his shoulders, his back . . . they fell onto the bed, and it was as if all the time they'd been waiting for this, and that waiting had exploded around them.

She twisted beneath him, gasping as his hands slid beneath the skirt, up her thighs, unsnapping her garters, easing up. That he had skill was undeniable—he had her out of her girdle before she knew it, and all she'd been aware of was his kiss, his touch. She arched beneath him. When he moaned and eased inside her, she wrapped her legs around his hips and moved with him, her whole body thrumming against his. She could not be still, she could not fight the rising sensation, the pleasure that spiraled, that did not stop until she was gasping and trembling and crying out, and she grabbed him to keep him close just as he too cried out and jerked away, keeping his promise, coming on her stomach, then sagging on top of her, their breathing ragged, sweating.

Lena closed her eyes. She rested her hand on the smooth skin of his back, then traced his spine.

He said nothing for a long time. She felt the steady rise and fall of his chest against hers, the prickle of his hair against her breasts, the faint itch of it. He was heavy but she did not want him to move. Walter had not been like this. She had never felt anything like this.

Finally, Paul raised his head to look at her. "I think you'd better start telling people we're a couple," he said.

"Yes," she told him. "I think I'd better."

CHAPTER 17

Hollywood—late 1953

She had met Paul in the bohemian world but they both lived in Hollywood, and Hollywood was changing quickly and not for the better. He stopped going to Larry Lipton's—she was the only reason he had been going for those last months and now it was too dangerous for him too. Harvey and Charlie would not let her or Paul visit, reasserting the riskiness of such an association, but she talked to them when she could, much less often now that *Confidential* magazine had hit. They had to take even more care: she could call only with important news, and they talked only from pay phones. She hated to admit it, but Harvey and Charlie were right. *Confidential* was vicious. It upended the gossip industry, and now the others had to compete, and the whole game changed. It had been bad before, but now it wasn't just gossip, it was scandal, the more destructive the better, and everyone was looking for it. The gossip queens had always had their own "investigators," but now retired policemen hired themselves out to suss out "news," and anyone could make money working as a private investigator. Studio publicity departments had to work overtime—not that they hadn't had their hands full before, with alcoholic stars and affairs that had to be smoothed over so as not to mar the image of happy marriages, or marriages designed to hide any rumor of homosexuality or any kind of aberrance.

Lena lived in fear that one of them would discover who she really was, or bring the men she had never stopped watching for down upon her. She had remained vigilant, and the close call with Jasper made her even more careful—sunglasses always, hats. She had the beautician lighten her hair to a champagne blond, and cut it in a fashionable bob with a side part, flipped under just past her chin.

She and Paul lived separately: she had her apartment and he had his rooms at the Chateau Marmont. They both wanted so much; they had to live with no hint of impropriety.

At least, they did to the outside world.

At home, however, they kept the blinds down and snuck out before dawn, but those in-between hours they spent in bed, especially their first months together, always using condoms. She was afraid to get a prescription for a diaphragm in case the rumor of it got out, and they were both too ambitious to do something stupid like make a baby—Paul's words, and if nothing else, Lena knew she could count on Paul's sense of responsibility. He respected her career, but he wouldn't be a man who lived off a woman, and though he'd sold a few screenplays, minor films in his eyes, two of which hadn't gone into production, along with a Western and another science fiction film, it wasn't enough. He winced at the thought of what the gossip columns would say: "'Ambitious Screenwriter Marries Costuming Star.' I'd never live it down."

She laughed and tangled her fingers in his hair. She didn't argue with him. As long as this mattered to Paul, she didn't have to tell him that marriage wasn't a possibility at all. "I'm not a costume star yet."

"You will be eventually, maybe sooner than later."

"Flavio will be there forever." She said the words, but Paul knew that she'd been troubled about her mentor, and she wasn't the only one. Flavio had been unreliable lately, enough so that Higbert Braxton, the studio head, had noticed, and that was not good. Braxton was a ubiquitous presence. He liked his fingers in everything. He liked striding the back lots and paying unannounced visits to the soundstages. Once he'd plunged through the door, sending everyone into a nervous tizzy. He'd demanded lighting changes and then he'd asked that Susan Hayward's lipstick be changed. The makeup person had had to take the actress back to the mirrors, blot what she already wore, and send her back out again. Higgy Braxton had declared the new shade perfect.

When he left, the grips moved the lights back to where they'd been, but Braxton saw the dailies that night and noted the change and ordered a reshoot the next day. You could never be sure what Braxton cared about, or whether he was just making a change for the sake of it, and everyone knew it. He liked to tour the costume department when he was bored. Lena could always tell when he was there: the sewing machines, which operated normally at a smooth and steady pace, became erratic, with starts and stops she could feel through the floor, and Flavio would roll his eyes and hurry downstairs to restore order.

Braxton was a tall, blond, beefy man who looked as if he'd be more at home on an African savanna than in an administration office, and the truth was that he often was in Africa, big game hunting. His sandy-colored hair was expertly cut and perfectly pomaded, his mustache an exact copy of Theodore Roosevelt's, as were his glasses, though he had sharply cut, classic Roman features. There was no Roosevelt roundness in Higgy's face.

"His office looks like he's studying taxidermy," Flavio told her once. "God knows why he thinks it necessary to keep rifles at a movie studio, but maybe he thinks a trained lion will get loose or something."

Lena herself had a respectful relationship with Higgy Braxton— that is, she respectfully kept her distance unless it was unavoidable, which it was the day Flavio didn't show up for the Joan Fontaine fitting. It wasn't the first time he'd missed a fitting; usually they were the first ones, where they took measurements and draped already chosen fabrics to see how they played with the actresses' complexions and the light. These weren't as important as later fittings, and Lena and one of the wardrobe girls had no trouble managing on their own.

But Miss Fontaine was not accustomed to being attended by assistants, and she complained to Higgy, who came galloping into Flavio's office the next day, early in the morning.

Flavio was not there.

Lena was. She came out of her anteroom at the sound of Higgy Braxton shouting at the secretary, his booming voice reverberating through the walls. It took her only a moment to realize who it must be, time enough to catch sight of the *Daily Racing Form* on Flavio's desk and tuck it away in a drawer—just before Braxton burst through the door, Flavio's secretary hovering helplessly behind.

"Flavio!" he bellowed.

"He's not in yet this morning," Lena said calmly. She turned to the secretary. "Thank you, Amelia. That will be all. I'll take care of Mr. Braxton."

The secretary gave her a grateful smile and left.

"Where is he, Lena?" He delivered his words in a sharp staccato.

"He had an appointment this morning," Lena said smoothly. "What do you need, Mr. Braxton?"

"I got a complaint from Joan Fontaine. He wasn't at her fitting yesterday."

"Ah, no. Cindy and I took care of that. Unfortunately Flavio had to leave early. His wife, you know . . ."

"No, I don't know." Higgy frowned, nonplussed. "What the hell's wrong with Sheila?"

"She had an appointment."

"Don couldn't drive her?"

Even his employees' employees couldn't escape Braxton's notice. "I don't know, exactly, but I believe Sheila wanted Flavio with her. It was"—Lena lowered her voice—"a woman thing."

"Ah." Braxton looked as momentarily uncomfortable as Lena had hoped. "I see. Well, tell him when he returns that I was here and I am most unhappy. This can't happen again, at least not with a star of Miss Fontaine's stature."

"Of course. I'll tell him."

"And, um . . . you." He put his hand to his chin, looked at her as if she were an interesting specimen, and Lena couldn't help but recall Flavio's comment about Braxton and taxidermy. "Miss Fontaine did say that you were very efficient. Very professional."

"Flavio has taught me to be."

"Hmmm." Higgy Braxton gazed at her consideringly. "She said you had a good eye."

Lena smiled. "That's very kind of her."

"How long have you been here, Lena?"

"Three years, Mr. Braxton."

"For God's sake, enough of that. Call me Higgy. Three years, is it?"

"Yes, Mr.—Higgy."

"How much of that have you served as Flavio's assistant?"

"Two and a half."

Higgy nodded thoughtfully. "Well. I can see you're loyal to him. That's good. I like loyalty. You're protecting him, and that's fine. But you let him know for me that this can't happen again. I don't know what's distracting him lately, but twenty years with Lux will only go so far. You tell him that."

"I'm sure it was important," Lena assured him, though she was not sure at all, and Higgy's words filled her with dread.

"You be sure to tell him," Braxton said.

When Flavio came in late that morning, hollow eyed, and sagged on the couch, Lena said, "Higgy Braxton came to costume today to find you. I told him you had to go to an appointment with Sheila, so if he sends her flowers or something, she has a 'woman thing.' I don't think he'll ask beyond that."

Flavio put his hand to his eyes with a groan. "Good thinking, my dear. What did he want?"

"Joan Fontaine complained about your missing the fitting yesterday."

"Of course she did."

"I promise that Cindy and I were perfectly competent. She didn't seem unhappy at all."

Flavio struggled to sit up. "I'm sure you were perfect. What did Higgy say?"

"That your twenty years at Lux would only go so far and not to let it happen again."

Another groan. Flavio got to his feet and lit a cigarette. "Have Amelia send La Fontaine flowers, will you? I'm sure her favorites are on file. And thank you for your help."

Lena headed toward her little office. "The racing form is in your desk drawer."

They spoke no more about it. They never did. Not his addiction to horse racing nor his other predilections that often had him asking his driver to take Sheila home after a party or a gala or a night on the town while he went elsewhere. Lena simply covered for him whenever she had to. Sometimes, one of her designs made it into a movie because Flavio had simply not done what he was supposed to do. He was always apologetic, and Lena loved him, so it didn't matter. It was a thrill to see her costume in a film, even if Flavio got the credit. He was the best teacher she'd ever had; she didn't begrudge him the occasional lapse.

She worried what would happen if he lost twenty years of his own career, and so she bent over backward to make certain that his more and more frequent lapses went unnoticed, especially by Higgy Braxton. She was sure she had succeeded.

The day she realized she was wrong, she was in the commissary. It was eight months after her first conversation with Braxton about Flavio. She sat alone, eating a deviled egg sandwich while she feverishly made changes to a costume sketch that a director had requested that morning. The constant activity of the commissary was better than the insanity of the costume department, which was in a frenzy today. Everyone was in a flurry about a wrong shipment of dye, and a cutter had made a mistake with a burgundy shot silk that they had bought from an estate sale and could not replace. In her office, she would have been interrupted constantly to solve problems, and she needed to finish in time for an afternoon fitting with Susan Hayward, which she did not want to run long because she had a date with Paul tonight. He had finished his new screenplay, *Club Medusa*, which he said was the best thing he'd ever written, and he wanted to celebrate.

Lena was so intent on her work that she didn't notice Higgy Braxton standing before her until his shadow crossed over the page. She looked up. "Oh. Oh! Hello."

He pulled out a chair and sat across from her, which was the most disconcerting thing that had happened all day, more so than anything in the costume department. "How are you, Lena?"

Even more disconcerting. "I'm . . . um . . . good. I'm—uh—finishing this—"

He twisted his neck to look. "For *Oh Oklahoma?*"

"Yes. I'm just adding the changes that Fred Stevens wanted. The director." Then she felt stupid, because of course Higgy would know who Fred Stevens was.

His little smile made her feel more stupid. "Really? I haven't seen the costume sketches yet for this one. Who designed that?"

His words felt like a trap. She had designed it, but she couldn't say that, not without revealing that she'd designed most of the costumes for this film. Flavio had been so distracted; she thought he might be ill. She'd never tell Higgy that. "Flavio, of course. Who else? He just asked me to make the changes—"

"I don't like being lied to, Lena."

She laughed nervously. "No one would trust an assistant with such an important film—"

"I know you did the ball gown for *All for Heaven*. And the picnic scene for *Margery Lawson*. You did the cabaret costumes for *Dawn Rain*. Do I have to list them all?"

Lena said nothing; she didn't know what to say, whether Higgy Braxton would think this good or bad, and which for whom. Would he be angry? He hadn't said whether he liked the costumes or not, had he?

"I'm not an idiot. Keep in mind, everything goes through me, and I've been approving Flavio's costumes for two decades. I know when I see his designs, and when I don't."

~

"There's something wrong with Flavio," Susan Hayward confided several weeks later. "I don't want to go to Higgy with it, but I don't have a choice anymore."

Early the next morning, Lena found her mentor exactly where she'd expected to, watching the morning workouts at Clockers' Corner at Santa Anita. He stood out among the horsemen and trainers, as fashionably dressed as he was in his black-checkered cravat and his hat, looking very louche as he drank coffee from a paper cup at one of the tables overlooking the racetrack and the San Gabriel Mountains.

He barely looked up from the day's *Daily Racing Form* as Lena took the seat across from him. Hoofbeats thundered on the track; the horses looked gorgeous in the morning sunlight, muscular and gleaming. A slight breeze brought the scent of dirt and the stables.

She pulled the brim of her hat against the sun. "You should be at the studio."

"I'm in hiding."

"You're going to have to hide from Higgy, too, if you're not careful. And Susan Hayward."

"Hmmm." He hadn't lifted his gaze from the form. "That is scary. I've seen her husband."

"I think he gives as good as he gets." Lena had heard plenty from the actress about her home situation. "Flavio, really. You have to stop this. Higgy loves you, but . . ."

"But he's starting to love you better." A raised eye, a lifted brow.

"That's not true."

"He likes your designs."

She sighed. "He has no choice when mine are the only ones he sees lately."

Flavio reached for his coffee. She noticed that his hand trembled—and that he'd pulled his hat low over his brow and the collar of his coat high. He'd said he was in hiding. It wasn't a joke, she realized.

"How serious is it this time, Flavio?" she asked softly.

"I can't go back to the studio. Not today. Perhaps not for a while."

"How long is 'a while'?"

Lena saw the answer in the way he finally met her gaze.

Flavio set his coffee cup on the table and Lena reached to cover his hand with her own. "What can I do?"

Flavio laughed shortly. "Find a way to appease Scotty Fields?"

Lena winced. She should have known. She wished she wasn't shocked that Flavio was involved with the LA mob, but Mickey Cohen had fingers in pies all over Hollywood. Studio bosses, actors, singers . . . she tried not to think of how many films had mob financing. Thankfully Scotty Fields was one of Cohen's lesser thugs, but that didn't mean this wasn't serious. She wondered what exactly the extent of Flavio's thralldom to Scotty Fields was. Extortion? There were obviously things Flavio wanted kept secret. Loan-sharking? Given Flavio's love for horse racing, it was probable.

She was afraid to ask. In the end, she didn't have to. Flavio let out a long sigh. "Fast women and slow racehorses, Lena. They've always been my undoing, and they always will."

"Does Sheila know about Scotty?"

He shrugged. A yes, then. Honestly, Lena would have been surprised to find it otherwise. Sheila's acceptance of her husband's . . . peccadilloes . . . along with her fierce protection of his reputation was a great part of the reason for the longevity of their marriage.

"All right." She infused her voice with purpose. "You and Sheila should take a long vacation until we can get everything sorted. I'll make your excuses to Higgy."

"It's long past time for excuses," Flavio admitted quietly, and the pounding galloping added a drumbeat of mourning that Lena ignored, determined as she was to save him.

She hurried back to the studio, hoping that Higgy had not heard about Flavio's absence, but it was a vain hope. She'd no sooner walked into the costume department when Flavio's secretary said, "Higgy wants to see you, Lena."

"Me?"

"He asked for you directly."

Lena winced. This could not be good. But there was no avoiding Higgy Braxton, and no delaying. Nervously, she went to the administration building, and Higgy's office. His secretary, who Lena thought wouldn't know her from any extra on the lot, said, "Ah yes, Lena, go on in. He's waiting for you."

Somehow, she found that even more nerve racking.

Lena went inside, and understood exactly what Flavio had meant when he said Higgy's office looked like he studied taxidermy. Higbert Braxton's sanctuary had been designed in every way to intimidate: his desk at the far end elevated on a two-foot dais, a bearskin rug laid before it—complete with the animal's open mouth baring menacing teeth—two African antelope heads, a lion, and an arching marlin decorated the walls. The chairs were covered in leopard skin. Crossed rifles had been placed on the wall to frame Higgy's chair. A sideboard held a decanter of whiskey—only bourbon, because apparently that was what you drank when you met with Higgy—and a box of cigars. The room smelled of maleness: cigar and musk and Higgy's particular bespoke cologne that evoked fire smoke and gunpowder and earth.

He barely looked up from his papers. "I don't want to hear any more excuses for him."

She was at a disadvantage already. "He needs to take a vacation, Higgy. Sheila is—"

"Sheila is perfectly well." Higgy raised his eyes to meet Lena's gaze. "And my head costume designer is done. He's out."

"Oh, no, you can't—"

"His time is over, Lena. I should think you'd be happy. Flavio's loss is your gain."

She stared at him, not comprehending.

"You're the new costume head for Lux Pictures," Higgy said. "Congratulations."

CHAPTER 18

The gossip columns went wild. Costume designers weren't usually the subject of such gossip, but no one had ever moved so quickly from sketch artist to the head costume designer, and Flavio was beloved and famous. Everyone assumed that she'd either slept with Higgy Braxton, or blackmailed Flavio, or otherwise organized his downfall. How else had a woman won the job so quickly?

Photoplay hinted that someone—perhaps an ambitious assistant?— had alerted Braxton to Flavio's predilection for betting the horses at Santa Anita or Hollywood Park. *Confidential* was less subtle. Rumor has it a certain single-named Costume Designer owed money to his up-and-coming assistant, and she called in his debt. The new star has made a bigger bang than the A-bomb!

Modern Screen only wrote, Lena Taylor is the new Head of Costume Design at Lux Pictures, and former head Flavio is out! Sources say that after Susan Hayward requested Miss Taylor for Oh Oklahoma! studio head Higbert Braxton fired the twenty-year veteran.

She should have expected it, given the speculation when Flavio made her his assistant, but she hadn't. "Ignore it," Flavio told Lena at the time. "It's only a matter of time before Hedda Hopper finds another hidden communist among the stars and everyone forgets all about this. Anyway, it will only bring more customers into my shop." He planned to open a place in Beverly Hills, very exclusive, catering mostly to the stars, and Lena could tell he was relieved, but still she felt horrible about the whole thing.

"I don't like people thinking I pushed you out."

"Lena," he said carefully. "Let them think it. Let them believe you're a barracuda. It can only help you."

"They can think me a barracuda. I just don't want them to think I betrayed you after you've done so much for me."

He smiled as he packed the last of his things into a box. "You and I both know the truth. The others don't matter. It's a blessing really. My severance will pay off Scotty, and all is right with the world."

Yes, he was relieved, but Lena thought he looked sad too. Twenty years ending so abruptly, and in such a way.

It didn't take her long to realize that she bore the brunt of it. No one would believe anything bad about Flavio, but they certainly believed it about her. In the beginning, she was too busy to notice, really, and the box office and the reviews for *Oh Oklahoma!* were so good that she shrugged off the snippy comment in Louella Parsons's column in the *Los Angeles Examiner* about the lackluster costumes by the notorious Lena Taylor, whose rise at Lux Pictures has been most extraordinary—the movie was set on a wagon train, for God's sake, the characters stranded in Indian country. It had taken weeks to dye and wear the pioneer dresses and sunbonnets so they looked appropriately weathered by the elements, and not a single scene required a ball gown or anything approaching fashion.

But the comments kept coming. As the months passed, her name appeared more and more often in *Photoplay* or *Motion Picture Magazine*, invariably accompanied by an adjective like *notorious* or *infamous*. It troubled her—not just the spite, but the fact that she was now so . . . visible. But nothing had happened, not for years now. If she had not forgotten Rome, it appeared that Rome had forgotten her. Maybe . . . maybe she didn't have to worry so much? Maybe she could relax? She was the head costume designer at Lux Pictures now. Maybe being so high profile could no longer hurt her. Maybe it helped her instead.

"Does all the talk bother Braxton?" Paul asked her.

"I think he likes it. He laughs whenever he sees me. 'Oh, there she is, the notorious Lena Taylor!'" She imitated Higgy's brusque manner of speaking.

Paul laughed. "Have any of the stars refused to work with you?"

"God, no. I'm busier than ever. You know how it is in Hollywood. They love to say they've worked with me. Then they can add to the gossip."

"It hasn't kept anyone from working with Lux that Steve can see. He says it's getting harder and harder to get in there." Steve Jameson was Paul's agent, and he was shopping around *Club Medusa*.

"Did he send *Medusa* to Higgy?"

"Last week," Paul told her.

"Could you imagine it? If I got to costume your script?"

He laughed again and held her close. "How would we work together, I wonder?"

"Perfectly." She nuzzled his chest. "Like we were made for each other."

His hand went to her hair. "I hope you're right, because I got the word today. Braxton bought it."

"Paul!" She nearly jumped out of bed. She threw a pillow at him. "You jerk! Why didn't you tell me right away?"

He grinned. "I liked the suspense."

"Oh my God! We have to go out. We have to celebrate. Ciro's—or . . . or the Cocoanut Grove—"

"What about right here?" he suggested, reaching for her. "Let's not go all Hollywood yet, sweetheart. It's just you and me, let's just stay that way for a little bit longer."

Something in his voice made her pause. "What is it?"

"It gets complicated from here on out. I just . . . I don't know."

"You're nervous." She marveled at it. She'd never seen him nervous before.

"A little."

"It's a bold premise," she said. "Four women opening a nightclub on their own. But it's brilliant. They won't want you to change it too much. I know they won't."

He pulled her back onto his chest and kissed her forehead. "I guess we'll see, won't we?"

"I won't let them."

"Sweetheart, we won't have a choice if we want it to go ahead. Usually I don't care. It's what happens. I just . . . I've never written anything I cared so much about before."

He was adorable when he was uncertain. She eased her leg over his hips until she was half covering him. "I'll be there to help you through it, though it will break my heart if they change a word."

"Really? Well, don't worry. I won't let anyone break your heart," he assured her.

"I'll hold you to that," she whispered against his mouth.

∼

It was impossible to worry when everything was going so well, and it was exhausting to be concerned about her past when she was so busy at Lux. The gossip about her "meteoric rise" died down as Paul's film entered preproduction. Maybe she had nothing to worry about anymore. Maybe Rome was truly behind her. Maybe no one cared.

She pushed her unfinished piece of chiffon cake across the table toward Flavio and said, "The Brown Derby is usually crawling with gossips, and yet there's not a single one here today to note us having lunch together."

Flavio took a bite of her cake. He was such an elegant man that even the way he wielded the fork had style. "No one cares that we're friends. Only that we're enemies. Besides, the columnists are all on their best behavior. They're still smarting over the Mitchum lawsuit, and it's not as if there isn't plenty of dirt all over Hollywood. Costume designers are small fry, especially if they keep their noses clean—which I assume you have? Or has my good influence waned since I've been gone?"

She laughed. It was true that Robert Mitchum suing *Confidential* for a million dollars had put a crimp in the magazine's style. He'd lost the suit, but only on a technicality. "Maybe *Confidential* is smarting, but I don't think the other gossip magazines are too concerned."

"You should be happy they've grown tired of you."

"Oh believe me, I am. I just get anxious when everything goes well, you know?"

He gave her a wry smile. "Enjoy it while it lasts."

"I'm trying to. Besides, I've got all I can do now that production is starting on Paul's movie. There's a new censor I have to meet in a few hours. I don't have a good feeling about him. I was hoping maybe . . ."

"What? That you would somehow avoid having a censor? What did I miss? Is the world so changed?"

"It's just . . . it's Paul's. I'm feeling very proprietary."

"Ah. Yes, of course. Have you given him my congratulations?"

"You can give them to him yourself. He's coming to your party tonight."

Flavio grinned. "Has he proposed yet?"

"Flavio—"

"Dear God, how long does he mean to wait? It's been, what . . . I can't even count the years. You'll be an old woman before long."

"It's fine," she assured him. "I like things the way they are."

"I see."

"I do. Really."

"Um-hmm."

Lena felt herself flush and looked into her cold coffee.

He shook it away. "My dear, ask that man to get you a diamond. It's absurd that he hasn't. What's he waiting for?"

Flavio did not know the truth, of course, and Lena wasn't going to tell him, as much as she trusted him. Harvey and Charlie had offered to look into the divorce laws for her, but she was too worried—even just suing for divorce, regardless of whether she had to find Walter, and regardless of the technicality of her name change, would catch the eye of some private detective or gossip columnist, and the fact that she'd been Elsie Gruner when she'd married him would lead anyone curious to . . . too many places she didn't want them to go.

So now, she deflected. "You'd love the screenplay. You would. It's such a beautiful story. A woman inherits her uncle's failing café and turns it into a successful nightclub with the help of all these other women. It's powerful and dramatic and funny, and—and—"

Flavio put down his fork and sat up straighter, devoting his entire attention to her. He had always known when to really listen.

"—he understands so well what women want, and if some idiot censor ruins it, I'll have to kill him."

"I'm sure Paul knows—as do you, my dear—the realities of this business. If they screw it up, he'll just write it again and again until someone gets it right."

Lena laughed softly. "You're such a cynic."

"I've been here a long time. An ice age really. You're still just a baby."

"Not really. Not anymore." She shook her head wistfully. "And Paul's not that pragmatic, either, you know. He has such high hopes for the film. Anyway, I've got to go. I'm supposed to meet this censor at two."

"What's his name?"

"Michael something—Runyon. Michael Runyon."

"Never heard of him."

"I told you he was new. Hopefully he'll be a little stupid too." She reached for her purse.

Flavio waved her away. "This one's on me. You get the next one. I'll see you tonight. Don't be late or you'll miss the champagne."

She blew him a kiss and hurried from the restaurant to her car. The Los Angeles sun beat relentlessly upon the roof, and the inside was sweltering. She took a deep breath of heated new leather upholstery and traces of L'Air du Temps, reveling in it for just a moment before she cranked the window. She'd had the car for several months. It was a 1954 Chrysler New Yorker Deluxe Newport in a peacock blue, and she loved it. The only thing in her apartment she cared about was her jazz collection, but this car felt like the embodiment of her career. How far she'd come from a pig farm in Zanesville. Sometimes she thought of how the artists at Larry Lipton's would sneer at her love for such a material possession, but when she drove the Chrysler, she was truly Lena Taylor, head costume designer of Lux Pictures.

When she reached Culver City, and the long, peach-colored stucco administration building, she parked at the sign with her name on it and headed into the costume department. She'd no sooner stepped inside than her head of wardrobe, Connie, came rushing over. "Where have you been? We've had a crisis."

As if there wasn't one every day.

"They dyed the georgette the wrong green."

"How wrong is it?"

Connie grimaced. "Lime instead of emerald. It will look terrible with Bunny's skin."

Lena stripped off her gloves and shoved them in her purse. "They'll have to re-dye it."

"There's no time. They shoot the scene this afternoon."

"No one checked the color before they made the dress?"

Connie bowed her blond head. Her updo was so loose it looked ready to fall, the sign of a hot and frustrating day. "They did. Somehow they had the wrong swatch."

Lena followed her assistant to the room where the dress hung, looking even more yellow than Connie had described it. Barbara Sweetin, the actress who would be wearing the dress, had dark auburn hair and milky pale skin. The dress would make her look sallow, and it would be worse with the lights they used for Technicolor.

Lena swore beneath her breath. "How long do we have?"

Connie checked her watch. "Three hours. I can maybe get us a half hour beyond that."

"Get Sammy." Lena fingered the delicate georgette. "And bring every dark green dress we have from stock that's not twenty yards with a crinoline. And Bunny's dress form."

"Lena, there's not enough time."

"There has to be enough time," Lena said grimly. "Find me a dress and I'll redesign it. Sammy can alter anything. Get him in here. We'll both have to help."

"But you have that meeting with the new censor."

"I've an hour until then. Meet me in the sewing room."

~

She was twenty minutes late to her meeting with Michael Runyon. Her beige dress was covered with tiny bits of green silk lint that she hadn't had time to brush away, and strands of her blond hair fell into her sweaty face. She rushed to the room where her secretary, Shirley, had put him, already apologizing, feeling worse when he swept her with a pale blue gaze and smiled, saying, "They did tell me you were a very busy woman."

"I had a last-minute emergency," she explained.

He stood and offered a hand, which she took. "Michael Runyon."

"Lena Taylor."

He wore a dark Brooks Brothers suit. Unexceptional shoes. His hair was blond and wavy, Brylcreemed into submission. But for the suit, he looked like Higgy's type, as if he should be in the mountains somewhere bagging antelope or whatever mountain men did. Not really the kind of man she'd expected.

"This is simply a formality," he assured her. "I'm sure you already know all the rules."

"No navels. No cleavage. I'm very familiar with the Hays Code. This isn't my first film, Mr. Runyon."

"Have you worked with George Gardner before?"

George was the director Higgy had hired for the film. "Yes, I know him. He's perfect for *Club Medusa*. I don't imagine there will be any problems. He's approved the costumes already."

Runyon gave her a strange look. "Didn't they tell you? It's not called *Club Medusa* now. It's been retitled."

Paul had said nothing. Neither had Higgy. "To what?"

"*The Doom of Medusa.*"

"*The Doom of Medusa?* But . . . that hardly sounds . . . triumphant."

Michael Runyon looked sympathetic. "It's like any film, Miss Taylor. Changes are just part of the process. I will want to take a look at the costumes."

"Yes, of course."

"You'll have them tomorrow morning?"

"They're already finished. Most of them."

"Good." The production censor went to the door. "It was a pleasure meeting you, Miss Taylor. I'll see you here at eight a.m. sharp."

Shirley poked her head in the door. "Lena? We just got a call from Tom over on soundstage three. Miss Hayward is complaining about her shoes. Should I send one of the girls?"

"No, I'll go." Lena put Michael Runyon out of her mind, and headed to soundstage three.

CHAPTER 19

She found Paul by the Chateau Marmont pool, where she knew he would be, where he was every afternoon at this time. She spotted him as she emerged from the winding path through the junglelike foliage. He lounged on one of the chaises, papers on his thighs, a cigarette dangling from his lips. He was, as usual, making notes on the pages and paying no attention to anyone around him, not young Natalie Wood in a leopard-skin bikini sitting on the edge of the small oval pool, nor Anthony Hopkins talking earnestly with two other men on the brick herringbone pool deck, nor the two girls splashing in the water. She knew from experience that the only time he would look up was when the single poolside phone rang, and then, like everyone else's, his head would jerk, and he'd wait for the bartender to call his name, and when he didn't, Paul would return to his work, pausing only to tap his cigarette into the ashtray beside him.

Paul was so absorbed it took him a moment to notice she'd walked up to him, and when he did, the smile that crossed his face made her remember seeing him that first time in Larry Lipton's Venice Beach living room, every space filled with louche poets and drifters and, as Larry called them, "seekers," Charlie Parker on the turntable, and the room gray with cigarette smoke.

Now, he reached for her wrist and wrapped his hand around it. His short-sleeved shirt was open to reveal the dark hair on his chest, and she wished to bury herself in his arms and forget the day.

He gave her a look. "Not that I'm sorry to see you, but why are you here so early?"

"I met the man from the production office assigned to the movie today."

He waited.

She didn't know if he knew about the title change. She told herself he'd be fine with it. He was a writer, he had to be used to such things by now. But she hated to be the bearer of bad news. "They're calling it *The Doom of Medusa*."

He laughed shortly. "Of course they are."

"You didn't know."

"The writer's always the last to be told."

"He didn't say anything about any other changes. I'm meeting him about the costumes first thing tomorrow."

"*The Doom of Medusa*," he said beneath his breath. "I don't like the sound of it."

She said quickly, "You know Higgy will bring you in to make the changes if there are any. He won't call another screenwriter if they can save money by having you do them first. And that way, you can—" She saw a movement in the branches just beyond them. Lena paused. It was best not to have such conversations there. It was too public. In a low voice she said, "We should talk about this inside."

Paul followed her gaze, then gathered up the papers on his lap. "Let's go upstairs."

Paul's room wasn't one of the penthouses, but like all the rooms at the Chateau, it had an iconoclastic charm. His balcony overlooked the busy and noisy Sunset Boulevard side, and the apartment had seen better days. It was dark and moody, too many things patched, mended, and remended. The Turkish carpets were stained and in places threadbare, the woodwork chipped and scuffed. None of the furniture matched—the previous owner had bought most of it at estate sales, and Paul's rooms were a perfect example of shabby old Hollywood decadence, a pink velvet love seat with carved mahogany arms and legs and trim, a knockoff Tiffany lamp with a curving, swanlike neck and a vaguely Moorish design in its mosaic of red, yellow, and green glass.

The bookcase, chairs, and table were equally mismatched. The artwork was . . . eclectic. A painting of a cocked-headed, dark-haired woman that looked like a copy of a Modigliani graced the main room, along with a smaller one of a rooster. In the bedroom, a pine dresser with a huge round mirror reflected a bed with a white vinyl padded headboard and a beige bedcover with a pattern of green swirls. On the wall hung a copy of a blobby-looking Klimt. Maybe. Or maybe it was just a blob of color with flecks of gold.

Paul had managed to make the place his own. His dark blue Royal typewriter sat on the table, next to a ream of paper, a typewriter eraser, and an overflowing ashtray; typed pages, some scrawled with notes and scratched-out lines and big x's, littered the floor. His phonograph held pride of place on top of a small bookcase, and piled on the shelves was a collection of jazz records that rivaled her own.

Once they were through the door, he dropped his papers on the television and pulled her close for a kiss. Sun-touched Brylcreem, sun-warmed skin, the taste of Marlboros. She fell into him, running her hand down his chest to the waist of his shorts. He grabbed her hand and pulled slightly away with a laugh.

"Tell me about this guy—what's his name? The censor?"

"Michael Runyon."

"Runyon?" Paul frowned. "Michael Runyon?"

"Yes. Why? Do you know him?"

Paul hesitated, then he shook his head. "I used to know someone by that name, but he didn't work in the movies."

"He's a suit. But . . . I don't know, he looks like maybe he was a boxer in another life or something. Blond. Blue eyed?"

Paul frowned. "Couldn't be the same guy."

"He may not look like a censor, but he's just like the rest of them. He wants to see costumes at eight tomorrow morning. He was fine, but . . ."

"There's always a but."

"I've never met a censor who wasn't impossible." She took one of the cigarettes from the pack on the TV and waited while Paul reached for his lighter. "If he changes this script, I'll—"

"The title change may mean nothing." He lit her cigarette and lit one for himself. "It's all about marketing."

"You don't believe that and neither do I. Flavio said you should do what everyone else does and just rewrite it for someone else. I had lunch with him today." She wandered to the balcony doors and opened them. The noisy rush of Sunset Boulevard swept inside, along with a warm breeze. "He said to tell you congratulations."

"He's a good man."

"Nobody believes me when I say that."

"Well, you ruined him."

She spun from the balcony. "How can you, of all people—" She stopped when she saw the tease in his eyes.

"How have you survived in Hollywood this long?" he asked with a smile.

"I don't know." She took a long drag on the cigarette and turned back to the balcony, and heard his slow and steady gait as he came up behind her. His arms encircled her then, drawing her back against his chest.

He gently took the cigarette from her mouth and settled it in the ashtray on the table beside them, and Lena turned in his arms.

"I like this view better," she said.

"So do I," he said quietly, the tease gone from his dark eyes now, replaced with an expression that curled and dipped into her, heavy and deep, erasing the day, the remedy she'd been hoping for, and before he got her to the bedroom, she'd already put the last hours behind her.

~

Ciro's was packed. After thirty-some years in Hollywood, Flavio had many friends, and none of them were likely to turn down an invitation for free drinks in celebration of his birthday. The nightclub was loud with talk and laughter, cigarette smoke hung about the pale green draperies like a fog and obscured the rose ceiling. The band on the small stage wasn't famous—Flavio wasn't going to pay for that—but they performed as if they were, with a vibrant, effusive, and Benny Goodman–like style that only added to the ebullient atmosphere.

The bronze urn lights flanking the bandstand and baroque stylings of Ciro's were as familiar to Lena as the costume department, and she felt right at home. Everything was perfect. She was sitting next to the man she loved on the red silk wall sofa, her gin martini was cold and delicious, and the mood was festive and no one had yet caused a scene. Louella Parsons was there, talking earnestly to Gregory Peck. Earlier, Lena had complimented Louella's gown and the columnist had turned to Paul. "And who is this handsome man?"

"Paul Carbone." Paul offered his hand.

Louella took it, but it wasn't a shake so much as a lingering caress she gave in return. Her gaze swept over him. "Oh yes, the screenwriter."

Lena suppressed a prick of irritation. Louella had mentioned the two of them a dozen times in her column. She knew perfectly well who Paul was. "He's got a movie in production at Lux," Lena interjected.

"Lux?" Louella raised a perfectly drawn brow. "*Your* studio? How interesting. Do tell."

But before either of them could say a word, Donald O'Connor stepped in with "Louella, you're looking well," and Louella smiled at Paul and said, "We'll talk later, Mr. Carbone."

"She liked you," Lena whispered as they stepped away.

Paul only rolled his eyes, but he knew as well as she did that it was a good thing when a woman who had the power to make or break your movie looked favorably on you, even if being handsome was the only reason.

She saw James Dean and Lana Turner—Lana had always loved Flavio and wore one of his gowns that night. Cesar Romero by the bandstand talking to Sheila Flavio. George Nader and Tony Curtis and Desi Arnaz and Lucille Ball, and she thought that was Shelley Winters but it was hard to see through the crowd.

Lena swallowed the rest of her martini and signaled the waiter for another. Paul was talking to a screenwriter on his other side. The band launched into "Happy Birthday," and attention turned to the cake a waiter wheeled out from the kitchen, many layered, frosted in Flavio's signature white and black, with sparklers shooting from the top, and everyone sang and clapped. Flavio bowed and laughed.

People got to their feet, several calling "Bravo!" when Flavio cut the cake to reveal a checkboard of vanilla and chocolate. Someone shouted, "Speech!"

"All right, all right." Flavio adjusted the bow tie of his tuxedo and grinned widely. "Here's my speech: Thank you all for coming, and thank you for making my time here so memorable. Here's to many more memorable years." He raised his champagne to cheers of *Hear, hear!* "To my wife, Sheila, without whom I would not be here—my love, I salute you! And last but not least, here's to the person to whom I owe a great debt—my lovely, dear friend, Lena Taylor. Lena, please—" He gestured for her to come up beside him.

Paul pushed her gently, and Lena forgot her consternation in the sheer sweetness of Flavio's generosity and wove through the illustrious crowd toward her friend. When she got there, he put his arm around her and whispered, "Don't cry, there are photographers." He lifted his glass again; she turned her head and kissed Flavio's cheek, which not only made a good picture for the columns, but also allowed her hair to fall forward and hide her face.

She left a red stain of lipstick on his skin, which he made a big show about after she stepped away, head down. She was skilled at avoiding a full face shot. She could only imagine the headlines. *"Costume Foes Kiss and Make Up."*

It took her some time to get back to the red silk sofa. Everyone stopped her to say how happy they were that she and Flavio were friends again. They'd just *known* all those rumors had been lies!

She reached Paul just as she saw Louella jostling toward them. Lena grabbed Paul's hand. "I need some fresh air. Let's go outside for a minute?"

"I was just going to suggest that," he said.

Together they zigzagged through the crowd and out the front door to the gallery lined with pillars and lights and sculpted trees at the entrance to Ciro's. Lena fumbled in her purse for a cigarette; Paul offered one of his own and lit it for her. The smoke felt good in her lungs, calming. Now she felt almost giddy.

"Thank God. I could not face Louella just now. She would have found some way to say something unsavory about all that with Flavio."

Paul smiled, but it was strained.

"You did perfectly with her earlier," she reassured him. "Don't worry, she thinks you're 'handsome,' so I think she'll be easy on you."

"I'm not worried about Louella Parsons. I had another reason for wanting to get you away from the crowd." He reached into his pocket and pulled something out, offering it to her.

It took a moment before she understood. A moment before she comprehended that the sparkle in the middle of his palm was no trick of the lights, but a ring. A diamond. Then, she didn't know what to do, or what to say. She could only stare at it, startled.

Paul said simply, "Marry me?"

She reached out gingerly to touch the ring, and he took her hand and pulled off her elbow-length glove, and then he slid the diamond onto her finger, where it threw all the lights of Ciro's into relief.

She dropped the cigarette to smolder on the cement. He hadn't let go of her hand, and she stared at him in shocked joy and in the moment before he kissed her there in the entryway of Ciro's, she let down her guard—only a moment, but it was enough. Enough for the photographer who had followed them, enough for the picture that would run in Louella's column the next day, Lena's face in all its blooming happiness on full display.

But just at that moment, all she saw was a flash of blinding light, and she forgot about it the next second, with Paul's kiss.

CHAPTER 20

It was odd, wasn't it, how once you got everything you thought you wanted, fate—or whatever—threw a wrench into it, so that you were left reevaluating your life once again? Things were never settled, never clear, never what you thought they would be for more than a day at a time. When Lena woke the next morning, squinting at the fierceness of the light screaming into her eyes, realizing in the next moment that it was the morning sun flashing through the diamond of her ring, joy and excitement surged through her—followed immediately by fear. How exactly was she to tell Paul that she had lied to him about her past?

Paul treasured honesty. As a writer, he took pride in reading people well. She had no idea what he would say or do if she told him that the Lena Taylor he knew and loved was an invention, that she was already married. The thought brought panic. As for Italy and everything that had happened there . . . only Harvey and Charlie knew the truth, and she knew they would never tell. It was a long time ago, and far away, and nothing had come of it after all. There was no reason for Paul to ever know.

She disentangled herself from Paul's arms. He made a sound in his sleep and she kissed his temple and went to the shower. It was the first time she'd stayed overnight, but she'd told Paul she'd wanted to. She hoped she wouldn't regret it. They were engaged now, so maybe that would calm the gossips if they discovered she'd spent the night. Besides, she had more important things to worry about this morning.

When she came out of the bathroom, Paul was awake, sitting up in bed, smoking. She wiggled her hand at him, showing off the ring, and he grinned and said, "Looks like I've made an honest woman of you at last."

Her smile faltered, but before she could answer, the phone rang. Paul reached over to answer it. "Hello?" A pause. "This is Paul Carbone."

Lena finished dressing in her usual beige ensemble, today a beige-gray sateen suit with a bit of a conquistador flavor, a take on one of her early sketches, as Paul's one-sided conversation rumbled in the background. She went to the mirror over the dresser to apply mascara, brows, Elizabeth Arden Oriental Red lipstick—though nothing really mitigated the beige and she didn't try. That was the point.

Lena finished pinning up her shoulder-length hair just as Paul hung up the receiver. "Well," he said.

"What was that about?"

He took a deep breath. "I'm wanted at Lux for script changes."

Lena tensed. "What kind of script changes?"

"I'm not quite sure. Apparently Braxton's made some kind of agreement with the government. They want pictures for overseas that promote the American way of life."

"Why should they change it for that?"

Paul shrugged and threw back the covers to climb out of bed. "You'll have to ask your boss. I'm supposed to be there at ten."

He blew her a kiss and disappeared into the bathroom. A few minutes later, she heard water running. The clock on the bedside table said she had to hurry if she meant to be at the studio on time, and given her tardiness to the meeting with Runyon yesterday, she did. She scrawled a quick note telling Paul she'd see him later, and then hurried into the warmth of the Los Angeles morning, and her car.

When she reached the studio, she found the costume design shop in its usual state of controlled panic. Connie had the costumes for *The Doom of Medusa*, still of course with their *Club Medusa* tags, hanging and ready for Michael Runyon's inspection, and Shirley offered Lena coffee the moment she came through the door. When Lena pulled off her gloves and reached for the coffee, Shirley gasped and let out an *eek*, setting the coffee aside before Lena could take it.

"Oh dear God, what is that?" Shirley asked. She grabbed Lena's hand. "Paul proposed!"

"Ssshhh! You'll alert the whole town!" Lena joked.

"Well, of course! Everyone's been waiting and waiting! Tell me everything. How did it happen?"

Connie stepped out from the wardrobe room. "Did I just hear what I think I did?" She took one glance at Lena's hand. "Paul proposed?"

"Last night. At Flavio's birthday party."

"It's about time!" Connie snatched Lena's hand from Shirley. "That's quite a ring. How big is that diamond, do you think? A carat? I wonder what it cost him?"

"I don't think it's that big."

"Of course it is." Connie offered her hand with her wedding and engagement set. "This is half a carat, and look—yours is easily twice that. I think it's a carat and a half. Look, Shirl, don't you think?"

Shirley nodded. "Oh yes. I didn't think writers made very much money."

"Well, he did sell the screenplay for *Club Medusa*," Connie noted.

"That's true. And I guess you're worth the investment." Shirley laughed. "When's the wedding?"

Lena pulled her hand back, feeling uncomfortable again. "It just happened. We haven't had time to discuss it."

"When Jeremy proposed to me, I had the whole wedding planned within the hour," Connie said. "I nearly had the hall rented before we left the park."

"You'd been waiting for Jeremy to propose for a year," Lena pointed out. "I think you bought the ring for him, didn't you?"

Connie rolled her eyes. "Don't tell me you haven't been waiting for Paul. I've seen the way you look at him, and how you go all moody if he doesn't call. You're as bad as the rest of us, even if you are the head costumer at Lux Pictures."

Lena said nothing. "Speaking of which, Mr. Runyon should be here any minute. We should get to work." She led the way into the wardrobe room, where the costumes she'd designed for Ruby Dennison, the actress playing the role of Helen, the heroine of Paul's script, hung waiting. The character was a naive young woman who became a brilliant leader and businesswoman when she inherited her uncle's café and was truly on her own for the first time. Lena's costumes reflected the burgeoning of Helen's personality over her coming of age and growing confidence as she formed the all-woman team that turned the café into the most popular nightclub in the city, Club Medusa.

Lena picked through the costumes, preparing for Michael Runyon's arrival. She didn't have to wait long before he came inside with a charm that had Shirley smiling and trailing after him with a cup of coffee. "Cream or sugar, Mr. Runyon?"

"Black is perfect, thank you, miss," he said, smiling back in a way that made Shirley blush and stand there until Lena raised an eyebrow at her.

Lena introduced Connie.

"Delighted to meet you, Miss Spencer. Should I assume you've both been informed of the latest changes?"

Lena asked, "Something beyond the title change?"

Runyon sat down, unbuttoning his suit coat, sipping his coffee, like a man comfortable with the world. Lena noted the way he put Connie at ease, but Lena herself remained wary.

He said to her, "Braxton is bringing in the writer. I've been told you know him?"

Lena found herself easing her left hand behind her back. "Paul Carbone. Yes."

"We'll be changing the nightclub to a jazz club."

"A jazz club? But . . . Pa—Mr. Carbone had imagined it as something like the Mocambo."

"We're looking for something that communicates American ideals overseas," Runyon said. "Jazz is prohibited in Russia, but it's got a big, illicit following. We want to show that you're free in America to enjoy it, and that it's not only for Negroes. The Soviets think we're racists. The clubs show that's not true."

Lena stared at him in surprise. Once, maybe, that had been so. "Which clubs allow mixing now, Mr. Runyon?" she asked. "No one white goes to Central Avenue anymore."

"Who's at Ciro's? Nat King Cole."

But of course, Ciro's wasn't a jazz club. It was a nightclub. With dancing and dinner. And you didn't see many Negroes there, except on the stage. It wasn't the same. But she didn't say it.

"The Medusa will have a great jazz band. A Negro one," Runyon went on.

"It had that when it was a nightclub," Lena said.

"Yes, but is it really plausible that women could run something as large and complex as the Mocambo?" Runyon shook his head. "It makes more sense that Helen tries something a bit smaller."

Lena struggled to understand the change. "You're saying—"

"She struggles with the club and ends up borrowing money from a mob boss, who takes it over."

The Doom of Medusa. It was beginning to make more sense now. "And the other women? The friends she engages to help her?"

Runyon rose without answering. He went to the rack of costumes, casually flipping through the hangers, barely affording any of them more than a cursory glance. "All those costumes will have to be changed. The colors aren't right. None of them. We don't want all those pale colors. And no gold."

"Shooting starts next week. There isn't time."

"We'll need to rebuild some sets, so you have two weeks."

Connie put in, "But our budget . . . that gold with all the embroidery cost . . ."

Runyon went thoughtful. "Yes, I see. Well, do what you can to save money. You can dye that blue to a darker shade, I'd think. The film's being shot with black-and-white stock, so . . . whatever works for the others. Just dark. I want these women to be down on their luck at first, and then, when Helen brings them all in, they dress better, but like . . . like—" He made a curvy motion with his hands, a figure eight. "The club corrupts them. They aren't *good* women. Not until they're saved at the end. Well, some of them."

Lena did not believe what she was hearing. "That's not the script."

"Not yet," he admitted.

Lena hesitated. Connie gave her a bewildered look. "Mr. Runyon, I don't wish to offend you or . . . or disagree with you really, but . . . but Mr. Gardner has already approved these, and I don't feel comfortable changing all this without a new script to follow and the director's instruction, or the producer, for that matter—"

"I see. Yes, yes, of course." Runyon smiled, but Lena saw the force behind the charm now. "You may be right. I have a meeting with Carbone at ten. What do you say we meet again at two and go over the changes for the character of Helen first? The others we can get to once Carbone has them written. We'll start over, as it were."

Lena stared back at him, disconcerted, uncertain.

Connie said, "Should I have Shirley clear your schedule, Lena?"

"Yes," Lena managed. "Yes. Two o'clock."

Runyon nodded. "I'll ask Carbone to send notes as soon as he has them. Until then . . . Miss Taylor. Miss . . . Spencer."

He left the room without another word.

"What the hell was that?" Connie asked. "These aren't just changes, they're . . . it's a whole new film! How are we supposed to costume it in two weeks? Please, please, please tell me we don't have to do this."

"Not if I have anything to say about it." Lena headed for the door, and Higgy Braxton's office.

~

She stormed into Higgy's office, where his secretary, the venerable Adele, stopped Lena in her tracks. "He's meeting with Eddie. It'll give you time to calm down. Want some coffee?"

Eddie Jackson was one of the studio executives, and Adele's comment about calming down did not go unheeded. By now Lena knew that Higgy Braxton hated tempers and he hated scenes, though he loved being the cause of them. She shook her head at the offer of coffee and sat down in one of the cheap moss green upholstered chairs, and then decided that coffee would be a good idea after all.

"Has Higgy said anything to you about Michael Runyon?" she asked, taking a cup from the secretary.

Adele shook her head, shivering the dark curls of her poodle cut, and turned back to her typing. "He's the new guy from the production office, isn't he?"

The coffee was stale. Lena should have known it would be. Higgy didn't drink coffee and didn't care about catering to anyone who waited for a meeting with him. In fact, he liked them as unsettled as possible. Thus the uncomfortable cheap chairs. Lena put the cup aside. "I wonder if he's *ever* worked on a film before."

Adele made no comment. Her fingers pounded on the typewriter keys with stern, quick precision. Uncomfortably, Lena contemplated

Higbert Braxton's closed doors, Adele's rapid-fire typing filling her ears, and Lena wondered if she was being naive to think that she had any say at all about Michael Runyon. If what Paul had been told was true, that Higgy had made some agreement with the government about overseas films, then this was truly a waste of time. Higgy was a member of the Motion Picture Alliance for the Preservation of American Ideals, and had been since its founding. If this had to do with the MPA, he would be intractable, and he'd be backed by too many important people. Not only that, but Lena would only hurt her own position by complaining. She was the head costume designer, yes, but she was also a woman, and lucky to be here. She knew that, in Higgy's eyes anyway, she was replaceable. Connie could replace her. Sam in the sewing room had an excellent eye. Lena knew her strengths: she was good at making stars look their best; she could make a size fourteen look like a ten. She knew that the right skirt and shaded hose could make stubby legs look long. She could make an actress happy with her appearance even when she played the role of a charwoman. It was tailoring and color and fabric, yes, but it was also her gift for listening and a bit of persuasion.

Lux's stars would miss her, and they would complain if Braxton fired her. But their complaints wouldn't save her if Higgy decided she was too much trouble.

Lena crossed her legs and rested her hand on her knee, and the movement caused her engagement ring to catch the light. There was that too. Once Higgy saw it, and realized, as he must, who it was from, he would only think she was defending Paul, who was perfectly capable of defending himself. Higgy would just consider her a typical woman standing up for her man. This would weaken not only Lena's position, but Paul's, too, and he would not want that. Paul more than anyone knew how much she loved her job, how lost she'd be without it. But this was Paul's first big script, and she loved it. She was letting her emotions get in her way, which she knew better than to do.

Lena rose.

The typing paused. Adele turned. "Decided you didn't need to see him after all?"

"Eddie isn't in there, is he?" Lena asked.

Adele shook her head.

"Thank you, then. For saving me from myself."

"It's myself I'm saving," Adele told her. "I'm the one who has to listen to him scream after."

"You're a pearl," Lena said with a smile.

CHAPTER 21

Lena showed up at Paul's door with a bag that held only bottles of gin and vermouth and a jar of olives. He answered looking frustrated and rumpled, his thick hair so disheveled from running his hand through it that even Brylcreem couldn't keep it in place. The room behind him was choking with cigarette smoke.

He kissed her in greeting and said, "It's not that I'm not happy to see you, but . . ."

"I know. The Medusa is a jazz club, and Helen is a mob moll, and I don't know yet what the rest of the women have to do with anything because you haven't written it yet, but I expect Runyon's ordered you to make them drug addicts or evil seductresses who can only be saved by a 'good man.'" She went to the kitchenette and pulled the bottles from the bag. "I thought you could use some moral support. Martini?"

Paul sank into the chair at the desk and lit a cigarette. "Yes please."

"Not to mention the fact that I now have only two weeks to recostume the entire film. So I thought I'd get the early word on who exactly the characters are supposed to be."

"I don't even know." He raked his hand through his hair. "Look, I was thinking . . . I could withdraw the script. Give back the money."

"You could," she said matter-of-factly. "But you know as well as I do that the only way to get any power in this town is to have a script produced."

He gave her a look, and she knew he was thinking about all the ways he'd have to bend, and whether he could. Whether he wanted to.

Lena dropped olives into the martinis and handed one to him. "Paul, you have so much talent, but this . . . it takes more than that. If you want this career, now is the time to decide. You don't want to fight with a censor. Especially not this guy."

"Why do you say that?"

"You won't win. You'll just get removed from the picture. I don't have to tell you that."

"No, I mean, why do you say especially not Runyon?"

"I don't know." She shrugged. "I just . . . there's something about him. He's very charming but I—"

"Charming? Does he flirt with you?"

"No. No, that's not what I meant. He's so smooth. He has Higgy's ear too. If you don't make the changes, they'll get another writer to make them and you won't get credit. That's how it works. You have to have successes under your belt before you can get away with being called difficult."

"I'm beginning to wonder if success is worth having if it means this much compromise. It's not the same movie, Lena."

"No. But it's a movie. With stars. From a studio. With your name on it."

Paul sighed and drank the martini in a single gulp. "I hate this."

"I know. You wrote a great script. Higgy knows that too. It will be your start. Your real start."

He put the glass aside and retrieved his cigarette. He turned to the typewriter. She felt his surrender, which she hadn't been sure of, despite the fact that he'd expected changes. But these changes were so extreme. He was right; it was not the same movie.

Lena wandered to the balcony, the open doors letting in the traffic noise of Sunset Boulevard, the scent of hot summer asphalt and exhaust filtering through the trees, the sound of rapid braking at the bend as a pedestrian no doubt tried to cross the street. Someone in another room was cooking with garlic. She liked this place far better than her own apartment, which too often felt lonely and empty.

She sipped her martini and listened to Paul typing until she felt soothed, and then she went back inside to order sandwiches from Schwab's. The *LA Examiner* was by the telephone, open to the entertainment section, Louella Parsons's column. Lena noted the photo of Elizabeth Taylor at some function, and then, right below it, the picture of Lena herself and Flavio at Ciro's, her kiss on his cheek, her face artfully hidden.

She hadn't known she was in the paper today. She wondered why Paul had said nothing of it, as he'd obviously seen it. He typed away, oblivious, and she picked up the paper to read the article. Her heart sank the moment she read the caption beneath the picture. A Snake in the Grass? Flavio welcomes rival Lena Taylor to birthday party at Ciro's. Apparently Lena's own imagined headline about kissing and making up was too good to be true. She read further, about the stars that had attended, and the black-and-white-checked birthday cake, and whether Flavio's remarks in his speech had truly been meant to forgive his traitorous ex-assistant, or whether he was abiding by the old wisdom "Keep your friends close and your enemies closer."

"Did you read this?" Lena demanded.

Paul paused in his typing. "Read what?"

"Louella Parsons."

"Oh, yeah." He reached for the cigarette smoldering in the ashtray beside him. "Sorry, I forgot to mention it. These changes . . . I suppose Flavio has to marry you or something to prove you don't hate one another."

Lena read aloud: "'More than one Hollywood insider is starting to ask: Can such a talent really spring from nowhere, as Lena Taylor seems to have done? Curious minds want to know!'"

"I'm sure all of Hollywood is wondering," Paul said dryly. He blew out smoke and started typing again.

"Paul—"

"She's just stirring up trouble, sweetheart. But look where it continues on the next page. She mentions us."

"She does?"

"A picture and everything."

Lena's heart stilled. She remembered now. The flash she hadn't expected—God, what had they captured? Warily, she turned the page and stared with horror at the picture, her face full on, smiling, dazed, Paul in profile. Impossible. After all these years, how could this happen?

"She was at least nice about that, don't you think?" Paul asked, and Lena let her gaze drop to the caption. Lux Costume Head says YES! to screenwriter Paul Carbone. More good news for the very LUCKY lady!

Nice, yes, but also insinuating. *Very LUCKY.* But Lena could not focus on that, could not keep from staring at the baldness of her face.

It doesn't matter, she told herself. It had been years. No one was looking. No one cared. Nothing would happen.

She wanted desperately to believe it.

~

On the way to work the next morning, Lena turned off the road and stopped at an out-of-the-way pay phone. She smiled when she heard Harvey's voice.

"Honey! Wait—why are you calling? Only on birthdays, remember? Or did I forget Charlie's?"

"Or good news, you said. Birthdays or good news."

"Or bad news."

"Well this is good news, and I've been meaning to call for days. I'm engaged."

"I saw it! Charlie and I are so happy! Congratulations. When's the wedding?"

Lena sobered. "Well, you know, that's the problem."

Harvey let out a big sigh. "Charlie's at work, but you know what he'd say. You have a birth certificate. You can get a marriage license with it. That's all you need."

She glanced around her empty office and lowered her voice. "If you read the *Examiner* you saw the rest. And the picture . . ."

"Yes, I saw that too."

"I don't know what to do."

"Nothing." He was definitive. "Have you seen any evidence that anyone's looking for you?"

"No."

"Good. You don't want to do anything to raise alarms. Business as usual."

"I never meant to keep secrets from him."

"Everyone keeps secrets. I'm sure he has some of his own," Harvey said. "Don't forget where you two met—and I don't mean that jazz club story you tell people. Any gossip about you will turn on him just as quickly. What do you think your Hollywood Red-hunters would make of us? Or all those Sundays?"

It didn't require an answer.

"Let me talk to Charlie when he gets home. We'll figure out what to do together. We'll be in touch, but let us call you, okay? The phones. Say nothing. Do nothing." Then he hung up.

∼

Her meeting with Runyon and the director, George Gardner—and Paul, who would be there too—was at one o'clock. After her call with Harvey, Lena spent the morning at the studio deciding on swatches for the sketches she'd made last night, doing a fitting for Anna Magnani, and trying to ignore her apprehension over Louella's column and her fear that Paul, who was with the censor and the director now, might lose his composure and get fired before Lena arrived. He'd come to terms with their requests last night, but if Runyon pushed too hard, or made too many more . . . she was relieved when it was finally time to make her way to soundstage six, where they were rebuilding the sets of *The Doom of Medusa* to reflect the changes.

The huge doors of six stood open to allow the set builders access; the lavish nightclub that they'd finished two weeks ago was now being torn apart and revamped as a dark and seedy jazz club.

Runyon was nowhere to be seen. Lena crossed the floor, dodging the scaffolding and tools, light stands and boxes of filters and gels and cords lying about. She headed to the set itself, which no longer looked anything like the original nightclub. It reminded her now of places in Italy, the close, hot clubs with their crooked, rocking tables and the dim sconces on the walls, the stage barely big enough to hold a quartet and the bar in the corner with the spotty illumination behind the bottles of booze. It took her back to Rome in a way that made Lena uncomfortable.

"Miss Taylor!"

She turned to see Michael Runyon and George Gardner sitting at a folding table off set, near a cart that held an urn of coffee and a tray of danishes from the commissary. She walked over to see a typewriter at one end, pencils and script pages scattered everywhere, and a pressed-tin Lux ashtray brimming with cigarette butts.

"Working hard?" she asked. "Where's Paul?"

"He went to the commissary for sandwiches," Gardner said. He was a tall man—six three at least—and stick thin. He walked with a habitual stoop, as if he'd been used to hiding his height as a kid. He was as dark as Paul, with that same thick hair, and a five-o'clock shadow that began at noon. A more competent director one could not find, but he wasn't much of an artist. She'd always liked George Gardner, however; he made quick decisions, and he'd never made a pass at her, which could not be said of many of the directors she'd worked with.

Runyon looked up from the pages he was reading. "I had no idea you knew the writer so well, Miss Taylor. I understand congratulations are in order."

"Thank you. I assure you we're both very professional, Mr. Runyon."

"I don't doubt it."

"Sit down, Lena. Can I get you some coffee?" George rose at her nod.

She took a seat and took the portfolio with her sketches, swatches attached, from her bag. "These are just for Ruby's character, Helen, and for the first couple of scenes. I'd like to get the seamstresses going. I haven't seen the changes for the other characters yet, so—" She paused at the look that Runyon and George exchanged as the director came back to the table and set her coffee before her. "What is it?"

"Paul's a brilliant writer, which I'm sure you know," George said. "I do."

"But maybe he doesn't grasp what we're trying to do here," Runyon filled in. "Since you have a . . . connection, we were hoping you could help . . . well, steer him, so to speak."

"What is he objecting to?"

Michael Runyon sighed. "Let me ask you a question: a woman inherits her uncle's failing café and turns it into a successful nightclub, despite overwhelming debt and the mob's constant threat to take it over. To do this, she hires brilliant women who work as a team to make the club the most sought-after place to be in Hollywood. What's wrong with this picture?"

"Nothing."

"Do you remember our conversation the other day? About sharing American ideals overseas?"

"Oh yes. Very well."

"No one doubts the great capabilities of women, but this? Where in this film are the family values? Women raising strong, happy children? Where are the self-made men?"

Lena looked over at George, who studiously poured sugar into his coffee and avoided her gaze. She looked back at Runyon. "Which one of those things did Paul object to adding?"

Runyon looked confused. "Do you know any women who want to run businesses instead of being wives and mothers?"

"Well, um—yes, actually."

"Are they happy? Fulfilled?"

"I have a career myself, Mr. Runyon—"

"And you're engaged to be married," he pointed out. "A fine thing. A wonderful thing. It's the American way. Happy families. Women helping their husbands raise strong citizens to create a strong economy. Women on their own, relying on each other, well . . . that's not the right message. It's vaguely . . . one could almost say it's morally decadent, don't you think?"

Michael Runyon smiled throughout his entire speech, a perfectly charming, sincere smile that sent such creeping irritation and unease through Lena that she didn't trust herself to answer. She turned to George and pushed her sketches across the table to him. "Are you still planning to shoot the opening of the jazz club first?"

He looked surprised to be addressed, but then he nodded. "Next week, if everything is ready."

"Here are the sketches for Helen and Roger and Simone." Lena spread the pages before him. "As you can see, I've changed the fabrics. Now Helen's in deep blue. The dark gray suit is from Richard Widmark's own wardrobe, but it will work for his character of Roger here and it saves us having to make one, and Simone's gown—"

"Roger needs a white tuxedo," Runyon said.

Lena looked over at him. "What?"

"White. To show he's our hero."

"But . . . a tuxedo's a bit much for the Medusa, and white especially. The gowns are not that formal."

"That's fine," Michael Runyon said. "A white tux gives Roger gravitas and power. It shows that the women are his helpmates, not his superiors."

Lena struggled to speak evenly. "Even with the changes, isn't this supposed to be a night of triumph for Helen? This is her idea."

The smile, that perpetual smile, died abruptly. "Do you share your fiancé's propensities, Miss Taylor?"

"I—I'm not sure what that means."

Runyon tapped his pencil on the table. "I need to know everyone on this production is working together. How can I trust the costumer if I know she and the writer are a couple, and the writer is fighting my every suggestion? Hmmm? You see my dilemma, Miss Taylor?"

"Yes," she said quietly. "I see. A white tux it is. And I'll speak to Paul."

"Thank you." Michael Runyon laid the pencil down and turned to George. "What would we men do without women, Gardner? They truly are the great civilizers."

~

Lena got the approval on the sketches for the first scene to be shot and left before Paul returned, unable to bear the thought of watching Runyon go after him. When she got to the costume department, she handed the sketch pad to Connie and said, "Let's get started on these."

Then she went into her office and collapsed into the chair. She breathed deep and shut her eyes and tried to think of how best to explain to Paul what had just happened with Runyon.

The knock on her door made her start and sit upright. Shirley came in, all bustling efficiency. "Should I have Paul pick you up at five for the Hearst gala?"

Lena stared at her blankly.

"The Cocoanut Grove?" Shirley reminded her. "Tonight? Don't tell me you've forgotten. The Louella Parsons thing?"

Lena *had* forgotten. It was Louella Parsons's thirtieth anniversary as a columnist for the *Examiner*, and Hearst was throwing a party. "Oh God. Call Louella and send my regrets. Tell her I'm . . . I'm ill."

"You can't not go. It's Louella Parsons! You don't dare sit this one out. You'll be in her column."

"I've already been in her column. That's half the reason I'm not going. Anyway, everyone will be there. She won't notice I'm not."

"It's because you've been in her column that she'll notice. It will just give her more to say if you don't show up. And your dress—that beautiful dress . . ."

The look on Shirley's face was one of both horror and disbelief, and Lena sighed, knowing that her secretary was right. Louella would notice, *and* she would assume that Lena wasn't there because of the column, and it would signal that Louella was right to be suspicious of Lena's past. The woman noticed everything. Shirley was right, too, that it would give Louella a reason to say something else nasty. It was the last thing Lena needed.

"Okay. Fine. Five then. You know best."

Shirley nodded, looking relieved as she left Lena's office.

Lena rubbed her temples and turned her attention to the mail on her desk. There was an invitation to a benefit for stage and screen animals and one to Sheila Flavio's luncheon to raise money for the retired movie actors' home next week, and a handwritten envelope. *LENA TAYLOR, COSTUMER TO THE STARS—*

Lena frowned. It had no return address. The postmark was from the post office down the street. She wondered how this one had escaped Shirley, who rarely let such junk mail get by her. Lena slit open the envelope. Inside she found a single piece of paper. Written upon it, in pencil, was only a phone number: *CR-18131 r116.*

She stared at it, puzzled, and turned it over. Nothing indicated where it had come from, or from whom.

"Lena?" Shirley's voice came over the intercom. "Estelle needs you down in the sewing room right away."

Lena tucked the note back into the envelope and shoved it into her desk drawer, already forgetting it in the rush to get to the day's next emergency.

CHAPTER 22

The gown waited for her in one of the studio dressing rooms, and it was beautiful, as Shirley had said. Lena had designed it originally in tangerine and had loved it in that color, but of course she couldn't wear something so ostentatious. She'd had it made in gray draped silk, gathered to cling about her hips and waist and breasts, a very Grecian style. Narrow panels fell over her shoulders and down her back in two narrow trains. Black and silver flowers and vines embroidered beneath and between the breasts, at the hips and the shoulders, and then again at the hem accented her curves. Such a crime that she couldn't use the tangerine fabric, but there would be a hundred stars there. She had worked so hard for this, she could not throw it away by outshining even a single one of them.

You shine.

Funny, now why had she thought of that?

She put her hair in an uncomplicated updo, did her makeup simply, but with her favorite red lips, pulled on elegant white gloves that reached above her elbows, and shoved her engagement ring over the thin satin. She didn't want to hide it away, not tonight, when it was so important to remind herself—and Paul—that they were together in this.

"You look gorgeous," Paul said when he arrived. He kissed her, but in the middle of the kiss she felt his hesitation.

"Long day?" she asked when she pulled away. She didn't really have to ask, it was written on his face, in the circles beneath his eyes.

He gave her a weary look.

"Runyon's changes," she said, grabbing the purse that matched her dress, gray with black-and-silver trim. She tried to be easy and calm as they went to his car.

"He wants me to destroy my story."

"I know."

"I want to buy it back, Lena."

She nodded. "Okay. So you're ready to start all over again?"

He looked startled by that, and a little defenseless. "I guess."

"Then we will."

"We? I'm talking about *me*. You don't have to get involved in this."

She took his hand to ease herself into the car and waited until he shut the door and got in on the other side. "Runyon threatened my job today." She didn't want to say it, but she already kept too many secrets from him.

"Because of me?"

She really did not want to say this. "We're engaged, and he's . . . doubting . . . I can be loyal to the project over you."

"He can't fire you. You're the head costumer."

"He can try."

"Braxton won't—"

"Oh, Paul." She sighed. "Higgy's a pragmatist. If I cause too much trouble, I'll be out as quickly as he threw out Flavio. More quickly, because I'm a woman, and I'm engaged, and he'll just assume you can take care of me."

Paul started the car and pulled from the studio lot, quiet for a long moment, long enough that it made her uneasy. Then he said, "Well, I can, you know."

"I—I'm not sure what you're saying."

"Just that . . . if they let you go . . ." He cleared his throat. "I can take care of you."

"Paul, I . . . I love my job."

"I know you do."

"I've worked so hard—"

"I know. I know."

"I don't know who I'd be—"

He grabbed her hand and squeezed it hard, pinching the engagement ring between her fingers and the satin of the glove so it almost hurt. "Forget I said it."

She tried to forget it, but she could not. The words lingered between them, the possibility he'd raised so easily—as if it *was* a possibility when the very thought of it sent a little worm of panic twisting within her—and she stared out the window at the passing neon lights and the palm trees reaching to a sky turning purple with evening and wished she'd feigned illness tonight.

He seemed as lost in thought as she, and they said little more before they reached the vast entrance gate of the Ambassador Hotel, with its name tower to the left and the palm trees and hedges and the beige expanse of the hotel stretching beyond. They went down the drive to the huge white glowing saucer of the circular entry, where valets stood at the red carpet laid over the red, green, and beige patterned tile. The elegant square clock beneath the elegant script of *The Ambassador Hotel*, everything so luxurious and beautiful that, as always, Lena could not quite believe that she was here.

Their car was right behind Joan Crawford's in a line that stretched as far as Lena could see down the drive ahead. She'd known that anyone who was anyone—though probably not Hedda Hopper, as she and Louella were currently enemies—would be here tonight.

The valet opened her door. Paul held out his arm for her. Camera flashes blinded, but they were for Joan and her party ahead. Lena gripped Paul's arm tightly and dipped her head as they went into the grand lobby with its huge Italian fireplace and crystal chandeliers. Those who lived in the Ambassador were fond of saying that the hotel was so vast, with so many amenities, that you could live your entire life there without ever once having to set foot off the grounds, and it was true that it had that feel of inexhaustibility, as if whatever you were looking for, whatever fantasy you wished, could be provided, if you only asked.

A maître d' and waiters led them down wide, elegant stairs. The Moroccan-style doors with the **COCOANUT GROVE** sign above were already opened to reveal the ballroom, where white-clothed tables and chairs of bamboo and wicker crowded full-size fake palm trees, and fronds brushed the embellished Moroccan arches and pillars. Papier-mâché monkeys with electrified eyes swung from the branches. The sounds of a waterfall came from the southern wall, above which a painted moon held pride of place. The blue ceiling glowed with scattered stars.

The ballroom was as crowded with people as with palm trees, and waiters scurried about with trays of drinks. Jewels glittered; silk and satin, georgette and chiffon rustled softly. The stage was draped with swaths of purple satin, the dais strewn with garlands to honor Louella Parsons. The word *excess* could not have found a better expression than in the Cocoanut Grove that night. It was also beautiful. If her parents could see her now . . . well, they would not approve of such excess. That thought led her rather guiltily to the bohemians at Larry's, with all their talk about the simple life, but then again, they'd never experienced anything like this, had they? When the waiter offered champagne, Lena drank it eagerly. She and Paul found their place settings, next to a producer and his wife, another screenwriter, and a press agent and his date, which made Lena more restless than she already was.

"I'm going to the ladies' room," she told Paul. He nodded, and she made her way through the crowd, smiling here at Debbie Reynolds and Robert Wagner, there at Elizabeth Taylor, who was surrounded by a crowd of mostly men.

Barbara Sweetin, resplendent in brick red chiffon, with rubies at her throat and dangling from her ears, laughed at something Robert Mitchum said and put out a hand to stop Lena as she passed. "Here she is, the most brilliant costume designer in Hollywood!" Barbara leaned to hug Lena, half spilling her champagne.

"Hello, Miss Taylor." Robert Mitchum smiled. He was more handsome in person. He took a sip of his martini as he scanned the crowd. "I guess we're all either trying for forgiveness or favor. No other way to explain why everyone managed to get roped into this tonight."

"If anyone could have managed to avoid it, I'd think it would be you, after your *Confidential* suit."

"Which I lost," he noted.

"On a technicality," Barbara said. "You put the fear of God into them, Bob."

"I'm not sure about that. It would be nice to think it, though."

Lena said, "At least we know Hedda's not here tonight."

"We could spot her by her outrageous hat if she were." Barbara laughed into her glass.

"That woman won't rest until she's got every communist in Hollywood," Mitchum said.

"I don't suppose you're scared of *that*, are you, Bob?" Barbara teased.

He laughed and glanced idly at the ring on Lena's finger. "Who's the lucky man?"

"Paul Carbone. He's a screenwriter."

Bob Mitchum looked as if he were searching his memory. "Hmmm. Don't know him."

"He's got a film at Lux. *Club Med*—no . . . *The Doom of Medusa*, I guess it's called now. It's really a wonderful movie. Or it was." Lena could not help saying the last bit.

Barbara sighed. "Censors got to it, have they? They've practically *ruined Twilight Fever*. I don't like the man they've assigned to it at all. He keeps telling me not to touch my hair. He says it's too provocative."

Mitchum grinned. "You are provocative by nature, Bunny."

"If they didn't want me to be, they wouldn't have hired me. I keep telling him that."

225

"There are a couple of them here tonight," Mitchum said, nodding toward the stage. "You can tell by the suits. Like I said, all of Hollywood turned out."

Lena followed his gaze, and yes, he was right. There by the stage stood three men in those blocky Brooks Brothers suits instead of the formal dress that most of the others wore tonight. One of them was Michael Runyon.

"Why are they here?" Just as Lena said it, Runyon's gaze turned to her. Like a spotlight, it was direct and piercing. She did not like the way he looked at her.

She turned away quickly and wished she hadn't left her champagne at the table with Paul.

"Have a good time tonight," she said to Barbara and Bob Mitchum, and then she tried to melt into the crowd and make her way to the ladies' room. She imagined she felt Michael Runyon's gaze on her even then, though there was no way he could follow her through these masses. She glanced over her shoulder to make sure of it, and saw the flash of another suit behind her. It raised a tiny, familiar panic. Following her?

No, of course not. She was overreacting.

She hurried to the ladies' room. She used the toilet and fumbled with her garters and inadvertently put a ladder in her stocking, cursed beneath her breath—at least the gown was long and no one would see it. Then she leaned against the sink and lit a cigarette, breathing in the smoke until her nerves calmed. By now Paul would definitely be wondering what had happened to her.

She gazed at the ring, that sparkling stone, so clean, so clear, so unlike anything she'd ever worn, a dream of a stone. She put out the cigarette and smoothed the satin of the glove, turned the band of the ring to settle it better into place. There. Perfect. Then she went out the door.

And there stood Walter Maynard, waiting for her.

CHAPTER 23

The shock of seeing him rendered her mute. He looked the same—a little older, a little more worn, but the same, with his pomaded dark hair and those hooded dark eyes. He was dressed better, in a white tuxedo (perfect for *Medusa*, she couldn't help thinking), but now she saw what she hadn't seen before in Walter: a seediness, a whine that curled through him like a warning, and she couldn't believe she had gone to bed with this man. Multiple times. Or that she had married him.

Good God, what was he doing here?

"Hello, Elsie," he said with a grin. "Or wait, I guess it's Lena now, isn't it? Good name. It becomes you."

The note abruptly made sense, the mocking *COSTUMER TO THE STARS*—how like Walter's petty little jealousies. "It was you."

"Imagine my surprise to see you in Louella Parsons's column! I mean, we talked about it all the time, but it was supposed to be me. You were supposed to be on my arm, remember?"

"What do you want, Walter?"

"Don't be that way, baby. I've come all this way to see you."

She wanted to turn away, to walk away. But if she did, he'd surely make trouble, exactly what she'd been afraid of when it came to Walter. The door to her past, the man who could ruin everything. "Just tell me what you want."

He shrugged. "A new name, a new life . . . I thought maybe you might want to see your husband, you know? The man who took you away from the pig farm and brought you here? The one who saved your life? That's what you said, anyway. I remember it. All those times in bed, you said—"

"I've got to get back." She felt hot and sick, and it got worse when he leaned close, and she smelled his aftershave, the same he'd always worn.

"Meet me at that tavern by your apartment tomorrow night. Eight o'clock."

It turned her stomach that he knew her address. She hoped against hope that he was bluffing. "Which tavern?"

"The Lucky 8."

Yes, he knew it.

"Miss Taylor, are you all right?"

The voice came from down the hallway. Both she and Walter started at the sound, though she was relieved to hear it, even when she realized it came from Michael Runyon.

She tried to smile. "Yes, thank you, Mr. Runyon. Mr. Maynard was just leaving."

"I was," Walter said. "Good to see you again, Miss Taylor."

He threw her another grin and sauntered off. The hem of his tuxedo coat was frayed at the back. The detail disconcerted her; it meant Walter was more desperate than he'd looked, and a desperate Walter was not good. But she had no time to think about it, because Michael Runyon stood looking at her with that too-intense stare, as if he saw something in her that disturbed him.

"I hope I didn't interrupt something," Runyon said.

"Of course not." She started to leave.

"A quick word, if you don't mind."

She stopped and turned back. The last thing she wanted was to talk to Michael Runyon. Walter had rattled her. "About?"

"I wondered . . . perhaps you know where Carbone was during the war?"

In the ballroom, the band started up. "He was in the army, with the troops who helped to liberate Rome. Why?"

Runyon's gaze shifted. "Ah."

"'Ah' what, Mr. Runyon?"

"Sometimes soldiers return with certain . . . attitudes. About war. About America."

"That's not Paul," she said, but she understood Runyon's implicit threat, and her tension over Walter shifted to a different kind of tension. She wondered what Runyon knew about Paul's past, and then her suspicions grew when the censor asked, "Where did you two meet?"

She had the feeling he'd asked Paul the same question, that he was comparing their answers. But she and Paul always told the same story. It was a joke between them, a protective one. "At a jazz club. I really have to get back to him."

Runyon's smile was the most insincere she'd ever seen. "Of course. Enjoy the party."

Lena gathered herself as she made her way back to the table and Paul. She barely heard the music, all she could think about was the danger threatening on all sides, Walter appearing out of the blue, Runyon's question that was not a question but a warning. Everything closing in, a meeting tomorrow night at the Lucky 8.

Paul stood to help her to her chair. He leaned close to whisper, "I was getting worried."

"I got caught in too many conversations," she whispered back.

She tried to concentrate on the evening, but it was too difficult. She drank champagne, she picked at the dinner. When Louella received her golden plaque honoring her thirtieth anniversary, Lena turned to Paul and said, "Do you think we could go?"

"You should at least say hello to Louella, shouldn't you?" he asked. "At least so she knows you were here."

He was right, of course. Lena nodded, and when the music started up again, she let him take her through the crowd to congratulate

Louella, who stood near the stage taking her laurels like the blue ribbon winner of a county fair baking contest. Her sharp eyes raked Paul, Lena's gorgeous gown in a drab gray, and of course, the ring on Lena's finger.

"I guess I should offer congrats of my own," Louella said. "Quite a match, the up-and-coming screenwriter and the costume queen. You must be grateful, Mr. Carbone, to have such an influential fiancée. I imagine she was crucial in getting you read at Lux."

Lena smiled thinly. "They bought his screenplay before we were engaged. I had nothing to do with it. It's a brilliant story."

Louella ignored her and said to Paul, "You're a lucky man. She has a way of getting what she wants."

The gossip maven turned to greet someone else, leaving Lena wordless for a moment, the insult—was it an insult?—resting uncomfortably on what had already been an unsettling night. Then she was angry, and the anger played on her fears, and she turned back to say something.

"Don't," Paul cautioned in a low voice, leading her away. "It won't help. Come on, I'll take you home," he said.

"I can't go home," she said quietly. "We have to talk."

Paul closed his eyes briefly. "Not tonight, Lena—"

"I spoke to Michael Runyon. He was here."

"This can wait. I'm exhausted."

"It can't wait."

They were as silent on the way back to the Chateau as they'd been on the way to the gala.

When they got to Paul's rooms, she put Thelonious Monk on the record player and poured them both a martini while he changed out of his suit and into shorts and a shirt. She traded the gown for one of his shirts. She sat on the pink sofa and sipped the martini and watched as he lit a cigarette and sat across from her—he was as tense as she was; his motions were tight and clipped.

"Runyon asked me what kind of man you were when you came back from the war," she said shortly. "He said soldiers sometimes return with certain 'attitudes.' Then he asked where we met."

Paul's face shuttered. He took a long, slow drag of the cigarette. "Did you tell him?"

"I said the usual. A jazz club. What did you tell him?"

Paul looked troubled now. "He's never asked. Why is he asking you?"

"I don't know. I think . . . it's a threat. I don't know what he knows or what he thinks he knows, but he told me before that your original screenplay was morally decadent."

Paul said quietly, "So he thinks I'm a socialist now."

"This changes things," Lena said. "Higgy is a member of the MPA, Paul. He made training films for the army." She watched as Paul rose and paced to the balcony doors. "Runyon will go to him, if he hasn't already. You can't quit without admitting you're not on board with the changes, and to them that means you're un-American."

Paul had his back to her. Now he turned to look at her, and she saw in that look everything he'd said to her before the gala. "And they'll fire you along with me. They'll say the same things about you."

She didn't look away. "Yes." She sighed. "There will be other movies. But not if you're marked as trouble, Paul."

Lena rose from the sofa. The dissonant harmonies of Monk's "'Round Midnight" surrounded them, smoky, jagged. She put her arms around Paul and pressed her mouth to his chest, at the opening of his shirt. "I love you."

He sighed in defeat and put his hands to her waist and kissed her. He tasted of gin and tobacco. He brushed back her loosened hair. "I love you too."

And unexpectedly she remembered Walter standing in the hallway of the Cocoanut Grove. Walter with that grin, with trouble weighting his every word. She should tell Paul about him now. But this moment . . . she wanted to keep this moment, and she recalled

Harvey's words this morning and she was afraid. There were so many wrong ways to go, so much to lose, and she could not lose this, she could not lose Paul. So she said nothing once again. She would work it out tomorrow. She would fix everything with Walter. It would be all right. It had to be.

CHAPTER 24

Ruby Dennison twisted to admire the way the deep blue silk skimmed her shoulders. At her movement, her chihuahua, perched on the arm of the love seat, barked sharply.

"Quiet, Kit! Oh, it's perfect, Lena. Just perfect. It makes me feel so confident. Kit, I said be quiet!—Connie, can you hand me that spray bottle?" Ruby brandished the bottle of water and the little beast went silent, still quivering with tension and suppressed rage. "How's that, you little monster, you don't like that, do you?" Ruby pulled at the neckline of the dress. "Can we go just a bit lower?"

Lena pretended to consider. "Hmmm . . . Ruby, you really do have the most beautiful collarbones—doesn't she, Connie? I hate to ruin how well this neckline accents them."

"Gorgeous," Connie said, eyeing the dog.

Ruby turned to study herself better in the mirror, then traced her collarbone with a graceful finger. "I suppose that's true. They are nice. I remember I caught Tony Curtis looking at them once." Kit made a tiny yip. Ruby spun on her heel with the spray bottle. The dog stepped back. "Well, I guess the neckline is fine. But I really need to catch Sammy's eye in the first scene."

Lena scowled, distracted as she bent to adjust the hem. "Sammy who?"

"Sammy the Ox. The Mafia guy? I'm supposed to seduce him later but I haven't seen the scene yet."

Lena sighed. Another revision she knew nothing about.

Ruby jiggled a little. Kit could no longer contain his outrage. He yapped like an insane thing, which he was.

Lena said, "Connie—"

"He likes to be held," Ruby offered.

Connie picked up the dog, who, while little, was rotund. He must have weighed twenty pounds. Kit struggled in her arms, but at least he was quiet.

Lena fixed the hem and sat back on her heels.

"I think it should be a bit higher." Ruby tugged on the skirt. "Just a tad."

"This is an evening gown, Ruby."

"Oh. Well." Ruby exhaled. "I suppose. But I think my legs are my best feature."

Connie yelped. "He bit me!"

"I'm sorry, Connie. He's in a temper today—you bad dog! Put him down. Could you please get the danish from my purse, Connie?" Ruby jerked away from Lena and bent to the dog, covering his little face and snout with kisses, letting him lick her bright red lips.

Ruby took the paper-wrapped danish from Connie and tore a piece off for the dog, who gobbled it as if he'd been starving to death.

"Be careful," Lena warned Ruby. "The butter will stain the—"

The door creaked open, and Shirley poked her head in. "Changes, Lena." She held out a piece of paper and made a sympathetic face. "From Mr. Runyon."

Lena took the paper and read the first lines. *Club Medusa opening scene changes: Helen's gown is now RED. She is triumphant and scandalous in scarlet.*

Lena threw back her head in exasperation. She looked at Ruby feeding that ridiculous dog a pastry, the deep blue gown they'd rushed to get ready for the first shot. "He must be joking."

"What is it?" Connie took the note from her and skimmed it. "This is impossible."

"I told him Helen should be triumphant," Lena said. "But I didn't count on scandalous. What the hell are they doing?"

"Scarlet," Connie murmured. "We still have that brown silk we used for *The Scarlet Bride*."

That particular shade of brown looked like bright red when filmed in black and white—unlike red itself, which didn't read well. Lena took a deep breath. "Let's get it cut, but . . ." She looked at Ruby in the dress. Lena was in a bad mood today, and if Michael Runyon wanted scandalous, scandalous was what he would get. "Ruby, would you stand for a minute?"

When Ruby did, Lena handed Kit to Connie and took a piece of tailor's chalk from the table. She slashed a line across the gown from one shoulder to beneath Ruby's arm, turning it into a single-shoulder dress. To Connie she said, "I want a bit of a flair here too—not a bow, but two panels that cascade over her shoulder. Short ones. They shouldn't go past her elbow. And ask Marge to take it in an eighth of an inch."

Ruby *eek*ed. "God, Lena! I won't be able to move!"

"He wants you scandalous," Lena said grimly. "And if you're going to seduce a mob thug, then you want it tight. But you'd better stop sharing danishes with your dog for a week or so."

~

After the fitting Lena went back to her office, feeling worn out, frustrated, and angry. The meeting tonight with Walter clouded her day like a fog; she couldn't get past her tension and rage to think of much else, and it didn't help that she was supposed to comply gracefully with Michael Runyon's changes on *Medusa*, especially since Paul had reluctantly agreed to stay on the film.

The others in the costume department had gone home by the time she'd finished reading the script and making notes for the next movie in her queue, *Moon Crazy*, and done some preliminary sketches for *Promise Me Tomorrow*, which was Higgy's attempt to cash in on the success of *From Here to Eternity* with half the budget.

She glanced at the clock. Nearly time to meet Walter. She left the studio and drove back to her apartment, and the neon sign of the Lucky

8 flashed at her from down the block like a warning light. She parked her car where she normally did, but didn't bother to go to her apartment first, knowing she looked tired and not her best. She didn't care. Walter was no longer someone she wanted to impress. She just wanted to find out how to get him out of her life as quickly as possible, and keep him far away from gossip columnists and especially Paul.

The bar was small and stank of beer and stale cigarette smoke and had the feel of a habitual stomping ground for retired men of the neighborhood. When she walked in, they all swiveled on their barstools and squinted through the cigarette smoke at the neon light shining through the open door. If they were surprised to see a woman, they didn't show it, but it was also obvious that women rarely came in this place. She cursed Walter for suggesting it and cursed herself for agreeing, because it was unlikely that anyone would forget seeing her here if someone asked, and she should have at least worn a hat and sunglasses to disguise herself.

But it wasn't likely these men had any connection to Louella or Hedda Hopper, nor did they likely care about the latest Hollywood gossip.

Walter was there already, settled in a red leather booth. At least he'd been smart enough to choose a table in the back. She slid in across from him. She thought he looked nervous. He was smoking. There were two beers on the table. "I wasn't sure you'd come."

"I was pretty sure you'd show up at my apartment door if I didn't."

"You know me so well, baby." He pushed one of the beers toward her. "I bought you a beer."

She reached into her purse for a cigarette and lit it. "I don't have time for a beer, Walter. Tell me what you want from me and let's be done with it."

"You're so cold now. What happened to my hot little farm girl?"

Lena exhaled into his face.

"Don't you care where I've been the last six years?"

She shrugged. "I guess you want me to know."

"I was in New York for a while. I did a couple of off-Broadway productions. A touring show or two."

The clock on the wall was half an hour fast, no doubt for last call purposes. "So what are you doing back in LA?"

"Well, now, that's why I wanted to talk to you. I was in Las Vegas— it's a booming city, Else, I think you'd like it—"

"My name is Lena."

"Okay, *Lena*. Whatever you want. Anyway, I was at a show there. Some Negro guy, Sammy something. Pretty good, you know? I was in the bar when he was there, and he left behind an *Examiner*, and I open it up and there you are! At first I don't recognize you. I think, who's that gorgeous thing, and then: she looks familiar, and then, bang! Why, that's Elsie! The love of my life! My long-lost wife who ran off and disappeared and I *looked*, baby. I looked everywhere for you for weeks. Where'd you go?"

She regarded him stonily. "Aliens took me."

Walter turned petulant, never his best look. "You left me with nothing."

"So you saw me in the *Examiner*."

"With some other guy."

Paul, of course. Lena tried to ignore a cold shiver. She wondered if Walter had read the caption.

"My wife, with a different name, in a Flavio dress, with some other guy." Walter shook his head as if the whole thing was too much to take in.

"It was my own dress, not Flavio's," she couldn't help saying.

"You looked good," he snapped, obviously annoyed. "So I thought, my wife's made a success of herself in Hollywood, in the movies, so why not come see her and see if she can't throw a little of that success my way?"

"I've moved on, Walter. I guess maybe you have too. Why don't we just get a divorce and be done with each other?" She was smoking too quickly. She smashed the butt in the ashtray and lit another.

"What? Walk away from my baby? I can't go into a pool hall without expecting to see you there looking like a goddess in that orange dress. Don't tell me you don't still think about me the way I think about you."

She debated whether to tell him about Paul, and decided not to. It would only give him more to work with, and besides, she had forgotten to take off her engagement ring. If he didn't notice it, he was blind, but she didn't want to broadcast it if he somehow missed it. "I don't. I honestly don't. I'm sorry. It was a long time ago. I'm thankful for what you did for me, but—"

"Thankful." He seized on the word. "You see, that's what I was hoping for. Thanks. I'd like a little thanks, baby. In a tangible way."

They'd got to it at last. Lena took a deep drag on the cigarette to calm her now racing nerves. "How much money do you want?"

"Money? No, what I want is nothing too hard for you, I'm sure. A leading role in something at your studio. I'm sure you've got something. A Western, maybe? I'd do one of those. I think I'd make a great cowboy. Or maybe in a musical. You know I can sing and dance."

She had a vague memory of him practicing tap to a song on the record player.

"Walter, I'm not a casting director."

He leaned over the table. "But you know people, baby. You can get me through the door. And I have a script too. You can get it read."

"You're a screenwriter now?"

"In fact, maybe you can have your fiancé read it."

So he already knew about Paul. Very bad. "No. Absolutely not." She said it so loudly the bartender asked, "Hey, everything okay over there?"

She turned with a quick smile. "Fine, just fine," she reassured him. She turned back to Walter, and in a quieter voice repeated firmly, "No."

Walter had always known when he'd pushed too far. "Then Marlon Brando," he insisted. "I want you to set up a meeting with Marlon Brando for me. It's got the perfect part for him. Once he reads it, I know he'll want to do it."

"Marlon Brando?" She stared at him in disbelief. "I've only met him in passing."

"Then get me into a party where he'll be. You get invited to these things all the time, don't you? Get me on the list."

"Walter, I can't do any of these things—"

"I see." He nodded soberly. He drank his beer, and set it down again, licking the foam from his upper lip. "I guess Louella Parsons has been asking around about you. Wondering where you come from. How you just 'sprang up' in LA. Hedda Hopper too."

Lena said nothing.

"Talk is that Hedda's offering money for answers. I guess either one of them'd be happy to hear from someone who knew you when. Before you got to LA. Wouldn't you think? Someone who maybe brought you here. When you were someone else. Maybe your screenwriter would be interested to read that his fiancée is already married. He might even want to talk to me about it. What do you think?"

Her fingers tightened on the cigarette. "A part in a movie, you said?"

"A good part. Not some extra. And a meeting with Brando."

"I don't know if I can do that."

"Well, you'll try, won't you?" Walter smiled. "You've always been good at getting what you want, haven't you, *Lena*? I guess you'll find a way to manage."

The echo of Louella Parsons's similar words the night before enraged her in a way nothing else he'd said had done. She took a deep breath. "If I do this, then that's it. Nothing else. I get you a job. I get you at the same function as Brando. Then you give me a divorce and you forget you know me and you're on your own."

"Of course," he said smugly. "I'm a man of my word. You know that."

She didn't know that. She honestly could not remember anything she'd trusted Walter to do, or any promise she'd trusted him to keep, and she had the sinking feeling that this was only the beginning, that now that Walter was in her life again, he would stay there. But what choice did she have? None. She had none. She looked into his satisfied eyes and hated him in that moment so sincerely she wouldn't have felt anything but happiness if he'd fallen dead to the floor, but mere wishing did not make things happen.

"Fine," she said, sliding from the booth. "I'll do what I can. But don't contact me in the meantime, do you understand? No notes, no phone calls. Tell me how to contact you, and I will when I've got something."

He smiled and took a card from his pocket. "I've got a service. You can call that. But I'll need to hear something in a week. And in the meantime, I guess I do need some money—would you mind fronting me a little cash? I'm a bit tapped out."

She opened her purse and took out all the cash she had. She threw it on the table with such force the bills scattered, which made her feel good until she turned on her heel and realized that the men at the bar were watching. She ignored them and left. When she stepped out in the still-warm night, her temples began to pound.

Walter followed her out, the bills crumpled in his hand. "Come on, baby, don't leave mad. Give me a kiss for old times' sake."

She turned to face him, and he stepped toward her, more quickly than she expected, a lunge really. She turned her face at the last minute, so the kiss landed on her cheek instead of her mouth.

She recoiled. "Don't touch me again. Never touch me."

Walter laughed. He held up his hands, still laughing, and then ambled away, and Lena stared after him, so furious that it took a moment to realize she was clenching her fists. She watched until he disappeared around the corner.

She wanted a drink. She wanted Paul. But instead she went to her apartment, wondering what made people say things about her like *she's good at getting what she wants*, and why that wasn't a badge of honor.

The hallway light was dimmer than usual. Lena made a mental note to tell the apartment management about it as she slid her key into the lock. Her hand trembled—damn Walter, anyway—and the key would not go, not right. She had to jam it in, and it wasn't until she tried it twice that she realized the lock was broken.

Her apartment door was already unlocked.

Lena hesitated. She nudged the door with her foot; it creaked eerily open. She heard no sound from inside, none at all, and she pushed the door again, fear tightening her muscles as it swung to reveal the narrow foyer, the little entry table, its small drawer and the notepad and pencil she kept inside tossed onto the floor. The mirror above hung crookedly, as if it had been bumped. In it, she saw herself reflected, eyes wide, pale faced, frightened. Yes, she was frightened. This wasn't how she'd left things; the sense of being invaded overwhelmed her so that for a moment she could only stand there.

"Hello?" she tried quietly. Her voice echoed back. She palmed her keys, shoved them between her fingers as a weapon—it was the only thing she had. There was no one there; she knew it, she could feel it. Such a profound sense of emptiness, more so than usual, but as she rounded the corner of the hallway and took in the living room, Lena gasped so loudly it filled the empty spaces.

Her apartment had been ransacked. Her sketchbooks had been thrown to the floor, and some of them had been torn apart. Her books and magazines were strewn everywhere. The drawers in the coffee table had been emptied of coasters and colored pencils. But worse . . . worse were her records. Every one of them was pulled out of its sleeve. Some had been broken. They looked as if someone had hurled them across the room. Her whole collection . . . Coleman Hawkins, Charles Mingus, Charlie Parker, Miles Davis's *Birth of the Cool* . . .

Lena dropped her purse and knelt on the floor, pulling them together, gathering them, trying to comprehend what had happened. Some of the sleeves had been torn apart. Thelonious Monk's *Genius of Modern Music* was shattered. Dizzy Gillespie was in pieces where it had been thrown against the wall.

What had happened here?

She abandoned the records. Her bedroom was in ruins. Every drawer of her dresser opened, clothing flung about as if by a tornado. Her closet, her shoes . . . the bathroom was no better. She shook as she made her way to the phone, but when she lifted the receiver, there was no dial tone.

Suddenly she couldn't breathe. She stumbled to the window and opened it, leaning into the dust-filled Los Angeles night, but it didn't help. She couldn't stay here. She gathered toiletries, and clothes for tomorrow, and then, half-blind with fear and shock, she hurried from her apartment and out to her car. The street was as empty as LA side streets were at night; she felt as if she might be the only person in the world as she fumbled with her car door, which became strangely recalcitrant thanks to her trembling fingers. She tossed her bag inside, crawled in, and pushed down the lock with such force it bruised her palm.

Then where . . . How to explain what she couldn't explain herself? The whole night. Walter . . . then this . . . she tried to put it all together, but she could see no reason for Walter to have done this, not when she'd met with him, not when she'd given him what he wanted, and she didn't want to think beyond that, could not think beyond that. The police . . . she had to call the police . . . but . . .

So many secrets. She was afraid to call. She was afraid of what the police would discover. There was so much she was hiding. She needed Harvey and Charlie, and Paul . . .

But she couldn't go to Paul tonight, not as shaken as she was. He would demand answers, and she had none that she could give him, not yet. Not until Walter was gone. Not until she was thinking more clearly.

She would go to the studio. She'd be safe there. No one could get past the gate. No one could get to her there. The studio.

She started the car. Its engine rumbling to life reassured her; it was a familiar sound in a day that had turned itself upside down.

It wasn't until she was nearly to Lux that she saw the blue Ford behind her and realized that she was being followed.

CHAPTER 25

Her office was hot, and the paint kept drying on her brush. She had a headache from everything that had happened the night before and her lack of sleep didn't help. She hadn't yet called the police and she hadn't figured out if she should. She was afraid to leave the studio, though the blue Ford had pulled off before she'd reached the gates, and so she knew she was right in feeling safe there. Images from her wrecked apartment wouldn't leave her mind, but even worse was the image of Walter across the table from her in the Lucky 8, his smug face when she realized that she couldn't ignore him and she couldn't run away this time. He'd expose her if she didn't get him what he wanted. But how to do that and get him out of her life at the same time? Otherwise this would go on forever. Forever and forever and—

The brush dried for the tenth time, and she jabbed it at the easel in frustration. If only she could send Walter to the ends of the earth, some nice location in the darkest reaches of the Amazon or something. Something like *The African Queen*. He could play a poacher or something. Maybe he'd get eaten by a crocodile . . .

She paused, remembering that there *was* a film in preproduction at Lux that would be shot on location in Mexico, and hadn't the screenwriter Philip Yordan put together a unit in Madrid? She thought she'd heard something like that, and yes, they were shooting films in Spain and Great Britain to avoid the blacklisting problems here. Walter had been right about some things, Lena did have contacts. She probably could get someone overseas to take a look at him. She'd put Walter on a plane, fly him to Spain to shoot some B movie, and let him find his own way back.

It was the perfect solution. All she needed was a list of directors and producers shooting overseas. Shirley could get that for her by tomorrow. Lena was off her stool and halfway to her door when there was a knock and Shirley stuck her head in.

"Oh good! I was just coming to—"

"The police are here to see you, Lena," Shirley said quietly.

Lena stopped short. She had not called them. "The police?"

Shirley opened the door wider to reveal two men who didn't look like police officers. They wore no uniforms, but instead suits and hats. Both had their badges, clearly marked as Los Angeles Police Department, in their hands; both were nearly six feet tall. One had brown eyes, the other blue. The blue-eyed one said, "Detective Joe Miller, Miss Taylor, and this is my partner, Detective John Von Colucci."

Lena sent a questioning look to Shirley, who only shrugged.

"We need to talk to you about a Mr. Walter Maynard?"

"You mean . . . this isn't about my apartment?"

Both men frowned. "Your apartment? No."

It took Lena a moment to recalibrate. She ushered them into her office and shut the door. "Look, whatever trouble Walter has got himself into, I don't want any part of it."

"He's dead, Miss Taylor."

Those were the last words she'd expected. "What? What do you mean? What happened?"

"We believe he was murdered."

Lena stared at the detective in shock. *Murdered?* How? Why?"

"That's what we're trying to determine, Miss Taylor. He was found at ten o'clock last night outside his hotel, about forty-five minutes after he left the Lucky 8 tavern. Do you know anything about that?"

The Lucky 8. Where she had been with him. Now Lena was afraid. How much did these men know about her relationship with Walter? "About his death? No, nothing."

"Do you know why he also had a screenplay in his room with your name and phone number on it?"

"No."

"Your fiancé is a screenwriter, isn't that so?"

"There are a thousand screenwriters in this town, Detective. I can't think what one has to do with the other."

"All right, all right. When was the last time you saw Mr. Maynard?"

She wanted to lie, everything in her screamed to lie, but she saw the way they were looking at her, and they'd mentioned the Lucky 8. She remembered how those men in the tavern had looked at her, too, and worrying she'd be recognized. She didn't know if the police knew she was Walter's wife, but it seemed stupid to lie about meeting him at the tavern. "Last night. At the Lucky 8."

She'd been right not to lie, she saw, when Von Colucci nodded. "Yes, witnesses saw you there. What was the meeting about?"

"He wanted money."

"And you gave it to him," Miller noted.

Another thing not to lie about. The men at the Lucky 8 had seen it all. "I was feeling generous. He was an old friend." She took a chance on the last. Surely they would have mentioned her marriage by now if they'd known about it. Walter was dead. She could say anything. At least, she hoped she could.

"You didn't seem happy to do it, according to those there. One man said you threw it at him. Another said there seemed to be tension between you," said Miller.

"Is that a question?" she asked.

"What is your relationship with Mr. Maynard?"

They didn't know. Lena felt a surge of relief. "I knew him a long time ago. When I first came to LA. I hadn't seen him in years. He asked for money, I gave it to him. As a favor. That was it."

"Why the tension?" Von Colucci asked.

"Walter was . . . troubled. He had a temper. And honestly, I was irritated to be asked for money after so long. As I said, I hadn't seen him for a while."

"Irritated enough to kill him?"

"No, Detective. I didn't kill Walter. I left him in front of the Lucky 8 and I went home."

"Is there anyone who can vouch for that?"

"I was alone."

"Anyone who saw you there? Anyone you might have called?"

When she got home, her apartment . . . her phone . . . she'd called no one. She'd come to the studio. The only one who knew otherwise was whoever followed her in the blue Ford—and why were they following her? Had it something to do with Walter? Or something else? Who had searched her apartment? What could she tell these men about any of it? They'd ask why she hadn't called the police and they would be right to ask. She couldn't explain, and now there was Walter's death on top of it, and it all felt weirdly connected and she was afraid. "No, no one. Am I . . . am I in trouble?"

"These are only preliminary questions," Detective Von Colucci assured her. "Right now, it's only a fact-finding mission, Miss Taylor."

"How was he killed?" she asked.

The detectives exchanged a glance. "We're keeping that information quiet for now," said Von Colucci.

"I think that's about all for the time being," Detective Miller said. "But we do ask that you not leave Los Angeles for the next few weeks, while our investigation continues."

"I'm too busy to leave LA," she told him.

A slight nod. "We'll be in touch."

Their departing smiles were thin and not the least bit reassuring. She showed them out, and shut her door behind them, ignoring Shirley's worried look.

Walter was dead. Why? He was a hustler and he could be irritating with all his grand ideas about himself, but that wasn't a reason to kill him. She felt sorry for it, but she didn't really grieve him. She'd moved on from Walter long ago, and his death relieved her of two problems: she didn't have to worry about divorce now, or his blackmail. She hadn't expected the problem that he'd left in his wake, however.

Because, of course, the problems of marriage and blackmail were gone, but not the problem of her past. The police would dig, and if she truly was the last person to see Walter alive—but she wasn't, how could she be? Someone had killed him. She hadn't seen him in six years; she had no idea what his life had been, or what enemies he had. But those men in the Lucky 8 had seen *her*. They'd seen her argue with Walter. They'd seen her throw the money down in anger. They'd probably seen the way she'd recoiled from his kiss in the street. The police would keep digging. How long before they dug up a long-lost wife? How long before they stumbled upon Elsie Maynard, née Gruner? And who had searched her apartment? What did they want?

∼

She did not want to go back there. But she wanted to see it again without the shock of Walter coloring the wreckage. She wanted to see if she could find any clue to who might have ransacked the place. By the time she left work and stopped at the grocery store, night had fallen, and her apartment building on Highland glowed with window lights. She got her mail and took the groceries upstairs to her apartment, her footsteps ringing hollowly. Uneasily she pushed on the door. It didn't budge. She inserted the key and found nothing wrong with the lock.

In puzzlement, Lena went inside, and with a dawning horror she realized her apartment was as it had always been. Nothing out of place. It was as if the nightmare of last night had not happened. No drawers were open, no sketchbooks thrown about, no records strewn upon the floor. The Charlie Parker was in one piece and back in its sleeve and in its place on the shelf—she would have thought she'd gone mad but for the fact that while the broken records had been replaced, the torn pages of her sketchbook had been taped back together.

All her clothes had been folded and put back into her dresser, even her panties. A cold shudder of violation ran through her. She had to sit down. Who could have done this? Why? There was no way now to report it to the police. Who would believe her? She wasn't sure she believed it herself. And it felt so tied to Walter, and Walter was dead. Unbelievably dead.

She didn't know how long she stood there before she locked the door with the chain and put a kitchen chair beneath the knob to bolster it. She felt she was moving in a dream as she changed her clothes, looking over her shoulder, expecting what? A ghost? She opened the can of spaghetti she'd bought for dinner but left it. She'd bought it because it had a drawing of the Colosseum on it but it looked so unappetizing, and she really hadn't believed it would taste like the pasta in Rome, but that picture . . . so many pasts to put behind her; she hated how one raised the others in her thoughts—why couldn't they stay separate, in nice little boxes, each with their own lock?

The silence was too much, that empty, un-lived-in kind. She opened the window to let in the night and the night sounds, turned on the television and went to look at the mail.

Lena spotted the envelope before she sat down on the beige couch with its low, rolling armrest. The familiarity of the address caught her eye: *LENA TAYLOR, COSTUMER TO THE STARS*. Another letter from Walter.

She started to crumple it and throw it away unopened, and then stopped. The police were obviously investigating her, she had to be careful. If they found out about the letters, they'd suspect Walter had been blackmailing her—which he had—and that would only lead to questions she did not want to answer. She looked down at the phone number written in pencil. *CR-18131 r116.*

A woman on the television screamed. Lena jumped. The shadows in the room reached from the corners; outside, a dog barked and a man snapped at it to shut up.

There was no stamp on the letter. He'd put it directly into her mailbox. But . . . she'd picked up the mail yesterday, so someone had put it in her mailbox today. And Walter had been dead since ten o'clock last night—or actually, probably a bit before.

Lena frowned. If it wasn't from Walter, then who could have left it? Did he have a partner? Someone who could tell the police about these letters? About their marriage? Was this the same person who had broken into her apartment and wrecked it? The same person who had set it so creepily back to rights? *Why?*

The music on the TV grew moody and ominous. Lena crossed the room and switched it off—a mistake; the apartment was too quiet then. She turned it back on and turned the channel, to an ad for Chevrolet that sounded familiar and normal. She picked up the note on the coffee table and looked again at the number, and then remembered Walter telling her he had a service. Lena went to her purse and searched for the card he'd given her. It was bent; she'd shoved it so hastily into her purse. *Walt Maynard, actor/screenwriter, MA 64671.*

Not the same number as that on the letter.

CR-18131.

The note wasn't from Walter. Then who had sent it? And why?

CHAPTER 26

The next morning Shirley handed Lena the newspaper when she walked in. Not only was she mentioned on the front page in an article about Walter's death, but Hedda Hopper's column featured her prominently as well. The first item. Lux Pictures Costume Star a Murderess? Police Question Lena Taylor in Actor's Suspicious Death.

"Higgy wants to see you," Shirley informed her.

Lena nodded distractedly. "All right."

"You have several messages too," Shirley said. "The *Times*, the *Examiner*, and a few other reporters—"

"I'm not doing any interviews. Put them all off. Everyone else too. I don't have time for this."

"You have to say something, Lena." Connie stepped from her office. "Otherwise they'll print whatever they want."

Lena let out her breath in frustration and tucked the newspaper beneath her arm. She marched from the costume department back out into the morning sun and crossed to the administration building. When she got to Higgy's office, Adele simply motioned her into the studio head's office.

Lena paused. "How is he?"

"How do you think? Today his costumer is mentioned in the paper more times than *Twenty Steps to Heaven*."

Higgy's most recent picture, *Twenty Steps to Heaven*, had opened only yesterday. So . . . he was furious. Lena steeled herself and knocked quickly on the door before she opened it. "Higgy?"

"What the hell is this about?" he thundered from the dais of his desk.

Lena closed the door quickly behind her. Higgy was intimidating on his best day, but when he was angry, his office had a distinctly locked-in-a-cave-with-a-spear-hunter feel. Even the lamps hanging from their thin metal poles seemed to shudder.

"Obviously I didn't know she was going to print that, Higgy. I don't even know how she knew. The police must have sent her the tip."

He rose. When he stood, it looked almost as if his head brushed the ceiling, though Lena knew it was an optical illusion created by his interior designer. Still, it was effective. He looked like he filled the room. "I don't give one rat's ass who sent her the tip. I want to know why I didn't know first that my head of costume was being questioned by police in a murder case. Why didn't you come to me before you talked to them?"

He made it sound as if she'd committed some cardinal sin.

"I—I'm sorry. I didn't have the chance. They came to my office."

"It never occurred to you to come to me after? Or that I might be able to make all this go away before it got to the papers?"

She bowed her head. "No. No, I'm sorry."

"I have men in the LAPD I *pay* to alert me to things like this!"

"I'm sorry, Higgy."

Higgy jabbed his finger at her. "You had better hope to God that I can take care of it now. In the meantime, you will meet with Hedda Hopper and give her a statement saying you had nothing to do with this."

"I *didn't* have anything to do with this."

"Then it will be easy, won't it? You'll do it today, Miss Taylor, do we understand one another?"

Miss Taylor. She didn't remember the last time he'd called her that. "Yes, of course. I'll call her right away."

"Good. Then get the fuck out of my office."

She was out the door almost before he'd finished speaking. She didn't dare to pause and crossed the office lobby with little more than a wave at Adele, who no doubt heard the entire exchange.

Lena still had the newspaper tucked beneath her arm when she got to her office. She unfolded it and looked again at the headline. Shirley looked up warily.

"See if you can set up lunch with Hedda Hopper, will you please?" Lena asked. "Someplace nice. Musso and Frank's if you can, or the Brown Derby? I'll give her the whole story, and she won't have to guess. That ought to get her there."

Shirley made a little scowl, but she nodded.

"And tell Connie she'll have to cover the fittings during that time, since I'll be charming the tiger."

"Better take some fresh meat," Shirley noted.

~

First, though, there was Paul. She had to tell him about the police, and what it had involved. Whether she'd tell him about her apartment she hadn't decided. Probably not. She was confused and afraid, and her instincts told her to keep it quiet for now. Walter was complication enough.

Anxiety and apprehension hurried her steps to soundstage six. She couldn't delay another moment, even if it meant she had to tell him surrounded by other people. In a way, that might be easier. She had no idea how he would react, nor did she know exactly what she would say.

The soundstage churned with activity. The jazz club set was still being assembled, and the sounds of hammering and drilling filled the air, along with talk and shouting as the lighting guys experimented with various setups and conferred with the cinematographer. The prop and art direction people bent over a long table covered with different types of table lamps and bottles. Lena paused inside, afraid to approach the writing table.

There he was, with Michael Runyon and George Gardner. Paul spoke intently, gesturing. Before him were several pages spread over the table, the typewriter, a half-crumpled pack of Marlboros. Runyon nodded, then motioned with his cigarette. The table was wreathed in smoke.

She shouldn't interrupt, Lena thought. But that was just cowardice, wasn't it? Warily, she walked to the table. The moment they saw her, the talk died, all three of them stared at her with various expressions of impatient *Yes?* She had eyes only for Paul, who looked tired, stubble rough on his face—he hadn't shaved—and his eyes hooded. There were no smiles for her, only tension.

Lena tried a smile of her own. "I'm sorry for interrupting. I was wondering if I could steal your writer for a minute?"

"It's a bad time, Lena." There was no doubt of Paul's strain now. It was more than that too. She read anger in it.

"I really need to talk to you."

"We're in the middle of something."

"That was quite the headline in Hedda's column," Runyon said.

Lena turned furiously to him.

"Shut up, Runyon," Paul barked.

"Why don't you go talk to her?" Runyon suggested. "Maybe it'll put you in a better mood."

George nodded in agreement. "Go on. I'm going to get more coffee."

Paul looked like he wanted to refuse. But then he grabbed his cigarette and rose, motioning for her to follow him outside, away from the bustle.

"I should have called you last night," Lena said. "I'm sorry. I was a bit shaken."

"So was I. Especially after the detectives paid me a visit." Paul stared into the distance and drew on his cigarette.

She stared at him in surprise. "They talked to you? Why?"

"They wanted to ask me if I knew any reason my fiancée might want to murder Walter Maynard."

"What did you say?"

Now he looked at her. His dark eyes burned. "What could I say other than I had no idea because I had no idea who the hell Walter Maynard was?"

"Paul, I had nothing to do with his death, I promise."

He laughed shortly and shook his head. "Who is he?"

She hadn't known exactly what she would tell him, but her worries about what the police might find if they traced back far enough in Walter's life, the truth of Elsie Gruner and Rome, kept her from revealing the truth. She was no longer married—that was the most important thing. Paul had agreed to work with Runyon on this script and she couldn't allow her past to threaten that fragile compromise. For now it seemed safer—better—to keep to the story she'd told the detectives. "An old friend. I knew him years ago, when I first came to LA."

Paul eyed her. "What kind of an old friend?"

"One I hadn't seen for six years. He was an actor."

"I see."

"I don't think you do. He saw my picture in Louella's column and wanted money. I gave him some."

"Why would you do that?"

She shrugged. "He was down on his luck. He'd helped me out a long time ago—"

"Really? How so?"

She probably shouldn't have said that. "He . . . gave me rides to work. That kind of thing. He needed a favor, and it was the best way to make him go away. I didn't want him hanging around."

Paul frowned. "You realize how that sounds?"

Lena sighed. "I didn't want him dead—why would I? I'm telling you, I hadn't seen him for years! When I left him last night, he was still alive. I have no idea what happened to him after that."

Paul considered her. He took the last drag on his cigarette and threw it down, grinding it out on the dirt, which clouded up and dulled the shine of his shoe. "They asked me if I had a reason to kill him. They asked me where I was. If I had an alibi."

"Oh, Paul. I'm so sorry."

"Fortunately I'd gone to one of those Mexican places on Olvera with Runyon."

"Good." Lena didn't try to hide her relief. "Though I'm surprised you'd want to spend any more time with him than you have to."

Paul didn't comment on that. Instead he said, "Is there some reason the police would think I might want to kill this Maynard, Lena?"

"What a question!"

He regarded her soberly. "You know what I'm asking you."

Lena touched his forearm, hesitating, wondering if he'd freeze or pull away and then realizing she'd never had to wonder that before. He didn't; she wrapped her fingers around his arm. "No. I promise you there's not. I don't know what Walter was involved in, but I had nothing to do with it. I met with him and I gave him money, and I was annoyed with him because he'd popped up out of nowhere and I felt obligated because he was down on his luck, but that's *all*."

"Okay." Paul nodded. "Okay."

She met his gaze. "You should know that Higgy's furious. He's making me have lunch with Hedda to explain, and . . . so this isn't going away yet."

Another nod. "I've got to get back. Let's have dinner tonight."

"I'd love to." She kissed him, and then she finally got the smile she'd been waiting for before he turned to go inside. She wanted to bury herself in that smile, though she was afraid of it, too; she was afraid that it absolved her and she did not deserve absolution, because she'd lied to him again—but she was doing it to protect him. Walter was dead; he couldn't come back to tell the truth, and she hadn't murdered him, so none of it could matter.

She found the thought strangely upsetting.

CHAPTER 27

The blue Ford trailed her again when Lena went to meet Hedda Hopper for lunch, though whoever was in it did not follow her inside. Even the familiar gloss of Musso & Frank's couldn't ease Lena's jitters. She tried to forget the car and concentrate on Hedda and Hedda's brief article. The gossip columnist had laid the details out shortly and clearly: Walter Maynard, an actor who had recently arrived in LA from New York, had been killed last night. He was last seen in the Lucky 8 Tavern with Lena Taylor, and according to witnesses, the two had fought. She'd thrown money at him and departed and claimed to know nothing of what happened to him after.

All true. But it was Hedda's parting lines that disconcerted Lena. How sharp and clever the gossip columnist was, implying without stating, nothing Lena could sue over, but still hinting at blackmail, or something unsavory. *"Lena Taylor has certainly flown high and fast among the Hollywood elite since she arrived at Lux Studios. One may well ask what Mr. Maynard had to say that flapped the unflappable Miss Taylor."*

Yes, one may ask. Lena hoped one didn't. In fact, she meant to guarantee it.

She had always liked Musso & Frank's; it had a Hollywood glamour that she associated with success, and the movie stars and writers who came here to be served by a discreet and efficient waitstaff only emphasized it. She took in the white tablecloths, the red leather booths, the mahogany bar and the gentle green-and-cream hunting-scene-illustrated wallpaper in the archways and between the wooden beams. Glass and mirrors and elegant light and the hum of talk.

She scanned the tables; Hedda hadn't arrived yet, which gave Lena time to compose herself as the maître d' led her to a table. She ordered a martini—just one, she told herself. She wanted to remain in control, but one drink would calm her, and she was glad she had time for a few sips before she spotted Hedda Hopper's hat bobbing at the entrance. Black today, with a band of red roses. It was a somber choice for Hedda. Lena, for whom dress meant much more than mere clothing, wondered if she should read anything into that, or if Hedda had simply chosen it to match her outfit.

She waved to catch the columnist's attention, and Hedda waved a gloved hand back and started over. She wore pearls, a strand of large ones and a multistrand of tiny ones looped thickly around her neck. The light glimmered off her large conch-shell earrings and a brooch with a red stone at the knot of the white scarf at her throat. She smiled as she approached the table, glanced at Lena's martini—disapprovingly? Otherwise? In any case she noted it and did not order one for herself but said "Coffee please" before she settled herself in the booth across from Lena with an alert officiousness that filled Lena with dread all over again.

"So nice to see you, Hedda," Lena said smoothly, taking a bigger sip of the martini. "How glad I am that you could come to lunch on such short notice."

"Well, you're all the talk this morning."

Lena smiled thinly and indicated the menu. "It's my treat."

A waiter brought Hedda's coffee. The menu lay untouched before her, but she said, "I'll have the lobster salad."

"The shrimp louie," Lena ordered.

When the waiter moved away, Hedda said, "I understand congratulations are in order. Engaged! How lovely. Of course, I had to learn that from Louella . . ."

"Only because of her gala. I'd been so busy, you understand, but it was thoughtless of me, Hedda, and I do apologize."

Hedda sipped her coffee, but her mouth was tight when she put the cup down. "I thought we were friends."

"We were—we are. It isn't Louella I've invited to lunch today."

"Hmmm. Well, let's see it." A quick gesture. "Show me the rock."

Lena pulled off her glove to show off her ring.

Hedda eyed it with the steady appraisal of someone who knew the value of jewelry. "That cost him a pretty penny. I'd guess maybe the entire amount of that screenplay you helped him sell to Lux."

"It sold on its own merit," Lena corrected gently, trying to keep the frustration from her voice. "It's a wonderful script."

Hedda gave her a whatever-you-say look and sat back. "I understand it's been given a new title."

"The Doom of Medusa."

Hedda raised a brow. "Not horror?"

Lena shook her head. "Oh no. It's very *Raisin in the Sun*. With Ruby Dennison, who of course is so charming. The film is . . ." *What?* Once, she would have said it was unlike anything else. A film about women's relationships and triumph. Now it was such a mess that she wasn't sure what to say. Fortunately, she didn't have to think of anything, because Hedda wasn't interested in the story of *The Doom of Medusa*.

"What about all the trouble I'm hearing about on the set?"

"I can't imagine what you're talking about."

"Nothing good ever came of getting ahead of oneself or taking advantage. People ought to be grateful when they've been given a shot. That's the problem in this town. Too little gratitude."

Lena frowned, uncertain who Hedda was referring to. Paul? Or Lena herself? She was saved from having to ask by the arrival of their lunch and the waiter's suggestion of another martini. It took all Lena's willpower to decline. She focused on the shrimp louie, though she wasn't very hungry in the sharp focus of Hedda's gaze.

"Especially now," Hedda went on, picking up her fork, "when the threat is everywhere."

Lena stiffened. "What threat is that?"

"Why, the Reds, of course. Anyone might take a lack of gratitude as un-American."

Lena didn't mistake the implication in the gossip columnist's voice—or that it was about Paul. "There's no conflict on the set, or lack of gratitude, for that matter. Who's been telling you that?"

"What does your fiancé think about this Walter Maynard business?" Hedda parried.

Lena wondered if Hedda Hopper ever lowered her voice in any situation. The restaurant was full, talk and the clink of glass and silverware a quiet, steady hum. The only saving grace was that everyone in Musso & Frank's was more interested in their own conversations than hers.

"He thinks it unfortunate, as do I." She finished the martini and wished fervently to order another, which she could not do. Hedda already had her too much on edge. "But we're both certain the police will find whoever killed him. I'm assuming the police tipped you?"

Hedda didn't answer her question about the police, but asked, "You'd known Mr. Maynard for some time?"

Lena kept to the story she'd told Paul and the police. "He was an old friend but I hadn't seen him for years. He was trouble."

Hedda paused over a forkful of lobster salad. "Mob trouble?"

Lena shrugged. *Why not?* Walter was dead, who knew what he might be involved with? Besides, it would give Hedda some other lead to follow, one that would take her far from Lena. "I don't really know, but I sure wouldn't doubt it."

"Hmmm." Hedda looked thoughtful as she chewed. She swallowed and said, "What did you fight about in the Lucky 8?"

"He wanted money."

"You didn't want to help an old friend?"

Lena gave Hedda a look. "I gave it to him, didn't I? I hoped it would be enough that he would leave me alone."

A small smile, a rock of her head in acknowledgment. "Leave you alone? Why?"

"He was a man looking for a gravy train. I didn't want to be that."

"He sounds like someone you might want to kill."

"Well, I didn't." Lena bit off the tail of a shrimp with a snap. "Like I said, Walter was always looking for trouble. All I can say is that he found it."

"Did you know his wife?"

It sounded like a foreign language at first, words so shocking she could only stare, and then they landed and she wasn't prepared and she knew Hedda saw it. "What?"

"Her name's on an old lease of his." The columnist's eyes glittered. "A woman named Elsie."

Lena had no words for the feeling rushing through her. Alarm, maybe? Or maybe it was terror. The lease, of course.

"You didn't know he had a wife?" Hedda asked, and that gleam in her eyes told Lena she was pleased at Lena's surprise, that she'd found something to use, that she reveled in her own cleverness.

"How do you know it? Did the police—"

"The LAPD?" Hedda laughed. "God no. My office found it. We have our own detectives. We're searching for Elsie Maynard now."

Another terrifying thing. The only saving grace was that she'd used Walter's last name only for a short time. But how long before they found Elsie Gruner? How long before they traced that name right to her? Lena tried desperately to remember what tracks she'd left behind.

"I didn't know he was married, no."

"Well." Hedda attacked her lobster. "It will be interesting to see what this Elsie has to say when we find her."

Lena put down her fork and gestured for the waiter. "I think I will have another martini after all."

Hedda said, "You'll let me know if the police have any more developments?"

"I'm sure you'll know before I do."

Hedda chuckled. "Probably true. If you get arrested, my dear, you will give me an exclusive?"

"You think that's funny?"

Another short laugh. "I like to have my sources nailed down."

"I don't need any more gossip. Higgy is already going crazy." Lena spoke before she thought, and then wished she could take it back.

But Hedda only waved that away. "Of course he is. But you won't be staying much longer anyway, will you?"

"What do you mean?"

"You'll be getting married."

"Yes. What does that have to do with it?"

"You'll be leaving Lux, won't you?"

"Well, I—"

"I don't know a single marriage that works when the wife does." Hedda pointed her fork at Lena. "A wife's job is to support her husband. Look at all these movie star marriages that fall apart when the wife doesn't give up her career. You mark my words, Lena, a marriage where the wife doesn't dedicate herself to being a wife and mother is one doomed to failure."

It wasn't the first time Hedda had said such things, in her column anyway, but it was the first time she'd said them to Lena. Lena fingered the stem of the coupe and smelled the fragrant herbal gin and watched the olive bounce against the glass.

"Wives are the strength of our nation," Hedda went on, finishing her lobster. "But only when they support their men. The Reds can only hope our women abandon their families for careers that 'complete them.' Such nonsense. Children will complete you when you have them. Mark my words. You don't want to be sorry. Your screenwriter is a handsome man. You keep working and he'll run off with someone who puts him first. Someone like that, my dear, can always find someone who will. I've seen it happen time and again." Hedda set down her fork with emphasis. "Now, I must run. Have you anything else to say before I go? On the record, of course."

The change in subject rattled her; Lena called herself back to the subject at hand, but when she said, "I had nothing to do with Walter Maynard's death," the words didn't feel forceful, she was still thinking about Hedda's advice, about leaving Lux. "And neither did Paul."

"Of course you didn't." Hedda's half smile wasn't reassuring. "Thank you for lunch. I enjoyed it."

She wobbled off, the sound of her heels clipping through the smooth murmur of talk, the roses teetering perilously, seeming disembodied against the black of her hat. Lena watched her go and sat there drinking her martini, ignoring the shrimp louie, mostly untouched before her, while Hedda's insinuations and revelations spun in her head. The woman had discovered Elsie Maynard. She had heard about conflicts on the set of *Medusa*. Lena didn't think she'd put Hedda off that scent, either, and what would happen if Hedda wrote about it? Runyon was already suspicious about Paul, and Hedda's words about ingratitude being un-American . . . and there was Lena's past, and the LAPD investigation and that note . . .

Lena finished the rest of her martini. She wanted to call Harvey and Charlie for their advice, but dared not. She had no one she could confide in, no one she could trust with this. She was more on her own than she had ever been.

~

Shirley gave her an anxious look when Lena returned. "How did it go?"

"You know Hedda," Lena said with a thin smile. "She'll solve the murder before the LAPD does."

"*Temple Street Pickup* is on your desk."

It was a relief to enter the quiet of her office, to let her mind change directions. The thumbnail she'd been working on yesterday hung on the easel half-done, waiting for color. A research book on late nineteenth century dress lay open on the low table near the couch. Fabric swatches and tear-outs from magazines were everywhere—she found the mess calming despite its chaos. This was who she was. She could forget about everything here.

Lena put down her purse and drew off her gloves. She saw the next screenplay in her queue where Shirley said she'd put it. Another spy movie. She put the screenplay aside. Beneath it was an envelope.

LENA TAYLOR, COSTUMER TO THE STARS.

She froze. What was this doing here? She thought she'd put it away. Unless . . . she pulled open her desk drawer and found the original letter still there.

"Shirley," she called. "Who left this letter on my desk?"

"What letter?" Shirley called back. "The mail isn't here yet."

Lena felt sick. So this was a third letter. A new one. Like the others, it had no postmark, and no stamp, which meant . . . which meant that someone had put it here on her desk. Someone had come into her office to place it here.

The hair on the back of her neck tickled. She had the strange feeling of being watched, a tightness in her chest. She turned the envelope over. It was sealed.

She wanted to run; instead she walked slowly and deliberately to the door. "Did anyone strange come into my office today?"

Shirley frowned, obviously perplexed by the question. "Strange how?"

"I don't know. A messenger, or . . . anyone?"

"Of course not." Shirley looked offended. "You know I don't let just anyone walk in."

"Yes, but . . ." Lena held out the envelope. "Do you know where this came from?"

Shirley came over to examine it. "Why, no. Where did you find it?"

"On my desk. Were you gone at some point?"

"I went to get my lunch, but I was only gone a few minutes, and I lock everything up."

Lena went back into her office and shut the door behind her. How the envelope got here was a puzzle; when she opened it, the message was the same. Just the phone number. Such a benign thing, and yet, it raised a sense of menace, of portent, that Lena could not sweep away.

She looked at her telephone. How ridiculous this was. Maybe it was nothing. Maybe it was . . . but she couldn't think of any reason why anyone would leave a note like this if it were innocuous. A friend would include their name. A salesman would at least provide a hint of what they were selling—or would they? Maybe it was meant to raise her curiosity. Maybe it wasn't meant to be threatening at all.

Maybe . . .

Lena picked up the receiver. She dialed the number. Her heart pounded as it rang. One ring, and then two, and then . . .

"Beverly Hills Hotel. How may I help you?"

This she had not expected.

"Hello?" The female voice prodded, very polite.

"Um—" Lena could not think of what to say. "Um . . . yes. Room 116 please?"

The phone rang. And rang. Lena tensed with each blistering *brrrr*, her fingers tightened on the receiver.

It picked up. There was a clicking sound. Something garbled. A voice? She couldn't tell. More clicking, and a weird sound that fell in and out, like someone speaking underwater. Beneath it all she heard music. Jazz.

"Hello?" Lena said. "Hello?"

Only the strange click, and the music. Music Lena recognized, a song that made her catch her breath, that threw her so far back in time she lost her grasp on the present; she forgot where and who she was.

"Nature Boy."

Lena slammed down the receiver.

CHAPTER 28

Lena was so distracted and jumpy that when Paul showed up at her office to take her to dinner, she was tempted to plead a headache. That morning's conversation with him felt so very far away. She didn't know how she could manage a conversation with anyone, but especially with him, when her secrets danced so busily in her head. Still, she smiled and kissed him, and when he noted that she didn't seem herself, she said, "It's been a madhouse today, truly, and lunch with Hedda didn't help."

"Maybe we should just order in sandwiches," he suggested.

But that sounded somehow worse, because it meant they would be alone, and she didn't want to be alone with him. Her tension held her tight and he knew her too well; she feared that he might see what she couldn't afford for him to see.

"Honestly, I feel like going out," she said as brightly as she could. "Maybe the Villa Nova?" The place was popular, and would be swarmed; it would be difficult to have a private conversation. She could see Paul's puzzlement, but he shrugged.

"If that's what you want. I'd prefer somewhere quieter. You're not the only one who's had a day."

"More disagreements with Runyon?"

"Always disagreements with Runyon." He frowned. "Today we were arguing about the friendship between Simone and Helen, and he said women didn't have true friends, only competitors. But he's a cynical bastard. He's used to seeing the worst in people."

"Well, he does work in the movies."

Paul looked puzzled for a moment.

"And I suppose being a censor means you're always arguing with everyone."

"Yeah, I guess that's true." Paul went thoughtful. "He asked about you and your women friends, actually, and you know, I couldn't think of any."

And there was Julia again. In her head, when Lena thought she'd excised her. Julia, and "Nature Boy," and the grief Lena had thought long gone. "Why would Michael Runyon care whether or not I have women friends?"

"It was just a question for argument."

"I have enough trouble in my life managing actresses." Lena tried to smile. "They take up all my time."

~

The Villa Nova was as crowded as Lena suspected, and the Italian music playing over the speakers was too loud and there was too much conversation beneath it, but she had the impression that the noise suited Paul equally well tonight. He was as distracted as she was, and it was clear he didn't want to talk about Walter, which was a relief, since Walter seemed a long-ago problem compared to the problems she had now.

Afterward, as they went to their cars, Paul said, "All this with the movie, and this Maynard fellow and the police . . . I'll admit I'm . . ."

"I've got sketches to do tonight." Lena nearly jumped on his words, relieved. "I really should go home."

It wasn't until he kissed her good night and went to his own car that Lena realized how relieved he'd looked as well, but she was too wrapped up in her own worries to add that to the list. She didn't want to go to her apartment, but she felt unsettled and bewildered, and the phone call earlier had brought back memories she didn't know how to manage. La

Grotta. Petra singing. Julia's enigmatic smile. Then that song again in Julia's room at the academy.

At least no blue Ford followed her home. She didn't check the mail. If there was another note, she didn't want to know. Her apartment was as hollow and lonely as ever, but it didn't feel like her own now, it felt invaded, and she locked the door and put on *Birth of the Cool*, which she'd never listened to in Rome because it hadn't been out then. She hoped it would help her forget the day.

But it didn't. She wished she were somewhere else. She was jumpy and distracted and uncomfortable, and Miles Davis's trumpet sounded alien and uneasy. She couldn't bear it. She turned it off, trading it for an equally unbearable silence.

The phone rang, jangling disquietingly, almost as if it sensed how vulnerable she felt. She started, staring at it, shaken by an odd foreboding. She did not want to pick it up. This afternoon, "Nature Boy" . . . no, she did not want to pick it up. She'd never been afraid of a phone call before, but now she was.

It kept ringing.

Lena swallowed hard. She told herself not to be stupid. It might be important. Someone from the studio. Maybe Paul, though she doubted it. *Answer it.*

But she could not lose her apprehension. Slowly, she went to the phone. If she took long enough, maybe they would hang up. Maybe she would never have to know who was on the other end.

Still ringing.

Lena lifted the handset, unaccountably panicked. Just as she put it to her ear, she heard the click. Whoever was on the other end had grown tired of waiting.

She let out her breath in relief and hung up, unsurprised to find she was shaking.

～

Lena went bleary eyed to work. She had to attend the Brandenburg gala that afternoon, and she wished she could send her regrets. But it was a charity event and Higgy had asked her to go to talk to Elizabeth Taylor, who he wanted to cast in *Every Day's a Holiday*. Before considering the role, the actress had insisted on having a conversation with the woman who had ousted Flavio, since the last time they'd worked together, Lena had been Flavio's assistant and Elizabeth had barely noticed her.

But Elizabeth Taylor didn't show. Lena ate finger sandwiches and drank champagne and mingled with Olivia de Havilland and Mickey Rooney and Susan Hayward and waited for it to be late enough to leave without appearing rude. The gardens were gorgeous; a string quartet played classical music that accented the classical touches like the bronze statues dotted throughout, and Nancy Brandenburg floated about in yellow georgette obviously designed by Flavio, though he wasn't there, and cajoled checks from every attendee for whatever charity the event was for—Lena was too consumed by other things to remember, but she donated and tried to make small talk. Cars continued to arrive, men and women still making their way down the flower-edged drive. Maybe Elizabeth Taylor would be a late arrival and it wouldn't be such a waste of time.

"The whole thing must have been terrible for you," William Holden said. "An old friend, you say?"

Lena nodded and tried to look sad. The questions about Walter had been coming all afternoon. "It was a shock to see him again. Even a greater shock to hear that he was dead."

"I imagine so. But you were no longer friends, it sounds like."

"Well no, not after he asked me for money. I'm sorry he's dead, but I wonder if he might have been involved with the mob." She was bored with the conversation, it had become wearying repeating what she'd said a dozen times today already and trying to look sad. The quartet was tuning up again after a break. So many people crowded the gardens that she thought she could probably get away without anyone noticing.

"He wouldn't be the only one," Bill Holden said. "I wonder if every studio in town is getting their financing from Mickey Cohen these days."

She made a small sound of agreement, took another sip of champagne—

And saw Julia.

There, near the string quartet. It was her. Chestnut hair. A gorgeous dress of coral silk—a dress Lena knew because it was one of her designs copied from the film *Sixpenny Lane*. And yet . . .

Lena blinked. It could not be Julia. Julia was dead.

But there she was, in a Lena Taylor dress, with Sam Rockdale, a young actor making a name for himself in Westerns.

Lena felt the blood leave her face. It could not be possible.

"Are you all right?" Holden turned his head to follow her gaze. "You look like you've seen a ghost."

"Do . . . do you know that woman? That woman in coral?"

"What woman?"

"Just over there. With Sam Rockdale."

Bill looked. "I've never seen her before. Do you know her?"

"No. No. I couldn't."

But then the woman who could not be Julia because Julia was dead looked toward Lena with a purposeful gaze, as if she had known all this time where Lena was. And at once the strange notes, the call with "Nature Boy" on the other end, made a terrible, terrible sense, and Lena's head went so light she thought she might pass out.

Julia smiled at her.

Lena looked for a place to set her champagne down. The glass crashed to the ground, shattering on the parterre.

"Lena, are you all right?" Bill Holden asked.

"Fine," she said. "I—I have to find the ladies' room. You'll excuse me, won't you?"

He frowned. "If you're sure you're all right."

She murmured something, she wasn't sure what, and moved away. Honestly it was all she could do not to run. She had no idea where the restrooms were and frankly did not need one. What she needed was to be away. Her thoughts spun too quickly for her to grab hold of them; she couldn't ground herself. She was back in Rome, at the train station. The man was saying, "*She's a part of it,*" and Julia was saying, "*Get up, Lena,*" and *Run* was in her head, and that was what she wanted to do. This couldn't be happening. Julia was dead. Lena had seen her fall. She'd seen the blood.

Julia was dead, and every day since then she'd been dead and Lena had been in hiding because of it.

She tried to move away from the crowd except the crowd was everywhere, people everywhere, drinking, laughing. Waiters carrying trays of hors d'oeuvres, little rounds of toast with caviar and shrimp dipped in cocktail sauce, and all Lena could think to do was to get away, and the farther away she moved, the more she began to think that it wasn't Julia she'd seen at all, but just some woman who looked like her. It couldn't be Julia. It was just that the days had been so strange lately, with Walter coming back, and "Nature Boy" and the blue Ford and the ransacking of her apartment and *everything*—

"Hello, Lena."

The voice behind her sounded so familiar, so fond. It stopped Lena in her tracks.

"You took your time calling."

Lena closed her eyes and let out a small laugh. "You were just waiting there with the record?"

"Don't be ridiculous. I was listening to it when you called. It was a coincidence. There's something wrong with the phone, I couldn't make you hear me."

"There's something wrong with the phone at the *Beverly Hills Hotel?*"

"I think they're bugged. My room anyway."

Slowly, Lena turned. Yes, it was Julia. Julia, who looked just the same, but also somehow not. Julia with the cat-shaped eyes that didn't look as bright as they'd once been and the chestnut hair now streaked with gray though Julia was far too young for gray streaks. Julia wore a fine gold chain that rested against a scar that crossed her collarbone. Her smooth skin was too pale, her finely sculpted face hollowed out, almost gaunt. She was still striking, but . . . "Why would your room be bugged?"

Julia shrugged.

Lena studied her. It was impossible. All so impossible. She did not know what to make of any of it. "How did you get in here?"

"I have my ways. There are so many people here, she doesn't know who half of them are."

"The last time I saw you . . . you're alive."

"Yes." A laugh. "It was touch and go. But yes."

"What happened? I don't understand . . ."

"Not here." Julia glanced around. "Listen, we have to meet. I've been looking for you for some time."

"Some time? It's been years. Why are you sending me cryptic notes instead of just writing like a normal person? Or . . . I don't know . . . sending a telegram?"

"It was the best way. You'll have to trust me on that." Another furtive glance. "Can you meet with me tomorrow?"

Those last hours in Rome. Running from those men. *"You can't escape."* The carabinieri escorting her to the airport and that long and lonely flight back to LA, where she arrived so changed it was as if she hadn't just shed a skin but been recast.

"It's better if you don't ask questions," they'd said. *"For your own sake."*

Kovalova. That had been the name. A Russian name.

"Pretend it never happened," Charlie had said. Lena's apartment had been torn apart and put together again. She was being followed. She'd lied to the police. She'd lied to Paul. Runyon had accused them both of

not being devoted to American ideals. Hedda Hopper. *Un-American*. How many times had Lena heard that word lately. Too many.

"I can't meet you, Julia. Not now."

"I'm in trouble."

"Whatever it is, I don't want any part of it. Not this time."

"It's too late. You are a part of it. You're still a part of it."

"What do you mean?"

"I mean you're in danger, Lena."

"No." Lena shook her head. "No, I won't. I refuse."

"You can't refuse." Julia looked sorry, but that didn't help. "You have to meet with me. Tomorrow. Clifton's South Seas at noon. Please."

"Julia—"

Julia squeezed her arm, and the touch too felt familiar, even through Julia's glove.

"What happened to you?" Lena asked.

"Your engagement ring is beautiful," Julia said softly, and Lena heard the warning there. "He's a handsome man. Don't throw it all away, Lena."

Lena's heart pounded.

"Tomorrow," Julia said. Then she slipped away.

CHAPTER 29

Lena couldn't concentrate all the next day. By midmorning, she was disoriented and the three cups of coffee she'd had only made her shaky.

"What about the jumpsuit?" Connie asked. They were in Lena's office, going through Lena's notes for *Moon Crazy*.

Lena said blankly, "The jumpsuit?"

"For the wolf scene at the zoo."

Lena struggled to remember. She flipped the pages of the script in her hand. "What page is that?"

Connie frowned. "What's wrong with you today? Your head isn't in this. I hardly ever see you so distracted."

"Oh, nothing." Lena reached for her cigarettes. "I didn't sleep well last night."

"Too worried?"

For a moment Lena thought Connie had somehow seen into her mind and knew about Julia's reappearance, and she struggled to reconcile her confusion with the fact that Connie could not possibly know, and in her pause, Connie gently prodded, "About Paul and the new script changes that came in this morning?"

Lena had hardly noted the changes. She lit her cigarette and looked at her watch. She had barely fifteen minutes before she had to go meet Julia, and she still hadn't figured out how to explain this impromptu appointment to Connie, but now was the time.

"Would you mind going through those and making a list of the changes?" she asked. "I've got a meeting at noon and I won't have time. I've got to meet with Runyon tomorrow morning with sketches."

"You don't have a meeting at noon."

"Very sudden. Just came up last night."

"You remember you have a fitting with Claudia Mazur at four?"

Lena didn't remember, but she nodded. "I'll be back for it."

"Remember, Lena, she specifically asked for you. She won't be happy if I have to handle it."

"I'll be back." Lena dragged on the cigarette, but it did nothing to calm her spate of uneasiness at the thought of actually going to this meeting with Julia.

"Lena, I don't see how you have time—"

"I won't miss it," Lena said firmly. "I know. I know. Believe me. I still have to do the sketches for *Medusa*, and I won't forget Claudia. I'll be back in time." She grabbed her purse and gave Connie as reassuring a smile as she could manage. "We'll continue with *Moon Crazy* when I get back, and if you could have that list of *Medusa* changes for me, I would appreciate it. I'll be here by two—I promise!"

Connie waved her off, but she didn't look happy about it, nor reassured by Lena's promises. But Lena would make it up to her later. Maybe she'd stop by Greenblatt's and pick up some of those hamantaschen Connie liked. Or maybe just get her a piece of chocolate cake from Clifton's.

The traffic made it take forever to get to the restaurant, but when Lena finally pulled up before the monstrosity of the vine-and-palm-tree-embellished exterior of Clifton's South Seas cafeteria—*Pay what you wish, Visitors Welcome*—she wished she were still driving. She felt more apprehensive than ever.

Clifton's was always crowded, and she understood why Julia had chosen it. In the noise of the cafeteria lines and the waterfall and the talk, and the lushness of its ridiculous decor of swaying fake palm trees and tiki huts and torches, they would go unnoticed.

She looked around, but didn't see a lone woman sitting anywhere, and so Lena took a white-clothed table near a palm ringed with lights just off a thatched hut and tried to keep from staring at the entrance. The restaurant was loud with talk and the gushing water of its twelve waterfalls, the sound of which ricocheted off the volcanic rock walls and grottoes. The cafeteria line was long, as always, people swarming the carving station, the hot meals of fried chicken and fish, meatloaf, sides, desserts, bread, Jell-O, puddings, cakes, pies . . . the mingled food scents mixed with the mist of the waterfalls and the perfumes and cigarette smoke of the patrons, creating a warm and heavy atmosphere set to the tune of organ music.

She didn't see Julia in the line for food either. Lena's tension ratcheted. She lit a cigarette and tried to look self-possessed when she felt anything but.

Twelve fifteen, and still no Julia. Twelve twenty. The busboys began to look at her strangely, and Lena grew annoyed. It felt like Termini Station all over again, that endless wait, the growing worry and irritation, the doors closing on the Venice train.

One of the hosts approached her. "Excuse me, ma'am, are you waiting for someone, or—?"

"Yes, I am," she snapped. "They're late."

The man smiled and retreated, but continued watching her. Twelve thirty and no Julia. By twelve forty, Lena ran out of patience. She wasn't hungry and she was done waiting. Danger or no danger, Paul or no Paul, she had no intention of sitting there all day. She picked up her purse and left, saying to the host as she walked out, "She must have been delayed."

"Have a good afternoon, ma'am."

The day was too hot, and her nerves were shot and she was beyond annoyed when she reached her car. She opened the door and got inside, rolling down the window and cursing in a long, slow grind of invective, and then she heard the click of the passenger door. When she turned, there was Julia, sliding in with a smile and a "Hello, Lena," as if this had been the plan all along. She wore a blue linen dress with a white pleated yoke and bright pink lipstick. "I'm sorry for making you wait. I wanted to make sure no one was following you."

"They are," Lena said. "I suppose you have an idea who they might be?"

Julia threw her a glance. "Don't you? I think you should drive."

"Drive where?"

"Is Paul at home?"

Now Lena was alarmed. "You know his name?"

"I've been watching you for days and days, Lena. That picture of you two in the newspaper? I know everything about you. My, what you've made of yourself! You did even better than I imagined."

Lena frowned. "You've been watching me?"

Julia exhaled heavily. "I'm not the only one. Go to his place at the Chateau. We need someplace to talk where no one will see."

"I can't put him in danger, Julia."

"He's already involved." Julia looked out the rear window. "You should hurry, before they find us."

"Who's 'they'?"

Julia's soft mouth tightened. "Just drive, Lena."

Lena did, distracted by Julia's constant watch out the back window. Julia said nothing more, and her obvious worry filled the space between them until Lena was seized by it too. She couldn't keep from glancing at Julia, from trying again to define the difference in her friend. When they finally pulled up to the Chateau Marmont, it was a relief to hand the keys to the valet—George, who had seen her there many times before and had a ready smile.

"Mr. Carbone is out, Miss Taylor," he informed her.

"I've just come to pick something up for him," she said. "I won't be long, so . . ."

He nodded. Julia had already gone inside. She waited by the elevator as Lena went the few steps through the small, shabby lobby to the compact, old-fashioned front desk, where Corinne bustled about. She was middle aged and delightful, and she smiled when she saw Lena.

"Good afternoon, Miss Taylor! A beautiful day, isn't it?"

"It is. How are you, Corinne?"

"Never better. How can I help you?"

"Paul asked me to pick up something for him—he said you'd give me the key?" Lena didn't expect it to be a problem; still, she was relieved when Corinne did not question it. Everyone here knew by now of Lena and Paul's engagement.

"Of course." Corinne turned to retrieve the key and handed it over the narrow counter. "Just bring it back when you're done."

Lena smiled, though she felt like doing anything but, and met Julia at the elevator. Once they were inside, Julia said, "That was easy."

"I'm here fairly often."

"How bohemian of you."

"We are engaged," Lena said shortly.

The elevator door opened at Paul's floor. Lena went down the hall to his room and unlocked the door, feeling strangely disrespectful as she did so. She'd been here alone before, but it felt different bringing Julia here, a sullying of a sacred space that belonged just to her and Paul. She didn't like it. She wished she hadn't done it.

But it was too late now. She watched the way Julia took in the room, her dispassionate gaze that was also somehow judgmental, though Lena couldn't decide what Julia was judging—the eclecticism? The shabbiness? Lena bit back the impulse to explain that these were the very things that drew artists to the Chateau. It was eccentric. It was discreet. At a time when what you were or what you thought or who you loved could get you banned or exiled or jailed, the Chateau Marmont did not judge. It welcomed anyone.

Lena put down her purse and took off her gloves. Julia moved to the windows. She looked out, made a sound of satisfaction, then closed the curtains, closing out the bright light, closing them in darkness.

Lena switched on a lamp. "Why are we here, Julia? Why did you want to meet with me? What happened that day at the station? Where have you been all this time?"

"Those are many different questions." Julia pulled off her own gloves and sat. She licked her lips nervously. "Have you something to drink?"

"Coffee? Water?"

"Vodka?"

"At noon?"

Julia looked at her watch. "It's after one."

"I have gin." Lena went to the tiny kitchen and pulled out the gin and vermouth to make Julia a martini.

"You'd better make yourself one too," Julia advised.

"Am I going to need it?" Lena asked.

A small laugh. "Oh, I think so."

Lena didn't like the sound of that, but she didn't like much about this Julia, who seemed so much the same and yet so different. And it wasn't that it was a vast difference so much as it seemed to exist at Julia's very core. That confidence edged by something Lena couldn't name, and that cynicism—was that what it was? The gauntness, the scar . . . Where had that scar come from? But mostly it was Julia's eyes, which were haunted—yes, that was the word Lena had been searching for. Haunted.

But she did as Julia suggested. She made herself a martini, too, but slowly, delaying. When she finally sat on the couch across from Julia, the room had already changed in tone and scope, it was no longer her refuge with Paul, but touched with an apprehension Lena knew it would be touched with forever, and God, she wished she hadn't brought Julia there.

Julia took a drink. "Where to start?"

"Maybe with where you've been?"

"I don't want to start there." Julia met Lena's gaze, and hers was so frank and pained that it took Lena aback. "But I suppose I will, because it will help you to understand. I've been in prison."

Of all the things she could have said, it was the last thing Lena would have expected. "Prison? Where?"

Julia ignored that. "Tell me something. That day we were going to leave for Venice—did you talk to anyone that day?"

Lena frowned. "Anyone? Like who?"

"Like CIA men? Asking you questions that you were stupid enough to answer?"

"I didn't tell them anything," Lena protested. "They showed up out of nowhere, and they asked me about your Mr. Bon Bon, and what I knew about him, and I didn't know anything, Julia. Just that he was dead, and he wasn't just some businessman, was he? He was someone important, and you'd told me nothing! What was I supposed to do? They frightened me, and I had *no* idea what was going on!"

"You were not that innocent, Lena. You'd been couriering for me for months."

"Cigarettes, yes. Packages . . . I didn't know what they were."

"I see." Again, that scathing tone. "It never occurred to you that it might not be in your best interest to tell anyone about it?"

"There were code words. I'm not a fool. Of course I didn't tell anyone."

"Except for the CIA."

"Julia—" Lena's hand shook, she had to put the martini down. "Julia, I never told them about being your courier. They didn't ask me anything about that."

"Then what did they ask you?"

"About . . . him. Mr. Bon Bon, like I said. How I knew him. What happened that night at Club LeRoy." *A classic pill drop.*

Julia's eyes narrowed. "What did you say?"

"I—I hardly remember. It was so long ago." It was only half a lie. The truth was that she didn't want to remember.

"Try."

Lena thought back to that day, the trattoria, the agent's searing blue eyes, the other one's reasonable tone, her panic and that sense that she'd been involved in something she didn't want to be involved with.

She picked up her martini and took a long sip, letting the gin linger on her tongue before she swallowed and spoke. "They said your last name was Kovalova. They said you had a few names. I remember how surprised I was that you'd lied to me. But then"—another sip—"I suppose that's why you were so good at coming up with another name for me, wasn't it? You were used to it."

Julia flinched in surprise. Lena couldn't remember ever catching her friend off guard before, and there was something disconcerting in it, catching a mentor in a mistake and having then to question everything you'd believed before that moment.

"Is it true?" Lena asked.

Julia's expression hardened. "It's a name. It doesn't matter. You told the CIA that I'd had a relationship with Terence Hall, and they ruined everything. Because that tipped off my . . . I guess you'd call them my bosses. That's how they found out that you and I were going to Venice."

Lena struggled to understand. "So?"

"We weren't coming back, Lena. I had tickets for Paris. We were to go there from Venice—you and me. We were suspects in Terry's murder."

"We weren't coming back? But . . . Cinecittà . . . and I didn't have anything to do with his death. They said . . . the CIA men said something about a pill drop. 'A classic pill drop.' Those were their words. They implied you'd poisoned him. Did you? Did you have something to do with his death?"

"Not really."

"That sounds equivocal."

"I didn't drop him any pills. I didn't kill him, but I knew it was going to happen. That's why I needed you to flirt with him that night. I wanted to start a fight with him, like I told you. God knows he'd never missed a chance to flirt with a pretty woman before. I wanted to make a scene—they would never have dared to poison him that night if I had. He would have been too conspicuous. Obviously he was in a mood and it didn't work. But Terry figured out he was marked because of that little meeting. It didn't save him, but it was a big mistake on my part. That's why they came after us."

"You knew he was going to be murdered?" Lena asked in horror.

Julia bowed her head in acquiescence.

The little gesture was as frightening as anything Lena had ever seen. "Who are these people, Julia? Who did you work for?"

Julia sighed. "Listen. The whole thing at Club LeRoy was a disaster. Because of me. Because I tried to save him. Which meant you and I were both marked for messing up. I made an agreement—let you take the fall, and I'd be forgiven. But I couldn't do it, Lena, so I tried to save us both. That's why we were going to Venice. To escape. Those men . . . they're ruthless. They would have . . . anyway, you saw what happened. They found us thanks to the CIA. That shot wasn't fatal. His aim was off, probably because he wouldn't have shot at all if you hadn't kicked him. Still . . . I went to prison. Insubordination. I've been looking for you since I got out."

Lena stiffened. "Why?"

"It wasn't easy to find you. I'm not the only one who changed my name. Why Taylor?"

Lena said nothing.

Julia sighed. "I came to LA because you'd been at Chouinard and I knew you'd never go back to Ohio. You know how many Lenas there are in LA? Quite a few, actually. Then I wondered if maybe you'd listened to me and took my advice about becoming a costume designer. After that . . . all it took was the column about Flavio's birthday party at Ciro's and your engagement and a little bit of research."

"Why look for me?" Lena asked. "What do you want from me?" She waited for the answer with a tight chest, afraid of whatever Julia might say.

"Would you believe that I missed you?" Julia dangled her martini glass, staring at it contemplatively. "I missed our days in Rome together. It was fun, wasn't it?"

Lena was startled at how she wished that was true. But she remembered the carabinieri, the insistence beneath their sympathy, and she saw that same hardness in Julia's face now. "The carabinieri were waiting for me when I got back to the academy. They questioned me for hours and escorted me out of Rome the next morning. They didn't believe me when I told them what happened at the station. They told me not to ask questions. I thought you were dead. I had to go into hiding. I had to stop thinking about Rome. I had to stop thinking about you."

Julia looked at her for a long moment with an expression Lena couldn't read. It wasn't blank, but it gave nothing away. Then Julia said in a strangely light voice, "When you left, something of mine disappeared too. I think you took it. I want it back. I'm not the only one who wants it either."

Lena was surprisingly disappointed. "I didn't take anything of yours."

"That day, you made a pickup for me. Remember?"

Lena shook her head, and then she remembered the kiosk, the boy who gave her the magazine. She'd totally forgotten about it. "Oh, yes. Piazza Fiume."

"That's right. What happened to it? The thing you picked up?"

"The Duke Ellington record?"

"Yes." Julia leaned forward eagerly. "Where is it?"

"Long gone."

"What?" Julia rose so quickly she sloshed martini on the floor. "What do you mean? Where is it?"

"Julia, it's been forever. I gave it away."

"The men who want it are very, very dangerous." Julia came to stand before Lena. "Where is it? Who did you give it to?"

"A friend who liked Duke Ellington."

"Where is this friend?"

Of course it hadn't been just a record, but it had looked like one. It had sounded like one, albeit scratchy. But the last thing Lena was going to do was direct Julia to Harvey and Charlie, even assuming they still had it. "What's on it?" Lena asked. "Why do these men want it?"

"It's not just these men, it's the CIA. They're following me. Those notes I sent . . . it was the best way I had to get in touch with you without raising their attention. I didn't know until after I'd sent them that they'd bugged my phone at the hotel. Lena, when I said you were being watched, I meant it. They're following you too. Do you understand?"

The words landed slowly, each one a visceral punch. "Is that what they're looking for? They searched my apartment. Is that what they wanted?"

"You've talked to the CIA. Would you like to talk to them again?"

"Is it the CIA who did it? Or your bosses?"

Julia's mouth tightened. "They'll come here next. To the Chateau. To Paul."

Lena went cold. "They'll never get past the desk."

Julia laughed. "Do you know how easy it was for me to leave that note in your office? You've seen these men, Lena. Do you really think they can't get past a front *desk*? And if Paul's here . . . well, they won't believe he doesn't know anything. Whether it's the CIA or the other men."

Lena rose and went for her cigarettes. She offered one to Julia, who took it, and lit them both with an unsteady hand. Lena drew on hers and said, "I need another martini."

"I'll make them," Julia said.

The sounds of pouring, stirring, clinking reached Lena from what sounded a far distance. When Julia put the martini glass in her hand,

Lena drank automatically, swallowing gin with smoke, Julia's words racing through her head.

"What's on that record really?" Lena asked again.

"You don't need to know. Do you think this friend of yours still has it?"

"I don't know."

"We'll offer whatever he wants."

"It's not that." It was the idea of leading peril to her friends, who needed none. The CIA? Those men in Rome, Julia's "bosses"? Julia had got Lena kicked out of Rome for . . . something she didn't yet completely understand. She wouldn't tip off anyone to her two friends, men on the FBI watch list, homosexuals who lived in secret. Lena wouldn't do it. "I can't."

"Whoever it is, he'll return the record, believe me. And if he won't, it will be taken care of."

"What do you mean, 'taken care of'?"

"Look, the sooner we get this record, the sooner I'm gone, and the sooner you can go back to your life."

"Tell me what you mean."

Julia exhaled heavily. "The people I work with are used to getting rid of obstructions, that's what I mean. Like your Walter, for example."

Her words didn't make sense. "Walter?"

"You remember him? Your husband?"

"I don't know what he has to do with this."

"He has nothing to do with this. At least, not anymore. I'm sorry." Julia pulled on her cigarette, and an awful, unsettling awareness tickled at Lena.

"Julia—"

"They thought he was in the way. A distraction."

Lena felt sick with horror. "What did you do?"

Julia shrugged. "I had nothing to do with it, I promise you. But he was blackmailing you, wasn't he?"

"Yes, but—you mean . . . your people . . ."

Julia nodded.

"But I didn't want that! I didn't ask for that. And now the police think I had something to do with his death!"

Julia looked painfully resigned. "You did, in a way. If not for you, he wouldn't be dead. But that's neither here nor there. It wasn't what I would have done. But I told you, these people are dangerous. He was in the way. If you don't want to meet the same fate, and you want to keep Paul from meeting it, too, you'll help me."

She had no choice. Still, Lena hesitated.

"You owe me, Lena. I saved your life. I nearly lost mine. *Please.* I can't go back to prison and I don't want to die. *Please.*"

It was true, everything Julia said. Lena did owe her, for her life and so much more. But it was that *please* that troubled her, that soft desperation, and Julia must have seen it.

"Let's go," Julia said, and before she knew it, Lena was swallowing the rest of the martini, throwing her purse strap over her shoulder, leaving Paul's in Julia's dizzy wake—or maybe that was the two martinis.

She took sobering pulls on her cigarette and returned the key to Corinne at the desk, and by the time George brought the car, Lena had caught the contagion of Julia's insistence—or no, it wasn't that. It was fear. The last thing she wanted to do was take Julia to Harvey and Charlie. The news about Walter shook her. The danger that came with Julia shook her. She wouldn't endanger the men who'd taken care of her for so long, but that meant she had to distract Julia for now. Pretend to take her . . . somewhere. Maybe get lost.

She hadn't driven far down Sunset Boulevard before she knew she'd made a wise decision.

Julia said, "Damn it! We're being followed!"

"By who?" Lena peered into the rearview mirror.

"That yellow car."

"Not very inconspicuous, is it?"

"They want us to know. Damn it. Turn here. We have to lose them."

Lena whipped the car around the corner so hard that Julia fell into her.

"Christ!" Julia said. "You're going to give me whiplash."

"You said to turn."

"I didn't mean like a lunatic. Are they still behind us?"

Lena glanced into the mirror. "No. No—wait, yes."

"Is there someplace we can go? Someplace close by and public?"

"La Rue? It's not far. We're not dressed for it, but—"

Julia nodded tersely, and Lena drove. The two-story colonial-style French restaurant was only a few blocks away. She parked and they got out quickly, hurrying inside. It was nearly empty this time of day, and the elegant pistachio-and-brown-striped booths were calmly serene.

Lena told the maître d' they were going to the bar.

"Of course, Miss Taylor." He didn't look approving, but neither did he stop them. The bar, red leather and ebony, held only a few other men, all of whom watched the two of them enter and sit. Lena felt like prey—a feeling she hadn't had since she'd last been in Julia's presence. She'd forgotten how Julia attracted men, that confidence, that bearing. Even changed, Julia drew attention.

The bartender attended them with alacrity; Julia ordered two martinis and glared at the entrance as if she were willing whoever was following them to stay out. It apparently worked, no one entered. The martinis appeared before them with magical quickness. Lena gulped hers. Julia took hold of the toothpick skewering her olive and dunked it up and down.

"So," she said. "Are you happy?"

Lena's pulse still raced; she turned to Julia in surprise. "What?"

"I wondered about you. All this time."

Lena watched the slow up and down of the dunked olive. They had left Paul's rooms so quickly that neither had put on their gloves, and Julia's hands were still bare. Her nails were very short, almost nonexistent. For the first time Lena noticed . . . were those *scars* crisscrossing Julia's knuckles?

Julia caught her look and brought her martini to her lips as if to hide her hands from Lena's gaze. Julia didn't want questions, that was obvious, and Lena didn't ask them. Instead she said, "What did you wonder?"

"How you were living. What you were doing with your freedom while I was locked away."

Lena lowered her voice. "You know, it seems to me that if you're doing something *illegal* you have to expect that one day you might get caught."

Julia popped the olive into her mouth. "How is it, working in the movies?"

"I like it. I'm good at it. You were right about that. I—oh my God, what time is it?" Lena looked at her watch. It was four fifteen. She was fifteen minutes late for the fitting with Claudia Mazur. The time with Julia had gone so quickly. "I'm late." Lena jumped off the barstool. "I have to go. I have to go right now. God, I should never have agreed to meet you today."

"We can't go now," Julia protested. "They might still be outside."

"You don't understand. *I have to go.* Now." Lena called the bartender as she fumbled in her purse for her wallet. "I have to go."

"You can't just leave me here."

"Call a cab."

"Lena, you *can't.*"

The panic in Julia's voice arrested Lena.

"You cannot leave me here," Julia said quietly and slowly. "You have to take me back to the hotel."

"I don't have time for that."

"Then at least take me with you. I can't stay here alone."

The fear in her eyes made Lena realize Julia wasn't lying. She was truly afraid.

"Okay," she said, "But I'm going straight to the studio, so don't argue with me. I can't lose my job over this."

Julia laughed shortly. "It's funny that you think it's your job you have to worry about."

CHAPTER 30

The yellow car was gone.

Julia breathed a sigh of relief. "Thank God."

Lena had no time to think about the yellow car or anything else. It seemed crazy that after all this, she had to concentrate on a fitting for an actress, but she did. She had to get to the studio. Once they got there, she didn't know what to do with Julia.

"Just wait here," Lena said. "I—I'll be back as soon as I can."

"You're just going to leave me here in the car."

Lena waved toward the back lot. "The commissary's behind the administration building, if you want. Ask anyone. They'll direct you. Please, Julia. I really *have* to go."

She raced from the car before Julia had a chance to protest. Lena hoped against hope that Claudia Mazur would still be there, but given Claudia's temperament . . . and Lena was half an hour late . . . If Claudia decided to complain to Higgy, Lena didn't know how she'd explain.

"Too late," Connie said when Lena stepped into dressing room B. "She's gone."

Lena sagged. "Damn it."

The costumes for Claudia were still hanging, and the dressing room looked untouched but for the cigarette butts in the ashtray. The lingering scent of Claudia's Chanel No. 5 fought with the cloud of not-quite-dissipated smoke.

Lena sighed. "How long did she wait?"

"Twenty minutes. I tried to fit her, but she refused. She said that she'd had you written into her contract, and she wasn't going to work for any studio that would do such a bait-and-switch. She was going right to Higgy."

"Wonderful. God, I don't need this now."

"I hope this meeting of yours was worth it," Connie said wryly. She dumped the ashtray into the trash can.

"I should talk to Higgy."

"Maybe tomorrow. I can smell the gin on your breath."

Lena made a face. "He won't be able to tell I've been drinking. Claudia will have caught him in the middle of his second bourbon."

"I don't know if that's a good or a bad thing. By the way, Paul dropped by. I'm to tell you he's coming here when he's finished today."

"Damn it." The curse left her mouth before Lena could stop it, and Connie looked at her in surprise. Lena fumbled for an excuse, though all she could think was *What am I supposed to do now?* Julia was waiting. Lena had to figure out what to do about Harvey and Charlie and a record they might or might not still have, and Paul knew nothing about Julia, and how was Lena supposed to explain her, not to mention the CIA and dangerous men and couriering secrets or whatever they'd been doing and all the rest of it—he would think her crazy. She'd have thought it, too, except that last day in Rome had been all too real, and the fear she felt wasn't her imagination.

Lena's head pounded. The three martinis, no doubt, but there was Connie, her eyebrow still raised, and Lena said faintly, "I haven't got to the changes for *Medusa* yet. I'm so late . . . I don't have time to do anything but work."

Her assistant's expression cleared. "I made the list you asked for. It's on your desk—"

"I thought I heard voices." Paul's voice came from the doorway. He poked his head inside. "There you are! I was just on my way to your office. Did Connie give you my message?"

"I just told her," Connie said.

How was it possible for a heart to both sink and rise? Lena forced a smile. "I'm running a bit behind."

"That makes two of us." His own smile was strained, and he looked tired, knocked about, and she wondered what he'd been through with Runyon today and realized how far that had been from her mind. "I could use a break. What do you say to La Rue tonight?"

La Rue. Of all the places. Lena had to restrain a laugh of pure disbelief. "Maybe somewhere else? I'm not sure I'm up to so much *fancy*."

"Come on," he said. "We can take my car. I have to be back here in the morning so you can just ride with me. Let's just stop at my place first so I can get out of this shirt."

She wasn't sure how to say no to that, or what excuse to use. She had none. There was no reason why she shouldn't agree, and so she said, "Okay. Just let me get something out of my car. I'll be right back," and then she hurried away before he could protest or say, "*I'll come with you*," or anything else. She nearly ran across the parking lot, and when she saw Julia leaning against her car door, lifting her face to the sun and to the nearly nonexistent breeze, Lena hissed, "Just what do you think you're doing? Someone might see you!"

Julia turned to her lazily. "It's about time."

"I can't go anywhere with you. Not tonight." She threw Julia the keys. "Take my car. Bring it back tomorrow. The guys at the gate know my car. Tell them you're bringing it back to me and they'll let you in. Don't forget, Julia, and don't do anything stupid with it. I have to go with Paul. I'm sorry, but I have to."

Julia let out an exasperated breath. "We don't have time for this."

"I don't have a choice."

"Why not just tell him I'm in town?"

"Because he doesn't know you exist," Lena said steadily.

Julia looked surprised.

"He doesn't know about Rome. He doesn't know anything. And I don't want him to know. Not now. Not ever. Do you understand? If you want me to help you, you'll do this for me now." Lena was surprised at the viciousness in her own voice, at the sheer intensity of her determination to keep things as they were. "Just go, Julia. Bring the car back tomorrow."

She turned away, hurrying back to Paul and the fitting room, half expecting Julia to call out for her. But Julia didn't, and Lena was grateful when she heard the familiar roar of her car engine and realized that Julia was going to do as she asked, and for tonight, at least, her life wouldn't change.

She stopped at her office and picked up the list of modifications for *The Doom of Medusa*, which were more extensive than she'd hoped, and then went back to the dressing rooms.

"I've got everything," Lena said. "We should go before Higgy takes it into his head to have a third bourbon and call for me. Are these all the changes, Connie?"

"There are more from today," Paul said grimly. "But I'll tell you about those tonight."

"What has Runyon done, made it into a science fiction movie?" Lena asked.

"He might as well. It'd be closer to the original."

Connie gave Lena a sympathetic look as she veered off toward the costume design building. "Well, then I'll wish you both luck. See you in the morning, Lena!"

Lena couldn't help scanning the parking lot as she and Paul went to his car, but thankfully Julia was well and truly gone, and she relaxed when she climbed into Paul's Oldsmobile Dynamic, which smelled reassuringly of cigarette smoke and Paul.

Paul, too, relaxed when he started the car, or no, it wasn't relaxation, it was more as if he released the cool persona he'd taken on for the day and now could be himself, and himself was a mass of frustration and intensity. He took his cigarettes from his pocket and shook one loose, offered her one, which she refused—she felt sick from today's smoking and drinking, and she didn't like the look on his face. He pushed the cigarette lighter on the dash with more force than necessary.

Lena forced her own worries and her own very difficult day to the background with a sigh. She didn't feel capable of managing any more problems, but she reminded herself that to ignore *Medusa* on top of Claudia Mazur would be a very bad idea. "What happened?"

The cigarette lighter popped. Paul lit his cigarette and took a few puffs before he answered. "Simone is out."

The character of Simone was Helen's best friend, and the book-keeper who convinced the bank to help fund Club Medusa. "What do you mean?"

"Well, they don't need her, do they, if the mob is going to finance the club," Paul said dryly.

"But Simone is—"

"Pivotal. Yes. The whole second act revolves around her bringing in Annie and Jess. I have to find another way to do it. Mob related, prefer-ably, though Runyon has no objection to it being related to smuggling."

Smuggling. Lena squirmed. A little too close. "Smuggling what?"

Paul shrugged. "He suggested drugs, since he wants Helen to end up with an opium addiction."

"Paul, no!"

"That's what I told him. At least let her marry Connor and have some kind of a life, if Connor is the one who saves the Medusa, for Christ's sake, but he says she can get in over her head and Connor can help her overcome her addiction."

The movie was disintegrating. The triumph of women overcoming all odds to start a successful club together, working as a team, now becoming another sad Hollywood story of women as victims and help-mates, saved only by the love of a good man. Lena wanted to cry.

"Runyon also suggested something with spies, but . . ." Paul dragged on his cigarette. "That makes them irredeemable, don't you think?"

"Spies?" Lena said faintly. The events of the day circled around, one thing feeding into the next, weirdly coincidental. Lena felt as if she were in a movie herself, a bizarre fiction. "You mean . . . the CIA?"

He frowned at her. "The CIA? No, of course not. Why would you say that? I mean the Soviets, of course."

"Oh, of course."

"I suppose if I put in Soviets it will help ease his suspicions that I might harbor communist sympathies, but . . . you haven't said anything to him about Lipton and all that, have you?"

"No, of course not." Lena was surprised by the question. "Why would I?"

"I don't know. He said something today . . . I couldn't figure it out." A quick sideways glance. "Was anyone in your family a member of the Communist Party?"

"*My* family?" She laughed. "Not that I know of. Why?"

"I said something about you being from Ohio today, and Runyon said it didn't surprise him, because the Midwest was the birthplace of the American Communist Party."

Which had nothing to do with her, because her parents couldn't have been further from Red sympathizers. "Not my parents. Why would he say that?"

Paul was quiet for a moment. Then, "He said you had radical opinions, and some of your friends were suspicious."

"My friends?" Lena went cold, but Michael Runyon couldn't know about Julia, or Rome, or anyone from her past. "He doesn't know about Harvey and Charlie. Who else could he be talking about?"

"I don't know," Paul said. "That's why I wondered if you'd said anything about Venice."

"Michael Runyon is the last person I would tell about Venice Beach," she said.

"Yeah." Paul went thoughtful in a way that made her nervous.

"So he wants to turn *Medusa* into a spy movie now? Does Higgy know? I just got a new script for another one. I can't imagine he wants two in the schedule."

Paul made a noncommittal sound. "Watch, they'll want to turn it into a musical next."

CHAPTER 31

Lena woke at 4:00 a.m., unable to get back to sleep. While Paul slept, she made coffee, and pulled out the list of changes that Connie had so helpfully compiled for her. She looked them over while the coffee percolated, but really all she could think about was Julia, and everything Julia had said. Julia being in prison and the CIA agents and she and Lena being targeted and how they'd go after Paul next. Was it true? Any of it? Julia had used her in Rome, was she doing it again? What she said about saving Lena's life—had that really been the way it was? So much of it was hazy with the passage of time. What remained was Lena's fear of those men, and the words *"You're part of it. You can't escape."*

No, those words she could not forget. And while Julia had dodged Lena's questions in the past and wasn't answering them now, Lena knew she hadn't misread the fear she'd seen in Julia today.

Lena drank the coffee bitter and black because Paul was out of sugar, and tried to focus on the costume changes for *Medusa*. When dawn peeked through the edges of the curtains, she'd managed two sketches, but they were uninspired and she knew it. If she hadn't let Julia take her car, Lena would have left by now, gone to her office where she could surround herself with work and better concentrate, but she was stuck until Paul was up and ready to go and by then she was so tense she was surprised he didn't notice.

But he didn't seem to, and she realized he was consumed with his own issues—most of them being the changes Runyon asked for. A kiss goodbye, and he was on his way to meet Runyon at the soundstage and she went to look for her car in the parking lot—not there yet—and tried to forget Julia for long enough to get something done.

Except that she'd forgotten about Claudia Mazur.

"Higgy wants to see you the minute you come in," Shirley informed her as Lena stepped through the door. Her secretary's expression was commiserating.

Lena sighed, but Higgy had eyes everywhere, and he'd know if she didn't do his bidding, and so she made her way to the administration building and his office.

Adele said, "Twice in one week. I think that's a record."

Lena winced. "Is he waiting for me?"

The secretary waved her in.

She knocked. At Higgy's brusque "You'd better be Lena Taylor," she stepped inside.

Lena spoke before she cleared the door. "I'm so sorry, Higgy. It couldn't be helped. I was delayed coming back from an estate sale. If she had waited twenty-five minutes—"

"She came to see me." Higgy leaned back in his chair, steepling his hands before him.

"Again, I'm sorry."

He swiveled to look at her. His brown eyes, magnified through the round lenses of his glasses, were cold and impersonal, which was not a good sign. "What do I like to say about actresses?"

"The only time you want to see them is in a movie, a gala, or your bed."

"That's right. So you can imagine what I thought about her showing up in my office."

"It won't happen again."

"I can't think what could possibly have been more important than showing up for a fitting. Isn't that what I pay you for?"

"Yes."

"It reminds me of something . . . What is it?" Higgy tapped his pencil against his temple. "Ah yes, I remember now. Your previous boss. I don't suppose you'd like to be the *previous* head costumer for Lux Pictures, would you?"

"No, I wouldn't." Lena swallowed hard. "Not at all."

"Then make it right. Today."

"I will. Absolutely. I'm sorry, Higgy." She turned to go.

"Oh, and Lena . . ." Higgy's voice stopped her. She turned back. "I hear your screenwriter is causing some problems for the production censor on *Medusa*, and that the costume department isn't keeping up. The film is important to the studio, do you understand? Runyon has my blessing, and Gardner is on board. Keep things on track, will you? I don't have time for all this trouble. Any more of it and I'll have to make some changes."

It was those words, more than the issue with Claudia Mazur, that unsettled Lena as she left Higgy's office and returned to her own. She followed Flavio's standard protocol and asked Shirley to send a dozen of Claudia's favorite flowers with an apologetic note and let Lena know when they were delivered. She would call then and offer a heartfelt apology and do what she could to soothe Claudia's feelings.

In the meantime, she had the sketches for *Medusa* and the morning to make up for the time she'd lost yesterday with Julia, not to mention the little matter of when Julia might show up with the car or what Julia might expect from Lena today and how that would throw a wrench into everything. So many complications. Better to just concentrate on what she could accomplish.

She got more coffee and settled down to work.

"Jonathan Martin is calling," Shirley announced. "He says it's very important."

Jonathan Martin was Charlie's alias. They insisted on using pseudonyms to prevent Lena from being associated with known communists and homosexuals. Neither he nor Harvey ever called unless it was from a pay phone. That Charlie had called meant that it was something important.

Lena was immediately worried. She looked to her door to make sure it was closed, and turned on the fan to keep anyone in the anteroom from overhearing. She picked up the phone. "Please tell me this isn't bad news. And this is very strange. How did you know I needed to talk to you?"

"You're all over the newspaper. We've been concerned."

"Oh, that. You shouldn't pay attention to gossips—"

"Not gossips. The LAPD. *Walter.*"

She'd forgotten that of course they must have seen the article about Walter's death and her questioning, that of course they would worry. She should have called them. "I'm so sorry. It's fine. I should have let you know. I'm fine. I had nothing to do with it."

"Of course you didn't. But you saw him."

"He decided to pay me a visit and ask for money."

"I always knew he was a bad sort."

"Yes, well . . ." She let the words trail off, knowing that he'd hear what she wasn't saying, that Walter's death solved her marriage problem.

"There's nothing to it? Nothing at all? You'll let us know if you need us?"

"I'm not dragging you into this."

"But you *will*, yes? If you need to?" She heard the warning in his voice.

"I won't need to, I promise. But there's something else."

"The reason you've been thinking about us?"

"Julia's back." She lowered her voice even more.

Charlie went quiet. "*Julia* Julia? From . . . ?"

"Yes."

"She's not dead?"

"Apparently not."

"Does Paul . . . ?"

"No. I'm trying to keep it that way."

"Listen, this sounds serious. We should meet with you—"

"*No!* Absolutely not. She's . . . I'll tell you later, but you should stay far away from me right now. Promise me."

Solemnly, Charlie said, "I can't promise that."

"It's too dangerous. I mean it. Remember that old record I had? That Duke Ellington record?"

"That scratchy thing?"

"Do you still have it?"

She heard the sound of a car honking, some kid laughing in the background. "Um . . . I don't think so. No, that's right—it was given to Larry, in fact. Some time ago."

"Why?"

"Who knows? I guess he thought Larry would find it interesting."

Lena took a deep breath. "Okay. Well that's one good thing at least."

"What's that?"

"You won't have to meet Julia."

"Honestly, I'd like to have a word with her. I have some things to say to her about what she got you involved with in Rome. Just tell me you're safe. And in no danger of being arrested for murder."

"I'm safe," she lied. "And in no danger of being arrested for murder."

"I don't like the sound of your voice."

"Goodbye, Mr. Martin," she said with a laugh. "If I need you, I'll call for an appointment."

"You promise?"

"Yes."

"I'll never forgive you otherwise. Neither of us will."

"Don't I know it."

The phone went dead on his end, and Lena hung up, both reassured and troubled. The record was no longer in Harvey and Charlie's possession, which was good—it kept them out of this. But Larry Lipton . . . how to finesse that? She wasn't sanguine about leading Julia, or CIA agents, right to Larry, where subversives gathered every

Sunday—even if most of them were harmless—and where she and Paul together had a history. And if Paul found out she'd made a visit there . . .

Her head began to pound. What she needed was a break and something to eat.

"I'm going to the commissary," she told Shirley. "Can I bring you anything?"

Shirley shook her head and tapped the *Family Circle's Reducing Diet Guide* on her desk. "I'm skipping lunch today."

Lena rolled her eyes—Shirley had a Marilyn Monroe figure and there wasn't a man on the lot who didn't look at her longingly—and went to the commissary. It was crowded, which didn't help Lena's headache or her impatience. Neither did the sight of Michael Runyon and George Gardner sitting at one of the tables, or the fact that the special was a hot chicken liver sandwich on toast, and the smell was faintly nauseating.

She stood in line to order. Just then, Paul came from the line bearing a tray of food, caught sight of her, and waved her over to the table with Runyon and George. Paul didn't look especially happy to see her, she noted. More . . . troubled, and she remembered what Higgy had said this morning and toyed with the idea of grabbing her pimento cheese sandwich and hurrying back to her office with it, but then . . . Higgy's demand that she "keep things on track" echoed in her head and she knew she couldn't retreat.

With a sandwich in hand, along with a Coca-Cola, she went to the table. They were in the midst of a conversation, George saying, ". . . what women in this country really want."

She tendered a thin smile for all of them. "Hello there. How intriguing that sounds. What is it we want?"

They all rose. Paul kissed her cheek. She placed her tray on the table and sat down. "Please sit. I'm dying to know. What do women in this country want and why are you asking?"

George glanced at Runyon. "We're just talking about the movie. About the message."

"Mmm." She took a long sip of the Coke. "Well I'm here to help. Given that I'm the only woman at the table, you can all pick my brain."

They looked uncomfortably at one another.

"What is it?" she asked. "Let me guess what you're thinking: women want diamond rings, nights on the town, fine restaurants, great shoes."

"At first. Of course women want a little fun at the start." Michael Runyon picked up a french fry and dunked it in ketchup.

George nodded. "But women aren't like men, are they? They're much smarter than we are. They get bored with fun all the time."

"Do tell." Lena picked up her sandwich. Paul looked uncomfortable.

"They like more serious things. Love. Marriage. Children. Family." George stirred his coffee thoughtfully.

"Men don't want those things?" Lena asked.

"Sure. Sort of. I mean, in general. But men get bored easily, and they don't know what's good for them." Runyon chomped on a fry. "But we do know how to keep women safe. Once a man has a family, he knows what's important."

"Still, he wants to have fun," Lena said.

Paul gave her a sharp look; she wasn't sure why. Lena bit into her sandwich.

Runyon nodded. "Why shouldn't he? After working all day, taking care of a family . . . a man should be able to let off a little steam."

"Is this all something to do with *Medusa*?" she asked.

"It's about how many of the women should have a happy ending," Paul said.

She couldn't read his tone. "A happy ending how?"

Paul very carefully did not look at her.

"That's what we're discussing," George said.

"How many women are in the movie now?" she asked.

"Three. Helen, Jess, and Hannah."

Lena frowned. "Hannah? Who's Hannah?"

"A new character." Runyon poured more ketchup onto his plate. "A Soviet spy."

She gave Paul a questioning look.

"It turned out to be a good idea," he said defensively, though the shift of his gaze told her he wasn't sincere.

"It does two things," Runyon said. "Hannah will of course realize that the American system is better suited to what women do best: raise strong families and support their husbands, and it also alerts moviegoers to the fact that the Soviets are infiltrating us in the very heart of our most treasured pastimes: jazz clubs, restaurants, Hollywood . . . you name it."

Lena said, "Why, Mr. Runyon, you sound like a member of the MPA. You see enemies everywhere."

"Enemies *are* everywhere, Miss Taylor." Runyon turned to her with his piercing blue eyes. "In places we least expect it. Your butcher, your neighbor. Friends."

Was it her imagination, or did he emphasize the last? She thought of Julia, who was the last person she wanted to be thinking about, and she remembered what Paul said last night, about Runyon's comment on her friends and family and the Midwest.

"How exhausting to be so suspicious." She took a sip of her Coke and changed the subject. "Who are you thinking of casting for this spy, anyway?"

"I thought Debbie Reynolds," Runyon said. "Gardner isn't sure."

Lena laughed. "Debbie Reynolds?"

"I hear she's looking for meatier roles . . . ," George said doubtfully.

"Not as a Soviet spy. America's sweetheart? She'll never do it. I can tell you now, put her out of your mind." Lena shook her head. "By the way, I'll have some new sketches for you tomorrow morning—but of course I'll need casting and script pages for Hannah the spy."

"I'm gratified. I'd rather thought you'd be running behind," Runyon said. "Given what happened yesterday."

Again, Paul looked troubled. So, in fact, did George.

Runyon kept talking. "The whole lot's talking about Claudia Mazur's temper tantrum. Braxton was furious."

Lena lost her appetite.

Runyon went on, "I've always heard good things about you, Miss Taylor. How professional you are for a woman. I admit it came as a surprise to me to hear how you misstepped on this one."

"Sometimes you have to give women an accommodation, Runyon," George said awkwardly, with a knowing smile for Lena. "They have . . . things . . . sometimes."

Things. Women's problems that men would never refer to by name—so embarrassing, a terrible weakness in the second sex. Periods and cramps and weird ailments connected to lady parts and all that. Lena had worked so hard to never let those things interfere with her job. They never had, that she could remember, and yet here she was, so casually being cast into that same lot, so carelessly assumed to need *an accommodation.*

"I'm sure Lena has a good excuse," Paul put in, his voice mild, very smooth. This, then, was the cause of the troubled expression she'd seen on him earlier. She'd said nothing to him yesterday of missing Claudia's fitting, and he must be wondering why she hadn't mentioned it.

"I got caught at an estate sale," she said. "They had some excellent fabrics and I hoped to buy some. There was a sateen that would have been perfect for the character of Jess. I was twenty minutes late, but Claudia didn't want to wait."

Michael Runyon stared at her for a moment as if he thought he'd spotted some dishonesty in her eyes—as if it could possibly matter to him whether she was lying or not. George only shrugged and said, "Did you get it? The fabric?"

Lena shook her head. "It was a waste, I'm afraid. Everything sold for far over my budget."

"Too bad." George took the last bite of his chicken salad and wiped his hands on a napkin. "We'd best be getting back to work. What do you say? Carbone? Runyon?"

Runyon nodded. He and George rose, and Paul got to his feet as well, but as the two others started to the door, Paul bent and put his hand on Lena's arm. "When George brought my car this morning he said something about you showing up yesterday afternoon," he said quietly. "You weren't really at an estate sale. Why were you at my apartment?"

Her heart sank, but she met his gaze. "I'll tell you all about it later."

He hesitated. He searched her face, and then he released her arm. His mouth tightened. He followed the other men, leaving her without a kiss, without a goodbye, and she watched him as he went to the door, that pounding in her head growing ever louder as he held it open for a woman to come inside.

Julia.

He passed her without a word and went out to join the others.

CHAPTER 32

Julia caught sight of her, came to the table, and sat down.

"What are you doing here?" Lena asked. Thankfully no one in the room paid attention. Not the table of writers, or the directors, or the cowboys in the corner.

"You told me to bring the car back to the studio."

"No. I mean here, in the commissary."

"I went to your office and your secretary told me you were here." Julia looked down at Paul's untouched roast beef sandwich. "Does this belong to someone? I'm starving."

"We aren't staying."

"Well, we are. For a bit anyway. We're not going anywhere just now." Julia picked up the sandwich and took a bite. "Mmm. Good."

Lena frowned. "What is that supposed to mean? You're right, I'm not going anywhere. I've got too much work to do. But you aren't staying."

Julia shook her head and took another bite. She waited until she'd chewed and swallowed before she said, "I need a place to hide for a couple hours."

"Not here!" Lena spoke as earnestly—and quietly—as she could. "Absolutely not."

"Why not? It's not as if anyone will notice. I mean, there are women dressed as whores over there and no one's even looking at them."

"They're obviously actresses. People will notice a lone woman walking around."

"Will they?" Julia ate more of the sandwich.

Lena had to admit Julia was right. No one was likely to notice another woman wandering the lot. If she'd got in through the gate, she belonged here, and no one would question it. But the thought of it made Lena twitchy.

"Maybe you should tell me why you're hiding."

"To protect you." Julia sipped the dregs of Paul's Coke. "And myself, obviously. I was followed last night, and I got a threatening call this morning. Who else did you give my phone number to?"

"No one."

"Not your lover boy?"

"I told you, he doesn't know you exist. Even if he did, why would he call and threaten you?"

"Because men are strange, Lena, and they are possessive, and maybe he thought you were having an affair."

The idea took Lena aback. "You said your phone was bugged, so clearly someone else knows it. What did this man say? How did he threaten you?"

"He breathed heavily. Like a gorilla."

"So he didn't say anything?"

"No. But I got the message." Julia finished half the sandwich and stirred the ice left in the glass. "If it wasn't your dreamboat, then let's just say it's someone neither of us wants around."

"One of your bosses."

Julia inclined her head in agreement. "What are you doing tonight?"

"Working. Hopefully rescheduling a fitting."

"Where does this friend of yours live? Maybe I'll go get the record myself."

"If you think I'm telling you that, you're crazy." Lena raised her voice without thinking, and lowered it again quickly, not wanting to make a scene in the commissary.

"Oh, all right. I suppose it's better if we go together. Besides, we always worked together so well." Julia smiled—that same smile, seductive and sweet at the same time. "Didn't you think so?"

Lena looked away, uncomfortable and distressed, and unable to put her finger on exactly why. She remembered dancing with Julia in the room at the academy, the feeling that there was nowhere else she ever wanted to be but there, in that moment, how close she'd felt to Julia then and how the life she'd known before had simply fallen away and she hadn't tried to hold on to it in any way but only released it. Such a strange thing. What a power Julia had had over her then. She could not explain it.

"Well." The commissary was clearing out, actors and production crew returning to the business of making pictures. "I don't have time to talk about this now. I have to get back to work."

Julia nodded. "I'll walk around for a while."

Lena didn't take comfort in that thought. "Stay out of the way. If the red light is on, it means you can't go inside. They're filming."

"Don't worry. I won't get you into more trouble today, Lena."

But Julia's smile was a bit wicked, and Lena worried as she left her old friend in the commissary. When she got back to the costume department, the look on her secretary's face stopped her before she'd crossed to her office door. More bad news.

"What is it?" she asked.

Wordlessly, Shirley handed her a newspaper, folded open to Hedda Hopper's latest column.

Lux Costume Head on the Way Out? The piece was short and to the point: *"Sources say that everyone's favorite costume designer may soon be bidding adieu to the studio where she so famously displaced the charming Flavio. Rumors that she's been missing fittings with major stars like Claudia Mazur and sending studio head Higbert Braxton into furies are everywhere in Tinseltown. Is the engagement ring Miss Taylor has been recently flaunting at Hollywood soirees her way of signaling she is giving up the fashion world for marital bliss?"*

"Oh dear God," Lena said when she finished. "Where did Hedda get this?"

"Claudia was *not* happy," Shirley said. "If I had to guess . . ."

It was worse than Lena had thought. "Did she get the flowers?"

"Half an hour ago."

"Will you get her on the telephone please?" Lena dodged into her office and leaned against the closed door, shutting her eyes against everything.

But then came Shirley's voice on the intercom. "She's out for the rest of the day, Lena. I've left a message."

Not good. Not good at all. She couldn't imagine what Higgy's reaction would be when he saw Hopper's column. Anger? Or would it spur him to make good on his promise to take things in hand if she didn't?

~

Claudia Mazur could not be reached all day. That afternoon, Richard Janx, the director of her film, called to ask if there was going to be a problem. He'd read Hedda Hopper's piece, and the schedule was very tight. Lena reassured him, and asked Shirley to call Claudia again.

Just then, Peter, one of the security guards, showed up, Julia in tow. "She says she belongs here, Miss Taylor?"

Julia only smiled.

"Yes, she's a friend. Is there a problem?" Lena asked.

"Just a bit of confusion, miss," Peter said, tipping his hat. "If she's with you, it's all right."

He left, and Julia seated herself on the couch in Lena's office with a sigh and shook back her hair with one of those elegant motions Lena had always envied. "It was nothing, Lena, don't get upset."

"It's been a long day—"

"The Roman Forum set is really bad, you know that, don't you? They've got the Basilica Giulia in the wrong place."

"It's for the cameras. They can move around more easily this way."

"So thousands of Americans will always believe it's where it's not."

"Thousands? It had better be *hundreds* of thousands, or Higgy will be very unhappy." Lena turned back to her sketchbook.

"That's not the point," Julia argued.

"Do you really care?" Lena asked. "Were you really even a student at the academy? Or was it just a . . . a front?"

"My God, Lena, how suspicious you've grown." Julia looked hurt. "Of course I was a student. I love archaeology. The rest was just . . . I needed money."

"Petra said you were all part of something."

"Petra was an idiot who liked thinking she was a revolutionary. They all were. But they were just artists, Lena, and you know how they are. Always wanting to change the world, but really they only care about themselves and their art."

"What ever happened to her?"

"I don't know. Keeping track of Petra wasn't a priority for me when I was locked up. She's probably married with thirteen children. Now we should go find this friend of yours, don't you think?"

"I'll be here awhile yet."

"Lena." Julia leaned forward, very intent. "I'm only causing you trouble and worry, which is not what I want. The sooner we do this, the sooner I'll be gone."

"Look, I know that, believe me. No one wants that more than I. But I messed up yesterday and I can't mess up again."

Julia looked surprised. "It can't be so bad. It's very impressive, you know, seeing how far you've climbed. You have an assistant, a secretary . . . all those people copying your fashions from the movies. Just as I told you it would be."

It *was* gratifying, and gratifying too to hear Julia say it. More than Lena expected. Still, she was surprised to hear herself confess, "I'm afraid I'm going to lose it."

"Why would you?"

"People are suspicious of my success. Everyone thinks I pushed out the old costume head, though I didn't. He just got distracted, and I'm . . . I'm afraid the same thing is happening to me."

She felt Julia's gaze, a long quiet moment. Then, "Don't let it."

"That's easy to say. But that fitting I missed was very important. I'm a woman—"

Julia said. "Being a woman means you have a perspective no man has. It makes you powerful, Lena. It makes you 'more than,' not 'less than.'"

Lena snorted. "Not in Hollywood."

"You sound like Elsie now."

The name made Lena cringe. Suddenly the smell of pig shit was in the air. Defensively she said, "I'm a long way from Elsie."

"Good. Don't let them tell you who you are, Lena. There is still so much for you to do. I can help you, you know. Like I did before."

"What does that mean?"

Julia said, "Only that I know people who can help you. If you want, depending on what you want."

Lena didn't like the sound of that, though she couldn't say why, or what it was in Julia's voice that made those words frightening. "I told you. I love my job."

"I know," Julia said. "You shouldn't have to worry about losing it either. You're too valuable. If you play it right, they'll realize it."

"I don't understand."

"You need job security, that's all."

Lena let the words sit for a moment, unsure what to say. Suddenly being here with Julia seemed so fraught, everything about her old friend perilous: prison, the couriering, murder, the men in the Cinquecento, her ransacked apartment, being followed. The CIA. Lena remembered Flavio talking about being in debt to Mickey Cohen's men. It was an open secret that the mob was involved in the movie business; so many studios in Hollywood had mob financing. She was sure Lux was no different. She'd seen the photos of Higgy Braxton at Ciro's and Mocambo with men rumored to have mob connections. "Are you . . . are you talking about . . . the mob?"

She felt Julia's gaze. "What?"

"I don't want to be beholden—"

"You think so small sometimes, Lena. That's the Elsie in you."

"Then I don't understand."

"You're so much stronger and cleverer than you know."

Lena remembered that Roman night, the impossible blue of the sky and the music trailing faintly into the courtyard, the marijuana cigarette, the tight feel of it in her lungs.

You shine.

"It's only the men who make you small."

"Not Paul," Lena said reflexively.

"Okay, not Paul. I'm sure he doesn't want you to quit your job and have babies. Do you have a cigarette? I'm all out."

"In my purse." Lena pushed her purse toward Julia, who reached into it for the package of Marlboros and shook out two.

She lit one for Lena without asking and handed it to her, and Lena took it. She needed it, she realized. Julia's talk had put her more on edge than she'd realized. "Paul's never said anything about my quitting," she said defensively. "Or about having babies."

No, he hadn't. But he had made that comment about taking care of her. Had she heard wistfulness in his voice? Had there been . . . what? A hope that she would say otherwise? Or were those only her own fears whispering?

"Hmmm." Julia breathed the sound on smoke. "What did he say when you told him about your marriage to Walter?"

"I never told him." Lena spoke more sharply than she meant. She saw Julia's surprise.

"You never told him?"

"There was never a good time."

Julia said nothing for a moment. There was only the sound of her exhalation. "You didn't tell him about Rome, or me, or Walter. Does he know your real name?"

Lena snapped, "No. Why do you care?"

Julia laughed shortly. "What, does he think you just appeared one day? You have no past?"

"I have a past," Lena protested. "He knows I'm from Ohio."

"Ah. Well. I guess that's something."

"I watched men shoot you and tell me I was part of something and could never escape," Lena snapped. "The police told me to leave Rome. I had no idea why. They questioned me for *hours* about communists and what I was doing in Rome. The CIA wanted to know about you and the murder of a British attaché. I was *escorted* out and told not to come back. You have no idea what's been going on here—what's still going on. Red-hunts and blacklists and McCarthy and everyone's scared to death of the bomb and the talk of war and treason . . . it's all so complicated and . . . and surely you can understand why I thought it best not to talk about Rome, especially because I didn't understand what had happened. And Paul didn't need the burden of my past on top of his own."

"Oh?" Julia's eyes lit. "That's interesting. What do you mean by that?"

"Nothing. Nothing." Lena thought Julia would push, but she didn't, which was good, because Lena had no intention of mentioning Paul's time at Venice Beach.

Julia only nodded and said, "What will you do when Paul finds out?"

Lena didn't want to answer that question. That fear haunted her day after day. "He won't. Will he?"

Julia looked away.

Lena said again, more forcefully, "Will he, Julia?"

"I don't want to spend any more time in LA," Julia said finally, without looking at Lena. "Everything about it feels insane. But the longer I'm here, the more certain it is that your dreamboat will start asking questions. I don't know how you're going to answer them. So let's get that record from your friend."

It wasn't what Lena wanted, but she trusted that Julia meant what she said. It made getting Julia out of LA more important than ever.

"Okay," she said. "I'll make the calls tomorrow."

CHAPTER 33

By the time Lena left the studio, it was near midnight and the main streets of LA looked surreal with neon and blinking lights while the side streets were as usual abandoned and lonely and it felt like being inside a movie set—a thought she'd had many times before. LA had an unrealness unlike anyplace she'd ever been, and lately her life had been feeling unreal too.

That sense grew stronger when she pulled onto Highland and saw Paul's car sparkling iridescent red in the glow of the streetlight before her apartment building. It was the last thing she expected. She parked behind him and got out of her car. He was in his front seat, sound asleep. She stood staring down at him for a moment, hesitant, not wanting to wake him because . . . well, it was midnight, and he would have questions, and what was he doing here? She remembered now his parting words at the commissary. He wanted to know why she'd really been late for Claudia Mazur, why she'd been in his rooms at the Chateau Marmont. He'd expected her to explain it all, and she still had no answers.

She thought about just letting him sleep, but that would be worse. His car was parked directly opposite the door to her apartment building; there was no way she could pretend she hadn't seen his distinctive Dynamic, and he'd know that. She knocked on the window. He started, looked around in obvious confusion, and then saw her. He opened the door. "What time is it?"

"I'm surprised to see you here."

He blinked and ran his hand through his hair. "I thought we were meeting tonight." How sweetly puzzled he looked, how concerned, as if it had to be a mistake and she would correct it immediately.

"I'm sorry. I—I should have told you I was working late. Let's go inside." She led the way to the door, to the elevator. By the time they reached her apartment, he was fully awake. Inside she threw her purse down and took off her gloves. Best to address it all head on. "I'm falling behind. I've got to make it up sometime."

"Has this anything to do with the estate sale you weren't at yesterday afternoon?"

"Yes," she said firmly. "I was . . . it was . . . Flavio, I'm afraid." She sent a quick *forgive me* into the universe, though Flavio would never know she was using him this way.

Paul let out a sound of exasperation. "Again?"

He believed her. Lena fought to keep her relief from showing. "I owe him, Paul. You know that. If not for him—"

"Yes, yes, I know. You'd still be in the sewing room. Except you wouldn't be, sweetheart, and everyone knows it. Your talent would have seen to that, if nothing else. You've got to stop jumping and running whenever Flavio calls for help. Has he ever considered that helping him with his mob friends might one day get you into trouble?"

"I know," she said, trying to sound contrite. "You're right. But he's been a good friend to me. He's been so much better about the gambling, but . . . a small slipup. He was in hiding. That's why I brought him to the Chateau." She prayed no one at the Chateau contradicted her; she didn't think anyone had noted that Julia was with her, but she couldn't be sure. For now it was the best she could come up with. "I'm sorry I didn't tell you right away, but I didn't think you'd mind, and then everything got so busy. I'm hoping it's all over now, but . . ."

"Yes, okay. I should call him myself and tell him to stop involving you."

"Please don't." She hoped he didn't hear the quick panic in her voice. "He'd only be upset that I told you. He'd be so embarrassed. He's very proud, you know."

Paul yawned. "God, it's late."

"Too late," she agreed. "We should go to bed."

She led him to her bedroom, and she was grateful when he fell asleep almost the minute his head hit the pillow. Grateful and both glad and perturbed that her lies had worked so well, that he trusted her so, and she thought again about all the things she hadn't told him, and the larger mess she was involved in and everything that could go wrong, and she became so distressed she could not sleep.

~

Lena had no time to call Larry Lipton the next morning, which in its own way was a relief. Claudia Mazur wanted a personal apology, so early the next afternoon, Lena drove to Claudia's new mansion in Beverly Hills with a vase full of pink peonies and a box of chocolates to prostrate herself before a robed Claudia, who looked as if she'd only just got out of bed.

"You can put them there," she said, pointing to a nearby table already loaded with flowers, including the pink peonies Lena had sent the day before, and at least three other vases of them. Apparently others had got the word that they were Claudia's favorite flower as well.

Claudia had tied her dark hair into a brightly colored chiffon scarf that fluttered behind her as she walked into a room filled with round sofas and low tables, a piano and shelves boasting her Academy Award for *Every Man's Favorite* three years ago, and a host of plaques for lesser awards and humanitarian endeavors. Lena made appropriate noises of respect and as quickly as was polite said, "I'm so very sorry for what happened, Claudia. I got delayed, and there was no excuse for it. I do hope you'll forgive me."

"You understand I asked for you specifically in my contract," Claudia said.

"I do. Again, I'm sorry. It won't happen again."

"It's not every day that I make such a request."

Claudia's contracts were full of such demands, but Lena refrained from commenting. She couldn't deny that Claudia's request was a credit to her. "It's an honor. I'll strive to live up to it."

"You're very talented, Lena, but even talented people make mistakes of arrogance," Claudia said sternly. "Flavio never would have treated me so abominably."

Lena did not remind her that Flavio had repeatedly treated stars abominably, which was why he was no longer at Lux. "No, of course not. Again, I apologize. Please let me make it up to you."

Claudia studied her for a moment, and then inclined her head as if she were a queen bestowing a favor instead of an actress no longer in the prime of her career—the reason she was doing one of Higgy's "prestige" films to begin with, a blatant attempt at another award grab. "I appreciate your coming all this way. It does my heart good. The younger set in Hollywood just doesn't realize how important common courtesy is anymore."

Hollywood was too competitive for courtesy, and what courtesy existed was all fake anyway. You couldn't trust it and the only favors in this town were quid pro quo. But Claudia could think whatever she wanted, as long as she showed up at Lux for her fitting tomorrow.

Lena was relieved when she finally finished smiling and genuflecting and was out the door. She was close to Rodeo Drive, where Flavio had his shop. After last night with Paul, she'd been thinking about her mentor. There was no reason for her to tell Flavio what had happened, and Paul didn't doubt her story and wouldn't bother to check, but she had a niggling, unsettling feeling. It would be reassuring to see his face.

Flavio's shop was small, very exclusive, and decorated in the designer's signature colors of black and white, the outside painted black with white trim, with a big showcase window holding mannequins posed in some of Flavio's most famous designs.

She looked for a parking spot, and it was then, as she began to parallel park, and glanced into her rearview mirror, that she realized where her unsettling feeling came from. A dark car pulled into the spot behind her. Two suited men got out and quickly approached her.

Dark suits. Both wore bowlers. They'd been following her and she hadn't known it.

Her window was down. The men appeared at her door in moments. One of them said, "Miss Taylor, we're with the FBI, could we have a word with you please?"

It was Rome all over again. That soft insistence, that courtesy that barely veiled a menacing force. Lena panicked.

"No." She threw the car into gear and jerked it into the road. The men jumped back in startled surprise. A car coming down the street slammed on its brakes and honked its horn but Lena kept going, speeding down the street, tires squealing, adrenaline pumping, until the men, the car, Flavio's store, receded into the background and then disappeared. She was sweating with panic, driving aimlessly, zigzagging until she was sure she'd lost them, and then she pulled over and buried her face in her shaking hands, calming herself.

It's over. Her heart raced. *It's over.*

Then she heard a noise, a car pulling up, and when she raised her face from her hands, there was a gray Chevy beside her, a man in a porkpie hat, and a camera flash blinding her.

A private investigator, and she knew he had seen the whole thing.

CHAPTER 34

The gossips made the most of it. The news of Lena's "assault" was all over the newspaper the next day; the morning columns were jubilantly gabby—Lux Costumer Assaulted on Rodeo Drive!! Attack just outside Flavio Couture. Coincidence? Is anyone safe in Tinseltown?—and the photograph that made the rounds had her looking horrible and upset. Though what disturbed Lena most about the column that morning was the final lines: Lena Taylor has certainly flown high and fast among the Hollywood elite since she arrived at Lux Studios. One may well ask if there is more to the attack last night than meets the eye. Was she just a random victim? Or was the costume queen targeted, and for what reason? Was the location in front of Flavio's a clue? Stay tuned to this space for more answers!

She'd known the incident would be in the papers, of course. Last night she'd told Paul she'd been followed and a PI had captured it all, and no she didn't know who or why but it was frightening. She'd trusted his worry would do the thinking for him, and she was right, it did, at least for then, and he asked no probing questions—yet. She'd called Flavio to reassure him and Harvey and Charlie, too, and then tried to forget it all and focus on work, but she was shaken and she felt ready to crack into a thousand pieces. Thankfully Claudia Mazur was too interested in punishing Lena for missing the last fitting to care about gossip. Claudia didn't let Lena forget for one moment that she was doing her a favor by forgiving her, and she behaved as badly as any movie star Lena had ever worked with. None of the fabrics were right, though she'd already approved them. "I don't remember that red being so *yellow*. It makes me look sallow." "I told you I will not wear gray." "I understand I'm supposed to be a housekeeper, Lena, but I should be a *pretty* housekeeper."

None of Lena's usual tricks worked. It was all the more frustrating because all the fabrics and colors and designs *had* worked for Claudia before.

Lena was relieved when the actress finally left, and she and Connie stood outside the open door of the fitting room to smoke and lament.

Connie exhaled smoke in a thin stream. "What are we going to do?"

"Nothing," Lena told her. "Richard's already approved the costumes, and she's just being difficult and she knows she liked everything before. Make the fitting alterations, and the next time she tries them on, they'll be perfect—you watch. Today was just to tell me to get bent."

Connie sighed. "I don't know how you do it. Especially after what happened yesterday. How are you holding up?"

"I'm fine," Lena lied. She tapped her ash onto the asphalt. "It was frightening, but no one touched me. It was hardly an assault. Probably just another private investigator."

"You aren't worried about it happening again? What if it's true that you're being targeted for some reason?"

Lena couldn't look at her assistant. "Targeted why?"

Connie was quiet.

"What, Connie? What do you mean?"

"Just that . . . never mind."

Now Lena did look at her. "What's the gossip on the lot?"

Reluctantly, Connie said, "Some people are saying it's the mob, that you owe them for helping you move up so fast. Others are saying it's the feds coming after you for un-American activities. I even heard"— Connie let out a harsh laugh—"well, I heard—it's so ridiculous—that you'd been, you know . . . there was talk of . . . homosexual talk." She lowered her voice to a nearly undecipherable whisper for the last words. *Homosexual talk?* Where did that come from? The CIA? Julia's men? Everyone at the studio knew about her engagement. The rumor was a lie, but it didn't matter. Lena felt the machinations behind it with despair. Whoever started it meant for her to feel threatened. Julia had said she was in danger, it seemed now to assail her from all sides. Lena didn't know how to fight it. She ground out her cigarette and tried to keep her voice even as she said, "This is all coming from the lot? Or have you heard it elsewhere?"

"Just the lot. For now."

"You know none of it is true."

"That's what I said, every time I heard anything. But you know how it is. People love gossip."

"That's not just gossip. That's—"

The phone inside the dressing room rang. Connie ducked in to answer it. The conversation was short. "Mr. Runyon is waiting for you at your office," she announced when she hung up.

One more thing to dread. "Did Shirley say why?"

Connie shook her head.

They walked to the costume department building in silence. The rumors played in Lena's head. The resentments over her rise and Flavio's fall had never fully gone away, but this wasn't just simple resentment or simple gossip. The accusation of un-American activities was far more serious, and as for the homosexuality bit . . . that was worse. The accusation alone would be enough to ruin her. Where was it coming from?

But Michael Runyon waited for her in her office, and that was the first thing she had to manage.

He smiled when he saw her and rose from the chair in the anteroom. "Miss Taylor, I'm sorry I haven't made an appointment, but your secretary tells me you're done with fittings for the day."

Lena turned to Shirley, who gave her a helpless shrug in return. "As it happens, she's right. How can I help you, Mr. Runyon?"

"I wonder if you have a few minutes to discuss costuming for *Medusa*."

She made a show of looking around. "Is George hiding somewhere? Usually the director is part of a costume conversation."

"George is with the art director."

"Shouldn't we wait for him?"

"As you already know, I have his approval on all discussions about the movie," Runyon said smoothly.

"Yes," Lena said. "You know, I've never seen a production censor quite so *involved* in a movie before. You'll forgive me if I'm finding it a bit odd."

Another charming smile. "Braxton is determined that it be a big overseas hit, and he wants to make sure this film is in line with the values of the Motion Picture Alliance. There's a great deal depending on it."

"Why this film? There are others more in line with the MPA's values, I think. *Moon Crazy*, for one—"

"Braxton chose this one."

"I can't help but wonder why, since so much needs to be changed."

"He saw the potential from the beginning, and he believed in Carbone's ability to change it, especially when he heard about the films Carbone had written for the army."

"For the army?" Lena was surprised. She'd known that Paul had written screenplays while he was in the army—he'd written them all his life. But not that he'd written anything *for* the army, which seemed an important distinction. "Is that what you said? *For* the army?"

"Propaganda films," Runyon said easily. "His experience was one of the reasons Braxton bought *Medusa*. You know Braxton produced army films himself, of course."

Yes, she did know that, but she couldn't imagine her fiancé writing such propaganda films for the military. As disillusioned as he'd been? She couldn't imagine it of the man she first encountered sitting on the floor in Larry Lipton's living room, talking about changing the system from the inside out. The man who believed in everything men like Runyon called un-American.

It clashed uncomfortably with the man she knew. Also, Paul had never told her about it. "I don't—"

"Of course, war changes men," Runyon went on. "I told Braxton that. Sometimes it gives them . . . strange ideas."

That same insinuation about Paul he'd made before. On top of the news about the propaganda films, it perturbed her. Abruptly, Lena said, "You wanted to discuss costumes?"

"Why don't we go to the commissary?" Runyon said. "Or better yet—let's go have a drink and discuss all this further. What about the Chapel?"

The Chapel was a bar not far from the studio. Lena nodded. After what Connie had told her about the studio gossip, she didn't want to go to the commissary knowing people were talking behind her back, and frankly a drink would help ease her way through any conversation with Michael Runyon.

"I'll meet you there," she said.

"We can take my car," Runyon said. "It's not far. Why take two?"

She followed him out to his car, a two-toned Buick, blue and gray—nice for a production censor, but then again, how many production censors' cars had she seen before? None. Maybe they were all nice. Probably censors were paid very well. It smelled of new leather, along with the ubiquitous cigarette smoke, and he had a tin of mints on the dash, which slid back and forth as he drove the short distance to the Chapel.

The bar was a popular after-work destination for Lux Studio employees, but the day wasn't over just yet, and the brown vinyl booths and round tables were just starting to populate. The sun sent multicolored light slanting across the parquet floor, and with its dark wood, and narrow windows with stained glass fanlights, the Chapel lived up to its name. Brick walls embraced a small stage where local bands played on the weekends. A jukebox played the other days of the week, but just now it was silent. Lena chose a booth nestled beside the stage. She had no desire to get drunk with Michael Runyon, so instead of her usual martini she ordered a gin and tonic. He ordered a Manhattan.

She reached into her purse for her notebook and a pencil.

"You won't need that," he said. "We're just—what do you call it?—brainstorming."

"Okay." She didn't put the notebook back. "About what?"

"The Debbie Reynolds character."

Lena couldn't resist a laugh. "Mr. Runyon, Debbie Reynolds is not doing this picture. She'll never play a Soviet spy."

He rocked his head back and forth in a *maybe* motion.

"Then you know something I don't," she said. "She's devoted to her image. *And* she's getting married. Who knows what she'll do after that. She may just decide to be a wife."

The waiter delivered their drinks. Runyon took a sip of his. "Is that the gossip? That she's planning to be a housewife?"

"I don't know. I don't have time to read the gossip magazines. But I wouldn't be surprised if that's the talk."

"You don't sound approving."

Lena laughed again. "I don't have an opinion on Debbie Reynolds's life."

"Oh? I think you do."

"Trust me, I don't."

"I see."

"But if she plans on living on the career of a second-rate Frank Sinatra, she should probably think again. Eddie Fisher probably has a limited shelf life. She, on the other hand, has endless potential."

"Ouch."

"I know you think women are the 'great civilizers.' Isn't that what you said? Or maybe that was George, but you agreed with him." Lena squeezed the lime into her gin and tonic. "But not all men deserve a woman who would give up everything for them, you know? And not all women want to."

Runyon considered her. "Are you saying you don't believe in marriage?"

"I'm engaged." She flashed her ring at him. "Obviously I believe in marriage."

"Then you think Carbone is a man worth giving everything up for."

Slowly, Lena sipped her drink. The gin was bracing, the tonic sweet and bitter at the same time. "Who said I have to give anything up?"

"Your job is very demanding."

"It is."

"Children are also very demanding."

"Do you have children, Mr. Runyon?"

"No. No wife. No family. It wouldn't be fair. My job consumes me."

"Then you understand."

"But *you* are getting married," he pointed out.

Lena stirred her drink, raising bubbles.

"I see. You're one of those women," Runyon said slowly. "Does Carbone know this?"

"You're very concerned about my future life, Mr. Runyon."

"I suppose you envision a world of shared responsibility, shared child-raising, that whole equality-driven, egalitarian marriage where both husband and wife have vocations."

"Is that such a bad thing? I think it rather modern."

"Modern? It sounds more like communism to me."

Lena's warning instincts stirred. She took a drink. "You wanted to talk about costumes?"

"I've been hearing rumors about you, Miss Taylor."

"Ah. I'm afraid those rumors have been about forever. But no, I did not get Flavio fired from Lux. I learned everything from him, and he and I are good friends. His leaving was mutually agreed upon—"

"I don't care about that." Runyon waved it away. "It's more the company you keep."

She stared at him, bewildered but also alarmed because it wasn't what she expected him to say and she wasn't sure how to interpret it.

What exactly did he mean? "The company I keep? Mr. Runyon, if you're questioning the company I keep, you'll have to question all of Hollywood, and believe me, there are more secrets in this town than I certainly am privy to."

"But you're privy to some of them, aren't you?" he asked, a bit too fervently. "If, for example, I were to ask you who uses marijuana, you would know, wouldn't you?"

"You could go to *Confidential* for that," she said. "I think they keep a running tab. But why would you care?"

"What about wife beaters?"

Lena tried to cover her squirming with a gulp of gin and tonic. "Why are you asking me these questions? What have they to do with *The Doom of Medusa*?"

"What about communist sympathizers?"

"I don't know," she said shortly. "I don't ask people their politics."

Runyon shook his glass slightly, swirling the drink around the ice. "Have you ever been to Italy, Miss Taylor?"

It was all Lena could do to keep her expression even. "Why?"

"Some of your designs have a distinctly Italian feel. Very Roman sometimes."

The chill from the gin had moved into her spine. "Classicism is a style. I was trained in it. I like the look. It speaks to me."

"Where were you trained?"

Elsie Gruner had trained at Chouinard. Lena Taylor had come to LA with nothing. Abruptly she remembered that long-ago meeting with Jasper Rutledge, reborn as Gaspard whatever, just as she'd been reborn. Carefully, Lena said, "Flavio trained me. I think he's been to Italy a few times."

"And Carbone, too, I think."

"Yes, I told you. He was in Rome for the liberation."

"Is that where you met him?"

She tried to laugh. It came out short and stifled. "No. I told you that too. I met him here in LA. At a jazz club. Why all the questions?"

Runyon ignored that. "Did Carbone base his writing of the Medusa on the jazz clubs he'd seen in Rome?"

"I don't know, why don't you ask him? If you remember, he wrote the Medusa club as a nightclub. You changed it to a jazz club."

"It reminds me of one I knew there," Runyon mused, his fingers on his glass, though he didn't raise it to drink.

"You were in Rome?"

"For a short while. I was working on a film there in . . . must have been '49? '50?"

She was afraid now.

"There was a little place on . . . hmmm . . . it was in the neighborhood of Via del Babuino," Runyon went on. "Anyway, lots of artists' studios there. The street of the artists, they called it. The neighborhood was known for anarchists and communist sympathizers."

It was Via Margutta that was known as the street of the artists, but she didn't correct him. "Is that right?" she murmured.

"The club Carbone described is like one in that neighborhood."

"So . . . is that why you think his political views have changed since he got out of the army? Because of a jazz club he *might* have visited in Rome?"

"I don't know," Runyon said, and his expression turned sharp again, his eyes piercing. "What do you think?"

"I think Paul is not a communist," she said. "Nor am I."

"A pity. I thought if you were, it might help us decide what a Soviet spy would wear." He said it casually, but it was not casual at all; Lena knew it.

She swallowed the rest of her drink. "That's what research is for, Mr. Runyon."

"Soviet spies are not obvious, that's why they're spies. They don't just come up to you and say 'Hello, I'm a Russian spy.' And that makes it difficult to research. They try to blend in. That is, if they're successful, they do."

"You know a lot about Soviet spies," she said.

Runyon said, "I'm only assuming."

"If that's the case, then it's easy, don't you think? We have her dress like everyone else. Quiet, unassuming. Drawing no attention to herself."

"Rather the way you do," he said.

She did not miss his implication, though he kept a friendly smile on his face. "I dress *movie stars*. I dress this way so I'm not competing with them. If you'd ever had to convince a gorgeous woman to look drab for a character, you would understand."

"Of course," he said, but the smirk on his face said differently.

Maybe he saw something in her. Maybe it was something in her voice. Maybe it was the memory that bit into the words, because it remained there, hovering, and she couldn't bat it away. Whatever it was, Michael Runyon downed the rest of his drink and studied her as if he understood something she didn't understand herself.

"You should be very careful, Miss Taylor," he said.

"I have no idea what you mean," she said. "But I should be getting back. I have plenty of work to do tonight."

~

Once she was safely back in her office, she realized how tense she was, despite the gin and tonic. She felt flayed, honestly, and the struggle to reveal nothing and yet still defend herself and Paul—*against what, exactly?*—had worn her to a frazzle. She still had no real idea what Michael Runyon had been about, or what he wanted, or what rumors he'd heard, but she was disconcerted. More than that, she was afraid. She had not mistaken the threat in Michael Runyon's words.

She eased off her slingback pumps and rubbed her feet and lit a cigarette. She'd received a few calls while she was gone; one from Paul. Another from Julia. Lena crumpled that message in her fist, though she knew she couldn't avoid Julia.

The last was from Detective Joe Miller, asking her to call him at her earliest convenience. *Regarding the Maynard case.* After the chaos of the last few days, she'd nearly forgotten all about poor Walter; she'd forgotten the police would still be investigating the case, because for her the mystery had been solved. Julia's bosses had happened to him, and the fact that she knew that, and the police didn't, and it was just one more thing she couldn't say, raised a terror in her she couldn't push away. Walter had been the start of her new life; what an irony if he were to be the end of it.

She couldn't bring herself to laugh.

CHAPTER 35

"Would you like a cup of coffee?" Detective Miller asked solicitously.

It was early. Very early, in fact. Lena had awakened with the dawn to go down to the police department in city hall, not wanting to be late to work and give Higgy another reason to be upset. She shook her head in answer to Miller's question. "No thank you. Why did you want to see me, Detective?"

The little room was close. A small fan spun in the corner but didn't lend much movement to the air. Miller gave it an annoyed look. "I'm sorry. It's not very comfortable in here, I know. The new building is supposed to be air-conditioned."

"That will be nice for you." Lena spoke politely and eyed the clock. She didn't care about the nearly finished new LAPD building a block away.

"We got the coroner's report back on Walter Maynard. What do you know about poisons, Miss Taylor?"

Lena tried to look surprised. "Is that what killed him? Poison? I know rat poison, like everyone else."

"Did you consider Walter Maynard to be a rat?"

"No. Was it rat poison?"

Detective Miller sighed. "As it happens, no. It was curare."

Lena gave him a blank look.

"Walter Maynard died badly." Miller watched her closely as he spoke. "It would have taken him almost fifteen minutes. Curare would have paralyzed and suffocated him slowly. He would have been aware that he was dying and been unable to do anything to stop it. The only thing that might have saved him is if someone had happened upon him and given him mouth-to-mouth resuscitation. Maybe."

"Oh my God." Lena didn't have to feign horror. The vision he presented was terrible. She wouldn't have wished a death like that on Walter, or any death, especially, beyond that fleeting moment in the tavern, which she felt guilty for, and hoped that Detective Miller couldn't see it resting uneasily upon her.

Miller said, "Have you been in a hospital recently?"

The question startled her with its incongruity. "A hospital? No. Why?"

"Have you been to Canada?"

"No."

"Not shooting a film there?"

"Lux has no films shooting in Canada. Why?"

Miller rubbed his nose. "Curare comes from South America. It was used by Indians there to poison arrows."

"I haven't been to South America either," she said.

"A Canadian doctor began using it as an anesthetic about fifteen years ago."

That explained Canada.

"But do you know what I find most fascinating about curare, Miss Taylor?"

She shook her head. "I can't begin to guess."

"The Russians use it as a poison. They inject it."

"The Russians," Lena said faintly. "How interesting."

"Don't you think so?" Miller's blue gaze held her tightly. "Do you know any Russians? Have you any Russian friends? Anyone you can think of who might wish harm to Walter Maynard?"

Lena's mouth went dry. Now Michael Runyon's questions last night held a heavy resonance. Russian friends, Russian spies. Paul's politics and her own. Revolutionaries. Julia's other last name and the fact that

Lena knew exactly who had poisoned Walter. With curare, a poison the Russians used.

Julia Keane's bosses were Russian. Which meant . . . Julia was a Russian spy.

The realization sank into Lena slowly, all the things that she'd denied until that moment, the suspicions she'd pushed away, falling into place. She'd thought Julia a communist, yes. But a spy? She had not allowed herself to believe it, though of course, *of course*, she'd known it. The scars on Julia's collarbone, on her hands, the haunted look in her eyes, prison—what prison? A Russian prison? An American one? *"She has a few names."*

Was it true, and if it was, what did it mean, and what really was this record Lena had given to Harvey and Charlie that Julia wanted back so badly? The FBI agents who'd approached her in her car, the men Julia had said were following her. Was *this* what they'd wanted to talk to her about? She was beginning to think she shouldn't have raced away.

Lena needed time to think. Time away from Detective Miller's shrewd gaze. She didn't know how to answer him or what to say or what to do. All she knew was that her instincts screamed danger, and she wanted out of this close little room with its clicking fan and Detective Miller's questions.

"I don't," she managed to croak. "I don't know any Russians. Unless they're actors. And actors . . . well, you know, they could just be pretending to be Russian to get a part."

Miller was quiet for a moment. Then, finally, he said, "I understand you were assaulted on Rodeo Drive the day before yesterday."

"It was hardly that. The gossips made more of it than it was."

"What was it then? You didn't file a police report?"

"I didn't think it was worth it. Two men followed me in a car. They approached me. I got scared and drove off. I'm afraid I caused a bit of a scene. It was stupid, but I thought then it was private investigators, and I still think it was."

"Why would someone hire private investigators to follow you?"

She gave him a weary look. "Gossip columnists, Detective. Since all this with Walter, I've been a bit of a target."

"Ah. I see. I'm sorry." He did not sound particularly sorry.

She smiled thinly.

"Just one more thing." He reached into the folder on the table before him and drew out a photocopy of some kind of form. Lena didn't recognize it. Not until he turned it and put it in front of her. It was the lease for the duplex in Edendale. She knew already that Walter had put her name on it because Hedda Hopper had told her so, and sure enough, here was Detective Miller, pointing to the front page, the cover page, where, beneath the fancy-fonted *LEASE*, the form stated that the duplex was rented to *Walter Maynard and wife, Elsie.* "Did you know Maynard's wife? This Elsie?"

Lena said, "Before my time." It wasn't exactly a lie.

Detective Miller nodded. "Very well. That's all then, Miss Taylor. We'll let you know if we have any more questions."

Lena did not delay in leaving the room, or city hall. It was all she could do to keep from running.

~

Julia called incessantly throughout the morning. Lena found a hundred reasons not to take her calls. Finally she told Shirley to tell Julia Keane that she'd left for the day. It wouldn't work for long, Lena knew that. She half expected Julia to burst into her office. But for now, she needed time to think. What was the usual course of action when one discovered a friend was possibly a Russian spy, especially when you'd been involved with her in running—what? Secrets? What kind of secrets? The kind that had something to do with the Italian government, or British assistant attachés to the Vatican? Or those involving the US government? Was this what the carabinieri had accused Lena of being part of? Those men in the Cinquecento? It wasn't just a game she'd been playing. It was *treason.*

What was this record that Julia needed so desperately?

Lena remembered the drink she'd had with Michael Runyon yesterday with discomfort, the things he'd implied. How close he'd come; how had he come so close? It was curious, wasn't it, the questions he'd asked. Not the usual questions from a censor. What had he said about Soviet spies? That they didn't just come up and announce themselves. *"They try to blend in. That is, if they're successful, they do."*

Wouldn't that be true of American spies too? CIA agents, maybe? Men who were maybe working to make propaganda films for the army, or for the Motion Picture Alliance. Men like Michael Runyon, for example, or maybe . . . just maybe . . .

Like Paul.

Lena fought the thought. She had no reason to believe it. Maybe Paul had once written propaganda films for the army, but he'd been singularly uninterested in continuing to play that game now. He'd fought every change for *The Doom of Medusa*. He didn't like Michael Runyon, and that Runyon thought Paul harbored communist sympathies was clear. But then, why hadn't Paul ever told her about the propaganda films? And why was Runyon working so hard to instill doubts in her about her fiancé?

Who was Michael Runyon, anyway? Why did he care so much about her associations or her friends?

The questions were a distraction, she knew. It kept her from thinking about Julia, and what to do about her old friend who worked for Russians—*the friend who'd tried to save the British attaché, the friend who* had *saved Lena's life*—but the drink she'd had with Runyon still troubled her, and here, at least, was something she could do, some action she could take that didn't cause any moral dilemma.

Lena grabbed the sketches she'd worked on that morning. She told Shirley she was off to soundstage six to get costume approval, and to tell Connie where she was.

The lot was furiously busy. Prop masters carried sheets of sugar plate glass to the set for the newest Bob and Mikey adventure, an animal wrangler wrangled a herd of dogs, raising clouds of dust and getting in the way of everyone. Lena wove her way through the actors and crew, focused singularly on reaching the soundstage. She got there during the rehearsal for the first scene. Ruby sat with the script pages, her assistant trying desperately to appease Kit with a donut while Richard Widmark looked as if he were desperately trying not to strangle the dog. George Gardner consulted with Paul near the actors.

Paul frowned as she came in. She waved to him with the sketch pages, and then pointed to Runyon, who sat alone at the writing table, and Paul nodded and went back to his consultation with the director.

It was just as she'd hoped. She didn't want to involve Paul in this, not yet. Though she had questions for him too, they were private ones, and she understood that accusing him of keeping secrets from her was an irony she had best tread carefully around. But for now, Runyon was who she wanted.

She marched to the table.

"Miss Taylor," Runyon said coolly. "New costume sketches? How gratifying."

"Yes, but that's not why I'm here. Do you mind if we have a chat?" She motioned to the door. "Outside?"

"I'm very busy at the moment."

"Doing what? There don't seem to be any un-American ideas for you to wrestle just now, or spies for you to corner—unless of course you consider me to be a spy, which I think you do. Or Paul. Or maybe he's one of you. I honestly don't know. But I would like some answers."

She'd alarmed him, she was gratified to see. He rose without a word and led the way outside, across the road from the soundstage to the Roman Forum set—how strangely appropriate, Lena thought, as Runyon went into the relative shade of the Basilica Giulia, in its wrong place. Runyon turned to face her and crossed his arms over his chest.

"Assuming I can give you answers," he said. "What do you want to know?"

"Why are you on my back?"

"Do your job and I won't be."

Lena regarded him grimly. "That's not what I mean, and you know it. You've practically accused me of being a spy. Why?"

"Because I don't think you're who you say you are."

"I wasn't aware production censors were trained to spot spies."

"We have many jobs."

"You're not a production censor."

"Now why would you say that?"

"Because I've worked with many, and while all of them are as irritating as you, none of them have shown such interest in my associations or my past, Mr. Runyon. I think you're with the CIA. Or you're a spy. Or maybe both. So maybe you could tell me why you're so interested in me, and we can stop with all the games."

He contemplated her, one long minute. Lena said nothing. She had no idea whether he would admit to it or deny it, but she had no doubt she was right. She didn't know why she hadn't seen it before.

Runyon took her arm lightly, pulling her behind one of the arches, out of sight.

"You've been a target of the CIA for a long time, Miss Taylor," he said. "Or should I say, Miss Gruner? Ever since Rome."

She was stunned. Stunned and frozen. Whatever she had expected, it wasn't this. *Deny it.* That was her first thought. Pretend she didn't know what he was talking about.

"Don't bother to lie. Do you think we stop tracking people who have been involved in communist spy rings?"

She swallowed hard. "Does Paul know?"

"Paul." Runyon let out a breath. "Carbone is complicated."

"Maybe you could tell me why that is."

"I'm not getting involved in lovers' affairs," he said.

"Just"—she hated how desperate she sounded—"does he know who I am? Does he know about Rome?"

Runyon shook his head. Lena closed her eyes for a moment in sheer relief. "But he will, soon enough. He has his own suspicions."

"Is he a CIA agent too?"

Impatiently, Runyon said, "You'll have to ask him that yourself. Look, Miss Taylor, I want one thing from you: you're in possession of a very important document. You left Rome with it."

Lena laughed. "If you mean the record, I don't have it."

Runyon looked surprised.

"I don't have it," she repeated. "The Duke Ellington record, or whatever it is. I gave it away years ago. I have no idea what's on it or where it is now. I'm sorry to tell you that you've all been watching me for no reason, and if you don't mind my saying, it's ridiculous that you've gone to all that trouble for it. Taking a job as a censor and all . . . all this? You could have just asked me for it."

Runyon looked amused. "Do you really think you're our only target? Or that the CIA spends so many resources on you? You're only one spoke on a very big wheel, Miss Taylor. I'm not the only CIA man working for the pictures, for one thing. The Psychological Warfare Workshop has many arms, and monitoring communists in Hollywood is only part of it. The record is one of my objectives, but only one."

"The Psychological Warfare Workshop?"

"The best way to fight communist propaganda is with our own campaign for truth. The movies are only one way to do that. Don't you agree? Where's the record?"

"I don't know."

"You're lying."

"No. I have no idea where it ended up."

"You know we could destroy you. One phone call to HUAC . . ."

The idea was terrifying. "Is the FBI all part of this too?"

"The FBI?"

"They approached me the other day in front of Flavio's shop."

"That was the attack reported in the papers?"

Lena nodded. "They wanted to talk to me. I don't know why."

"Damn FBI," Runyon said. "They are a pain in my ass. They probably got word of your friend. Speaking of which, Julia Keane is another part of this mission. How well do you know her?"

Lena eyed him warily. "Why ask questions you already know the answers to?"

"She's a Soviet spy. Her job is to find you and get this document back."

"What happens once she gets the document?"

"We're not sure. It depends upon your loyalties, we think."

"My loyalties?"

"Yes. We, of course, are aware of her every move. Will you help us retrieve this document, capture her, and testify against her?"

"You're asking me to betray a friend," Lena said slowly. The scars on Julia's hands, on her collarbone. That haunted look. The execution of the Rosenbergs was not such ancient history. "What happens to Soviet spies, Mr. Runyon?"

He said nothing, but she didn't need him to.

"You're asking me to condemn her to death."

"Are you a patriot, Miss Taylor? We have reasons to doubt it, you know."

"What's on this Duke Ellington record anyway?"

Runyon only smiled.

CHAPTER 36

Murder Case Closed—Chief of Police William Parker today announced that the murder case of Walter Maynard, who was found dead in front of the Hollywood Hotel two weeks ago, has been closed. There will be no other statement or information released about the case.

Autopsy results reveal that Maynard died of a heart attack. He had last been seen at the Lucky 8 Tavern on Highland in an argument with Lena Taylor, the costume design head of Lux Studios. Miss Taylor was questioned and released. She is not a suspect.

∽

Lux Costumer off the Hook!—Today police announced that Lena Taylor, Lux Pictures' head costumer, is no longer a suspect in the death of her old friend actor Walter Maynard, who died under mysterious circumstances. They've given no other details in the case, and won't, so we are left to wonder: What did the star tailor fight with Maynard about an hour and a half before he died? And who attacked Miss Taylor two weeks later in front of Flavio's Couture on Rodeo? Nothing but questions for this reporter, especially because there are rumors that Maynard had underworld connections, and his wife, Elsie Maynard, has disappeared. Could Mrs. Maynard have something to do with her husband's death? This reporter is dying to know. Anyone with any information about Elsie Maynard should get in touch with this office immediately. Another curious element to this case is that Lena Taylor has recently been seen in the company of a mysterious woman—très intéressant! Given the stellar fashion designer's new missteps, could we be watching a fall as spectacular as Miss Taylor's rise?

~

"What's this?"

Paul tossed the newspaper to where Lena sat on the couch in her office. She caught it—and caught also that he looked . . . not angry, or not exactly angry, but conflicted. Sad and angry both.

She looked down at the gossip column, scanning it quickly first, then reading it more closely, because she needed time to think of an answer. That stupid private investigator. Or maybe it was even the CIA or the FBI who had planted this item; she had no idea. She wondered which of them had told the police to back off the Maynard case. But it didn't matter. What mattered was that she'd told Paul nothing about Julia, and that Runyon's words weighed heavily on her, Paul's suspicions, her own, the decision she must make.

She decided to lead with the good news. "Thank God they closed the case."

"That's not what I mean. Who's the 'mysterious woman' they're talking about?"

"Oh. An old friend who came in from out of town."

He raised a brow. "Another old friend? You didn't tell me that."

"You were working. I probably just forgot."

"You just forgot."

Lena tried to smile, it was a miserable failure. "She came into town, I took her out . . . it was nothing, Paul."

"You're lying to me."

"Don't be silly."

"It doesn't say 'one night' here. It says 'recently been seen in the company of.'"

"It's just a gossip column. You know how they exaggerate—"

"Lena." He sank into a chair and put his head in his hands. "Don't do this to me. Please."

Her chest tightened so she could not get a breath. "Maybe you already know. Didn't Runyon tell you, since he's so busy filling your head with suspicions about me anyway?"

Paul's brow furrowed. "I don't know what you mean."

"Of course you do. Just like he's filling my head with suspicions about you. Like the fact that you wrote propaganda films for the army. I didn't know that. Runyon works for the CIA—I think you know that too. Maybe . . . maybe you work for the CIA too. Do you?" Lena spoke the words quickly, so she didn't have to think about them.

Paul said, "The CIA? Is that what you think?"

"You think I'm a spy, don't you?"

He took a deep breath. "No. No . . . I don't know. You never talk about your past, and I . . ."

"I do talk about it," she protested—a small protest, very small.

"What do I know? You're from a pig farm in Ohio. You don't share memories, Lena, not like most people. It's like you're . . . you're frightened of them, or . . . or something . . ."

"No," she said. "No."

"This Walter Maynard, who just pops up out of the blue, and this 'mysterious woman'—I have to hear about these things in gossip columns, for Christ's sake."

"You never told me about writing films for the army. And Runyon implies you're a CIA operative—"

"I wrote *training* films for the army! I guess if you want to call them propaganda, go ahead. It's not completely wrong. Yes, I did, so what? I hated it. I hated it all. I hated the army and those films. They were half lies, and I didn't want to admit that I'd helped make them, and I didn't want to talk about it. I came out looking for something that was right in the world, something true and beautiful, and I found you, and—" He shrugged helplessly. "But you're a lie, too, aren't you?"

His words broke her heart, and how could she say that no, she wasn't a lie? How could she say she was something true, when she wasn't, and when she was so afraid of her past? When she'd lied, but not just that, when she had a friend who was a Soviet spy, when she'd couriered secrets she was afraid to think about, when she was the reason Walter Maynard was dead. Could Paul bear those things? Was it right to ask him to, especially when associating with her could ruin his career?

"You can't believe what Runyon tells you about me." She heard the desperation in her voice. "Why do you believe him?"

"I've known him for a long time, Lena." Paul sounded resigned. "We were in the army together, in the signal corps. He left before I did. When I got out, he approached me to come work for the CIA. I refused. I was done with all of it. He doesn't trust me, but he's never quite let me go, and I've never known him to be a liar."

"Why didn't you tell me you knew him?"

"He warned me to be careful. I didn't know what to think."

"I'm not a spy," Lena said.

"Okay." He nodded shortly.

"You don't believe me."

"You're not a spy. Okay. Tell me something real."

"I love you."

He closed his eyes and sighed. "That I believe. But I don't think it's enough, Lena. Not now. I think you're keeping things from me. Secrets. How can we go into marriage like that? What are you not telling me?"

She wanted to cry. *Tell him.* It should be easy. Open her mouth. Tell him her real name. Tell him who Walter really was. Those things weren't so hard, were they?

"Just one thing," he said softly.

She closed her eyes. "Lena Taylor isn't my real name. My real name is Elsie Gruner. I changed everything, even my age. I'm not thirty. I'm twenty-six. I came to LA with Walter, and actually . . ." The next part was hard to say. "Actually, he was my husband."

Paul was quiet. She could not bear his silence, or not seeing his face. She opened her eyes. What was his expression? She couldn't tell. Sorrow? She couldn't read it, she didn't know.

She could think of nothing to do but keep talking. "We weren't together very long. I hardly knew him, but . . . he was a small-time pool hustler and I helped him. We came out here because he wanted to be an actor and I wanted out of Zanesville. But he was a terrible actor. I mean really terrible." A half laugh, half cry. "Then I met Harvey and Charlie and they liked my designs and Charlie got me into Chouinard and I left Walter. Well. We left each other."

Paul looked so helplessly confused. Like a small boy really. "Why didn't you tell me this?"

"Because we weren't divorced, and . . . and I was afraid that if I tried to divorce him, he would come back and . . . do exactly what he did."

"Which was what?"

"Try to blackmail me."

"About what? Was he a criminal or something? Did the two of you . . . I don't know, do something illegal?"

"No. Nothing like that. He threatened to tell you I was married, and he wouldn't give me a divorce because he saw me as his way into an acting career. He would have caused a scandal, and that would have led to . . ." She paused, trying to find the words. "Led to other things."

"Other things?" Paul asked warily. "Like what? You aren't telling me that you—"

"No. No. I didn't hurt him. I gave him money, just like I said."

"Then what?"

"Even though I didn't kill him, Walter's dead because of me. Oh . . . please believe me when I tell you I don't want you involved in all this."

He frowned deeply. "What are you talking about? Involved in what?"

"I can't tell you."

"Another lie?"

"No, not a lie." Lena spoke desperately. "It's just . . . it's dangerous, and I can't . . ."

"You're involved in something dangerous?" Paul rose from the couch. "Lena—Elsie—whoever you are—for God's sake. Does this have something to do with that attack the other day? Those men?"

"It wasn't an attack, but yes. I'm being followed. The FBI. Maybe the CIA too. I don't know, Paul, but please—don't you see how you can't get involved in this?"

"Are you telling me Runyon's right? You're some kind of . . . of agent?"

"No!" The word came out with more force than she intended. "No! Paul, please. Please, just listen to me. I love you. I just . . . I can't tell you this yet. Please just trust me."

He gave her a look—such a look. Amused, wondering, perplexed, angry . . . she saw all those things. "How can I trust you, when you've just told me you've lied to me about something as basic as your name?"

Lena's vision blurred. "Because I love you, and I don't know how this is all going to work out, and I'm trying to protect you."

"How *what* is going to work out? You're scaring me, Lena. It's supposed to be the other way around. I'm supposed to protect *you*."

"You didn't do something stupid years ago. Believe me, Paul, I'm trying to fix everything."

He stared at her in obvious disbelief. "You're really not going to tell me what's going on."

There was too much at stake, and Paul was too important. Until Julia was gone—really, truly gone—Lena refused to endanger Paul, whatever it cost her. "No."

He exhaled, obviously frustrated, a great rush of breath, a muttered curse. Then, without another word, he went out the door.

She watched him leave with a slow and terrible sadness. She could do nothing else. She had taken a risk. All she could hope was that eventually Paul would understand. For now—

The constant hum of the sewing machines downstairs stopped abruptly.

Lena sighed wearily. What now? She was in no mood for another emergency.

Then Lena heard the boom of Higgy's voice reverberating through the floor. God, not this, not now.

Reluctantly, Lena left her office, ignoring Shirley's watchfulness— Lena didn't want to think about what her secretary might have heard between her and Paul. Lena went down the hall and down the stairs, setting herself to Determined Costume Head, but the moment she reached the sewing room and saw Higgy pacing, she realized she should have stayed in her office.

"You!" he thundered the moment he saw her. "You are just who I wanted to see."

"My office is upstairs." Lena tried for calm. "You didn't need to disrupt the entire costume department."

"I wanted to see if Runyon was right."

"Right about what?"

"About the schedule."

The seamstresses wouldn't meet Lena's eyes. "I don't understand. But maybe we could talk about this somewhere else so everyone could get back to work?"

"I've been patient with you, Lena," Higgy said. "The gossip and Claudia Mazur, and now this thing with Runyon—"

"What thing with Runyon?" They all watched, every seamstress. Lena was afraid to look behind her; she feared the cutters were gathered in the doorway.

"He wants you off the film unless you can find a way to work together. I don't have time for all these histrionics."

"What histrionics?" Lena asked, but she knew. She knew exactly what this was. Runyon's pressure. She heard the message clearly, though Runyon had obviously told Higgy only that he could not work with her. *Do what we want, or you lose your job.* Get the CIA the record. Get them Julia. This now, on top of what had just happened with Paul. Desperately she said, "Higgy, I don't know what he's talking about. Everything is going well—"

"The schedule is right here. You're behind, even I can see that. And what's all this?" He pulled the newspaper from an inside suit coat pocket. "Suspect in a murder case? Mysterious women? Falling stars? Goddamn it, Lena, I *warned* you! Do you know what the papers have been saying about *Twenty Steps to Heaven?*"

"Um, no—"

"*Nothing,* that's what! The gossip columns are all about you, not about the feud we planted between Helen Richards and Tony Curtis. *Not* about the expensive location shoot in New Mexico. And *not* about the Oscar talk we paid for. How do you think I feel about that?"

"Not good," Lena said quietly.

"Not good. Ha! Not good!" Higgy laughed and took in the very alert staff. "She says not good! Yes, Lena, I do not feel *good* about it. So make nice with Runyon before I do what he wants! That's an order!"

The humiliation itself was too much to bear; her face burned as she turned to go. But these seamstresses were her employees; she would not run away. Her cheeks might be a furious red, but Lena lifted her chin and walked with dignity back to the stairs, ignoring their looks, ignoring the cutters gathered, as she'd expected, in the doorway. Everyone knew Higgy Braxton's tempers. She would not give him the satisfaction of breaking her before her staff.

Upstairs, both Connie and Shirley waited for her. Connie said, "What happened? I heard him yelling."

"Nothing I can't handle," Lena managed through a constricted throat.

She went into her office and collected her purse, her sketchbooks, the things she thought she couldn't do without for the next several days. Then she went to find Michael Runyon.

CHAPTER 37

"You could just go get it," Lena told Michael Runyon. "I'm not sure why I have to be involved now that you know where it is."

They were back at the Chapel. The place felt close and weirdly sacred, with the low lights reflecting off the stained glass and the darkness outside. The jukebox crooned Frank Sinatra and the customers murmured quietly as if they understood the momentousness of the decision Lena had forced herself to make. Well, *forced* . . . she had no other choice. She didn't want to think about what the CIA might do to her if she refused to help. Losing her job was the least of it.

Runyon ignored her comment. "We've tried to make things easy for you, Miss Taylor. The police are no longer investigating Walter Maynard's death, and the FBI has been warned off. I'd think this little thing would be easy for you."

This little thing. "You're telling me that you told the police to close Walter's murder case?"

Runyon inclined his head in acknowledgment.

"But . . . why would you do that?"

"It was an unnecessary distraction," was all he said.

She was flummoxed by the notion that they could so easily dismiss a man's death.

He went on. "Once you've arranged the pickup with Julia, you let me know. I'll be waiting there with a half dozen men."

"A half dozen? For one woman? That sounds excessive."

"If you worked for the CIA, Miss Taylor, you'd understand how tricky Soviet spies can be."

"It seems I have joined the CIA," she said glumly, eating the olive out of her martini.

"We'll be hiding. You won't see us. When the record is in her hands, and you're coming out of the house, we'll arrest her. Nothing easier."

"I won't have to do any signaling, or any code words or anything like that."

"It's not like a movie."

"There was a lot of that in Rome."

"Like I said, the Soviets like tricks."

"Well, they've been doing it a lot longer than we have, so . . ."

Runyon's eyes narrowed. "When you say things like that, I start questioning which side you're on."

"I wonder myself. It's hard to trust you, you know, when you do things like make a perfectly good movie bad."

"Ah, we're back to that, are we?"

"He had a beautiful vision, and you made it ordinary. No, you made it sordid. All these things you're trying to promote about America . . . it's just a fantasy, you know. You're putting Negroes at the tables in the Medusa club but in reality there's no place where they can mix with whites to listen to jazz, not anymore. Women being saved by good men . . . When does that ever happen? Women who are opium addicts are more likely to die alone or be murdered. Does anyone really forgive a woman who goes bad? It's all a fairy tale. That's all you do, tell fairy tales."

"That's rich, coming from a woman whose whole life is a lie."

She finished her martini, tired of the depressing reality of the conversation, tired of him. "Well then, on that note, I guess I'll do my part and get in touch with Julia. She's been calling. I'm surprised she hasn't tracked me down in person."

"You'll let me know when it's all arranged?"

"You'll be my first call," she assured him.

~

She met Julia at the Polo Lounge the next evening. Lena was a mass of swimming anxiety that even a martini did nothing to ease, equal parts dread, regret, fear, and sorrow.

Fortunately Julia didn't seem to see it. "You're sure? You're sure it's at this Larry Lipton's house?"

"I can't guarantee Larry still has it, but he has a huge collection. It's probably there somewhere."

Julia laughed lightly, disbelievingly. "I can't believe we're so close. After all this time."

Lena said nothing. She willed herself calm as she drank her martini. Calm, not someone who was ready to betray someone she'd cared so deeply for. Julia had saved her life, but more than that, she wouldn't be who she was if not for Julia—Lena knew that indisputably. She owed Julia so much. It was such an awful way to pay her back.

She's a Soviet spy.

Julia started to slide from the booth. "Well, let's go get it."

This Lena hadn't expected. "Julia, wait—we can't just go get it."

"Why not?"

"Because it's late. Because we can't just drop in on him unannounced. I should call Larry."

Julia frowned. "It's not that late. Is he in bed by eight or something?"

Lena struggled for an excuse. "It's an odd time to show up at someone's house when you aren't really friends. He hasn't seen me in years."

"Tell him the truth, that you found out that he has something you've been searching for and you couldn't wait to get it."

"I'd rather call first."

Julia leaned close. In a low voice, she said, "Lena, do I have to remind you that we're being watched all the time? There are listeners everywhere. They've probably bugged your phone. That 'attack' the other night—who was it really? The FBI? The CIA?"

"The FBI," Lena admitted.

Julia rolled her eyes. "They'll have someone at the pay phone too. They have ways. You won't see it, but if you make a phone call, I can promise you they'll be at Larry Lipton's waiting for us."

That was true, if not for the reasons Julia thought. "You sound paranoid."

Julia laughed shortly. "You'd be paranoid too if you knew what I do."

Lena rolled her eyes. She had to make the call, not to Larry, but to Runyon. Lena hadn't thought that Julia would want to leave immediately, but she should have realized that of course Julia would want to go the moment she knew where the damn record was. Lena couldn't even plead work as an excuse. The news of Higgy's tantrum had already hit the gossip columns—Lena was sure that, too, was Runyon's work.

Star Costumer given notice at Lux Pictures! Studio Head warns Head Designer Lena Taylor to BEHAVE only a year after she ousted rival Flavio!

Julia had brought the newspaper with her and set it on the table with a flourish when she'd first arrived. "Fast work," she'd said with a wry grin. "What'd you do? Sass the producer?"

Something else that was a little too close to the truth. "I took up more newspaper space than Lux's latest picture," Lena explained.

Now Julia asked, "What does Paul say about all this?"

Lena went hot. "He's not happy."

"Then don't you think that the best thing to do is end all this quickly? It's getting late. Let's go."

"Wait. What's so important about this record, anyway?"

"I've told you." Julia slung her purse handle over her arm and slid from the booth.

Lena could think of no way to delay, Julia was on her way out of the bar. Lena couldn't stop her short of tripping her and causing a scene. Lena followed Julia, then stopped. "I need to use the ladies' room. Meet me at the car, okay?"

Julia paused, for a moment Lena was sure Julia was going to protest; there was something in her expression, a fleeting something, maybe distrust or maybe it was only impatience. Lena smiled her best smile, though that noxious mix of anxiety and dread churned.

"I'll only be a minute."

Julia's answering smile came slowly, but she turned away and started toward the doors. Lena hurried to the bathroom, then dodged to the pay phone nearby. She fumbled with the clasp of her purse. Michael Runyon's card was in her wallet. She pulled it loose, then searched for change, feeling the seconds pass, nearly dropping the coins before she got them into the slot. The dial moved too slowly, everything too slow, but then, thank God, the phone was ringing.

"CIA, Michael Runyon's office." A weary male voice came on the line.

"This is Lena Taylor. I need to get a message to Mr. Runyon immediately." She spoke as quietly as she could into the receiver.

"He's on a movie set."

"Send a messenger. Tell him I'm on the way to Larry Lipton's house with Julia Keane right now."

A pause. Then, "Where are you now?"

"We're leaving the Beverly Hills Hotel."

"Lena?"

The voice came from behind her. Lena hung up and turned to face a frowning Julia.

"I decided I should visit the bathroom too," Julia said. "Who did you call?"

"Oh, well . . . I saw the phone here and thought I'd try to call Larry, but then I realized I'd forgotten his number."

"Who were you talking to then?"

"The operator." The lie came easily, thankfully. "But I guess you're right. We don't need to call him. I'd hoped it would save time, you know, if he had the record ready to go, but oh well."

Lena couldn't tell if Julia believed her, but to her relief, Julia nodded.

"Oh well," she repeated.

After the ladies' room, the valet brought Lena's car. Julia was uncharacteristically silent as they drove off. It was uncomfortable and nerve racking. Lena reached for the radio.

Julia stilled her hand. When Lena looked at her in question, Julia ran her hands under the dashboard. She turned down the visors; she searched beneath the seats. She was obviously checking the car for something. When she'd finished, she twisted in the seat to look behind her.

"What are you looking for?" Lena asked.

"Bugs," Julia said shortly. "A van following us. They wouldn't be too far behind. The transmitters don't have a long reach."

"Transmitters? Are you talking about the CIA again?"

Julia settled herself in her seat and let out a deep breath. "In the Soviet Union, jazz is officially banned. It's easier to find Russian cigarettes in LA than a saxophone anywhere in the Soviet Union."

"Why are you telling me this? How do you know?"

Julia ignored her. "But it sneaks in. People love it. The black market thrives on jazz. The *stilyagi* especially have their own market for it."

"What are *stily*—whatever it was you said."

"*Stilyagi*. They're like your hipsters. Russian kids with long hair and ugly clothes."

"How do you know this, Julia?" She had to ask, even though she knew the answer, and Julia didn't pretend or dance around it.

"You know how I know this, Lena," Julia said sharply. "Now listen, will you? I'm trying to tell you something important. The *stilyagi* make bootleg recordings from the radio stations. The Voice of America and the BBC are jammed, but they can still get programs from Radio Iran and some others. Every now and then, someone manages to get the VOA. They record these on used x-ray sheets they get from the hospital trash bins. Have you heard of these? They call them 'bone music,' or 'ribs.'"

It was all Lena could do to keep her eyes on the road. "No. You mean the recordings are on chest x-rays?"

"Chests, knees, pelvises, ribs, whatever."

"And these actually play on a turntable?"

Julia made a sound of disapproval. "Yes, but the sound isn't very good. It doesn't matter. It's better than nothing."

"So . . . are you saying this record Larry has is one of these record-ings? This bone music?"

"The record you gave to Larry is Duke Ellington," Julia said. "But inserted in a false cover is a bone music recording, yes."

So that was why her own records had been torn apart. They'd been looking for a false cover. But Lena frowned. "So we're going to Larry Lipton's at seven thirty at night to pick up a bootleg recording of . . . what? Benny Goodman or something? And *this* is the reason why the CIA is following us and the men you work for are determined to get it back and we're both in danger? *This* is what I picked up for a Soviet spy ring in Rome?" It sounded ridiculous when she said it, and she half expected Julia to laugh it off, to admit that it was ridiculous. Why would the CIA want something like that? Why would they be in danger over it? Why would anyone care?

But Julia did not laugh it off. "Yes, Lena, *this* is the reason. But it's not a Benny Goodman recording. It's comment on Hedda Hopper's Hollywood gossip show about footage of Hiroshima and Nagasaki shot by a Japanese newsreel team after the bomb was dropped."

"I've never heard anything about this."

"Of course you haven't. No one has. The next day Hopper went on and retracted it. She claimed there is no movie footage of those cities after the attack. Except there is, and it's terrible."

"I've seen pictures—"

"No one's seen anything like this," Julia said bluntly. "You can't imagine. The US government seized the film. They don't want it seen, because they're trying to convince Americans that what you really need is more bombs to keep you safe. They're trying to convince you that you can survive them. Imagine what would happen if Americans saw footage of people without skin, or burnt skeletons, or people dying of radiation, or how the only thing remaining of people was their shadows blasted onto walls."

They had reached the Venice Speedway, oil derricks looming like shadowy aliens in the near darkness. Beyond, a bank of fog was rolling in.

"The film has disappeared," Julia went on steadily. "But there was a US crew, too, and they shot in color. There was supposed to be a Warner Brothers film based on it. Training films too. All stopped by the government. But what do you imagine would happen if word got out that such footage existed? Do you think Americans would insist on seeing it? And if they saw it, do you think they might start protesting arms buildup?"

Regardless of the pamphlets about surviving it, the bomb shelter plans, the warning sirens, there was no doubt that people were afraid of the bomb. It colored everything, an existential dread. The fear that the Soviets would use the bomb against them was reason enough for the US to proliferate their own arsenal. Everyone hoped that what the government said was true even if they feared it wasn't—that it did not mean the end of civilization.

"Hiroshima and Nagasaki were wastelands." Julia's words were very soft. "The bombs today are even stronger, Lena. Much stronger."

"I don't know what this means. How does this recording help anything? What can it do?"

Julia paused. Lena realized Julia was trying to decide how much to reveal. Finally she said, "We have contacts. Radio stations. Television. If we can get this recording out. If people hear it . . ."

"You hope to start a mass protest."

"Yes. Yes. The CIA doesn't want that, of course. They'll do anything to stop it."

They *were* stopping it. They were waiting at Larry's even now, meaning to seize the record, meaning to seize Julia. Lena saw it all before her as if it had already unfolded. Picking up the record at Larry's, walking out the door, the agents descending upon them. Julia's confusion the moment she realized that Lena had betrayed her. *Trust me*, she'd said long ago. *Can you trust me?* and Lena had. In the end, hadn't she been right to do so? Julia had tried to prevent the murder of Terence Hall. She had refused to leave Lena to take the fall for the plot gone wrong, she had taken a bullet to give Lena a chance to run.

Yes, Lena would not have been in danger if not for Julia.

But she would not be Lena Taylor either.

This record at Larry Lipton's . . . If Lena betrayed Julia, what would happen? The bone music would fall into the hands of the CIA, and the public would never learn about the movie footage of the devastation of the Japanese cities. They would just go on, knowing nothing, believing everything they were told about the bomb. Just as Runyon and his cronies would continue their propaganda, and studio heads like Higgy Braxton would keep acceding to them, and gossip queens like Hedda Hopper would keep destroying the lives of anyone who didn't live the lives they thought they should live. What was American freedom, anyway, but just words?

But that wasn't the reason Lena pulled the car to the side of the road and stopped. Her debt was too great, her heart too full of everything

Julia had given her. It was the memory of Julia saying, "*Get up, Lena.*" It was the memory of the voice in Lena's head. *"Run."*

"What are you doing?" Julia's voice held a note of fear. "Why are you stopping?"

"I want you to get out," Lena said steadily. She reached into her purse and pulled out an old receipt. On it, she scrawled Paul's number. "Go to Ocean Park, and call this number. It's Paul. Tell him you're a friend of mine, and I'm asking him for a big favor. I'll explain it to him later. Ask him to pick you up and take you—I don't know, wherever you want. Wherever you think you'll be safe. But get out of LA as quickly as you can. Do you understand me?"

Julia frowned. "The bone music—"

"There are CIA agents waiting at Larry's to arrest you. If they do, Julia, you know what will happen. You'll be in prison for life if you're lucky. If you're not . . ." Lena couldn't say the words. "I'm saying to you what you said to me in Rome. *Run. Hide.* The bone music is already lost, I'm sorry. I didn't know. I can't save it now that the CIA knows where it is. I wish you'd told me sooner, but I understand. I know why you couldn't. But I don't want you to die."

Julia stared at her, and in her gaze Lena saw understanding, and more than that, sorrow and regret. Julia closed her eyes for a moment, and opened them again on a deep breath. "Okay." She took up her purse. "Is anyone following us?"

"No. They think I'm bringing you to them. I don't see a blue Ford. Or a yellow car."

"No," Julia said. "There wouldn't be. They're waiting for me to deliver it." She scrunched the paper with Paul's number in her hand. "What will you tell them?"

"I don't know. I'll think of something. I'll give you as much time as I can."

Julia opened the car door. She had one foot out before she turned to Lena again. "I didn't lie to you, you know, Lena. You do shine."

She stepped out. It was all Lena could do not to put out her hand, to say, *Wait*, to say *I don't want you to go*, except . . . then what? It was over, there was nothing left. Rome was so far away. It was another time and there was no getting it back and the truth was that Lena didn't want it back anyway, but only what it represented, that time before she understood that not everything was possible.

The car door closed. Julia walked down the street toward Ocean Front, and with a lump in her throat that she didn't try to swallow, Lena watched her until she disappeared.

CHAPTER 38

After that, what was there to do but drive to Larry's? When Lena got there, she saw no parked cars but for Larry's own, and no evidence of Michael Runyon or his CIA agents, but then again, he'd said they would be hidden. She supposed it was possible that they hadn't arrived yet. It had been a very last-minute plan, and maybe the agent hadn't got the news to Runyon.

It didn't matter now. All Lena could hope to do was give Julia time. Lena took a deep breath and went up the walk to Larry's house. She heard music from inside. The porch light was off or out, the porch cast in darkness. When she knocked, she heard a rapid back and forth of talk, and then footsteps, but the music didn't stop. Larry opened the door and peered out.

"It's Lena. Lena Taylor."

"Lena Taylor?" He couldn't have sounded more surprised. "What are you doing here?"

"I . . . um . . . I know it's late—"

"Yeah, it is."

"—and I'm sorry to disturb you, but I wouldn't have come if it wasn't important."

Larry frowned, but he stepped back to let her in. As he shut the door behind her, she caught sight of his wife, Nettie, sitting on the couch, her forehead furrowed.

Lena waved. "Hello, Nettie. I am so sorry. I don't know if you remember me? Lena Taylor?"

"She came with Harvey Chesterfield and left with Paul Carbone," Larry provided helpfully.

"Ah," Nettie said.

"What can we do for you, Lena? As you said, it's late," Larry asked.

"Well, I gave something to Harvey—a record by Duke Ellington? It turns out he gave it to you."

"Duke Ellington?" Larry looked perplexed. He put his fingers to the bridge of his glasses. "Hmmm, I don't—"

"Yes, you do," Nettie provided. "It was so scratched up we couldn't listen to it. Remember, Larry? I wanted to throw it out, but you insisted on keeping it." She looked at Lena. "The Duke was always one of his favorites."

"Oh, I'm so glad." Lena didn't hide her relief. "It belonged to my father, and he recently died. My mom was looking for it."

"I'm so sorry to hear that," Nettie said. "Of course you must have it. Larry, give it to her. It's at the end of the first shelf."

"If you don't mind," Lena put in.

"Not at all, man, not at all." Larry puttered to the shelves of records and began flipping through those at the end of the first shelf. "Happy to, if it will comfort your poor mom—ah, here it is." He drew it out, and Lena was flung back to the day she and Harvey and Charlie had put it on the record player and winced at its damage, the clothes she'd packed for Venice piled on the floor.

Larry handed it to her. "Here you are."

She clutched it to her chest. "Oh, thank you so much, Larry—"

The knock on the door was not a knock, it was a blow, loud and thunderous. *Bang bang bang.*

The CIA, Michael Runyon. Lena's mouth went dry with fear.

Larry looked to Nettie, who half rose from the couch. "What the—?"

"So late. Are you expecting someone?" Nettie asked.

"Open up! It's the CIA." *Bang bang bang.*

"The what?" Larry hurried to the door. "Who?"

The doorknob rattled, the door opened to reveal Michael Runyon and three other men behind him.

"Hey, man, you can't just do that!" Larry protested. "I'm a US citizen!"

Runyon held up his hands. "We're not looking for you, sir."

"Do you have a warrant?"

"They won't need a warrant." Lena stepped forward. She held out the record. "They're looking for this."

Runyon snatched it from her hand. "That's not all we're looking for."

"She's not here," Lena said.

"I got the message," Runyon said. "Where is she?"

"I don't know."

Michael Runyon turned to Larry, who watched them with an astonished and bewildered expression. "Did this woman come here alone?"

"Look, man, I'm not answering any of your questions without a lawyer."

Lena sighed. "It's okay, Larry. Please tell them before they tear apart your house."

"Yeah, she came here alone."

"There wasn't another woman with her?"

Nettie said, "No, there was not."

Runyon took Lena's arm and smiled at Nettie. "We're sorry to trouble you both so late. We'll take this elsewhere." He turned to the men behind him. "Jones, Davis, check the house perimeter."

"You won't find her. She didn't come with me." Lena stumbled after Runyon as he pulled her onto the porch and down the stairs to the narrow lawn. "She was going to, but then . . . I don't know, she caught on that something was going on. She told me to get the record and she'd meet me tomorrow."

"Meet you where?" Runyon asked, brutally intense. He didn't sound like the censor she knew, but the hunter she'd imagined him as when they'd first met.

"At the Chapel." It was the first thing that popped into her head.

"What time?"

He'd bought it. She fought to hide her relief. "Two o'clock."

"Really? She didn't want to meet first thing?"

"I don't know. It doesn't open until eleven. I said two and she said okay."

Runyon frowned. "That's odd."

"Why?" A cat screeched in the bushes. Lena jumped. "Sorry, I'm a bit jumpy. Why is it odd?"

"Her contact was growing very impatient."

"Maybe they caught on to something."

Lena felt Runyon's contemplation, though she couldn't see his expression in the darkness.

The two men Runyon had sent to search the yard returned.

"Nothing," one of them said.

Runyon nodded. He pulled apart the cover of the record, revealing the false one beneath. Lena watched curiously as he drew out a flimsy x-ray sheet. He surveyed it too quickly for her to get a good look at it—it was round, there might have been a hole in the middle, she had only a fleeting impression of a gray image upon it—before he slid it inside again, apparently satisfied. "Let's go back. She's not here. You two go on. Get someone to the Beverly Hills Hotel. Someone else at the airport. I want someone at the Chapel in Culver City tomorrow as soon as it opens, but"—a quick glance at Lena—"Somehow I don't think she'll show up. I think Miss Taylor is right, and our target has caught wind that we're on to her."

Lena assumed an expression of guilelessness. "Is that it, then? Do you need anything else from me, or am I free to go?"

"You're free to go. But you'll let me know if she attempts to contact you again?"

"Of course. What is that really?" she asked. "Why does the CIA want it so badly?"

"If I told you that, I'd have to kill you," he said, and then laughed at her startled expression. "No, really, Miss Taylor, it's best if you don't know."

"It's just going to disappear, then?"

He exhaled heavily. "It's better this way. Trust me."

"Trust the government, you mean," Lena said.

"Don't you? In times of crisis, we all must decide what to believe," Runyon said. "It's our job to point the right direction."

"You sound so certain you know what the right direction is," Lena said.

Runyon walked her to her car. "I'll put in a good word for you to Braxton. I'm sure he'll understand your latest . . . transgressions. See you on the set?"

Lena got into her car and watched Runyon and his men walk down the street to wherever they'd hidden theirs. The fog had started to stretch its fingers into the neighboring streets; she started the car and turned on the headlights, and the dashboard lit her against the hazy gloom of the night so that she caught her reflection in the windshield, brown tones that highlighted the shadows in her face, her cheekbones, and the slope of her nose, and for a startling moment she remembered another night when she'd looked at her reflection in the windshield just like this, in the light of a pool hall sign, when she'd been Elsie Gruner, and when she'd been so sure that she could take the world in her hands and it would give her what she wanted and . . . She'd done that, hadn't she? She had, and here was another face staring back at her now, the same in some ways, but otherwise changed, just as inside she was a different person entirely. She knew now something she hadn't known then, that it wasn't only what you believed, as Runyon said, but also who believed in you.

Her parents hadn't. Walter hadn't. But Harvey and Charlie had and so had Julia. Flavio had and so had Paul. And now here were Runyon and the CIA saying it was their job to point her beliefs in the right direction, and the rest of the world's, too, and asking her to help them do it.

Paul had been right when he'd wondered if his career was worth having if it required so much compromise.

Now she understood, as she hadn't then, what that compromise truly meant. It wouldn't be hard to tell one more lie. God knew she'd told plenty. But Julia had said *enough* when she'd chosen prison over helping to murder Terence Hall, and she'd said it again when she chose to save Lena instead of leaving her to take the fall in Rome. Even with the bone music, Julia had chosen truth.

Now, Lena wanted that too. Runyon wanting her to use her talent to keep telling a story she didn't believe was a lie she didn't want to tell. Continuing to corrupt Paul's story . . . she no longer wanted to do it.

She was done with lies.

What would happen, she wondered, if she just said no?

No to the CIA's Psychological Warfare Workshop and their propaganda machine? No to the Motion Picture Alliance for the Preservation of American Ideals? No to Hedda Hopper and Louella Parsons and all the others?

"I didn't lie to you, you know, Lena. You do shine."

She knew someone else who did too.

CHAPTER 39

She showed up at his door with the dawn the next morning. Lena hadn't slept, and it looked like he hadn't either. He was unshaven and wearing a pair of pajama pants and smoking a cigarette. His rooms were foggy with smoke.

He stepped back to let her in and wordlessly made a pot of coffee. She opened the drapes to reveal the city waking, Los Angeles in its morning glory, saffron and pink, and stood at the window staring out while the percolator bubbled. It wasn't until he handed her the coffee that he said, "Who was she?"

For once, she could hardly hear Sunset Boulevard beyond the trees. It was so quiet. "What did she tell you?"

"That she was an old friend of yours. Julia. Not much else. She told me not to tell you where I took her in case they asked questions. Who would 'they' be?"

"The CIA, probably. Maybe the FBI. Anyone else who cared to ask, I think. She's a Soviet spy."

Paul choked on his coffee. "What?"

"It's probably not a good idea to tell anyone that. Or that you know her. Or yeah, where you dropped her."

"Christ, Lena—"

"I owed her. She's an old friend, though she did get me kicked out of Rome, but she saved my life, too, so I guess I have to forgive her. She was the one who first suggested I try costume designing."

Paul stared at her. "There are so many things in that sentence . . ."

"I know." She gripped her coffee cup tightly and turned to meet his gaze. "There's so much I have to tell you. I couldn't before."

"Why? What changed?"

"She's gone. For good, I think," she said quietly. "I was advised to say nothing of what happened to me in Rome and it was good advice until I met you, but then I was . . . afraid. We both had so much to lose and I couldn't bear the thought of losing you. I . . . I think we could have a future together—a good one. But only if I tell you the truth about everything, and then you can decide if you still want to be with me. So . . . I knew you would help with Julia, and I knew you would want an explanation, and here I am, ready to tell you everything."

Paul was quiet, his dark eyes serious. She waited. He could have said no, that he was done, and she thought she could handle that, but when he said, "Then I guess we'd better sit down," her relief was stunning in its intensity.

They went to the couch. She wanted to curl up in his arms, but she didn't, she kept her distance. It was easier than she'd thought, in the end, to tell him. It was as if the story had been waiting to come out, and she was just the conduit, as if she'd been unconsciously forming the tale in her head, all its disparate parts, and how easily it fit together, the story of her life, how one thing led to another. He already knew some of it, but she started at the beginning. Elsie Gruner and the pig farm in Zanesville and her parents who she didn't hear from because she'd never given them an address to write back and never checked the post office to see if they'd sent a letter to her at General Delivery—and everything about Walter and Harvey and Charlie and Chouinard and then Rome.

Paul said nothing, only listened and drank his coffee as she described her friendship with Julia, and how she'd changed herself there. "She made me who I am. She gave me the confidence to be Lena Taylor. I suspected what she was, but the truth is that I didn't want to know. I didn't want to see, not until I had no choice."

Then the rest, the CIA and the shooting at Termini Station. How she'd thought Julia was dead and the carabinieri and the escort from Rome. Harvey and Charlie telling her to say nothing to anyone ever.

"You didn't trust me," Paul said quietly.

"They told me to trust no one," she answered. "In the beginning . . . I didn't know what we would be to each other."

"Yes, you did."

Lena swallowed. "Even so, Paul, they were so insistent, and they were right. This business is a minefield. You know it yourself, and for a woman . . . I'm sorry, but I believed what they told me, and then . . . by the time I realized I loved you, I didn't know how to turn it around. I was afraid for both of us. I was afraid it would destroy you too if my associations got out. And then, Walter showed up and . . ."

"What did he want? Just money?"

"A job in the movies. A screenplay meeting with Marlon Brando."

Paul let out his breath in a low whistle. "Not asking for much."

"I was ready to send him to a film in Mexico, but it would never have been enough. Then Julia showed up and her people took care of him for me."

Paul laughed in disbelief. "What?"

"Poison. I didn't ask for it and I wouldn't have. I wish they hadn't done it. If I'd known, I would have tried to stop it. They felt he was in the way. Poor Walter. He was harmless, or . . . well, he wasn't. He would have made my life a misery, and he never would have given me a divorce. But I wouldn't have wished death on him."

"Do the police know this?"

"Michael Runyon put a stop to their investigation." Lena explained the rest.

When she was finished, Paul sat there quietly. She said nothing for a few moments. It was a lot to take in, she knew. Her stomach was a tight knot. She had no idea what he would say or what he would think and so much depended on it.

He said thoughtfully, "When Runyon left the army and joined this new intelligence group, I told him he was crazy. I told him he would always be lying. I asked him how he could in good conscience take on such a job. You know what he said to me?"

Lena shook her head.

"That he'd seen enough suffering during the war, and he'd chosen a side, and that side was America. He said that when your adversary has no scruples, you shouldn't have them, either, and if that meant he needed a dead conscience, then he was fine with that, and one day I'd be grateful he'd made that decision."

Lena sighed. She supposed she *should* be grateful that there were men like Runyon who had made that choice so that other, softer people didn't have to. But somehow she wasn't. And she was glad Paul had decided not to join them.

"When word got out about Braxton threatening your job, I knew Runyon had put a bug in his ear. We had an argument. I quit the movie."

"Paul!"

He shrugged. "I told him you and I were a team. I told him I was done playing his games."

"Me too," Lena said. "I'm sending Higgy my resignation."

Paul looked at her in question.

"I don't know exactly what I'll do, but I'm not going to keep working for a studio that's a member of the MPA. I won't."

Paul nodded slowly. "Well. My guess is you can get a job at any studio in town. You're in demand, and the gossip can only help you."

She had the feeling he wanted to say something else. She waited, but when he said nothing, she touched his wrist. Softly, she said, "But you can't. Why do I have the feeling you're about to tell me something I don't want to hear?"

"I'm going to Madrid for a few months. Philip Yordan has a whole script factory there. Lou Brandt, Sidney Harmon, Frank Capra. He says there's room for me if I want to go. I thought I'd try it out. Maybe write a new version of *Medusa*."

Her heart squeezed. "Just keep writing it until someone makes it the way you want it."

Paul nodded. "Good advice."

"A few months. That's not too long."

"It's pretty long to be away from you." He twisted his arm to take her hand, twining his fingers through hers. "I wasn't going to ask you to leave your job, but now . . . maybe you could come with me. It's up to you. I'll come back to you, you know. I'll always come back. But maybe we could start something new in Spain. Put the past behind us. Start over."

Lena smiled. The past never went away; she knew that now. But she also understood, as she hadn't before, that it made them both who they were; it had shaped them, it had taught them. "Or we could embrace it," she said, squeezing Paul's hand hard. "We could be who we're meant to be. We could be something true."

"We're already something true," he told her.

Costuming Star Says No to Studios, "I'm Done with Lies"—Former Lux Studios Costume Design head Lena Taylor is putting the studio life behind her. This reporter can confirm that sightings of La Taylor at elegant dining spots about town with various studio heads, including former boss Higbert Braxton, were indeed job offers. Taylor turned them all down. A source tells us that Braxton is furious over the loss of his popular costumer. What the next steps are for the star designer no one is saying, especially Lena Taylor herself, who is currently on her honeymoon in Madrid with screenwriter Paul Carbone.

~

February 14, 1956, Los Angeles Times

ANNOUNCING the Grand Opening of FLAVIO & CARBONE, Designers to the Stars!

The famous fashion designers Flavio and Lena Carbone (née Taylor, formerly of Lux Pictures) are pleased to announce their newest collaboration: an atelier for the discerning and the self-assured, fashion for those with a singular sense of style. Well known for their distinctive and transformative designs, discreet, iconic, and avant-garde, Flavio & Carbone have years of experience making fashion for the movies and costuming the stars.

Bringing Confidence through Dress is our trade. We Can Make You Shine.

915 Beverly Drive

By Appointment Only.

AFTERWORD

In September 1945, Lieutenant Daniel McGovern was one of the first Americans to arrive in Hiroshima and Nagasaki. As a director with the US Strategic Bomb Survey, he was there to study the effects of the bombing, and to film the official American record. While there, he learned that a Japanese film crew had shot black-and-white documentary footage of the atomic bomb's devastation of Hiroshima and Nagasaki in August, and that the crew had been ordered to stop shooting by American military police in October. All their footage was confiscated, and they were banned from further filming.

Lieutenant McGovern hired some of the Japanese crew to edit the seized footage. At the same time, McGovern's own crew shot color footage of the destroyed cities, as well as affected patients in hospitals.

The negative of the finished Japanese film was sent to the US in May 1946. McGovern's ninety thousand feet of footage was returned to the Pentagon. Once the government viewed the footage, it canceled a Warner Brothers feature film that was to be based on the project. The Atomic Energy Commission also did not want the film shown. It was generally felt that that footage would work against US government goals to increase the nuclear weapon arsenal. Both the Japanese and US footage were classified top secret and filed away. The Japanese film would remain concealed for more than twenty years, and the US film for more than thirty. For readers wishing to learn more details about this footage: https://apjjf.org/-Greg-Mitchell/1554/article.html.

In the Soviet Union, the government considered jazz a decadent capitalist campaign intended to destroy the USSR from the inside out, and by the 1930s, it was officially suppressed. By the end of World War II, it was effectively banned. There was, however, a vibrant underground scene and black market for jazz, and bootleg recordings from radio stations (recorded on x-ray sheets) were popular. Voice of America and the BBC were jammed, but resourceful fans found ways around that, and Radio Iran, Radio Luxembourg, and others had jazz programs that could be accessed. *Red and Hot*, by S. Frederick Starr, is an excellent history of jazz in the Soviet Union, and the website https://www.x-rayaudio.com has plenty of information on "bone music" for readers who wish to explore further.

The story of the US government using popular culture during the Cold War to influence both Soviet and American thought was the inspiration for this book. Many Americans opposed the shaping of minds through propaganda and would have been horrified to learn what the CIA was doing in the Soviet Union and throughout the world. They would have been more horrified to learn that the CIA was also using propaganda to influence Americans. The CIA not only helped to produce several books and articles with the intention of demonizing communism and to warn of a monolithic aggressor, but also used popular culture to urge a "normal" American way of life; that is, "the people's capitalism," blissful domesticity, American strength reflected in whole families with healthy children, and a racially diverse and happily blended society with equal opportunity for all.

The US Psychological Strategy Board, established in 1951, united several departments of US national security bureaucracy behind one goal: utilizing a campaign of psychological warfare in an effort to defeat the Soviet Union. The organization had a Motion Picture Service that employed director-producers who were given high security clearance and pursued film assignments (it cultivated directors like Frank Capra and producers such as Walt Disney) that fulfilled US messaging objectives. They searched out allies who were prepared to insert in their scripts the right actions and ideas, and employed men who worked undercover as producers, and agents whose job was to influence scripts, casting, and directors into portraying a "healthy" America. One such man was Carleton Alsop, who worked for the CIA's Psychological Warfare Workshop, and reported to the Psychological Strategy Board. My character Michael Runyon is based on Alsop. Excellent resources for the Hollywood culture wars are *The Cultural Cold War*, by Frances Stonor Saunders, and *Parting the Curtain*, by Walter L. Hixson.

The blacklist, McCarthyism, HUAC, and the Motion Picture Alliance for the Preservation of American Ideals effectively got communists and alternative thinkers out of Hollywood, or so frightened them that they felt straitjacketed creatively and philosophically, and many of them fled to Mexico, Spain, Great Britain, or other more forgiving locales to write and produce screenplays.

The Hays Production Code that kept every movie "clean" of sex, violence and "moral turpitude" was in effect from 1922 until it was struck down by the US Supreme Court in 1952.

Lawrence "Larry" Lipton was a real person, a writer, a poet, and the author of *The Holy Barbarians*, a book about the Beat scene in Venice Beach in the 1950s. He is also the father of James Lipton, host of *Inside the Actors Studio*.

This is a work of fiction. I've played with dates when it better suited the plot, and while some of the locales are real, some are purely imaginary. As always, I've done my best to be accurate when it comes to the facts, but any mistakes are purely my own.

ACKNOWLEDGMENTS

Many thanks to my agent, Danielle Egan-Miller, Marianna Fisher, Scott Miller, and everyone else at Browne & Miller—you guys went above and beyond on this one, and I am so very grateful for all the help. I could not have done it without you. Also so much gratitude to my editors at Lake Union: Danielle Marshall for her insight and support, Chantelle Aimee Osman for her positive and supportive attention, and developmental editor extraordinaire Jodi Warshaw, who remains brilliant. Thank you to project manager Karah Nichols and the copyeditors and page proofers and cold readers—again, none of this could be done without you. Thank you to Spencer Fuller at Faceout Studio for a truly wonderful cover.

Last but not least, my thanks to Kristin Hannah and Kany Levine, my brainstormers, readers, and strategizers. And to Kany, Maggie, and Cleo, your support and love are everything.

ABOUT THE AUTHOR

Photo © 2024 C. M. C. Levine

Megan Chance is the critically acclaimed, award-winning author of more than twenty novels, including *A Dangerous Education*, *A Splendid Ruin*, *Bone River*, and *An Inconvenient Wife*. She and her husband live in the Pacific Northwest, with their two grown daughters nearby. For more information about Megan and her books, visit www.meganchance.com.